© 2023

# Also by Lynn Emery

**Dr. Zen Mystery**
The Lodestone Puzzle
The In Situ Murders
The Titan Paradox

**Joliet Sisters Psychic Detectives**
Smooth Operator
Hunting Spirits
Dead Wrong
Dead Ahead
Die Trying
Spirited Sisters

**LaShaun Rousselle Mystery**
A Darker Shade of Midnight
Between Dusk and Dawn
Only By Moonlight
Into the Mist

Third Sight Into Darkness
Devil's Swamp
Blood Bayou
LaShaun Rousselle Mysteries Books 1-3

## Triple Trouble Mystery
Best Enemies
Devilish Details
Pretty Dangerous

## Standalone
After All
Louisiana Love City Girls Boxset
A Time to Love
One Love
Sweet Mystery
Night Magic
Good Woman Blues
Gotta Get Next To You
Soulful Strut
Tell Me Something Good
Tender Touch
Louisiana Love Box Set

Watch for more at www.lynnemery.com.

"En parlant du diable, on voit sa queue."
(When you speak of the devil, you see his tail.)

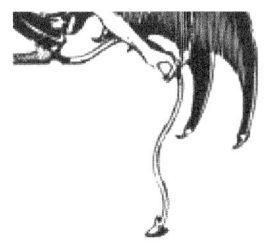

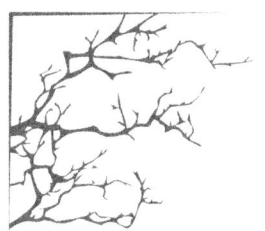

# Chapter 1

L aShaun sat in the principal's office feeling like she was the one in trouble. She'd been before at least three stern school administrators during her childhood. Always defiant and never giving an inch. She glanced to her left at Chase. His impassive expression gave away nothing to most. But LaShaun knew her husband. The cop in him would look at the evidence and go from there. The father in him... well, even LaShaun didn't know what kind of punishment he would decree for their oldest child.

"Could just be a misunderstanding," LaShaun murmured aside.

"Don't start making excuses for Ellie." Chase's deep voice dripped with controlled fury.

"I wasn't—" LaShaun stopped when the door swung open.

The principal bustled in, followed by a younger woman. Mrs. Richardson was a formidable-looking woman somewhere past forty-five. Her smooth, dark brown skin meant she could pass for thirty-something easily. Keys jangled from a stretch band around her left wrist. She took it off and placed them on the desk with care.

Ms. Armstead, the school social worker, wore a softer expression, though just as serious. "We'll bring Joëlle in after we have a chance to chat."

"Hmm," Chase said with a nod.

The two women exchanged a quick glance. Mrs. Richardson squinted at him with an appraising eye. Ms. Armstead's throat worked as she swallowed hard. LaShaun could almost hear their thoughts. The mother a well-known psychic from the notorious Rousselle family. The father a celebrated cop with the Vermilion Parish Sheriff's Department who'd caught at least four killers. No wonder the child had issues.

LaShaun smiled to ease the tension. Not that it would help, this being their third trip to the school since the term began.

"That's fine," LaShaun said.

"Mr. and Mrs. Broussard, Joëlle is a fine student. She's reading above her level. She's even developing into a talented athlete," Mrs. Richardson said.

"Gymnastics and softball," Ms. Armstead put in with enthusiasm. "Ellie is a leader, too. Other children look up to her."

"Not always entirely a good thing," Mrs. Richardson added, throwing cold water on Ms. Armstead's positive spin.

"Yes, well…" Ms. Armstead cleared her throat and took a step back. She stood next to the principal's desk and clamped her lips together.

"What's she done this time? You didn't bring us here because she's talking too much in class," Chase said in a sharp tone.

Ms. Armstead spoke up first. "The situation is sensitive, and I thought it was best if we discussed it before putting anything on paper. Creating a written record can follow a child for years."

"I agreed because Ellie isn't a disruptive child normally, but this—"

Mrs. Richardson looked at the social worker. She opened one of the drawers in her desk and held up a little unicorn, a pink enamel body with a mane and tail in rainbow colors. Light made the chain gleam, also silver. Two small keys dangled from the end of it.

"This isn't hers."

"Children love shiny, playful objects," Ms. Armstead offered in a faint voice.

"Unicorns, like in her bedroom." LaShaun glanced at Chase. His expression remained clouded.

"So, she stole that–" Chase pointed at the keychain. "From another student."

"To say she stole it is a bit strong," Ms. Armstead replied.

LaShaun studied the social worker. Ms. Armstead wasn't naïve, but LaShaun sensed that she was fond of Ellie and protective of children by nature. Before LaShaun could add her own view, Chase gave a loud grunt.

"My daughter took something from another student and didn't want to give it back. We call that theft in my line of work. Dressing it up won't do her any good." Chase shifted in his chair. "I know Ellie is charming. She's got a way about her. But as her father, I don't plan to sugarcoat this latest problem."

"I agree, Mr. Broussard. We have concerns about what seems to be a developing pattern of misbehavior." Mrs. Richardson's stern demeanor eased for the first time since they'd arrived. She hissed out a sigh. "I don't believe in suspending young people. Not unless their actions are extreme violence against students or staff. However, Ellie must have consequences. Ms. Armstead provides individual and group interventions. One hour after school on Wednesdays and Saturday mornings."

"A combination of behavioral and talk therapy. I've completed a short preliminary assessment. You signed consent, if you recall, when she was enrolled." Ms. Armstead looked from Chase to LaShaun.

"Part of our holistic approach here at Abbeville Charter School," Mrs. Richardson put in as if to head off any objection.

"Yes, of course. But twice a week seems a bit much, don't you think?" LaShaun clenched her fists. The need to defend her little girl bubbled up inside her. *Ellie isn't a master criminal*, she wanted to blurt.

"She knows right from wrong. As her parents, we can give her consequences at home and talk to her," Chase added, though his statement stopped short of agreeing with LaShaun outright.

"Hmm, well, we can talk about it more after we bring in Ellie." Ms. Armstead glanced at the principal who nodded. She left and returned with Ellie a few seconds later.

Ellie came in, her usual bubbly mood absent. At nine years old, she looked like the typical tween. She wore a blue long-sleeved t-shirt tucked into her school uniform skort. Blue knee socks and navy-blue sneakers matched the colors of the plaid bottom. When she started to sit on LaShaun's lap, Chase patted the empty chair between them instead. With a look at LaShaun over one shoulder, Ellie eased onto the cushioned seat. She glanced at Chase. He turned to her with one dark eyebrow raised. Ellie faced forward to stare at a point on the wall behind Mrs. Richardson. LaShaun took one of Ellie's hands and Chase transferred his grim look to her. His expression said not to baby her. LaShaun held on anyway.

"Now, Ellie. We're all here to help you. Not that what you did isn't serious, but we need to talk about it. You understand?" Mrs. Richardson's tone was earnest yet caring.

"Yes, ma'am." Ellie's gaze went from the principal to her shoes. She tapped her toes at a nervous pace against the low-pile taupe carpet.

"You remember what we always say, communication is key," Ms. Armstead added. "So, tell us about the unicorn keychain. It doesn't belong to you."

Ellie shook her head no. "It belongs to someone else."

"I can't believe we have to explain how wrong it is to take something that's not yours. You know I arrest people for stealing all the time, Joëlle Renée," Chase blurted out as if the words could be contained any longer.

"But Daddy—"

"Don't 'but' at me, young lady. I don't want to hear excuses," Chase clipped.

"She said I should take it, Daddy. Zee said to go in her locker when they dragged her away." Ellie's voice rose with each word. Her eyes filled with tears that then rolled down her tawny face.

"Calme-toi, mon petite. Who dragged her away?" LaShaun took a tissue from the box on Mrs. Richardson's desk. She dabbed Ellie's face with gentle pats.

"A man and a lady, but they weren't in uniform. You have to help her and—" Ellie's voice hitched as she continued to cry.

Chase looked from the social worker to the principal with a frown. "What exactly is going on? Who is Zee?"

"She's an older student from our high school campus. She tutored the younger children in math," Ms. Armstead said.

"The point is, Ellie didn't have permission to go through another student's locker. She somehow managed to stay behind on the school bus. The driver picked up students for the high school. Elle then got off and found the locker. Ellie claimed she'd dozed off when a teacher's assistant found her wandering the halls. The bus driver was kind enough to bring Ellie here at the end of her run." Mrs. Richardson fixed Ellie with a hard stare.

"I wasn't late either," Ellie declared.

"The day she missed the drop-off two weeks ago," LaShaun said. The teacher had called to tell her about the incident, but assured her Ellie was fine.

"Apparently, that was the second time. Ellie managed to hitch a ride back with a parent the first time," Ms. Armstead said.

"It's not that far. I could have walked," Ellie mumbled.

"Ellie!" LaShaun glared at her and then turned to Mrs. Richardson. "Why are we just hearing about this?"

"Because the parent only told us today. Her son is in the sixth grade here and he told us first. His mother confirmed it." Mrs. Richardson gazed at Ellie.

"It's less than a half mile away and there's a sidewalk. Plus, I—" Ellie's voice trailed off at the scowls aimed her way.

"Not the point, young lady," Chase snapped.

LaShaun sighed. Chase reverted to talking like his mother when he was angry. "Queen B," as LaShaun and her other daughter-in-law called her behind her back. As did her adult children, Chase's brother and three sisters. Except for the in-laws the "B" didn't stand for "bee."

"You wanted to help your friend who was in trouble," LaShaun began. She paused and glanced from the principal to the social worker.

"We can't discuss another child's... situation. Student confidentiality." Mrs. Richardson pressed her lips together as if to emphasize they would remain sealed.

"She asked me to get her notebook. Maybe she wanted to study?" Ellie blinked at Chase. She sighed when his severe expression didn't vanish.

"There's no reason good enough for you to disobey school rules and *our* rules," Chase replied.

"Yes, Daddy." Ellie resumed examining the tops of her sneakers. She swung her legs, making the motion-activated light in the soles twinkle.

LaShaun studied her daughter for a few moments. Ellie had avoided lying with a disingenuous question. Which meant there was another reason she wanted the teenager's notebook. The keychain was a mystery. Still, LaShaun decided it would be best to probe more at home.

"I'm sure we can work out appropriate consequences without the extra Saturday session," LaShaun said.

"I think that's reasonable," Ms. Armstead spoke before the principal could reply. She avoided looking at the older woman's faint frown of disapproval. "The extra session is for children who have serious issues relating to others. I think we can all agree that doesn't apply to Ellie."

"And Ellie is going to be the one who returns her belongings with an apology. Maybe even to her parents as well," LaShaun said with a sharp look at Ellie.

Ms. Armstead wore a pained expression. "The thing is—"

"We'll make sure the items are returned. No need to worry," Mrs. Richardson interrupted with a pointed look at the young social worker.

"Right. It might be best if we put some distance between the two for a bit," Ms. Armstead said.

"Sounds like a good idea to me." Chase nodded.

LaShaun blinked in puzzlement. "Yeah, okay."

"Do I have to go home now?" Ellie whispered as she looked up at LaShaun. Her large brown eyes sparkled with more tears threatening to fall.

"We have two hours left in the day. I think it's best for her to stay in school," Mrs. Richardson said in a crisp, "I'm in charge and that's final" tone. She raised both eyebrows at LaShaun and Chase.

"That's fine. I need to get back to the station." Chase placed his large hand over Ellie's tiny one. "We'll talk about your behavior when I get home. I'm glad you're safe, but you have to make better decisions. The *right* decisions. Now, you're going to listen to your teacher, Ms. Armstead, and the principal. Right?"

"Yes, Daddy."

Ellie jumped from her chair and onto his lap. She hugged him. Her worried expression faded when he patted her back and kissed the top of her head.

Ms. Armstead held out a hand and smiled. "I'll take you to class."

"Yes, ma'am," Ellie replied in a dutiful voice. She let go of Chase and went to LaShaun. After a hug and quick kiss on LaShaun's cheek, she took Ms. Armstead's hand.

"The Wednesday sessions are no longer than an hour. I'll send you the outline of what we cover. Ellie can ride the bus home, too," Ms. Armstead said. She patted one of Ellie's shoulders and Ellie beamed up at her. A bell rang to signal a schedule transition.

"I'd prefer to pick her up those days," LaShaun said. "She'd be riding with older children, right?"

"Middle schoolers and a few high school kids who have extra activities like band practice. So, Ellie staying later won't look unusual, if you're concerned. And there aren't any problems on afternoon transportation routes. She can sit up next to the bus driver," Mrs. Richardson put in.

"All the same, I'll pick her up," LaShaun said.

Ellie's smile faltered. She started to speak but stopped at the look LaShaun gave her. "Yes, Mama." She waved good-bye to her parents.

"No problem at all." Mrs. Reynolds gave a nod to the social worker.

"Miss Janet should be starting story time about now," Ms. Armstead chirped, putting cheer in her voice to leave behind the serious air of their meeting. Her and Ellie's voices faded as the door bumped shut.

"I appreciate how upsetting this must be, but I don't think Ellie meant any real harm. She became good friends with this teenager. It's quite believable she thought she was helping out a friend." Mrs. Richardson stood as a signal their meeting was over. Taking the cue, Chase and LaShaun stood as well.

"Is she okay? The young girl, I mean," LaShaun said.

"Honestly, I'm not sure." Mrs. Richardson frowned and let out a sigh as she looked away. "As I said, I can't go into specifics. But Ellie and the other children aren't in any danger, if that's your worry."

"Right." LaShaun exchanged a look with Chase.

"Good-bye and thanks for being so responsive." Mrs. Richardson walked them out of the office, down the hall, and out to the school's main lobby.

LaShaun glanced around the spacious first floor. A small raised garden sat at the center of the wide hall. Plants, cared for by the students, gave the entrance a welcoming touch. Above the atrium, a large skylight allowed late-fall sunlight to flood the area. To their right, a class of fifth graders chattered as they applied Halloween decorations to a huge cork board. A second bell chimed. Children on the second floor scurried to avoid being late.

"I know what you're thinking," Chase said as he followed LaShaun to her SUV.

"Our 'psychic stuff' is rubbing off on you now, huh?" LaShaun quipped as she tapped the remote. The lock clicked on the driver's door and she opened it.

"Funny. You know what I'm talking about." Chase waved at the buff-colored modern school building. "You wanted Ellie to attend that wizard academy instead of here. She wouldn't be having problems if she had."

"Harmony Charter School is approved by the state with a curriculum not very different from this one," LaShaun clipped. She tossed her crossbody purse onto the center console and faced him, arms folded.

"Most of the staff are TEA members, and the students are all 'gifted.' " Chase leaned on the open door. He brushed a strand of hair from her cheek.

"Don't try flirting with me," LaShaun said and gave his hand a playful slap. "The Third Eye Association has no official role in the school. They serve as a resource for the 'gifted' students. And not all of the students are like Ellie. Some of their siblings attend who don't have paranormal-enhanced senses."

The Third Eye Association, or TEA, had been organized over one-hundred fifty years ago. Their mission had started out as providing a safe haven for those who in earlier times had been branded as witches. Over decades, TEA evolved into both spiritual and scientific research. Depending on the era, their public face had been that of fortune tellers, hippies, and new age eccentrics fascinated with mysticism. They realized quite soon the advantage of playing along. Much better than being burned at the stake. In fact, they had developed cutting-edge technology proving the science of certain psychic abilities.

"Anyway, you wanted her at Harmony. But I think being around normal kids and teachers is better for her. In the big picture," Chase added before LaShaun could reply. "The majority of the world doesn't see ghosts or any that other woo-woo stuff."

"Ellie and CJ are *normal*." LaShaun felt a hard knot of anger form in her chest. She scowled at him. "You've been listening to your mother too much."

"Don't start, alright? I'm talking about kids who can't hear thoughts or move things without touching them. If that's even real." Chase shrugged.

"Seriously, Chase?" LaShaun squinted at him.

"Hey, I'm not saying it's all made up. You and your TEA pals talk about physics and medical science that might explain a lot of supernatural abilities," Chase countered.

"Is that what you tell your parents, especially Queen Bee?" LaShaun snapped.

"I've been spending more time with my parents to build a bridge." Chase stepped close and pulled LaShaun to him, both hands on her waist. "She's not the enemy."

"Isn't she? Ask your daughter how welcome she feels in Queen Bee's house," LaShaun snapped. "I don't give an inch when it comes to my kids."

Chase hissed out air and stood back. "My mother loves her grandkids, LaShaun. You need to let go of the past."

"Whatever."

"I'm going to bring you two hard-headed women together kicking and screaming if I have to," Chase shot back. When LaShaun let out a cynical grunt, Chase pulled a hand over his face. "Okay, so about Ellie. First, she's bullying other kids and now stealing. Maybe we should limit her playing with the other wiz... I mean, kids from that TEA play group."

"Ellie was defending a child who was being bullied. Even her teacher said so," LaShaun replied.

"Listen." Chase glanced around and lowered his voice even though they were alone in the parking lot. "Ellie can do that thing where she gets into your head, influence people to do what she wants. What if she decides to use that power to do bad things."

"Chase..."

"I'm telling you, LaShaun. I don't like the direction she's headed."

"Exactly the reason she should be in a TEA children's play group. They have child therapists who understand the temptations a child with gifts faces daily. Once they realize they can do things most kids can't, they can take the wrong path," LaShaun argued.

"TEA again. Your solution to everything," Chase muttered.

"What the hell do you mean? The reality is—" LaShaun broke off with an irritate huff when his work mobile phone chimed a notification. Three bells meaning an urgent alert demanded immediate attention.

Chase pulled it from the leather holder clipped to his belt, glanced at the screen, and frowned. He tapped a short text. "I gotta go. Look, we'll talk more about Ellie later. For now, she doesn't get to play on her tablet. Give her some extra study work related to following rules or something. And no TV for a week at least."

"Sounds reasonable," LaShaun replied in a grudging mumble.

"We finally agree on *something*." Chase turned to leave.

"Hey, find out what you can about that girl," LaShaun called.

"We don't know her name," Chase said and faced LaShaun again.

LaShaun stared in the direction of the high school. The twin buff colored building was visible down the two-lane highway. A short feeder roadway had been constructed to connect what Mrs. Richardson had called the sister campus. Both were run by the same charter school company.

"Zulime Glapion. Nicknamed Zee. She's sixteen I think."

Chase studied LaShaun's distracted frown for a beat. "Mrs. Richardson didn't tell us her name. Ellie..."

"Whispered it when she hugged me. No wizardry," LaShaun clipped.

"I just—" Chase broke off when his phone beeped a text notification.

"Right, gotta go. Dead body. Crime fighting time." LaShaun pointed to the phone.

"Cut it out. No supernatural powers looking into my cases," Chase tossed back. He stepped closer to her, pecked her forehead, and pulled back. "We'll get through this rocky patch, cher. Kiss CJ for me."

LaShaun waved good-bye as he walked backward toward his Vermilion Parish Sheriff's F-10 truck. The tension between them remained. She could feel it hanging in the air. Even their last joke hinted at the source. She sighed and got into her Honda CRV. Her next stop would be to pick up their toddler son from her Aunt Shirleen's house. Maybe music would banish her sour mood.

Cool air blew across LaShaun's face as she drove with the window down. A rare crisp fall day with low humidity was a treat in late September. Louisiana weather rarely gave a definitive change of seasons. The sixty-degree temperatures could vanish fast, replaced by tropical heat. LaShaun breathed in the faint scent of water. Marshland leading to Vermilion Bay lay not many miles to the south of Highway 335. Her aunt lived in a tiny unincorporated community called Rougonville. Sugar cane and soybean fields stretched on either side as she drove. Soon she reached more houses separated by prairies. Aunt Shirleen lived twenty minutes from their home just outside Beau Chene. A retired school cafeteria supervisor, she happily filled in as an occasional babysitter. LaShaun used the hands-free button to call and let her know she was on the way. Aunt Shirleen was on the porch when LaShaun pulled up to her house. The CRV's tires crunched up the crushed gravel driveway. CJ, dressed in denim jumper and plaid flannel shirt, jumped up and down as LaShaun waved to him. He was a tall four-year-old, a sign he'd shoot up and match his father's height one day.

"Hey, Mama. It's Mama!" CJ grinned back at Aunt Shirleen and faced LaShaun again.

"Yes, it's your mama. Back from her mission down at that school. Again." Aunt Shirleen rose from the white rocking chair and stood next to him. She was dressed in a red and black flowy tunic over black leggings. "Go on, Chase Justin."

Given the green light to leave the porch, CJ jumped over the four steps leading to the ground. Aunt Shirleen yelped at his daredevil maneuver. When he landed with a solid thud, Aunt Shirleen shook her head. CJ raced into LaShaun's outstretched arms. She picked him up and kissed his round cheek with a smack.

"Hey, my baby. You been behaving yourself? You best not be giving your auntie trouble." LaShaun shook him playfully from side to side.

"I was good," CJ declared and hugged her neck. Seconds later he squirmed to be let go. He was off and running the minute his little feet hit the ground.

"Mercy, that boy got energy for days." Aunt Shirleen beamed at CJ as he romped on the neatly cut grass of her lawn. Their dog Beau appeared from his position lounging on a corner of the porch and joined him. They played their version of dodge, circling each other. CJ's joyous shouts matched by Beau's short barks.

"I hope they didn't wear you out." LaShaun climbed the porch and pressed her cheek against her aunt's in greeting.

"Lawd no. Keeps me young. Don't get to see my grands so much, you know." Aunt Shirleen sat again. She pushed the rocker back and forth. All four of her adult children had moved away from Vermilion Parish for better career opportunities. Two lived in Houston, Texas, a third in Michigan, and her oldest son was in California.

"How are my cousins doing?" LaShaun knew her aunt was always happy to discuss her kids, the good and bad.

"They're fine. The question of the day is how's Ellie doin'?" Aunt Shirleen gave LaShaun a knowing squint.

Before LaShaun answered, a 2019 white Lexus sedan pulled in beside her CRV. Her cousin Azalei emerged. Dressed in a designer jogger suit, she swung braids down to her waist dramatically. She had to make an entrance no matter how small the audience.

"Afternoon everybody. Hey, baby boy!" Azalei called to CJ.

"Hey." CJ barely acknowledged her as he darted around Beau.

"Child, ain't this a pretty day." Azalei strolled up to LaShaun. "Girl, how's Ellie? Don't let them folks persecute my child. You know how they be about any member of the Rousselle family."

"With good cause. Tell the truth and shame the devil. Rousselles been hell-raising in Vermilion Parish for years," Aunt Shirleen said.

"Here she goes," Azalei whispered aside to LaShaun with a chuckle.

"C'mon now, Tee Shirl," LaShaun said, interrupting her aunt's recitation of family dirty laundry. "That's all in the past. Most of us have mellowed."

"Says who?" Aunt Shirleen punctuated her question with a cynical grunt.

"Back to Ellie," Azalei put in before their aunt could get going again. "She's not in too much trouble, I hope."

"She took a couple of things that belong to another student. Ellie insists she was trying to help her. Says 'they' dragged the girl, a sixteen-year-old tutor, away. The principal wouldn't explain. They're not allowed to release information about other students." LaShaun sat on the top step and watched CJ playing. He tossed the ball and Beau retrieved it each time.

"Sounds serious Who's the girl?" Aunt Shirleen raised an eyebrow as she gazed across the yard, her mind clearly elsewhere.

"Zulime Glapion. Pretty name. They kin to us?" LaShaun looked at her aunt over one shoulder.

"Lawd, no. You never heard about them Glapions? Now I'm wondering which one she is."

"Sounds like there's a juicy story there," Azalei said.

"Oh, started way back before I was even born," Aunt Shirleen murmured.

"Ancient history then?" Azalei smothered a cackle at the scowl Aunt Shirleen fired her way. Their aunt had a sore spot about her age and Azalei relished poking it.

Aunt Shirleen brushed away the wisecrack. "You better hope you look this good at sixty, youngster."

"What about the Glapions, Tee Shirl?" LaShaun said to distract them from an argument. She shot a pointed side-eye at Azalei. A silent warning not to mention Aunt Shirleen had shaved off a few birthdays from that number.

"I don't know. All I heard was the Glapions don't set with the Rousselle family. Not that it's many of the older generation left." Aunt Shirleen frowned in concentration as though sorting through memories or details. "You say somebody took her? A kidnapping?"

"I didn't say any such thing. So, don't start a rumor," LaShaun said and wagged a finger at her aunt.

"Well, something has happened. Let me get Chase Justin's little bag. He's been such a sweet joy, that one. Love to see him coming, hate to see him go." Aunt Shirleen went inside the house.

"Hey, give me some of that action." Azalei skipped off to the game of fetch. She took turns throwing the ball to CJ and Beau.

LaShaun laughed at their exaggerated seriousness in getting to the oversized tennis ball. She found a plastic bat left in the grass, raced over, and hit the ball when it came her way. Ten minutes later she was a bit sweaty and less tense about her meeting at Ellie's school.

"We better get home so we can meet Ellie's school bus. And get dinner going, too." LaShaun lifted the collar of her shirt to let a cool breeze dry her neck. "And take a quick shower while I'm at it."

"Ok," CJ called back but tromped after Beau anyway.

"Tee Shirl is a character. She's the only one that insists on calling CJ by his full name," Azalei said as she blew out a breath.

"Says it's more dignified than calling him by letters," LaShaun said. "I had a time convincing his daddy to give him the same name. He didn't want a Chase, Jr. So, I named him after one of our great-great uncles. A reputable one."

"As far as you know. There are a lot of twisted branches on the Rousselle family tree," Azalei quipped.

"Like *you*." LaShaun wore an impish grin.

Azalei arched both shapely eyebrows at her "And *you,* dear cousin."

"Ouch. Here's to rehabilitated bad girls." LaShaun shared a fist bump with Azalei.

"She's been in there about ten minutes. Bet you a cool twenty-dollar bill we'll get the whole story." Azalei glanced behind her into the house. The glass storm door gave them a shadowed view of the living room.

"Mrs. Reynolds made it clear that info is strictly confidential, especially when it comes to minors—"

Aunt Shirleen returned to the porch. She had CJ's superhero duffle bag in one hand and her cell phone in the other. She dropped onto a chair. "Yep, Zee Glapion. Her grandmother been raising her. The mama's in jail in California or somewhere. Not the first time. Drugs. Looks like Miss Zulime is headed down the same road."

Azalei smirked at LaShaun and held out a palm. "Told ya. CNN of Acadiana strikes again."

"CNN?" LaShaun playfully slapped away Azalei's hand.

"The Creole News Network. Got reporters covering events from the Texas state line to New Orleans and down to the Gulf Coast," Azalei said. "Pay up."

"I didn't take the bet, girl." LaShaun turned to their aunt. "Are you saying she was arrested?"

"Sure enough. Pretty serious, too. Attacked some woman who was supposed to be her court-appointed volunteer mentor. Or something. She was already doing community service to stay out of one of those juvenile group homes. The woman is in the hospital. Keeping it quiet cause Zee is a minor." Aunt Shirleen tsked-tsked as she shook her head.

"Apparently not hush-hush enough," LaShaun drawled with a glance at Azalei.

"Girl, you know they couldn't keep that kind of action quiet around here," Azalei replied with a shrug. "At least they ain't gossiping about me this time."

"Why, you been up to something? *Again*?" LaShaun squinted at her.

"No comment." Azalei smoothed down her hair. "I'm going to round up the youngster and his sidekick for ya." She strolled across the grass, full hips swaying.

Aunt Shirleen cocked an eyebrow at LaShaun. "That girl gonna get her butt whipped messing with married men. Her latest manages a car dealership in New Iberia."

"Ah, the Lexus. I wondered how she could afford one." LaShaun jerked a thumb at the spotless shiny sedan.

"Azalei needs to settle down. Get a good man and have a baby. Done good for you." Aunt Shirleen gave a nod.

"Hmm." LaShaun thought about the chafing issues she and Chase seemed to skirt more often.

"If you can stay out of them crazy voodoo investigations you keep getting into," Aunt Shirleen added as if reading LaShaun's mind.

"Not voodoo, Tee Shirl. When folks need help with things outside the ordinary..." LaShaun searched for a way to explain how she had been drawn into supernatural investigations.

"All I'm saying is your babies can have a regular life. I think even Odette would agree with me. Toward the end she had her regrets. Mostly about how she raised you. But I think she done good making up for it. Holding onto grudges for generations is like passing on poison to your own seed." Aunt Shirleen sat in another rocker. She pushed it back and forth as she studied Azalei and CJ yards away.

Monmon Odette had despised the St. Julien family, Antoine St. Julien in particular. She blamed him for Francine's death. Even though LaShaun's mother had died in a fire with another man. But for years Monmon Odette blamed his rejection of Francine for another woman as the real cause. She'd passed her hatred to LaShaun, who in turn bullied their only child, Savannah. In a strange twist, Monmon Odette trusted the adult Savannah to be her lawyer and handle her estate at the end. LaShaun and Savannah became friends. An even stranger development.

"Like the Glapions, you mean. But time brings changes. Ellie said Zulime asked her to get a notebook. Maybe there's something in it to prove she's innocent," LaShaun said.

"Humph. No question Zulime attacked the woman. Plenty of witnesses. You best keep Ellie far away from the girl," Aunt Shirleen said in sober voice.

"Yeah, I know for sure Chase would agree with you. But there's something about all this..." LaShaun stared ahead without seeing her surroundings. A tingle ran down her arms, a sign they were swimming into deeper waters.

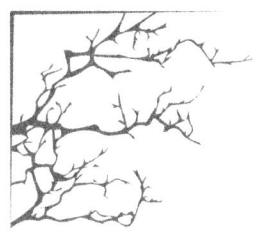

# Chapter 2

Later that evening at dinner, Ellie didn't argue for once about eating her vegetables at dinner. She sat subdued, pushing food around on her plate. Chase prompted her to eat a few times, and she complied. CJ, perched on his yellow booster seat, happily slurped up his green peas by the fistful. LaShaun was busy keeping him from spreading his dinner all over himself and the table.

"Well, little man, at least I'm glad you enjoy veggies," LaShaun said with a laugh. She used a damp towel to wipe rice from his face. "But this shirt is a lost cause. Not sure if I'll be able to get these food stains out."

"Wings!" CJ yelled. He waved a chicken bone in the air.

"He'd eat those things at every meal if we let him." Chase ruffled CJ's thick curls with one hand. "Dude, you need a good dunking to get cleaned up."

"I'll go to my room now. And CJ, don't follow me. He's always messing with my things." Ellie shot a glare at CJ and then slid from her chair to leave.

CJ scrambled from his seat with the awkward moves of a toddler. He landed on his butt but popped back up to his feet. "Play with sissie."

"No," Ellie snipped. "You just want an excuse to snoop around my room."

23

"CJ, we talked about this. You should ask Ellie if it's okay to go into her room. And no wandering when she's not there." LaShaun smothered a grin when CJ gave her his wide-eyed innocent look.

"See? He's not going to listen," Ellie grumbled. She wore a sour face as if the world was conspiring against her.

"He's still learning about boundaries, honey," LaShaun replied.

"Ellie has extra schoolwork to do," Chase said in a firm voice. He studied Ellie for a few seconds. "Then we need to have a talk."

"Yes, Daddy." Ellie didn't look back at him. She turned and trudged to her room with heavy steps.

CJ seemed not to notice the somber mood. He turned his attention to Beau. Their Great Weimar looked relaxed on the large doggie bed in the family room next to the kitchen. Beau yawned widely as if to give CJ a hint he wasn't up for more activity. He rested his large head on both front paws. The four-year-old ignored the cue and sat next to Beau. He babbled about going outside to look for tigers, an argument for play in the backyard.

LaShaun used a large kitchen towel to swipe up the mess CJ had made. "You could lighten up on her a bit, you know. I looked at the walking path between the two schools. It's quite safe. In fact, a school crossing guard was still on duty the day—"

"Don't start with the excuses." Chase stacked plates and other dishes onto a tray. He went to the large island and set it down.

"I'm only saying she wasn't as reckless as it sounded at first." LaShaun huffed out a sigh, looking at the floor. "We gotta get CJ better table manners. I have to sweep and mop at least twice a day."

"Maybe if we didn't have to spend time corralling Ellie..." Chase muttered.

"First, it was just a joke, Chase," LaShaun snapped. "CJ's messy eating has nothing to do with Ellie. Lord, you're sounding like Elizabeth."

Chase dropped forks into the dishwasher. Then he stacked plates in the racks. He made enough noise to make LaShaun clench her teeth. The crack about his mother came out before she could stop it. Neither spoke for a few minutes. The only sound between them was the angry thump of pots being moved from the stove top to the sink. LaShaun got the broom and then the mop. She made quick work of cleaning up the floor around the table. LaShaun shot glances at his broad back as he put pots in the bottom shelf of the dishwasher.

"I shouldn't have brought up your mother. It's just..."

LaShaun blew out air. She stored CJ's booster seat in the walk-in pantry. She straightened the chairs around the table. CJ had settled next to Beau with a picture book, pretending to read.

"You always do that," Chase clipped finally.

LaShaun used another damp dishcloth to wipe the quartz surface of the kitchen island. Then she wiped down the gas cooktop harder than necessary. She let a few beats pass before she took the bait. Might as well get it over with. "Do what?"

Chase turned after punching the button to start the dishwasher. It hummed to life behind him. He crossed his arms. "Make my mother the villain as a way of making points or getting me to back down and apologize for her. We should be talking about Ellie's behavior problems. Instead, you bring up mama."

"Ellie is different, Chase. You've known that from the time she was able to walk and talk," LaShaun shot back.

"See? *That's* the problem. We should have the same standards, the same rules for her like any regular kid. She's gotta live in a world of—"

"Of what, Chase? Normal people?" LaShaun looked over at CJ to check if he'd noticed the gathering storm. She lowered her voice. "You're wishing for a *regular* family life now, is that it?"

"My mother—"

"Hold up. I thought this wasn't about your mother," LaShaun shot back with heat.

"Both my parents are worried Ellie can't just be a kid with all the... supernatural baggage. I want her to have an uneventful childhood. Okay, I'll say it. Normal. Fishing with her grandfather. Picnics. School field trips that don't involve, you know... magic. And not make friends with criminals for God's sake." Chase threw up both hands.

"You told them she's telepathic and can sometimes influence how others behave?"

"Of course not. I don't want to freak them out anymore than—" Chase broke off at the scowl his words brought. "I mean, Ellie's abilities should be kept quiet until we figure out exactly what's going on with her."

"You're embarrassed about her. Which means me, too," LaShaun said low. Her body vibrated with a combination of rage and hurt. "What's next? Should we hide CJ in the attic?"

"I don't want them to be targets for superstitious idiots. Or tools for crazies like those cult members who show up on our doorstep every few months it seems. I'm not ashamed of my children."

"*Our* children, Chase Broussard," LaShaun hissed with a glare.

Chase rubbed his jaw hard. He squeezed his eyes shut and opened them again. "This isn't the time to fight each other. Let's agree about that. This thing with Ellie and the girl—"

"Zulime Glapion," LaShaun broke in.

"Information on juveniles is kept real quiet. I had to do a lot of talking to get anybody at OJJ to tell me anything," Chase said.

"OJJ?"

"The Office of Juvenile Justice. Look," LaShaun, this girl sounds like she's real trouble. She attacked a court-appointed mentor. She has a history of being kicked out of school. I'm more than a little pissed somebody thought community service tutoring younger kids was a good idea." Chase frowned. "I let them know it, too."

Before LaShaun could answer a crash came from the family room. CJ had thrown one of his balls into the built-in bookcase. Framed family photos lay scattered, along with a vase that miraculously wasn't broken.

"Oops. Beau, you know better." CJ shook a tiny finger at the dog. Beau woofed a denial back at him.

"Bath time and bed, mister," LaShaun yelled from the kitchen. She glanced at the decorative wall clock. "It's almost seven-thirty. When you start getting sleepy you also start getting into big trouble."

"Not sleepy, Mama. Beau needs a walk," CJ countered with toddler logic.

"Beau's already been out. And it's dark outside. By the way, you'll get a bath tomorrow, too." LaShaun aimed her last comment at Beau, who ducked his head at the mention of soap and water.

"We can take a bath together!" CJ said with glee. He beamed at a dubious Beau. The dog seemed to shoot LaShaun a pleading look.

"Nice try but no way," LaShaun retorted.

She directed CJ on helping pick up after himself. Once everything was back on the shelves, LaShaun herded him to his room. Chase stayed behind to finish tidying up the kitchen. LaShaun took off his rumpled and stained clothes. A warm bath in the tub helped CJ begin to wind down. LaShaun had his routine fixed. She dimmed the lights in both the bedroom and bathroom. She dressed him in his favorite cozy pajamas. Within ten minutes of story time his eyes drifted shut. LaShaun rubbed his back one last time before she made a quiet exit. When she returned to the kitchen, Chase was on his work cell phone. He ended the call and faced her with a grim set to his jaw.

"We really need to talk to Ellie about the Glapion girl."

"Before you go back to the station," LaShaun replied.

When Chase nodded, she headed to Ellie's bedroom. Minutes later they returned. Dressed in her mermaid lavender nightgown, Ellie looked like any nine-year-old. She held onto LaShaun's hands tightly as she darted anxious looks at Chase. LaShaun checked the baby monitor video on the smart home device. CJ lay on his back sleeping. Beau had curled up on the floor next to the toddler's single bed. At least two members of the Broussard household were at peace, she mused.

"Come over here." Chase patted the cushion next to him on their sofa in the family room.

LaShaun gave Ellie a gentle push to get her feet going toward Chase. "Go on. Daddy and I need to ask you more about Zulime."

"Okay, but I didn't steal her notebook and keychain." Ellie bit off her words at Chase's expressionless face. She eased onto the sofa at least twelve inches away from him.

"So, let's talk about it," LaShaun began before Chase could respond. She sat on the wide leather ottoman near the sofa.

Ellie took a deep breath. "Zee said I could help her. She asked me to keep her notebook because her private thoughts were in it. Not class work, though."

"Her journal?" LaShaun glanced at Chase and back to Ellie.

"Yeah. She said bad people would try and stop her from... I didn't really understand. But Zee said it didn't matter. Just get her things cause I was the only one she could trust. Those girls only pretended to be her friends. Mama, she's in big trouble. You have to help her." Ellie gripped LaShaun's right hand. "Please."

"Ellie, Zee is in trouble. You're right about that. She hurt someone really bad. So bad, the lady had to go to the hospital." Chase glanced at LaShaun.

A chill shook LaShaun as she third eye saw clearly Zulime's situation had gotten worse. Ellie glanced at LaShaun first and then Chase. She stood with a solemn look on her face.

"Mama, Daddy, Zee didn't do what they're saying she did. At least it didn't happen the *way* they say. I don't know why." Ellie frowned and blinked rapidly as if sorting through her thoughts.

"You know I've told you about my work, right? My job is to arrest people who've broken the rules. Sometimes serious rules called laws. But we don't put people in jail without evidence," Chase said in a patient tone.

Ellie blinked back from her reverie and looked at him. "I remember."

"Well, the reason Zulime, Zee, was taken away was because evidence, strong evidence, says she hurt someone. And that's against the law. I get that you were trying to help your friend. Helping a friend is a good thing. But not when they've done something wrong. Understand?" Chase rubbed her little shoulder.

"Yeah, but she didn't do the wrong thing like they say. I know she didn't. Zee is like me. People think she's a weirdo and bully her. Just because her grandmother lives in a house out on Blood River next to the bayou. And her family is like ours, like I read in Great-Grandmother Odette's journal." Ellie's eyes grew wider as she talked. "You have to believe me and help her. Mama, you understand. You told me about how other girls treated you in school."

"Ellie, I thought we agreed you wouldn't read your Monmon Odette's journals anymore. At least not until you're older and can understand them better." Chase stared hard at LaShaun over Ellie's head as he spoke.

"I—" Ellie bit her lower lip and looked at her bunny slippers, realizing she'd admitted to breaking another rule. "Yes, Daddy. Sorry. It was only the one with family recipes and how her great-great-great grandpapa came to Louisiana from La Española."

"Where?" Chase blinked hard at her.

"Haiti was first called La Española before the Spanish ceded it to France in the seventeenth century," LaShaun explained. "Monmon Odette was a history buff, especially when it came to our ancestors."

"Ah... right. The point is you're going to give mama the journal you're reading, okay?" Chase pulled Ellie against his body, one arm cradling her gently.

"Yes, Daddy."

"You did your best to help Zee, but you can't do anything for her now. No more breaking rules, especially leaving school. Even if it's for a friend. You tell a teacher, me, or your mama if someone needs help," Chase said.

"So, you'll help Zee? Like I said, I know she didn't do it. And even CJ—" Ellie stopped and bit her lip again. She glanced at LaShaun. "Sorry, Mama."

Chase's jaw tightened. "What about CJ, Ellie."

"We have to know everything. No keeping secrets from us about Zee or what's happening with her." LaShaun avoided Chase's hot gaze.

"CJ knows things just by touching them. That's why I brought Zee's keychain home. I was going to take it back to her locker. Honest! I just wanted CJ to read them. That's what Monmon Odette said in one of her journals. Some Rousselles could just hold a thing that belonged to someone and tell you a lot about them. I figure if we can get CJ to do it then Mama could really know how to help her." Ellie shuffled her feet making it appear the bunnies were dancing.

"CJ doesn't know that many words. How can he tell you anything?" Chase said in a tense voice.

"Oh, he talks real good. Better every day. I help him read some of my books to know more words. And he can draw!" Ellie slipped from the sofa and raced off before either of her parents could react.

Chase let out a slow breath. "Did you know?"

"No. Well, not exactly. A few times he'd do things like step into your slippers and say Daddy is at work. A few weeks ago, he grabbed one of Ellie's stuffed rabbits and said she was talking too much in class. Later, I got an email from the teacher. A note to discuss it with her. But that wasn't definitive. You're mostly away at work when you're not home. And... well, we both know Ellie is a chatterbox." LaShaun frowned as she tried to recall any other signs.

"Not exactly," Chase clipped. "But you didn't say anything to me."

"Maybe you haven't noticed how busy I am taking care of two small children, this house, the dog, and managing our investments. You're at work a lot," LaShaun snapped.

"Your investments mostly. From the Rousselle holdings," Chase replied.

"And what's that supposed to—" LaShaun stopped when Ellie ran back into the family room.

"Here, see? He drew Zee and there's this dark thing next to her. CJ drew it after her schoolbook. He says the baddies are there." Ellie held up the paper sheet ripped from her drawing tablet. Her cute face screwed up as she looked at it. "Though I'm not sure what it means. But if Mama talked to Zee—"

Chase took the drawing from her and placed it face down on the coffee table. "Ellie, no more playing kid detective. The trouble that your friend has gotten herself into is for grown-ups to handle."

Ellie nodded with enthusiasm. "Like Mama. I know, which is why I was going to tell her about..." Her voice trailed off at the dark look on his face. "Yes, Daddy."

"Sweetheart, Zulime has a lawyer and a social worker to help her. And the police will gather all the facts. If there are extenuating circumstances, they'll find out. I'm sure the judge will take them into consideration. Especially since she's so young," Chase said.

"What does extenamating..." Ellie blinked at him as she struggled to untangle her little tongue. "Whatever you said mean?"

"Extenuating circumstances. That means there may be reasons why Zulime did what she did that maybe makes it not so serious for her," LaShaun put in.

"Then that's what you have to find, Mama," Ellie said, her frown clearing into one of hope.

"Like I said, a lawyer is working on Zulime's case," Chase cut in. "She's not all alone like you think. So, we're going to trust in the system and let them handle it."

"You find the evidence then, Daddy. You're a policeman," Ellie said in a firm tone as if assigning Chase to the task.

Chase heaved a sigh as if he had a tenuous hold on his temper. "I promise you good people are doing the best they can for her. I looked into it."

Ellie glanced at LaShaun and back to Chase. She nodded making her thick curls bounce. "Yes, Daddy."

"Listen to your teacher and Mrs. Richardson. Obey the rules and absolutely no walking off from school again." LaShaun pointed a forefinger at Ellie's cute nose.

"Yes, Mama."

"Now, time for bed so you can be rested and ready for school tomorrow morning." LaShaun smiled at her.

"I'll put my hair into sleepy time pony tails and wear my bonnet." Ellie brushed a small hand through her hair.

"Good girl." LaShaun tucked a thick lock behind one of Ellie's ears.

"Yes, ma'am." Ellie assumed her most dutiful daughter face. Then she spun around fast and wrapped both arms around Chase's neck. "Thank you so much for helping Zee, Daddy. She's a nice person. Really."

"I never said..." Chase's words trailed off as Ellie skipped away, humming a tune. He blew out a noisy sigh.

LaShaun waited until Ellie had disappeared. Then she faced Chase. "Now about CJ."

"I know. I didn't mean to imply you kept things from me. And I'm not embarrassed about our children," Chase said with force.

"Okay." LaShaun crossed her arms. "So, what is all this stuff about your parents? Sounds like you've been talking to them instead of discussing your concerns with your wife. Their *mother*."

"Both my parents want the best for all of their grandchildren. But—" Chase cut her off when LaShaun opened her mouth to speak. He held up a palm. "But Ellie and now CJ face different hurdles than the other kids."

"Which is why TEA children's educational resources are beneficial." LaShaun pressed forward despite Chase's grunt of dissatisfaction at the mention of the Third Eye Association. "Look, I know you're not comfortable given some of the issues they've had."

"Issues? What an understatement. A crazy cult of evil wizards infiltrated TEA and they're scrambling to clean up."

Chase stood as he shook his head. "I can't believe you'd trust our children with them."

"TEA has taken serious steps to root out any Legion members or influence," LaShaun argued.

"You sound like a press release. You working in the PR office?" Chase retorted.

LaShaun tamped down a tart reply, counted to five, and then spoke. "They some of the best-trained cops in this or any country. Ex-military members. Even folks who have been intelligence officers. If they say it's handled, then it's been handled."

Chase still wore a tight-jawed expression. "Yeah. Uh-huh. I've got to head out. A body has been found."

"You've been gone most of the week. You have two very competent detectives in your unit, Chase. You don't have to show up every time," LaShaun shot back.

"Dave will want me there," Chase replied in a stiff tone. "He's the big boss, remember?"

"Oh, so that was Dave on the phone ordering you to the scene?"

LaShaun followed Chase as he walked to the laundry room. A locked closet in there was where he kept his duty belt. A second locked box held his service revolver.

"Look, LaShaun. There's a lot of stuff popping off right now. Meth labs, overdoses. This could be the start of gang fights. I've got a lot on my mind. We can talk about the kids when I get home," Chase spoke over his shoulder.

"Right. And who knows when that will be." LaShaun stared at his broad back. "Maybe you'd prefer not to come home.

Between going to your parents' house more and being on your shift, you're hardly here."

Chase turned around and sat on the bench. He pulled on one of three pairs boots he wore to work. "Don't be silly. Next, you'll say I've arranged a crime spree to avoid you and the kids."

"Do you have to go tonight? It's almost ten o'clock and you put in extra hours already." LaShaun stared at him. When he didn't meet her gaze LaShaun had the answer. "Damn it."

"A cop doesn't keep regular hours," Chase replied in an even tone.

"You didn't answer either of my questions. Did Dave himself call—" LaShaun stopped when the back doorbell chimed. She and Chase exchanged a glance.

"Who the hell..." Chase strode off and down the short hallway to the kitchen.

LaShaun followed him. "One of your detectives maybe."

"Nah, they're already at the scene."

Chase pulled out his work cell phone and opened the home security system app. He grunted and held the phone up so LaShaun could see. Jonah and CeeCee, two Third Eye Association operatives, grinned into the doorbell camera. Jonah gave a jolly wave as if they hadn't showed up unannounced. Chase muttered a string of expletives and then unlocked the door. He didn't open it but instead stepped back, arms crossed. Jonah entered first.

"Hey, hey, and good evening to all. Excuse the surprise visit, but we were in the area and couldn't resist seeing our favorite crime-fighting couple." Jonah's voice trailed off the longer he looked at Chase's granite expression. "Bad timing?"

"You're the psychics. You should know," Chase snapped. He spun on his heels and went back to the laundry room.

"Whoa. Big chief is in a foul mood." Jonah craned his neck to gaze after Chase.

"Sorry for dropping in unannounced. Really, but it's urgent and we were in the area. TEA business," CeeCee said and closed the door. She engaged the locks and faced LaShaun with an apologetic smile.

"I'm guessing we shouldn't mention TEA to Chase right about now." Jonah raised an eyebrow at LaShaun.

LaShaun motioned them to follow her. "A TEA Regional Operations Manager and criminal investigator show up in the middle of the night. I think he knows you're not here for milk and cookies."

"Though both sound good right about now." Jonah looked around the kitchen. "If you have any of those tea cakes from your grandmother's recipe..."

"I'll take coffee for sure," CeeCee put in.

Chase stuck his head around the doorframe from the hallway. "I'm gone. Leaving out through the mudroom. Nice seeing you two."

"Liar," Jonah said with a grin. His wisecrack made Chase uttered a short laugh before he ducked out again.

LaShaun heaved a deep sigh as the security system chimed, a signal he'd left through the second rear door they had. She ignored the pointed glance CeeCee exchanged with Jonah. Both sat down on chairs at the kitchen island. Neither spoke as she prepared the coffee maker. Then she pulled out the large cookie jar and set it down in front of Jonah.

"CJ ate the last of the tea cakes. Tante Shirleen made ginger cookies this morning. Sent a large batch home with us."

"Oooh, yes! No wonder I don't mind working cases in Louisiana. Best cooks in the country." Jonah removed the lid and grabbed a cookie. He bit into it, chewed, and sighed. "Make that the world."

CeeCee shook her head at him as he finished that cookie and stared on a second one. "Damn, Jonah. We just had dinner a couple of hours ago."

"Exactly. It's been so long." Jonah licked a crumb from his finger. "So, what trouble in paradise did we step into?"

"It's called none of our business," CeeCee clipped. She slapped his shoulder with a light touch.

"We maybe could ease the tension," Jonah protested. "I mean, we're family."

"Read the room. *We're* the source of tension." CeeCee looked at LaShaun. "Right?"

"Not you two specifically. But yeah, TEA is a sore spot with him right now. Well, it has been for a while. And then Ellie had some trouble at school." LaShaun waved a hand and turned to find mugs to serve up the coffee.

Jonah's playful expression faded. He was close to Ellie. "My little sis okay?"

"She's fine. Seems she takes rule-breaking after me," LaShaun quipped.

"You don't have to tell us what's going on," CeeCee offered.

LaShaun put mugs down in front of them with a solid thump. She retrieved the now-full glass carafe from the coffee machine and filled them. CeeCee thanked her and took a generous sip. Jonah, mouth full of cookie, waved away her offer.

"Her teenaged tutor, who's been arrested, asked Ellie to get some of her belongings. The principal at her school considers it theft. Anyway, Ellie insists the girl's being persecuted for being different and she's innocent." LaShaun shook her head as she poured coffee for herself. She sat down hard on a third barstool. "I don't know. Then she dropped the bomb that CJ has extra senses. He can 'read' objects."

"Object telepathy. He's able to tell people about themselves or about events in their lives." Jonah went to the refrigerator, got milk, and poured himself a glass from the cabinet.

"He's like a big kid. Cookies and milk snack." CeeCee rolled her eyes and sipped more coffee. She studied LaShaun for a few seconds. "You want the kids to take part in TEA-sponsored activities for children. Chase doesn't."

"To put it mildly," LaShaun replied with a snort.

"Hey, living with psychics is hard for folks limited to five senses. You'll work it out." CeeCee patted LaShaun's forearm.

"Yeah. Somehow, I guess. Anyway, what brings you to bayou country? At this hour no less." LaShaun swiveled the stool around to face CeeCee.

"Maybe we shouldn't drop anything else in your lap." CeeCee frowned as she drummed her fingers on the island's smooth surface.

Jonah drained the glass and set it in the sink. He rejoined them, hands on his slender waist. "Not an option. We need to get LaShaun's take as a local. Orders from the top."

"You mean a mission directly from God? Neither one of you is known for following orders from TEA leadership." LaShaun raised both eyebrows as she looked from him to CeeCee.

"We follow instructions. Mostly," Jonah replied with a cheeky grin.

"More like we use our discretion in the field," CeeCee added.

"And view most orders as suggestions, TEA policy as... guidelines." Jonah leaned on the counter, both palms flat on its surface. "Anyway, James Schaffer is—"

"Oh Lord!" LaShaun hissed like an angry cat. "Not that reality show, so-called, bogus ghost hunter jerk."

Jonah barked a laugh. "Tell us how you really feel, sis."

"Don't tell me TEA is taking anything that guy says seriously. Two seasoned field personnel for him?" LaShaun gazed at their twin grim expression.

"Schaffer says TEA murdered one of his colleagues and he has solid leads that make it plausible? Oh, hell yeah. They're taking it seriously," CeeCee said.

"Wow." LaShaun drank coffee and shook her head as the information sank in. "Wow. So, what do you need from me."

Jonah nodded. "Tell us what you know about the Glapion family. Current info, family history. The kind of stuff an internet search can't provide."

"Oh crap." LaShaun's entire body lit up with extrasensory needles pricking her skin.

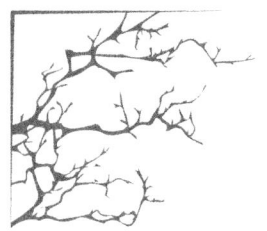

# Chapter 3

Wednesday morning at breakfast, Ellie ate her grits and eggs with gusto. Then she drained the orange juice from her small child-sized glass. "Eat your food, CJ. You want to grow up big and strong like Daddy, don't you?"

"Hmmm," CJ mumbled.

He stretched out his toddler arms and flexed his muscles. Then he stuffed the last wedge of buttered toast into his mouth. He'd only eaten half his scrambled eggs, but LaShaun wasn't going to complain. One disgruntled Broussard male in the house was enough. She took CJ's plate with a superhero on it and scraped the remains into the trash bin. Then she put a tiny bowl of red grapes and two orange slices in front of him. He attacked the fruit with gusto. Chase strolled in dressed in his pajama pants and a white t-shirt. He held a mug of his first cup of coffee.

"You ready for a great day at school?" He looked at Ellie. His tone clearly communicated the answer he should get back.

"Yes, Daddy. I've got my extra reading done for history and social studies. But they left out some of the Civil Rights facts. Cousin Azalei says that's the problem with public schools these days." Ellie started to say more. The look on her father's face brought her up short. "I'm doing just what the teacher told us to do."

"Your cousin Azalei isn't the one giving you grades. Remember that," Chase said.

"Yes, Daddy." Ellie assumed a respectful demeanor as she nodded agreement.

"Remember, you can find more information in the books I got for you. Right?" LaShaun put in.

Ellie nodded eagerly. "I told Miss Kincaid and she said those are great books, too. I think she might even use them if they let her. I think it's wrong if they don't."

"Either way, you let the adults fight that battle. *Your* job is to get the most out of your lessons. Pay attention in class," Chase said.

"Yes, Daddy."

"Good girl."

Chase kissed the top of her head. Then he stood back and leaned against the counter. He studied their children with a thoughtful expression as he sipped coffee. CJ was in high spirits, not noticing the underlying hint of tension in the air. LaShaun was grateful he didn't. For now, CJ was still a normal toddler enjoying life's simple pleasures: grapes, cartoons, and his dog. Whatever his extra senses were, he wasn't finding them distressing. LaShaun glanced at Chase but continued clearing up dishes. She had fallen into a deep sleep despite the events of the previous day. She barely registered his solid presence as he climbed into bed next to her.

"You're up early after working so late. What time did you get home? Two a.m.?" LaShaun said. She took a warm plate of breakfast from the oven for him.

"Hmm, around there. Yeah. Thanks."

Chase sat next to CJ at the table. Fall sunlight streamed in through the bay window of the dine-in alcove. He dug in, chattering with CJ in between bites. LaShaun squinted at his avoidance of her but said nothing. Instead, she steered Ellie to her room to finish getting ready. After she supervised Ellie's teeth brushing, she helped her select a sweater against the crisp October morning. Then she walked with her down the driveway. After about ten minutes the school bus pulled up. Ellie waved good-bye and climbed the steps. Once the big yellow vehicle rumbled off, LaShaun left. She rubbed the long sleeves of the light sweatshirt top she wore over denim leggings. She found Chase and CJ sitting next to each other in companionable silence. CJ still munched fruit as juice dribbled down his chin to his pajama top. Chase stared out of the bay window as if his mind was still on work.

"Well, you're going to be a big boy today. School like Ellie," LaShaun said in a cheerful tone. They were easing him into kindergarten three days a week at Ellie's school.

"I think in no time my boy will be going to school every day like his big sister. Right, champ? High five." Chase held up one large palm as a prompt.

CJ gave his father a solid slap with his tiny hand. "I know my colors and I can count to twenty!"

"That's what I'm talking about." Chase beamed at him. "I'll take him so you don't have to."

"You've earned at least the day off. You should get some rest. Sleep in after finishing a hearty breakfast to keep your strength up." LaShaun forced a light tone. "Then we could talk."

Chase grunted and shrugged. "I would but this new case is going to be touchy. Press is starting to swarm already. Good thing I went last night."

"Oh? I haven't looked at the morning news yet." LaShaun forgot to be annoyed with him, her thoughts on what she'd learned from Jonah and CeeCee.

"Umm." Chase used a wet towelette to swipe CJ's face clean. "So, tell me. Does the body we found have anything to do with Jonah and CeeCee popping in last night?"

LaShaun got busy scraping food scraps from plates. "Why would you ask that?"

"Huh." Chase studied LaShaun for a moment. Then he found CJ's tablet. "Here you go. Look at your show."

"Adventures with Trey! Yaay!" CJ clapped his hands as the educational animated series played on the screen. His focus became the bright figures of diverse characters.

Chase took his plate to LaShaun and handed it to her. "You dodged my question with a question. First sign a suspect is guilty of something,"

"Suspect, huh? So, you're going to interrogate me." LaShaun put the plate in the dishwasher and closed the door. She turned away to wipe the cooktop's surface.

"Are Jonah and CeeCee in Beau Chene because of this latest homicide?" Chase crossed, took the towel from LaShaun, and hung it up. "You've cleaned that spot enough to pass a health inspection."

"I can answer accurately if you tell me about it," LaShaun countered. She went to the kitchen island and sat on a stool.

"Fair enough." Chase crossed and sat next to her. "Tranicia Banks was found dead in an abandoned house. Her body had been there at least forty-eight hours. Evidence on the scene of drug use. She was a known drug user and occasional sex worker."

LaShaun gazed at him for a few moments. "Is that everything you know so far?"

"Everything I can tell you because Dave authorized a statement for the press. A local reporter knew a body had been found. Except we didn't release her name or the part about being a sex worker," Chase replied. "No postmortem yet. The State Police Crime Scene Unit hasn't finished a full forensic on the scene or her clothing."

"And you wouldn't tell me what they've found anyway because it's none of my business," LaShaun quipped.

"The details of a criminal investigation should not be disclosed to non-law enforcement individuals," Chase replied.

"What I said. It's none of my business." LaShaun grinned at him.

"LaShaun..." Chase squinted at her.

"No. CeeCee came because there's more TEA drama. Something about a leak and James Schaffer being hot to expose a secret organization."

Chase squinted at her. "What is it he thinks they've done?"

LaShaun sucked in a breath and blew it out. Chase wasn't psychic, but he had the instincts of a good cop. He knew something about the workings of TEA to be suspicious of the organization. And he knew LaShaun well.

"They wouldn't have shown up late at night unless it was something big," Chase said as if he was indeed reading her mind.

"A so-called paranormal expert slash investigator has gone missing. One of Schaffer's rival colleagues. He doesn't believe reports that the woman simply took off after a scandal screwed up her career. He believes the secret organization had her killed because she was getting close to the truth." LaShaun shrugged when Chase gave a snort of disdain. "I know. It sounds like a corny Hollywood script."

"Your friends." Chase shook his head.

"Might be a great idea to not tell your parents about my friends. They're shook enough about me and the kids," LaShaun retorted. "Jonah and CeeCee have become family. They're *good* people. In fact, the work they do keeps the public safe from supernatural bad actors."

"C'est vrai ça?" Chase replied.

"Yes, that's is the *truth*, Chase Armand Broussard. Believe me, you don't want the paranormal chaos not having them would cause." LaShaun poked a finger into his chest.

"If you say so."

"You're the one who gripes 'Give me normal everyday criminals any day of the week!' Well, because of people like CeeCee and Jonah, that's all you have to deal with, Chief Deputy Detective Broussard. Same goes for the rest of your law enforcement colleagues across the country. Even globally."

Chase waved away her statement. He gazed over at CJ, who was still engrossed in his favorite characters. Then he rose and filled his mug, emptying the glass coffee pot. He sat next to LaShaun again and lowered his voice. "I get sucked into y'all's spooky stuff a little too often."

"Not as much as you could be. There's more in heaven and earth, Horatio," LaShaun said.

"Yeah, yeah, yeah. So, the good news is my case has nothing to do with your sorcerer pals." Chase chuckled at the fiery look

LaShaun gave him. Then he grew serious again. "And tell me it doesn't mean you have to get involved."

"Schaffer is sniffing around in New Orleans and he might be headed this way. So, there's a Louisiana connection. For now, CeeCee and Jonah are strictly gathering information. There may be some local history that plays into what's going on with TEA."

"They want you to provide voodoo gossip from the bayou," Chase said, cocking his head to one side.

"Seems this woman was working on a story connected to Louisiana and groups of psychics. I don't know all the details because CeeCee and Jonah don't know them yet." LaShaun choose her words with care to dance along the line between truth and lie.

"Uh-huh. Nothing to do with Tranicia Banks though?" Chase scrutinized LaShaun as he asked the question.

"Nothing at all."

"Good."

"At least not based on what they told me so far," LaShaun added.

"LaShaun..." Chase pointed a forefinger at her nose.

"Hey, I don't know what all this Tranicia might have gotten up to. Lots of folks dabble in stuff they got no business messing with. You know that from past cases," LaShaun shot back.

Chase rubbed his jaw. "Humph. I'm going to do a thorough background check on my victim. Make sure she doesn't have any spooky friends. Or family, for that matter. Including contacts with Schaffer or his friend. Ask them to look into it."

"They might be like you and want to keep their case details confidential." LaShaun picked up his coffee mug and sipped. She grinned at the scowl on his handsome face.

"Y'all better not play with me. You tell them I want to know about this ghosthunter woman. More than what I'd have my staff pick through on the internet." Chase grabbed the mug from her. His scowl deepened when he saw it was empty. "I'll get more coffee at the station, I guess."

"I fixed you lunch. Leftover jambalaya and a side of coleslaw. Oh, and garlic bread," LaShaun called after him as he retreated to their main suite.

"I'll keep you I guess," Chase yelled back without looking around.

"You better." LaShaun laughed. Her smile dimmed at the thought of her mother-in-law's influence.

"A is for apple, made into sauce. B is for ball that we like to toss." CJ happily sang along with a puppet bouncing around on the tablet.

"LaShaun crossed the space where he still sat at the table. She scooped him up into her arms. "Let's get you cleaned up and ready for school. My goodness! You're getting to be so big."

"Not a baby. I can walk." CJ scrambled from her hold to land on the floor with the tablet still held tight.

LaShaun ruffled his thick curls so like his father's as they went to his room. For the next forty minutes she wrestled with the easily distracted toddler. Luckily, he didn't put up a battle when told to put away his tablet. LaShaun reminded him about school activities he loved. Though it was cool outside, the class would be in the garden that day. CJ loved the outdoors. Beau padded in from his own morning ramble in their expansive yard. He sat on his haunches, content to watch his humans. By the time LaShaun had CJ ready, Chase was dressed. He already had the look of concentration that signaled he'd heard from someone at the department. Still, he brightened at the sight of his son. CJ whooped with joy at riding to school with his daddy. With one last round of good-bye kisses and hugs, they left. LaShaun went to the kitchen to the smart home device. It had an app synced to her email account and instant messenger app. She scrolled through emails. Nothing but bills for online payments, ads, and other routine correspondence. An alarm bell rang on her cell phone; the signal an important text message waited. Aunt Shirleen's face appeared when she unlocked the screen.

"G'morning. Hot tea to go with breakfast, cher. Your friend Savannah St. Julien is Zulime's lawyer!" LaShaun read out loud. She could almost hear her aunt's Louisiana Creole accent, delighted she'd tapped into inside scoop. She clicked her tongue at the news. "*Ooo-kay*. So, I'm going into town."

MORNING SUNSHINE ADDED to the quaint look of downtown Beau Chene. LaShaun had stopped by Tante Marie's Bakery, founded by Savannah's aunt and now run by one of her adult grandsons. The box of Savannah's favorite pastries would serve as a gift. A method to smooth the way when LaShaun started asking questions about Zulime. Long shot, but it might work. Maybe she should lead with how Ellie was involved? LaShaun walked along the bustling sidewalk. Two busloads of tourists were the source of crowds. They made Beau Chene look almost like a thriving metropolis in miniature. LaShaun paused to allow a knot of chattering middle-aged women enter an antique shop. She only half paid attention, her thoughts steps ahead to her friend's law office. A familiar voice at her shoulder jerked her back.

"How you doin'?" Azalei seemed to appear out of thin air beside LaShaun on the sidewalk on Main Street. She grinned at LaShaun, a brown paperback in one hand.

"Don't you have a job?" LaShaun frowned at her cousin and gave her a head-to-toe scan. "Nice fit."

Azalei did her version of a short runway strut, twirled, and faced LaShaun again. She modeled a teal oversized sweater and matching floral slim pants. Teal, yellow, and orange petals on vines seemed to climb her legs. "Ivy Park. Bey rules my world today."

"Hmm. I don't mean to be catty, but..." LaShaun tilted her sunglasses down to peer at her cousin over them.

"Yes, I do have a job. Two lucrative hustles. And no, I don't mean the guy I'm dating. I have a thriving channel on YouTube serving up local gossip. Well, mostly about hip hop and reality show celebrities in Louisiana or with roots here. And I do feet pics." Azalei tossed her thick hair back.

"Feet pics?"

"Yep. Girl, I had no idea the foot fetish community was so huge. Guys go wild for a sweet pedi in stiletto sandals." Azalei stuck out a foot clad in expensive sneakers. "Well, you can't tell with these on, but my feet are quite fab."

"Aunt Leah must be losing her mind. Her debutante destined to marry the next Barack Obama." LaShaun blinked at her, mouth open. "And the family loves to talk about my shady past!"

"My identity is secret behind the best encryption system ever. I'm Miss Kiss My Pinkie. Look." Azalei held up her smartphone, swiped, and found the website. Various bright shades of polish on the nails matched different shoes. Some showed her bare feet with only toe rings.

"Jesus be a fence," LaShaun muttered. She shook her head at the shots of her cousin's toes. She started walking again.

Azalei matched her pace. "Don't judge. Ya girl pulling in a solid four thousand a month. I'm teasing just the feet for now. I'll move up to ankles and calves to test the market potential."

"Aunt Leah is probably *not* bragging about this at the ladies club meeting," LaShaun quipped. She could picture her socially ambitious aunt fainting from the shock.

"I'm a successful entrepreneur. Since it's all anonymous, she got over it. Sort of. Plus, her and Daddy aren't having to fund my lifestyle. She's taking a glass half full point of view. Oh, and it's legal." Azalei slipped her phone into a pocket of her fancy leather handbag. "So, where are we off to this fine morning?"

"*We* aren't going anywhere. I'm... running errands and going to visit a friend," LaShaun paused in front of a picturesque hardware store's window. She feigned looking at the display of gardening tools and decorations.

"Uh-huh. I'm guessing that friend would be attorney-at-law Savannah St. Julien. Her office is right off Main Street." Azalei looked at the colorful potted plants. "That's cute. I might get one for my new house."

"A house?"

"At the rate my business is expanding, I should have a down payment soon." Azalei lifted her chin in the air. "I'm investing to retire young."

"You know, I can't even criticize you this time. At least you're not causing trouble," LaShaun conceded.

"Thank you. We didn't all inherit a bundle from Monmon Odette," Azalei murmured.

"Don't start—"

"I'm not complaining. In fact, getting stiffed because you were the favorite spurred me to take initiative."

"Aunt Leah and our uncles got healthy chunks. Blame your daddy for losing it on business deals that went south."

Azalei hissed a sigh. "And Mama's wild spending."

"She wasn't alone," LaShaun shot back.

"Ouch. Anyway, we've all cleaned up our acts. Daddy will retire from the sugar and soybean mill soon. And Mama keeps a close eye on the budget," Azalei replied.

"So happy for you all. Now if you'll excuse me." LaShaun started walking again. She gritted her teeth when Azalei stayed with her.

"Speaking of hot topics around town. I heard Zulime Glapion is in big-time trouble. That woman she put a whoopin' on ain't doing so hot. Your friend has got her work cut out for her. Oh, and Zulime's grandmother has all but washed her hands of the girl. Seems she tired after dealing with her mama and daddy for years. She—"

"I thought your specialty was celebrity gossip."

Azalei pulled LaShaun aside to make way for approaching foot traffic. She sat down at sideway café table under a yellow striped awning. She gestured for LaShaun to join her. "Turns out the Glapion family is well-known around town."

"Azalei, I have things to do," LaShaun clipped.

"I have news you can use. We both know you're going to get involved. Ellie asked you to after that little dust up at her school.

Oh yeah, I know all about it." Azalei wore a smirk. She pointed to a chair again.

"Five minutes and I'm gone." LaShaun sat. She took out her cell phone, set the timer, and crossed her arms.

Azalei smiled even wider. "I knew you couldn't resist. Aunt Shirleen was right. The Glapion family has a reputation that matches the Rousselle legends. I won't go into the dry details that go back almost a hundred years. T' Shirl almost drove me nuts with the 'begats' and who was kin to who for almost an hour."

"Okay." LaShaun maintained her façade of mild interest. But she took note to follow up with their Tante Shirl later. What Azalei thought of as dusty facts might be revealing.

A teenager wearing a white shirt and black pants approached. He took their order for two café au laits and left. Azalei watched him leave. Then she leaned forward and dropped her voice to a confidential tone.

"The Glapion family came over about the same time as our ancestors from that island, what-its-name or whatever." Azalei waved a hand at the detail she found insignificant.

"Seriously, Ellie knows more about our history than you do. Take more of an interest," LaShaun said.

"You want to hear this story or not?" Azalei stopped again when the waiter returned. Once the cups were set down and he'd left, she resumed her account. "Didn't take long for the Glapion clan to clash with one of our ancestors. Over land at first. Then one of the LeGranges, or was it a Rousselle. Doesn't matter. One of the two said a Glapion stole some livestock. And things escalated. Our relatives came out on top and that's why the Glapions live way out on Blood River. Well, Zulime's grandmother lives in a house about a half-mile from Blood Bayou. Things went downhill for a lot of the descendants. Including Zulime's parents; and now her obviously."

"Her grandmother is Eunice Glapion Vidal." LaShaun took off her sunglasses. She gazed past Azalei as she sipped from the cup.

"Yep. Oh, and both husbands were distant cousins, so there's the whole intermarriage thing. Folks say that's why they're crazy." Azalei sipped as well. She winced and added sugar to the café au lait.

"Marrying cousins was common back in the day. Think of Britain's royal family," LaShaun replied in a distracted tone.

"The Glapions are anything but royalty, child. And Miss Eunice married a cousin t*wice* if you can believe it. Ew!" Azalei replied with a sniff.

LaShaun tapped a finger on the side of the warm coffee mug. "Anything else you find out about Zulime?"

"Like Aunt Shirleen said, she's been in a lot of trouble. Though she's not exactly an only child. Her daddy has another child, a boy. He's in college. Seems his mama's people did a better job raising him. Got him away from Zee's daddy early. His mother cleaned up her life, went back to school, and she's a nurse." Azalei reached into the box and snagged a beignet. She yelped when LaShaun slapped her hand.

"I meant about Zee attacking the woman," LaShaun said.

"Hmm, you mean Karlene Pattison. She's a part-time employee with the Brighter Futures program. Sorta like the Boys and Girls Clubs. They got a contract with three local juvenile courts to provide mentorship and other services to troubled kids. She has an apartment in New Iberia." Azalei jerked a thumb in the direction of the small town in a neighboring parish. New Iberia was a twenty-minute ride east of Beau Chene.

"Did you get her dress size while you were at it, Shirleen Junior?" LaShaun quipped.

"Give me a couple of more hours, cuz." Azalei grinned back and bit into the pastry.

LaShaun stood and snatched the box out of reach when Azalei went for it again. "You're flush with coins. Buy your own."

"I just gave you valuable info!" Azalei protested. She wiped powdered sugar from her hands with a paper napkin.

"Nothing I wouldn't have found out myself. I'll pay for the coffees and you've had one free beignet." LaShaun took out enough for the bill and a tip. She dropped the money on the table and stood.

"Hey, a seafood platter from Crawfish House for even more." Azalei leaned back in the chair and crossed her shapely legs.

LaShaun put her sunglasses back on. "I don't need you to dig dirt."

"There's only so much Savannah is gonna tell you," Azalei tossed back with a raised eyebrow.

"If the Glapions are as touchy as folks say, maybe you don't want to be on their list. And they already don't like members of the Rousselle family," LaShaun said.

Azalei chewed more beignet for a few seconds. "You know what, cuz? I'm going to let you take it from here. I've got a business to run and my good looks to protect. I don't want that Zulime girl looking for *me* when she gets out."

LaShaun laughed. "Good plan. See you later, cousin."

Azalei grinned at her and waved goodbye. She seemed content to sit a while longer and enjoy the morning. A man at a nearby table gazed at Azalei until a woman joined him. He snapped to attention but the woman had noticed. They got into a muted hot conversation. Azalei shot a side glance at them. She shrugged when LaShaun gave her a pointed look. With a shake of her head, LaShaun went on her way. Azalei stirred up turmoil without even trying.

LaShaun arrived at Savannah's law office ten minutes later. The one-story building had a frosted glass front. A female figure holding the scales of justice was painted in gold. The words "Savannah St. Julien, Attorney" was above it. LaShaun entered through the door with office hours printed on it. Savannah's latest legal secretary, Rai'lette, sat at the front desk of the small reception foyer.

"Good morning, ma'am. How can I help you today?" Rai'lette spoke while tapping the keyboard for a few seconds more. Then she stopped and looked at LaShaun.

"I'm afraid I don't have an appointment. I—"

"Oh, no worries. We take walk-ins, ma'am. Trouble pops up whenever it wants to. Now, is this a civil or criminal concern?" Rai'lette wore a look of sympathy.

LaShaun smiled at her. "Well..."

"I'm not being nosey, ma'am. We have an intake form. It's short, but it helps Ms. St. Julien get started on your business quickly. And, of course, it's for your record. Which we keep secure." Rai'lette beamed at LaShaun as if to reassure her. Then she tapped on her keyboard again. A form blinked into view on the wide computer screen.

Savannah appeared in the short hallway leading deeper into the building. She wore a light green button-front blouse tucked into dark olive-green pencil shirt. She held a thick brown open folder. Reading glasses perched on her nose. She slapped it shut when she glanced over and saw LaShaun in the lobby.

"Don't bother checking her in, Rai," Savannah said as she walked toward the desk. "This is my friend."

"Ok, cool." Rai'lette made the form vanish with a keystroke. She brought up a different document.

"Good morning." Savannah gazed at LaShaun as she tucked the folder under one arm.

"We haven't talked in a minute. I figure you're ready to take a mid-morning break." LaShaun held up the box.

"Right on time then." Savannah grinned. "Hey, Rai, we have goodies."

"Yum. Fresh coffee is in the break room," Rai'lette called over one shoulder, still working away.

"I'll take a few for us and leave some for you, Rai'lette," LaShaun replied.

She went to the compact kitchenette at the end of the hall opposite Savannah's office. A unisex restroom was across from it on the other side of the storage room. LaShaun found paper plates and mugs in the cabinet. She went to Savannah's office with everything on a tray. Savannah was already seated at the round table in a seating area left of her desk. She'd cleared it of papers that now sat on a small sofa beneath a window. Sunlight streamed through it. A potted Ficus plant brightened up one corner. One wall held Savannah's framed credentials. Prints showing swamp scenes hung on the other three walls. A dark green blazer that matched Savannah's skirt hung on a coat rack in another corner of the room.

"I was hoping this was a social visit, but the box from my aunt's shop says otherwise. I'm trying to guess what kind of tribulations and trials you're bringing to my doorstep this time. Pun intended." Savannah accepted a mug of steaming Louisiana dark roast.

"You've grown cynical in your approaching middle age, dear friend," LaShaun wisecracked. "Maybe I was in the area and decided to stop by."

"You show up at my office with a bribe when you want something," Savannah replied. She sipped, sighed, and leaned against the leather chairback.

LaShaun placed a hand over her heart. "You wound me."

Savannah made a rude sound and started to reply when her phone rang. She picked up the handset. After a cryptic set of replies to the caller, she tapped the button at the end of their conversation. "Well?"

"How are the girls?" LaShaun succeeded in pulling Savannah into the honored Southern tradition of small talk.

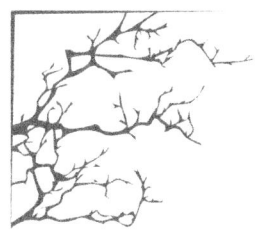

# Chapter 4

"Okay, okay, stop with the chitchat," Savannah broke in to stem the tide of minor updates on CJ, Savannah's twins, and even about Beau. "Let's hear it then. What trouble have you gotten yourself into now?"

"Not me, it's Ellie. Not legal trouble," LaShaun added when her friend's eyes widened. "She's attending the after-school behavior clinic. Ellie left school and took items from another student. The principal and Chase consider it stealing. Ellie says she was helping out a friend."

"They've accused her of theft. The parents of the other child making a fuss?" Savannah leaned forward.

"No, No. Nothing like that." LaShaun sighed as Savannah continued to look at her with an inquiring expression. "The friend is Zulime Glapion."

"I see," Savannah replied, her tone and facial expression neutral. She put her mug down on the table's wood surface.

"It was right about the time Zulime was arrested for attacking Karlene Pattison. The mentor assigned to her by Brighter Futures. Not that Ellie knows the details. But she says Zee asked her to get the notebook. So, Ellie sprang into action. She walked the short distance to the high school campus and got into Zee's locker."

"She's got your genes alright," Savannah quipped.

LaShaun squinted at her but went on. "A school aid saw her walking back. So, Ellie got busted."

"Let me guess. Ellie's broken rules before." Savannah peered at LaShaun over the mug's rim as she took another sip.

"Yes. The thing is Ellie begged me to do anything to help Zee and—"

Savannah held up both palms like a cop stopping traffic. "Donuts won't work this time, LaShaun."

"I know but—"

"Client-attorney privilege. Ever heard of it? Not only do I take is seriously, but so does the Louisiana Bar Association. I'll only discuss a client with her permission. In Zulime's case since she's a minor, with the legal guardian's permission," Savannah replied. The casual tone had vanished from her voice.

"I have information that might help," LaShaun said.

"Were you or Ellie a witness to the offense Ms. Glapion is accused of committing?" Savannah raised both eyebrows as she studied LaShaun with care.

"Well, no..." LaShaun admitted.

"You know of any mitigating circumstances that would explain Ms. Glapion's behavior on the day in question?" Savannah pressed on.

"Stop with the courtroom tactics like I'm on the stand." LaShaun waved a hand at her friend. She brushed hair away from her face. Then LaShaun tugged at her brown denim jacket over a light sweater. Savannah's silent, sharp scrutiny made her fidget a few moments longer. "Okay, okay."

Savannah crossed both arms. "Okay what?"

"Ellie's sixth sense tells her that Zulime is innocent. Or at least it didn't happen exactly the way the DA says it did. Mitigating circumstances like you said."

"You want me to build a defense based on the psychic insight of a nine-year-old?" Savannah snorted. "Thanks for the donuts anyway."

"Look, you know Ellie is gifted. If she says something is going on, then something is going on. There's that look." LaShaun jabbed a finger at her.

"Thank God this coffee is strong. I need it for this conversation." Savannah picked up her mug again.

"Your girls babysat Ellie when they were still in high school. I know they told you how she could... sense things," LaShaun shot back.

Savannah stared at LaShaun for a few beats. Then she nodded. "Telepathy."

"More than telepathy. Ellie can see into thoughts and motivations. Call her ability intuition on steroids if the psychic thing makes you jumpy. She can sometimes... push people to do what she wants."

"Hey, wait a minute. The girls would let Ellie eat sweets even though you told them not to. I just thought they were spoiling her." Savannah gaped at LaShaun.

"Now you know why I didn't fuss at them back then," LaShaun said with a smile.

"Holy crap." Savannah gulped more coffee and fell against the chairback.

"So, if Ellie says something else is going on, then there's a layer we're missing."

"Okay, fine. You don't have to convince me the Rousselle women are psychics. Remember I knew your grandmother. I can't use Ellie's belief in her friend. You got facts?"

"No, but if I could talk to Zulime it might help. She'd probably see me because I'm Ellie's mom," LaShaun added when Savannah scowled at her.

"The court would question me allowing you to visit her. So would her court-appointed child advocate. Judge Thibodeaux is very strict about what she calls vulnerable minors. Especially in this case," Savannah said.

"What sets Zulime's apart?"

"Her family history of drugs, domestic violence, and mental health issues. Her grandmother is... let's just say Mrs. Vidal is unconventional." Savannah finished her coffee and put the mug down. "I think the judge would be open to mitigating circumstances."

"Great."

"Concrete evidence, LaShaun," Savannah shot back. "I can't justify why you should be granted permission to see Zulime. You're not a relative. Or even a family friend acting on her grandmother's behalf."

LaShaun drank from her now-lukewarm cup of coffee without noticing. "Right. I see your point."

"Exactly. But I'll bite. Tell me why Ellie is so convinced there's more to the story. But I'm gonna need a refill and some sugar from a donut first," Savannah said.

"Yeah," LaShaun murmured,

She barely noticed Savannah's exit. LaShaun stared through the window, her thoughts far away. Savannah returned a minute later with the full carafe. She poured more coffee in both their mugs.

"Okay, go." Savannah selected a chocolate-covered donut. Then she settled in as if waiting for a good story.

"Actually, Ellie doesn't know details. She's trusting me to find out."

Savannah took time to finish chewing her first bite. Then washed it down. "Like I said, thanks for the donuts."

"It's a thread, and you know how good I am at following a lead," LaShaun protested.

"Sweetie, you don't have a 'thread.' What you have is a piece of lint. Look, I can't go into specifics about the charges or the defense I'm building so far. Juvenile cases are closed to the public and the press haven't gotten their eager paws on more yet. That's one good thing about Mrs. Vidal's eccentricity. She won't talk to them."

"Ellie says there's more to why Zee attacked the Pattinson woman. Maybe she was mistreating her?" LaShaun studied Savannah's expression for a clue.

"Speculative," was all Savannah offered in response.

"Damn it." LaShaun frowned when her phone beeped a text message notification. She pulled the phone from a jacket pocket, glanced at the screen, and dropped it back in.

"Okay, listen. Ellie took Zulime's journal out of her locker. She carried it everywhere with her. Ellie also took a keychain. Though it's strange the girl would have a keychain in her locker."

"Did I mention the Glapion family is strange?" Savannah gave a short grunt. "Talking to Zulime left my head spinning. When she wasn't glaring at me, she gave short answers that told me nothing. And her grandmother? The woman gave me the creeps. Reminded me of..."

"My grandmother. She mellowed toward the end. Even had you handle her legal affairs," LaShaun said with a grin.

"Yes, she did. I was still intimidated. She had a way of looking right into you. Then she'd become a sweet little old lady in a blink." Savannah shook her head with a smile. "Funny thing is I miss her."

"Me, too. Mrs. Vidal reminds you of Monmon Odette."

"Minus the sweetness." Savannah winced. "That woman is piece of work. Lives out on Blood Bayou in an old house that has to be a hundred years old. Doesn't see people."

"There's generally a reason when people isolate themselves from the world," LaShaun gazed off again, thinking about the Glapion family. "Maybe if I talked to her, I would understand more. Oh, and get permission to visit Zee."

"You're not listening to me, LaShaun. Eunice Vidal doesn't like *anyone* showing up at her door, not even relatives."

"I'll give her a call first," LaShaun said.

"Good luck. She has a landline and rarely picks up. Same for voice mail. That would be too modern. Zee somehow managed to get her a flip cell phone, but Mrs. Vidal refuses to touch it. Bad spirits or something, she says. She'll pick up if Zulime calls. Though how she knows..." Savannah shrugged.

"Caller ID, of course. Wait, she has an old-school phone with no features."

"Bingo. Rotary if you can believe it." Savannah took another generous bite of donut and licked icing from one thumb.

"Mrs. Vidal has a sixth sense, too, then. Yes, that makes sense. The Glapion family immigrated to Louisiana around the time of my LeGrange ancestors. At least one side of the family. They were friendly for a while but then had a dispute." LaShaun lapsed into turning over what she'd learned.

Savannah was quiet for a few moments as she finished off the donut. "So, let's review. You don't have any new evidence to help my case. You're not a witness to the offense, and you only know dusty gossip about the Glapion family."

"Well, if you're going to put the most negative spin on it..." LaShaun puffed out air in annoyance.

"And what do you expect me to say to the judge? I'd have to explain why you're involved," Savannah went on despite LaShaun's irritated scowl.

"Ellie knows Zulime and she—" LaShaun broke off at the pointed look from Savannah.

"If you want to ruin my career, just say that, LaShaun. Listen, I appreciate your willingness to help. Tell Ellie that Auntie Savannah is working hard to get justice for her friend. Zee is in good hands." Savannah waved a hand and went back to eating the last of her donut. "Subject covered and closed."

"Wait a minute. Ellie said Zee's journal might prove she's not the bad seed everyone thinks. Which is why Zee was so desperate for her to get it. Whatever is in there it must be important for her to ask my nine-year-old to break school rules. Maybe there's something that would explain the attack on Karlene Pattison. Or something negative about Brighter Futures," LaShaun said.

"Ellie's seen this journal and read it?"

"Umm, not exactly. She got busted and the principal took it away from her. And the keychain."

"Okay. Where's the journal or diary now?" Savannah put the last piece of donut in her mouth. She wiped her hands on a napkin and stood.

"I'm assuming Mrs. Richardson, the principal, has it. Real evidence." LaShaun stabbed a forefinger at Savannah. She took out her phone. "I have the school's number."

"Humph."

Savannah read the saved phone number on the screen. Then she went to her desk. LaShaun helped herself to a donut and coffee as Savannah called the school. It took a time for the staff to get the principal on the phone. Savannah identified herself as Zee's attorney, which no doubt helped.

"Yes, Mrs. Richardson. I understand you have items that belong to my client that might be material to her defense." Savannah grabbed a legal pad and wrote notes. She listened as the principal talked for a good three minutes. "Okay. I see. Thank you, ma'am. Of course. Bye."

"Well?" LaShaun leaned forward. "You going to pick up the diary?"

"Nope. An uncle or some relative came to pick up the few items from her locker. Two notebooks, a sweater, and 'various knickknacks' as Mrs. Richardson called them. I'd guess that includes the keychain." Savannah dropped her pen onto the legal pad. She swung her chair to face LaShaun, who still sat at the meeting table.

"A unicorn." LaShaun gazed out of the window again without seeing the scenery.

"Excuse me?" Savannah blinked fast with a puzzled expression.

"The keychain has a little unicorn dangling on a chain. Ellie took it so CJ could read the thing and give her clues."

"I'm gonna regret asking but..." Savannah let the question hang in the air.

"CJ is showing signs of extrasensory ability. He can touch objects and know events connected to them."

"Lord have mercy. I'll bet Chase is *shook*," Savannah joked.

LaShaun winced as she remembered Chase's reaction to the news. The sweetness of the beignet turned flat and she dropped it on the paper saucer. "Shook is one way to describe it."

Savannah walked back to the table and sat next to LaShaun. She placed a hand on her shoulder. "You two had another spirited discussion. Pun intended."

Strange given they started out as enemies in childhood, but Savannah had become LaShaun's good friend. More like a sister. LaShaun had confided her worry about Chase pulling away. She'd also vented to Savannah about slights from the Broussard family. Especially her mother-in-law.

"You're psychic, too? Better not tell Paul," LaShaun said, referring to Savannah's husband. "Trust me, it doesn't make for marital bliss."

"I think between my drama and raising feisty twin girls my guy could handle it," Savannah replied with a grin. Then she grew serious again when LaShaun didn't smile back. "He's crazy in love with you. Hell, he knew exactly what he signed up for marrying notorious LaShaun Rousselle."

"The phrase *buyer's remorse* comes to mind." LaShaun swallowed hard. The image of Chase's retreating back as he left after the last heated argument flashed in her mind.

"You listen to me; every marriage hits a few potholes along the way. Some bigger than others. You'll fight, but he's not going anywhere. Neither are you. One sour old monster-in-law won't break up the dream team."

LaShaun laughed hard. "I appreciate the pep talk."

"Any time. I meant every word." Savannah's supportive smile faded. She crossed her arms. "We have another problem though."

"What?" LaShaun frowned at the somber expression Savannah wore.

"Like I told you, Eunice Glapion Vidal doesn't keep in touch with anybody except Zulime. So, I'm wondering who she would have sent to the school to pick up Zulime's belongings?" Savannah looked at LaShaun. "You might be rubbing off on me, but my gut tells me something ain't right."

"I should go see Mrs. Vidal, Savannah. If you talk to Zulime to smooth the way..." LaShaun's voice trailed off. Then she nudged Savannah in the side after silence stretched between them. "What about it?"

Savannah blew out air. "Fine. I'm scheduled to visit Zulime in the morning, so I'll tell her about you. I'll try to call Mrs. Vidal, too. But no promises."

"You'll pull it off because you're fabulous!" LaShaun beamed at Savannah and sipped the last bit of coffee in her mug.

"Now, crossed fingers I can find Zee's diary and it has new details that will help her case," Savannah replied. She didn't look hopeful.

"You met any of Zulime's or Ms. Vidal's other relatives to get background?"

"Mrs. Vidal made it clear she didn't want me talking to them. I contacted a few cousins that are local. They weren't helpful.

I got the feeling they were scared of crossing her. In fact, they told me upfront she'd be pissed if they talked family business to anyone. Which means..." Savannah gazed at LaShaun.

LaShaun's sixth sense sent a tingle along her arms and down her back. She shook her head. "Yeah. Who picked up Zulime's diary and why?"

LASHAUN STOPPED BY the pet store to pick up food for Beau. While there she got him another rawhide chew bone. After a grocery run, LaShaun headed home. She still had about two hours before CJ would come home. He would stay for lunch, an afternoon nap, more play time. Chase had texted her he would let CJ ride the small school bus. The colorful school van would deposit him at the end of the driveway. He was so proud to be riding the bus like his big sister.

A Beyonce tune played on the music streaming app from their smart home device. LaShaun hummed along as she chopped up seasonings. She would make a pot of gumbo Friday in honor of the first temperature dip of the season. Cool weather with low humidity was a cause enough for celebration in subtropical Louisiana. All the ingredients would be set aside to make the task easier. The doorbell sounded.

"Now who is this?" LaShaun said to Beau.

The dog cocked his head to one side as if saying, "How would I know?" She giggled at his response. LaShaun gaped in surprise as she looked through the door's window. CeeCee's smiling face gazed back at her.

"Pretty sure you weren't expecting to see me so soon," CeeCee said when LaShaun let her in. CeeCee sniffed. "You smell like onions and bell peppers."

"Yeah, well, you smell like problems coming to call," LaShaun shot back. "Lucky for you I've got enough lunch fixings for both of us."

"Sounds good. I'm easy to please. Oh, I don't have the bottomless pit with me, so you don't have to lay out a buffet." CeeCee perched on a barstool at the island. "Hey there, sweet thing."

CeeCee patted Beau's large head when he came over to her, tail wagging. LaShaun bagged up the seasonings she'd cut up and put them in the fridge. Then she took frozen shrimp and crab legs from the large freezer in the pantry. She smiled at CeeCee, who engaged in lively conversation with Beau. LaShaun washed her hands, dried them, and made two chicken salad sandwiches. She filled two glasses of sweet tea. Then she sat next to CeeCee.

"Okay, what do you want?" LaShaun leaned one elbow on the smooth quartz surface.

"At least let me take a bite of my sandwich." CeeCee made a big show of enjoying her food. "Chips?"

"Sure thing, ma'am. Café Broussard at your service." LaShaun opened a drawer set below the island. She pulled out three bags.

"I'll take the cheese puff." CeeCee ate with enthusiasm. "Let me guess. Your grandmother's chicken salad recipe. Sweet tea, too. Got a special flavor.

"Sweetened with a bit of pear syrup. We got a few trees out back. I canned some."

"Nothing like coming down to the land of great food." CeeCee dabbed her mouth with the napkin LaShaun provided. "Hmmm, good."

"Thanks."

LaShaun gave her a side-eye but said nothing more. She ate and sipped tea as she waited for CeeCee to get to the point. CeeCee stopped a few times when her cell phone came alive with notifications. Taking it from a pocket in her jacket, she glanced at it each time. CeeCee's expression remained neutral. She then turned it face down on the quartz surface. LaShaun didn't bother trying to get a peek at the screen. They both finished eating and sat wiping their hands on napkins.

"Well?" LaShaun swiveled around to face CeeCee.

"I'm not even gonna insult your intelligence and say I just stopped by to say hello," CeeCee quipped. She brushed the coat on Beau's back one last time. The dog seemed to sense their time was over. He trotted off.

"Saves us both time," LaShaun shot back.

CeeCee squinted at LaShaun as she drained the last of her sweet tea. She put the mason jar-shaped mug down with a thump. "Don't get snippy with me, sister. When were you going to tell me about Ellie and the Glapion girl?"

"You asked if I knew the family. I don't. Nothing but local gossip, and old stuff at that." LaShaun drank from her own glass. She returned CeeCee's steady gaze with her own. Then she heaved a sigh. "Look, until I met with Ellie's principal, I didn't know Zulime Glapion existed."

"Huh. You also didn't tell us the Glapion and Rousselle families have history," CeeCee countered.

"I didn't find out until I talked to one of my aunts and—Cut the TEA hostile witness routine, CeeCee." LaShaun put down her mug. "The Glapions have a history of psychic capabilities. TEA wouldn't be interested in them otherwise. You and Jonah didn't tell me much either you know."

CeeCee tapped her fingertips on the island's surface for a few seconds. "Got word from the office to be cautious. They gave me the tip about Zulime and Ellie."

"TEA is running surveillance on my nine-year-old?" LaShaun frowned at the implications.

"No. Well, not exactly. Ellie has extraordinary extrasensory gifts. Not to mention she was exposed to monazite," CeeCee replied. The rare mineral had the incredible effect of enhancing paranormal attributes. "You and Chase gave permission for the testing. Remember?"

LaShaun's frown deepened at the memory of another source of Chase's discontent. His worry about the effects on their daughter overcame his aversion to TEA involvement in their lives.

"Yeah. So far, she's normal."

"Sure. Just the average tween with telepathy, possibly enhanced by a magical ore," CeeCee wisecracked. Her grin vanished at the hot look LaShaun gave her. "TEA only checks in on her a few times a year. Like you said, she hasn't shown any of the negative side effects. Unlike a few other subjects."

"Don't use words like 'subject' around Chase. He allowed TEA doctors to examine Ellie. But he's never going to be okay with it." LaShaun shook her head.

"I'll never let TEA medical researchers treat Ellie like she's a lab mouse. Those nerds can get carried away, but they've got reins on 'em." CeeCee studied LaShaun in silence for a few beats. "You and Chase good?"

"We're fine. So, what's the deal with you and Jonah being here?" LaShaun crossed her arms as she gazed back at CeeCee.

"James Schaffer thinks his fellow ghost hunter was onto the true extent of our activities. He's decided to 'expose the secret world of all powerful psychics really running world events.' Direct quote from his crackpot radio show," CeeCee said with a grunt.

"Please say you're kidding. I'm gonna need more tea for this discussion." LaShaun went to the fridge, got the pitcher of tea, and refilled both their glasses.

"Thanks. Ghost Team USA was cancelled, so he doesn't have a tv series anymore."

"Good," LaShaun retorted.

"He does specials on one of those streaming channels. It's called True Paranormal Tales, I think. Something like that. According to our division that tracks media." CeeCee gulped tea.

LaShaun scrutinized her friend. CeeCee avoided her gaze. "You're about to give me news I won't like."

"Hmm, all the tea is kickin' in. Gotta use it." CeeCee slipped from the stool.

She went to the powder room without needing directions. LaShaun only resisted a second when she noticed CeeCee's phone still on the counter. Though she tried, LaShaun's psychic sense couldn't come up with the passcode. She thought hard about possible dates or number sequences CeeCee might favor. Nothing. Guilt made her stop after two attempts. CeeCee strolled back into the kitchen ten minutes later. She glanced at her phone, looked at LaShaun, and slipped it into a jacket pocket.

"Did you crack it?" CeeCee wore a crooked grin.

"Sorry. I was out of line touching your secure TEA phone. You'd tell me if anything threatens my family. Right?" LaShaun stared at her.

"You know I follow TEA classified intel protocol, LaShaun," CeeCee said.

"To the letter. Unless you don't agree when it comes to a friend," LaShaun countered.

"Humph. Those alerts were routine by the way. The only thing you would have learned was the weather forecast. And seen my dental appointment reminder and notice of another stupid meeting I plan to miss." CeeCee laughed as she took her seat again.

"So, you drove out here to chastise me not mentioning Zulime Glapion? Yeah, sure." LaShaun stared at CeeCee with a stony expression.

"A local TEA field operative was undercover for the last fourteen months. She was working on a lead that Legion had activated a cell here again. They haven't given up dredging or mining monazite. It's too valuable to them," CeeCee replied.

LaShaun' sixth sense went into overdrive. She got up to pace around as she rubbed her tingling arms; a sensation of electrified insects crawling on her skin. CeeCee watched without speaking, content to sip tea. Then LaShaun faced CeeCee.

"The recent murder Chase is investigating. It's her, a TEA agent." LaShaun rubbed her forehead with one hand.

"Yep," CeeCee said with a somber nod. "Her unit thought she'd gone underground and it was too risky to keep in touch. But once her photo appeared in news reports..."

"Shit, CeeCee. Talk about the worse damn timing."

"Yeah, our dead agent would agree with you. Then again, I can't think of a good time to die," CeeCee replied with dark humor.

"I didn't mean to sound cold-hearted."

"TEA will complicate your relationship with Chase. Again. I haven't forgotten about your in-laws." CeeCee wore a look of sympathy. "Don't join our investigation if it's going to make things worse. Jonah and I can handle headquarters."

LaShaun sat down. "What's all this got to do with Zulime Glapion?"

"Nothing so far as we can tell. The Glapion family is another matter though. They have a history of profiting with the help of Legion. Could be that was the source of conflict with the Rousselle family back in the day?" CeeCee shrugged.

"Humph. My ancestors were known to be just as shady. I doubt they were on the side of truth and virtue. My grandmother would say the same if she was here," LaShaun said with a tight smile. "No, their fight was over property."

"I see. So, the two families have made up in the last hundred years or so?"

"More like stayed out of each other's way. I seriously doubt Zulime knows anything about ancient history. Or would care even if she did." LaShaun shook her head. "No, her meeting Ellie is likely to be a coincidence."

"Vermilion Parish isn't exactly dense with population. Kids crossing paths in the school system isn't out of the realm of possibility," CeeCee added. She gazed at LaShaun with raised eyebrows.

"Zee gets assigned to tutor Ellie. A TEA agent ends up dead. And Zee is arrested for attacking someone. I don't like the hint of an invisible thread linking it all, CeeCee." LaShaun gritted her teeth when the electric ants marched again.

"Yeah, glad you said it first. Look, for now my instructions are to let the local police investigate. They know Chase is good at his job. He gets the killer or strong leads we can follow at the very least. Then we can handle the supernatural angle. You know we like a hands-off approach. Keep *normal* folks out of TEA business at all cost."

LaShaun nodded. She gazed through the window at the peaceful warm autumn day. Trees ringing their property swayed gently in the breeze. "Sounds great to me."

"Zulime Glapion is away from Ellie. We're looking into her adult family members. I'll make sure Chase or his officers get tips if we find evidence about the murder. Discreetly so he won't know the true source. You won't be involved," CeeCee added at the sharp look LaShaun gave her.

"Thanks. I—" LaShaun broke off when her cell phone rang. She got up and went to the desk against one wall where it sat being charged. "Hey, Savannah. Look, I'm not going to get involved with the Zulime issue. What? Yeah. Yeah. Talk to you later."

"Your face tells me Savannah St. Julie gave you bad news," CeeCee said.

"The woman Zulime Glapion attacked died this morning." LaShaun turned to CeeCee. "The DA is going to charge her as an adult. Murder."

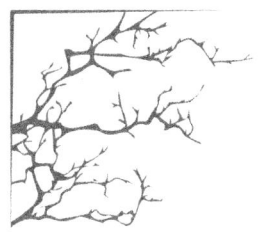

# Chapter 5

Chase sat eating dinner without speaking. LaShaun knew her daughter well. Usually, Ellie would attempt to pull Chase out of a dismal work-related mood with chatter. Not tonight though. Ellie stole glances at him but said nothing. CJ finished his dinner, happily eating fish sticks. He didn't notice his older sibling's silence for a while. The toddler's bouncy mood diminished during the meal. Soon it felt like a dark cloud hung over the eat-in dining alcove. Not even the cheerful décor succeeded in brightening the atmosphere.

LaShaun kept a close eye on Ellie. She tried blocking her from looking into Chase's thoughts. But her little psychic had grown stronger each year. LaShaun needed to distract her to add impact to her efforts. So, she asked Ellie questions about her latest favorite subject, marine life. Her school had a partnership with a local university's marine biology department. Ellie had become an ardent protector of turtles, dolphins, and pelicans.

"How did the project go? They're learning about coastal erosion now," LaShaun said aside to Chase, who only responded with a distracted nod.

"Mr. Willis showed us a video on how Christmas trees are put on the beach. We should get another big one this year," Ellie said. She glanced at her father.

"Santa!" CJ interjected with a hopeful smile.

"A bit early, baby boy," LaShaun replied with a laugh. "Let's celebrate Halloween first. Speaking of which, what do you want to be this year? It's not too soon to plan. Trick or treating is only a few weeks away."

Ellie blinked hard. "Maybe an astronaut. We learned about the first Black woman to stay on a space station."

LaShaun felt a wave of relief when Ellie chattered on about asteroids and stars. Then she switched back to Halloween. The school had recruited some of the children to help with decorations. To satisfy conservative Christian parents, the theme would lean more toward fall harvest.

"We're learning about the history of All Hallows' Eve. That's what it was called, Daddy," Ellie said and ate the last of her scalloped potatoes.

"Very interesting," Chase replied with a faint smile.

"Will Gran Elizabeth have a Halloween party this year? Jessica says she used to have one every year." Ellie's older cousins kept her up to speed on Broussard family news. "But Jessica says something happened one year, so Grandmama won't invite bad spirits in."

Chase went still for a second. He slowly chewed the last bite he'd taken. Then he cleared his throat. "Gran Elizabeth and Papa Bruce are getting on in years. They can't have big parties like they used to. It's a lot of work. You know, decorations, cooking."

"Aunt Katie and Sharon help," Ellie countered, referring to two of Chase's sisters. "And Auntie Adrianna." Adrianna was his brother's wife.

"They're busy with their own families," Chase offered. He drank sweet tea. "Finished your school assignments?"

"Yes." Ellie studied Chase's every move as she gazed at him.

"Me, too!" CJ chirped and jumped down from his seat before LaShaun intervened. He made a solid landing on both feet. Then he raced over to the small kitchen desk and grabbed a large art sheet. "See?"

"Very nice, CJ." Chase took the drawing from him to look at the loops and scribbles. "Hmmm, it's a..."

"Beau playing in the backyard," CJ said.

"They were supposed to draw an animal," Ellie put in. "CJ, the teacher meant like in the woods or at the zoo."

"D is for dog. Doggie door. Dog food. It counts." CJ took the drawing back. He gazed at his handiwork with a smile and put it back on the desk.

"The assignment was not only to reinforce the first letter in the name, but things related with the same letter," LaShaun explained. She smiled at CJ. "I'm sure Miss Trudeau will approve."

"I guess. Too bad CJ can't go to Gran and Papa's party. Jessica says there were games and pumpkin cupcakes. One year Papa Bruce had a fog machine in the backyard. Jessica says it was spooky, but a lot of fun." Ellie looked at Chase.

"Like I said, such a big production is a lot of work," Chase said. "Hey, it's getting about time for—"

"Are *we* the bad spirits Gran Elizabeth doesn't want?" Ellie asked, her voice muted. "She says things always seem to go wrong when me and Mama are around."

"When did you hear her say that?" Chase said sharply.

"A long time ago. CJ was still in mama's tummy. She told Aunt Elaine..." Ellie flinched and her voice faded away.

Chase avoided looking at LaShaun. His stony frown eased into a tense smile. "I'm sure she wasn't talking about you, baby girl. You misunderstood."

"Okay." Ellie's small face remained serious."

"Hey, I'll get you and CJ started on our night-time fun schedule. Bath time, a story, a song, and prayers." Chase stood and slapped his palms together. He held out a hand to CJ. "What do you say, champ?"

"Story time, yaay!" CJ grabbed his father's hand. Then he held out the other hand to Ellie.

"Mama?" Ellie glanced at LaShaun instead of joining in. "I'll help with the dishes."

"You'd rather work than listen to a story of how the fifolet led little Evangeline out of the swamp? Pa-sha," Chase said, his Cajun accent exaggerated to temp her.

"You take care of CJ. It's okay," LaShaun replied.

Chase's smile didn't reach his dark eyes as he looked back at LaShaun. He started to say something but seemed to change his mind. Instead, he swung CJ into the air, which brought on a squeal of delight. "Suit yourself. Me and CJ are gonna have us a time."

Once they were gone, LaShaun braced herself for uncomfortable questions. Instead, Ellie concentrated on following LaShaun's instructions to wipe the table. They loaded the dishwasher together. LaShaun explained to Ellie once again the proper care of their cast iron skillet, handed down from Monmon Odette. Older cooking tools from LaShaun's great-grandmother sat on a floating shelf. Ellie's favorite was a ceramic serving gumbo pot with crawfish, shrimp, and crabs painted on its yellow background. They talked about Rousselle family history. LaShaun sensed that Ellie drew comfort from stories about Monmon Odette.

LaShaun hung the dish cloth on a towel bar to dry. She placed both hands on her hips when she faced Ellie. "We made fast work of cleaning up. Thanks, sweetie."

"You're welcome. CJ didn't make as much of a mess as usual. Maybe because we didn't have green peas. He likes throwing them more than eating them," Ellie said and rolled her eyes.

"He'll grow out of it. At least I hope so." LaShaun chuckled when Ellie screwed up her face in a skeptical scowl.

"You should see some of the boys at lunchtime in the school cafeteria. They like throwing food at each other. So childish." Ellie shook her head in disapproval.

"Gee thanks for crushing my hopes," LaShaun quipped. "I think CJ will be different though. He's got an old soul as they say."

"Yeah, we're not like the other kids," Ellie murmured.

LaShaun brushed a hand through Ellie's thick dark curls. "All children are unique and beautiful in their own way. Just as the good Lord intended."

"That sounds like something Monmon Odette would say," Ellie replied.

LaShaun felt a shiver as she looked into Ellie's eyes. Her daughter's tone held an odd note. "Cher, have you..."

"What, Mama?" Ellie gazed back at her.

"Um, picked out your uniform for tomorrow? You can wear pants with the new school sweater or the jumper dress. The weather report says it's going to get a bit cooler."

LaShaun chattered about ordinary life to make sure they steered clear of more family talk. She wasn't ready to hear the answer to her unasked question. Ellie had a shown a strong interest, even a connection, to Monmon Odette. Despite the fact that her great-grandmother had died three years before Ellie was born. She'd pretty much forbade Ellie from reading Rousselle and LeGrange family journals. Especially those left by Monmon Odette in her florid handwriting.

"All my sweet girl. Lights out time." LaShaun kissed Ellie on the forehead. She pulled back the lavender comforter and matching sheets on Ellie's bed.

"Night, Mama." Ellie slipped beneath the covers. "Nightlight, please."

LaShaun paused to study Ellie for a few seconds. Ellie only used it when she was having nightmares. Yet she didn't look anxious. She hadn't awakened in fear during the night for weeks.

"You feel okay, baby?" LaShaun bent over her for a closer look and feel.

"I'm okay." Ellie smiled and closed her eyes. "I like the fairies dancing to put me to sleep."

"Ah."

LaShaun smiled back at her. Then she turned on the nightlight. A rotating shade casted figures of tiny winged mythical creatures floating on the ceiling. LaShaun set the timer so that the light would turn off after an hour. She glanced at Ellie a final time. Ellie's face looked serene as she gazed up at the shadow show. Her breathing became regular while her eyes fluttered shut. LaShaun went out and gently closed the door.

She went to the combination laundry and mudroom to load the washer. Chase was there already. He emptied a basket of towels into the machine and turned it on.

"CJ is down for the night. As usual he was asleep almost before his head hit the pillow," Chase said. "I went in to kiss Ellie, too."

"Good." LaShaun watched him fold clothes for a few seconds. "Was she sleeping?"

"Dozing off. She woke up long enough to say goodnight."

LaShaun stacked the folded t-shirts in the laundry basket. "I'll put these away. Hmm, about Ellie..."

Chase leaned against the counter and watched LaShaun pull the last few items from the dryer. "What about Ellie? She seemed fine to me."

"No questions about Zulime Glapion?" LaShaun folded the last of Ellie's little blouses and put them in a neat pile.

"No, thank goodness. Things are not looking good for that girl." Chase gazed at LaShaun. "So, let's avoid the bringing her up around Ellie."

"We live in a small town, Chase. She's going to find out sooner rather than later. Zulime's arrest is big news."

"Maybe, maybe not. Kids get easily distracted into their own world. Just keep her busy with her friends, school, and those shows she loves. Oh, and her tablet computer." Chase headed to the kitchen. Dressed in light grey sweat pants and a long-sleeved t-shirt, he looked relaxed. He went to the refrigerator and pulled out a covered dish of bread pudding.

"Once Ellie sets her mind on something she doesn't let go. Especially when it comes to a friend. I don't think she's going to let it go." LaShaun shook her head.

Chase heaved a sigh. He scooped bread pudding onto a plate and put it into the microwave. "She will if you do. And keep your TEA pals away. Them showing up only means trouble."

"Um, I have to tell you something. Your latest murder victim, the woman? She was TEA working undercover. But CeeCee and Jonah will be hands off," LaShaun added quickly when Chase muttered a curse word. "They're going to let the regular police investigation play out."

"How generous of them since TEA has no authority to mix in a homicide," Chase snapped. "Give me CeeCee's number. I expect them at my station to give statements. Full information, no holding back."

LaShaun went to her cell phone. She texted the information to his work mobile number. "There, you have it. What are you going to tell Dave and the detective assigned?"

"Sure as hell not about TEA." Chase padded over to the phone, glanced at the screen, and put it back to continue charging.

"Thanks." LaShaun sighed.

"I'm not doing it for *them*. I don't give a crap about their magical secret agenda." The bell on the microwave pinged and Chase removed the dish.

"What will you tell them then?" LaShaun sat next to him at the kitchen island.

Chase frowned for a few seconds. "I'll stick close to the truth. That they knew and worked with the victim in the past. Tried to stay in touch after she went off the rails. Something like that. At least now we can notify her family."

"I'm sure CeeCee will give you any information she can," LaShaun replied.

"Humph, we'll see. Not that it matters. My job is to catch whoever killed the woman. Period. I don't want to know about anything TEA related she got up to. A murder is a murder is a murder."

LaShaun studied his taut expression as he spooned bread pudding into his mouth. She said nothing, content to let him savor his dessert. "Speaking of Zulime's case, Savannah told me Karlene Pattison died from her injuries. The DA has started the process of charging Zee as an adult. Seems excessive. She's still a kid; only a few years older than Ellie."

"A kid who beat somebody to death," Chase replied with blunt force.

"She's had it rough from what Savannah told me. Plus, she didn't mean to kill the woman. They got into a fight," LaShaun argued.

"No, she went after the woman when they argued. That's all I'm going to say." Chase concentrated on his bread pudding.

LaShaun stared at him. "You're investigating the crime now. The DA turned the case over to your unit since Zee is going to be prosecuted in adult court."

"Look, I'm not discussing the case. Especially because Ellie's gotten herself mixed up in it." Chase took an angry stab into the bread pudding.

"Mixed up—" LaShaun pushed down a biting reply. She counted to ten. "Ellie was helping her friend, Chase. She's not an accessory to a crime."

"Okay, fine. Whatever. Talk to Ellie about right and wrong. She's not excused from the rules the rest of us follow because she's special."

"I've never expected anything more or less because of who she is," LaShaun shot back. "And please explain what you mean by 'the rest of us,' Chase?"

"People who don't see, hear, smell... the spirit world. It's just... a challenge dealing with all the woo-woo magic." Chase huffed a deep sigh.

"I see. I didn't realize *dealing* with us was such a burden to you." LaShaun crossed her arms and turned away from him.

"You're twisting this into something I never said." Chase rubbed his face hard with one hand. "Try to see it from my point of view. I can't have interference with my criminal investigations. These two murders are high profile as it is. I don't want you or Ellie to get caught up. James Schaffer is in town sniffing for his next big meal ticket. All I need is for him to hear your name. You know what will happen. I want Ellie protected."

"Yeah."

Chase dropped the spoon and pushed away the saucer. "I've got two messy murder cases on my hands. A little consideration would be nice."

LaShaun felt a prick of guilt at the tired and harassed note in his voice. Her hot temper cooled down. "Sorry. I know your job is tough enough as it is; and stressful. CeeCee really does intend to stay out of your way."

"And Jonah? He's known to ignore orders and go his own way."

"CeeCee does better keeping him in line than anyone. He'll follow her lead." LaShaun studied him in silence for a few moments. Chase finished the remains of the bread pudding.

"One thing I will say about Rousselle family magic—it makes for some real good cooking." Chase licked sauce from the spoon.

"Nothing but the usual ingredients in Monmon Odette's bread pudding recipe," LaShaun replied with a smile. She grew serious again. "About Zulime Glapion—"

"Off limits. I'm going to follow the evidence. She attacked the woman. Pattison died from injuries sustained as a result of the attack. No dispute about the facts."

"But the DA is charging her like Zee intended to kill her. What really happened sounds like manslaughter. And we don't even know if she was provoked or why," LaShaun countered.

"Savannah's job is to argue with the DA. Not *mine* and not yours either. She's got her work cut out for her is all I'll say," Chase said.

"The word justice should mean more in the 'criminal justice' system, Chase. You always say the object is to find the truth, or as close to it as possible. Zulime Glapion seems to have started out with the cards stacked against her," LaShaun pressed on.

Chase's jaw tensed. He tapped the counter top for a few minutes before he spoke. "Of course I'm looking for the full story. I would think you'd know me better than to suggest otherwise, LaShaun."

"I'm not just talking about your part in it. My point is a sixteen-year-old girl has the state with all its resources cranking up to put her away." LaShaun clicked her tongue in frustration. "If I can get information—"

"Whoa, whoa, back it up. You're going to do what exactly?"

LaShaun pursed her lips for a few seconds. "Offer to be Savannah's investigator."

"So, ignore what I said about not getting involved. Humph. I almost wish you'd have TEA crap to distract you," Chase retorted and looked away.

"As it happens TEA is also interested in the Glapion family. Not because of Zulime though. James Schaffer is trying to prove TEA is responsible for another self-styled paranormal investigator's disappearance. The Glapion family has history with Legion." LaShaun frowned as she mentally shuffled all of the cards she knew so far. "The entire picture isn't clear yet."

"Which has nothing to do with Zulime causing a woman's fatal injuries," he countered.

"But what if it was self-defense or Pattison pushed Zee in some way? Then those facts should come out as well."

Chase faced LaShaun. "Obviously, I can't stop you. It's not like you respect my opinion or the position you might put me in by going off half-cocked."

LaShaun sucked in a deep breath and let it out. "I never do anything half-cocked. I wouldn't be arguing against hanging this *child* out to dry If I didn't think—"

"Yeah, yeah. And her maybe being psychic or from a magical family doesn't have anything to do with it, I suppose."

"Is that what all this is about?" LaShaun clipped.

Chase picked up the spoon and saucer. He turned his back to LaShaun as he washed both in the kitchen sink. "All this what?"

"You're willing to see Zulime tried as an adult who deserves to be punished because she's like me. The person your mother thinks is the cause of most of the evil around here." LaShaun slid from the barstool to cross the floor. She grabbed his muscular bicep and turned him to face her. "Well?"

"Now you're really reaching. My mother doesn't know anything about Zulime Glapion or my case. For the last time, I'm going to follow the evidence. Karlene Pattison deserves justice, too. I'm sorry but so far, the evidence doesn't favor Zulime getting off, LaShaun."

"Daddy, you're going to send Zee to prison? But you said you'd help her. She's not a bad person, and you said the police only go after bad people." Ellie stood clutching her favorite stuffed animal, a bunny rabbit. She stood in the archway of the kitchen dressed in a pink nightgown and no slippers.

"You should be sleeping, young lady. Now go to your room. You have school tomorrow." Chase pointed in the direction of her room.

Ellie's eyes widened. "You are! You're going to lock her up without even trying to prove she didn't do it."

LaShaun crossed the space separating them. She placed an arm around Ellie's slight shoulders. "Honey, we've talked about Daddy's job before. He collects statements and details about crimes. The district attorney presents those to a judge and—"

"But you can find things that show Zee isn't a criminal," Ellie said to Chase. She stepped free of LaShaun's embrace and walked to Chase. She looked up at her father.

"Ellie, sometimes even good people make mistakes. I know she's your friend, but she did a bad thing that hurt someone," Chase said in a firm tone.

"Yes. I know Zee was accused of battery, which means she beat up that lady. Zee wouldn't have done it without a reason." Ellie didn't back down when Chase frowned.

"We agreed you'd let the people hired to help Zee do their jobs. You should focus on school and doing as you're told. Right now, you're too young to understand everything."

"You and mama said it's always the right time to do the right thing. Well, I don't think what you're doing to Zee is right,

Daddy." Ellie stood her ground as she continued to stare at Chase.

"I'm not doing anything to Zee, Ellie. I'm doing my job. If Zee is innocent or there are circumstances that prove—"

"So, you *are* going to prove she's not bad after all." Ellie's intense expression relaxed.

"That's not what I said," Chase said in a taut voice. He glanced at LaShaun. "I wonder where you're getting all of these ideas."

LaShaun glared at him but pushed down the impulse to lash out. Instead, she plastered a smile on her face. "Ellie, honey."

Ellie turned to LaShaun. "Yes, Mama?"

"Your father's job is to collect every bit of information. Aunt Savannah will put together a strong case to defend Zee. Everybody has a different job to do when it comes to enforcing laws." LaShaun took Ellie by the hand as she knelt to be at her eye level. "So, like Daddy says, there are people on Zee's side."

Silence stretched as Ellie gazed back at LaShaun. She shot a couple of side-eyes at Chase. Then she hugged LaShaun's neck. "Okay. Please help auntie help Zee, Mama."

"Let's get back to bed. And you know better to walk around on the cold floor with no slippers."

LaShaun led Ellie toward the hall leading to their bedrooms. She looked at Chase over one shoulder once as they left. He watched them go with a grimace stamped on his handsome face. LaShaun tucked Ellie into bed and returned to the kitchen. Chase wasn't there. She looked in the laundry room but he wasn't there either. The clean laundry remained on the folding table and basket. So, she went to their main suite. He had already pulled on a pair of jeans.

"Why are you getting dressed?"

He didn't answer. LaShaun watched as he pulled a dark green sweater over his head. Then he brushed his dark hair back in place. Chase vanished into their walk-in closet. One side held his clothes, the opposite hers. LaShaun sat on the padded bench in the center of it. Chase sat on one end to pull on a pair of boots.

"We don't do the silent treatment in this family. Remember?" LaShaun said in a quiet tone.

"I'm not sleepy and I have tomorrow off since I've worked so much overtime. My detectives have things in hand at the station." Chase tied the laces of one boot and then the other.

"So, you don't have to leave. At least not for work," LaShaun replied.

"I need fresh air."

"You mean you need to get away from us. You feel like you can't breathe with all of this *sorcery* in the air." LaShaun knew her bitter tone wasn't helping but it came out anyway.

"Your take on it, not mine. I could just do with some time away."

Chase avoided looking at her as he stood. He smoothed down his sweater and walked back to their bedroom. LaShaun followed him. He stuffed his slim wallet in one pocket. Then he grabbed his keyring from the dresser top.

"You're away a lot already. Or maybe long hours at work is an excuse to avoid being at home," LaShaun snapped.

"Now that you mention it, home isn't the most welcoming place these days. I've got a lot of stress out there. I don't need to it here, too." Chase strode out and down the hallway.

"Where..."

LaShaun cut off her loud, angry question. She glanced toward the closed doors of their children's bedrooms. No sounds indicated either had been roused. Relieved, LaShaun hurried after Chase to catch him.

"I'll call you later. Probably pick up breakfast out," Chase said without looking at LaShaun when she entered the kitchen. He stuffed his work mobile phone into a pocket.

"This is ridiculous, Chase. Where do you plan on spending the night?" LaShaun struggled not to shout at him. She stood with both fists balled.

"Somewhere I'm not made to feel like the bad guy by my own family," Chase shot back. He strode out through the side kitchen door that led to their double driveway.

Fury caused heat to flow down LaShaun's arms and into her fingertips. The power of her psychic energy crackled, pent-up lightning that needed an outlet. She looked around, found a small ceramic rooster on the quartz island and threw it across the room. It exploded against the cabinet with more power than simple impact.

"Damn it, Chase!"

"Mama?"

Ellie's soft voice brought LaShaun back from the edge. She spun around to face their daughter. LaShaun kept up a stream of chatter about dropping something accidentally and why Ellie should still be in bed. Shaken, LaShaun knew Ellie didn't buy any of it, but it would have to do. Until she figured out her next moves.

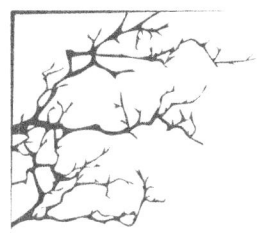

# Chapter 6

"It's only Wednesday and you've already had an action-packed week." Savannah shook her head in sympathy.

LaShaun had joined her at Tante Marie's Bakery for a late coffee after getting the kids sent off. The morning's temperatures had dipped into the low sixties. By ten o'clock it had eased into the low seventies. A sunny day with a clear blue sky contrasted with their twin glum moods.

"Understatement." LaShaun still hadn't eaten breakfast. Her stomach was too twisted into knots to tolerate food.

Savannah set down her iced coffee and waved to her cousin working the counter. "So, where was he all night?"

"At his sister Katie's. She called me on the sly last night knowing I'd be frantic. Still didn't get much sleep." LaShaun sipped mocha latte. One of her favorite fancy hot drinks didn't taste quite so good that morning.

"Yeah, you look it."

"Thanks a lot, best friend," LaShaun clipped.

Tante Marie herself bustled into the small café and over to their table. She carried an insulated box. "Now I baked these biscuits this morning. You put them in the refrigerator when you get home, LaShaun. Wrap them in my special parchment paper to heat them for breakfast. It's microwave safe. Part of the new product line my grandson developed."

"You're a national treasure, Tante Marie. Thanks so much." LaShaun brightened in the glow of maternal attention.

"Pshaw, cher. Oh, and I wrapped up a few cinnamon rolls for Chase and CJ. Their favorites from the way they gobble 'em up when they come." Tante Marie beamed at them. "My two girls. Now I know things look kinda dim but the good Lord is workin' it out."

"Yes, ma'am," LaShaun and Savannah replied dutifully in unison.

"Let me get back to the kitchen. Gotta make sure quality control is maintained. Not that I don't trust my boy. But team work makes the dream work." Tante Marie scurried off.

"Is this your aunt's version of retirement?" LaShaun smiled. Brandon, Tante Marie's grandson, wore a look of patience as Tante Marie rattled on with questions and instructions.

"Yep. Pestering my poor cousin, church work, and traveling. The fact that he's a culinary school phenom doesn't count. To quote Tante Marie, 'He's still a baby.'" Savannah laughed.

"He's twenty, but looking sixteen probably doesn't help," LaShaun wisecracked.

"Graduated from high school and college early, but short on lessons from the school of life," Savannah replied, imitating Tante Marie's deep contralto voice and lilting Creole accent.

"At least he's headed in the right direction. Speaking of young folks on the wrong path..." LaShaun leaned forward and lowered her voice. "Did you get a chance to talk to Zulime and her grandmother."

"Yes and no. I visited Zulime to tell her about the DA's decision. Her grandmother hasn't returned my call yet." Savannah frowned.

"Will Zulime talk to me?"

"She will but I still have to get her grandmother's permission, LaShaun. The youth detention center is strict about visitors, and the judge has been in touch with the director." Savannah nodded when LaShaun's eyebrows went up. "This case is ramping up. Karlene Pattison's family has been talking to the press. Someone told them about Zulime's troubled past."

"Which means DA Hazelton will do the 'tough on crime' dance," LaShaun retorted.

"He's an elected official and knows what plays well with the conservative voters of our fine parish." Savannah shrugged when LaShaun grunted with contempt. "Girl, it is what it is."

"So, they're willing to bury a poor Black sixteen-year-old girl. Treat her like a grown woman," LaShaun said.

"Part of my defense will include a child psychologist who has evaluated Zulime twice already. Once when she got in trouble a year or so ago. She'll testify about the developmental stages of adolescents; how they don't have the judgements of adults. Having her as an expert witness plus introducing Zulime's family history are key." Savannah gazed out of the wide glass windows. Sparse foot traffic flowed by.

"She's blessed to have you as her attorney."

"The odds are stacking up against Zulime by the hour. I've got a fight on my hands." Savannah heaved a sigh and drank from the tall cup.

"Same thing Chase said," LaShaun murmured.

Savannah studied LaShaun for a few beats. "He's probably home by now. A few hours before the kids show gives you two time to talk."

"I think we said more than enough last night."

"No, you went after each other. Look, I'm no therapist but I've been through rocky times with Paul. *Not* talking is a death sentence to a marriage," Savannah replied.

"Oh, we'll have a conversation for damn sure," LaShaun snapped.

"LaShaun..." Savannah squinted at her. "I mean without attacking each other. Mutual respect even when you're on opposite sides of an issue."

"He's listening to his mother. You know, the woman who told him not to marry a voodoo witch. I never thought he'd actually put stock in her opinion about me. I could deal with Elizabeth slamming me all the time. But my kids... Oh hell no! He damn well better pick Ellie and CJ over Miss Queen Bee. And I don't mean 'B' as in the insect either." LaShaun's fingertips grew hot, heating up the lukewarm latte. Steam rose from the white ceramic cup.

"Um, please don't supernaturally combust here," Savannah said softly. She gave a slight nod toward the window. "We don't need that kind of publicity. Look."

LaShaun breathed in and out to tamp down her psychic surge. She followed Savannah's gaze. James Schaffer stood on the sidewalk across the street. He talked into the microphone of a wireless headset while another man filmed him. He appeared to be interviewing a woman.

"Have you done something to attract that creep again?" Savannah asked.

"Not me. He's onto a story about the Third Eye Association. For once I'm not the center of his attention." LaShaun scowled at the subject of their mutual scorn.

"Not yet. He loves dogging your footsteps. Almost like an obsession. I have a feeling he'll find an excuse to hunt you down."

"I'll steer him away from Zulime if that's what you're concerned about," LaShaun said quietly.

"Not really. No paranormal angle to interest the creep. Unless you know why I *should* be worried." Savannah switched her gaze back to LaShaun.

"Not sure." LaShaun gazed at Schaffer. "Who's the woman?"

"Marianne Sinclair, a local minister and all-round pain in the ass. She's opposed to anything fun, like Halloween and Mardi Gras parades. She sees Satan around every corner." Savannah snorted and drank coffee.

A large Chevy Tahoe with the sheriff's office medallion on both sides drove slowly down Main Street. Sheriff Dave Godchaux leaned from the open driver's side window, smiling at passersby. He stopped to chat with a mother with two small children in tow. He handed out candy after the mother nodded.

"The election is still two years off, Dave," Savannah drawled.

"Never too early to schmooze the voters," LaShaun said.

Schaffer noticed the sheriff and cut off his interview with Reverend Sinclair. The woman scowled after him, obviously unhappy about losing the spotlight. Schaffer scurried down the sidewalk toward Dave. Either by chance or design, Dave gave a last wave to the young woman and her children and drove away. The Tahoe picked up speed as Schaffer, videographer in tow, scrambled to catch up. Pursuer and pursued disappeared around a corner.

"At least we can finish our coffee in peace," Savannah wisecracked.

"Schaffer knows his way to the sheriff's station. He'll make a nuisance of himself anyway. If I know Dave, he'll pass him off to either Chase or MJ," LaShaun said with a laugh. "They'll *love* him for that."

MJ Arceneaux headed up the property crimes unit and functioned as the Sherriff's Chief Deputy Sheriff. Chase was in charge of crimes against persons. MJ had become their friend. Like Chase, MJ preferred "ordinary human" crooks.

"Speaking of Chase, you really should fix things between you two." Savannah gazed at LaShaun.

"Me fix things? You're starting to take his side." LaShaun took an angry swig of coffee.

"I'm on both your sides because I want you to be happy. Or at least not at war," Savannah added with a crooked grin.

"I'm sick of apologizing for who I am, for my grandmother, and for my ancestors. The same bullying I faced is starting to happen with my children. Well, I sure as hell won't have it, Savannah. They're babies." LaShaun's grip on the coffee cup tightened. Steam rose from the brew until the surface bubbled.

"I'm the same way about my girls. I'd go ham on anybody messing with them. I also understand that Chase has been distant from his family."

"Oh, and that's my fault, too, I suppose," LaShaun retorted with a frown.

"No, he's grown and makes his own choices. And he chooses *you*. Every day. In spite of the local bobble heads whispering."

"Humph. His mother leads the pack. She'd love to see me burned at the stake for taking her precious son." LaShaun clenched her jaws so tightly her back teeth ached.

Savannah winced. "I wouldn't go that far. But even knowing how she is, Chase still loves his mother. You know, the way you still loved Monmon Odette and your mother," Savannah said softly.

"Nobody's perfect. Yada-yada," LaShaun muttered into her cup and drank more latte.

"Chase has a tough balancing act. If he decides to cut all ties with his parents, it has to be his decision alone. I think he's struggling to find a way to keep both his families." Savannah shrugged.

"Look, I've made sacrifices, too. I stay out of TEA investigations. I didn't enroll Ellie in the charter school they have right down the road in New Iberia. He seems to have forgotten my concessions once he talks to Elizabeth and his father."

"Then remind him." Savannah glanced at the decorative clock on the café wall. "I have motions to prepare and a deposition later. I need to get cracking. And you have a chance to talk to your husband before the kids get home. Calmly."

"Wait a minute. About me visiting Zulime—"

"I've left two more messages with Mrs. Vidal. Crickets. That woman is a tough nut to crack, but I'll keep trying." Savannah swigged the last of her iced coffee and stood. "Call me later?"

"Yeah, sure." LaShaun smiled at her friend. Her stomach growled and she placed a hand on it. "Maybe I'll have a biscuit and some eggs first."

"Can't go into marital battle on an empty tank," Savannah joked. She patted LaShaun's shoulder and left.

LaShaun ordered food. The café had cleared out of the other customers. They'd probably left for work like Savannah. She lingered over her breakfast. A few high, fluffy white clouds had appeared against the blue skies. Early October sunshine painted the quaint downtown main drag. When the bells from Sacred Heart Catholic Church rang the half hour, LaShaun glanced at the clock. Ten thirty. Savannah's advice clanged in her mind. She texted Chase. He replied that he was home.

"No more excuses, girl. Go face the music."

She paid for her meal and left. She used the fifteen-minute drive to go over what she'd say. Her heart thumped hard at the sight of Chase's truck in their driveway. Beau bounded around the back of the house to greet her. LaShaun petted him as another reason to delay but finally went inside. Chase stood in the kitchen leaning against the counter, cup in hand.

"I'm guessing you've had breakfast," he said.

"Yeah, with Savannah. Um, had an errand after I got the kids off." LaShaun took off her jacket and draped it on the back of a chair.

"Okay." Chase stared ahead at their property outside through the bay window.

"We talked about Zulime and—" LaShaun stopped when Chase raised a palm.

"She's being charged as an adult because the victim died. My detective is assigned. I can't work a miracle and get her out of trouble, LaShaun. You and Ellie have to understand." Chase looked at LaShaun and then away again.

"I know. Don't get mad but..." LaShaun fidgeted with her keys as her voice trailed off.

"Let's have it then," Chase said after letting her stew in silence for a few beats. "Guess I'll need a refill for what's coming."

LaShaun said nothing as he padded over to the coffee pot. Dressed in dark gray sweats and slippers the kids had given him last Christmas, Chase was the quintessential hot dad. He worked out. And unlike most men, Chase didn't protest her healthy versions of Louisiana meals. Less salt, more vegetables; easy on the fried foods and andouille sausage. Just one of the ways their marriage was unconventional. They stood strong as a team. She felt a rush of love and desire as he strolled over to her.

"Well?" Chase raised one dark eyebrow at her.

"I talked to Savannah about Zulime's defense," LaShaun said. She walked over to stand close to him.

"I'm so shocked," Chase drawled.

Encouraged by the seeming lack of anger but cautious, LaShaun pushed on and told him about the missing notebook. "I think, we think, a key piece of evidence has gone missing."

"Doesn't sound mysterious. Her grandmother sent somebody when the school called her." Chase studied LaShaun for a second. "But wait, Chase. There's more."

LaShaun clicked her tongue. "Very funny. Look, this girl's entire life is on the line. I'm not sure her grandmother understands how serious things have gotten. She doesn't return Savannah's phone calls. Eunice Vidal is like a hermit out in the swamp. It's odd."

"Which means?"

"Savannah says Mrs. Vidal doesn't have much to do with anyone, so she's skeptical about this uncle or cousin who picked up the notebook. And there's something important in it. Has to be because Zee went so far as to ask Ellie to get it," LaShaun said.

"She didn't want to lose her school work." Chase sipped from the mug.

"Zee is not into academics, to say the least. She's smart but resists authority," LaShaun replied.

"Sounds like anybody you know from back in the day?" Chase gazed at her with a faint smile.

LaShaun chuckled. "I resemble that remark. Her trouble hits close to home, not just because of Ellie."

"Huh."

Chase drank from his cup. Silence stretched between them. She could almost hear his cop's mind turning over data. LaShaun decided to let him be for the moment. She used their smart home device to start a load of laundry in the washer. Then she went outside to their backyard with Beau on her heels. Trees and low shrubs ringed the trimmed grass. Monmon Odette had left four acres of land and the house to LaShaun. Beau investigated the perimeter of the mowed lawn. No ordinary family pet, Beau could alert to any supernatural menace lurking. His tail wagging, he took off into the woods at a relaxed, loping run. She heard Chase's footsteps behind her on the back.

"So, what do you think?" LaShaun said over her shoulder. She turned back to stare after Beau.

"He's gonna need a bath," Chase replied with a grunt.

"About Zee, Mr. Funny Man."

"The way I see it, anything connected to the notebook is of interest to Savannah. She'll need whatever is in it to defend her client. Our job is more straightforward." Chase stood, legs apart, arms crossed on his broad chest.

"The facts are?" LaShaun sat on a wicker chaise lounge, elbows on both knees.

"Zulime was assigned to a Brighter Futures mentor. Part of the juvenile court diversion program."

"What had she done to end up before a judge?" LaShaun asked.

"Juvenile procedures aren't public record." Chase shrugged when LaShaun frowned as her silent response. "Okay, okay. Zee has a history of running away from home. Petty theft from her grandmother. She's gotten into a couple of fights at school."

"A history of violence then. Not good."

"Ellie is right about one thing. Zee seems to have been targeted by a group of girls at school. Relentless bullying is how a teacher's aide put it. You know how kids are when someone is seen as 'weird'. Her grandmother showed up to school a couple of times. That made it worse. She's 'a piece of work' is how the aide described Mrs. Vidal." Chase gazed at LaShaun. "Sheesh. The more I think about it, the more Zee sounds like…"

"Alright, just keep going with the story. We're talking about Zulime, not *me*," LaShaun said when he didn't finish the sentence. Still, she couldn't help but agree.

"Yeah, Zee does have a 'catch these hands' approach when crossed. The aide didn't think her teacher or Mrs. Richardson did enough to stop Zee from being targeted." Chase raised both eyebrows at LaShaun.

"Savannah will be interested in that angle. Very interested. Of course, as a former school bully, I know how creative kids can be. I found so many ways to harass kids that couldn't be proved. And then there's catching her outside of school."

"And kids don't always tell anyone what they're going through. I don't think she had much support at home." Chase sat on the cane chaise lounge next to LaShaun. "I don't want Ellie to think she can't talk to us, LaShaun."

"Honey, Ellie isn't going to become Zee in a few years. We're keeping channels of communication open. You know that." LaShaun placed a hand on his thigh.

"Do I? With everything said about the police in the news and now this thing with Zee... Ellie looked at me differently the other day. I'm not her hero anymore." Chase's voice held a hitch of emotion as he looked off into the distance.

"Nonsense. Ellie is still a big-time daddy's girl, and you're the best girl dad I know." LaShaun grabbed one of his large hands and kissed the back of it. "You're my hero, too."

"Even when you think I'm siding with my mother?"

"Yes." LaShaun grinned at him.

"Hey! You weren't supposed to agree." Chase faked a scowl.

"Well..." LaShaun shrugged.

"I'm not siding with mama. Okay, so it does *sound* like it sometimes. The supernatural stuff gets to me. I'm still getting used to not being as close to them these days. I grew up with Sunday dinner at their house, big crawfish boils with uncles, aunts, and cousins, family holiday parties. Now..." Chase's voice trailed off.

"When we go you can feel the friction. Folks giving me the side-eye. They barely hide the whispered conversations. Doesn't make for a fun time." LaShaun leaned into him and wrapped her arms around his waist. "I'm sorry."

"Look, I won't lie and say your little private investigations aren't a problem," Chase began. He yelped when LaShaun pinched him.

"Little investigations! Let me remind you I helped wrap up some pretty big cases. And I've so far kept you from having to deal with the 'supernatural stuff', Chief Detective Broussard. And you're welcome."

"Okay, okay. No more pinching. Unless we're naked and in the bedroom. Or the kitchen. Heck, the porch will do. The kids won't be home for *hours*." Chase snaked a hand up LaShaun's thigh.

"Behave."

Despite her feeble protest, LaShaun didn't resist his passionate kiss. Chase pulled her into his lap and laid back. His hand reached inside the pullover sweater LaShaun wore. He tugged until his fingers eased into her bra. LaShaun moaned as he caressed her.

"Mornin', neighbors!"

Mrs. Betty Marchand yelled and waved at the edge of the pasture that separated their properties. She wore knee boots with denim coveralls stuffed into the top of them. Betty Marchand was a dedicated member of the local grapevine; a blessing at times but mostly a nuisance. Not minding her own business was a favorite past-time.

Chase reluctantly removed his hand with a sigh. "So, the porch is out."

LaShaun sat straight. "Good morning."

"I swear, she pops up more than those spirits you fight," Chase said as he smiled and waved at her.

"You're silly," LaShaun stammered around more giggles.

"The woman probably has binoculars with night vision, too. I'll bet she's better equipped than we are down at the station,"

Chase continued. He cupped one of LaShaun buttocks and squeezed.

"And we keep giving her fresh gossip material. Now stop." LaShaun cleared her throat and tried to ignore the spike of lust his hand inspired. "How are you and the family, Mrs. Marchand?"

Their neighbor decided to get closer. She chattered away, bragging on her children as she crossed the grass to get closer. LaShaun took the lead in exchanging small talk that their kids were fine.

"We're out enjoying this cool, dry weather. Nice break from the hot summer we had," LaShaun called.

"Yeah, at least it was mostly quiet. Looks like crime is getting out of hand again. Lord knows what the world is coming to; young folks these days," Mrs. Marchand said and shook her head as if bitterly disappointed in life. "Well, at least we have our local sheriff's department doing its job. A reason to be grateful for sure."

"Thanks for the vote of confidence, Mrs. M," Chase replied with a neutral smile.

"That poor woman just doing her job to help and look what happened." Betty's round face held traces of expectation as she gazed at Chase.

"Hmm." Chase cast a side glance at LaShaun as a silent plea of help.

"Yeah, and then that other one dying of an overdose. Why folks like being half out of their minds on that stuff I'll never understand. I tell my kids all the time, start talking to my grandbabies early. Temptation is everywhere." Betty clicked her tongue.

"So sad. We better get moving. Loads to do before the kids get home," LaShaun called back.

"Yes. I imagine you do." Betty chuckled as she gazed at LaShaun.

LaShaun tugged her sweater back in place. "Well, have a great day."

"Yep. I'm just tending the horses. Then going into the chicken coop. I'll send y'all some fresh eggs later on. I'll be sure to *call* first though. I'll let you young married folks get back to doin'... whatever." Mrs. Marchand smiled at them one last time before she turned away.

Chase leaned close to pull LaShaun's back against him. His fingers found the snap of her jeans and tugged until it opened. "Getting back to 'whatever' sounds like a plan."

They started undressing each other in the laundry room. By the time they got to their main suite, both were down to their underwear. The rush of knowing the kids might be home soon only added to their excitement. Almost two hours later they were sweaty and blissful.

Chase hummed a Cajun song as he prepared lunch for them both. They traded jokes over their meal of roast beef po-boys and sweet tea. LaShaun wanted to believe they'd passed through this storm of family friction unscathed. But she knew better. Still, she enjoyed seeing Chase's genuine easygoing happiness for the first time in days. Then he grew pensive after a while.

"So, you forgive me for spending the night away from home? I noticed you didn't jump my ass about where I'd been. I was at—"

"Katie's house. She called me so I wouldn't worry," LaShaun said with a crooked grin.

"My sister the traitor," Chase quipped. "I admit to being petty and waiting late to send a text."

LaShaun shrugged. "I admit being petty and ignoring it."

"We're a pair, huh?" Chase brushed a thumb down LaShaun's nose.

"We are and a lot of folks have said the same," LaShaun said, her grin wider.

"Yeah." Chase chewed on the last bit of his sandwich. "CeeCee and Jonah; heard from them about my case?"

"No, and I'm surprised. I'll call CeeCee. Give them a nudge," LaShaun replied.

"I should be the first to know anything they find out about Ms. Banks. And if the Glapion case has any wizard connections." Chase raised one dark eyebrow at LaShaun.

"Ha-ha. You're trying to push my buttons with the wizard crack. Well, it won't work."

"But you're so sexy when you're mad." Chase grabbed at LaShaun with a comical lustful chuckle.

LaShaun gave his arm a playful swat. "Straighten up, mister. The kids will be home soon and I've got laundry to fold, houseplants to water, their snacks to prepare—"

"Dad to the rescue," Chase cut her off. "I have another day before I return to the station. So far, my people have things under control interviewing witnesses. Nothing urgent is happening, so Dave is cool with me not going in."

"Wonderful. I get to clean up after you, too," LaShaun wisecracked. She reached for his plate but Chase pulled it away.

"Nope. I'm going to play house-husband. Give my woman a break. Plus, I'm sure you want to do some supernatural snooping."

"Okay, Broussard. Don't push it." LaShaun hissed a sharp breath when he gazed at her without speaking. "Investigate, not snoop. I'm curious about the Glapions. A couple of generations ago they got into it with some of my family."

"Uh-oh. Bet the Glapions got the short end. You Rousselle folks are brutal." Chase ducked when LaShaun took a swipe at his head.

"Funny. It's ancient history. My grandmother never mentioned them. That tells me whatever beef they had was buried long ago." LaShaun watched Chase clear their lunch dishes. He went to the sink.

"Maybe there something in those family journals Ellie seems addicted to. I don't get why our modern baby loves reading that old stuff. My nieces and nephews doze off when us 'old' folks talk about back in the day," Chase said over one shoulder.

"She's fascinated with Monmon Odette. Nothing to worry about," LaShaun added when Chase turned to face her with a frown. "No messages from the great beyond. Because we're different, Ellie wants to explore more about our family."

"Broussard family history is pretty bland by comparison. Still, showing her old photos and talking about the Acadian migration is a good idea. What do you think?" Chase washed up the dishes and then the interior of the microwave.

"Hmm. Yeah." LaShaun only half heard him. Her thoughts had traveled miles away.

"I think it will help the whole thing with Mama," Chase continued. He used a yellow checked cloth to dry their plates as he talked. "Hey, you haven't heard anything I said."

LaShaun was startled to find him sitting next to her at the kitchen Island. "You're going to tell Ellie and CJ about how Cajuns came to Louisiana."

"Uh-huh," Chase said with a grunt. "When are you going to see Zulime?"

"Not until her grandmother gives permission. And she won't return Savannah's calls." LaShaun frowned as she looked out of the bay window.

Chase crossed his arms. "Make sure your cell phone is charged."

"Say what now?" LaShaun blinked back from her musings and stared at him.

"When you drive out to pop in on Eunice Vidal uninvited. I hear she's got a temper and doesn't like many people at all." Chase cocked his head to one side.

"Lover, you know me so well it's scary." LaShaun smacked a kiss on his lips.

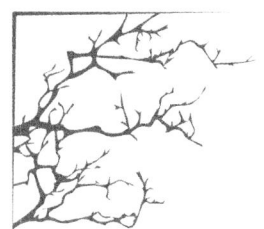

# Chapter 7

"**I**'m telling you, LaShaun, this is a bad idea."

Savannah squinted into the sunshine. She opened a fold-down compartment between the visors of her Volvo SUV to retrieve sunglasses. Then she heaved a sigh for the third time.

"I agree. I should be the one driving," LaShaun shot back. "If you're going to grumble the whole trip, I can leave your butt here."

They sat in the parking lot next to Savannah's law office. After getting Ellie off to school and dropping CJ at daycare, LaShaun met up with Savannah. Sunshine and seventy-seven-degree temperature made for a lovely day. LaShaun had pulled Savannah into her scheme to use the surprise element with Eunice Vidal. Even Savannah's assistant, Rai had, expressed doubts about the plan.

"Not grumbling. Just dropping a dose of reality." Savannah checked her look in the mirror. She applied lip gloss and fluffed her should-length auburn hair.

"Girl, we ain't going to one of your sorority soirees." LaShaun rolled her eyes at her friend.

"Oh, shut it."

Savannah primped for a second longer and then started the grey SUV. They drove down Main Street and took a right onto Railroad Avenue. Twenty minutes later, Savannah turned left onto Highway 167. Neither spoke for a long time. LaShaun read messages from Chase, CeeCee, and Jonah on her phone.

"You left her a voice message, right? It won't be a complete surprise." LaShaun looked up from the screen and squinted behind her own dark sunglasses.

"Yeah, well... we'll find out if she takes a shot at us," Savannah replied.

"Mrs. Vidal listens to messages. She just doesn't answer or call people. She's been hurt a lot in her life, but she's also hurt others. She's passed that pain onto her bloodline," LaShaun murmured. She breathed in and out, letting her sixth sense expand as they neared Blood River.

Savannah took one hand off the steering wheel to tap LaShaun's arm. "Stop the psychic thing while I'm driving. You're creeping me out."

"Oh, get over it. Besides, my third eye might help us avoid bullets." LaShaun barked a laugh when Savannah gasped. "I'm kidding. I'll bet Eunice doesn't even own a gun."

"Bet? Put that telepathy to some good use and find out for sure," Savannah replied, her voice sharp with anxiety.

LaShaun blinked back from her efforts to know Eunice Vidal. She turned to her friend. "You're scared of her."

"No, not exactly. I mean... the stories about her aren't reassuring. She stabbed her first husband, you know. Of course, he was abusive. And she'd caught him trying to fondle a kid," Savannah added.

"I like her already," LaShaun quipped.

Savannah laughed. "Well, Eunice Cecille Glapion Vidal is a mixed bag. Definitely not the *sweet old lady baking tea cakes* type. Her second husband was Jules Vidal, a fourth cousin three times removed. Or something. Anyway, he stayed drunk or high a lot. They had two kids. She had two with the first husband. Her oldest daughter died in a car accident back in the seventies. The other two adult kids live out of state. And you know where Zulime's father lives."

"Yeah. The Raymond Laborde Correctional Facility." LaShaun looked out at the landscape that whizzed by as Savannah drove.

"Sentenced to twenty-five years as a habitual offender. Another excuse to put poor Black people in prison for decades." Savannah's pretty face scrunched into a fierce scowl. "Non-violent offenses can lead to a life sentence."

"So, he's innocent?" LaShaun glanced at her.

"Oh, he did the crimes all right. I think the police and DA just finally had an out to get him off the streets."

"Louisiana's harsh three strikes law came in handy," LaShaun replied.

"Exactly. How did you..." Savannah tapped her temple as she shot a side-eye at LaShaun.

"I've been doing my own research on the family. When I wasn't wrangling an active four-year-old, making sure Ellie acts right in school, and—"

"Fighting with your husband," Savannah cut in. "Did you two work things out?"

LaShaun stretched her legs out. She smiled at the yellow wildflowers swaying in the breeze. "Yeah. We talked."

Savannah studied her for a few seconds. "Your goofy grin ain't got nothing to do with *talk*. Chase hit you with that good-good."

"We did have a conversation... before." LaShaun laughed when Savannah hooted like a high school girl sharing hot chitchat.

"I knew y'all would come through it."

"Back to Zulime though," LaShaun said, her expression turning serious again. "Tell me more about Brighter Futures. Any negative reports about the program?"

"Nothing in the official records that I could find. There were several citations in 2021 from the state licensing agency that said their background checks needed work. But a follow-up report cleared them and said they'd tightened their procedures," Savannah replied.

"Before, after, or while Karlene Pattison was a mentor?"

"I see where you're going." Savannah shook her head. "No recent complaints, and nothing refers to Pattison as one of the employees concerned. I'm not one to be cynical, but Brighter Futures management has political connections."

"Meaning any serious problems could be smoothed over or even concealed." LaShaun looked at her sharply.

"I'm not making any accusations. But like I said, none of it seems to involve Karlene Pattison. Though her background is a bit of a mystery. She grew up in upstate New York until she was fifteen. Her family moved to Pennsylvania. Left home at seventeen. She fell in with a bad crowd, had some juvenile offenses, but went to community college and turned her life around. Worked as an EMT and took a few criminal justice classes."

"She got interested in helping other people stay out of trouble," LaShaun said.

"Yep. All looks so normal on the surface. Former juvenile delinquent sees the light and wants to share her wisdom with our youth. I'm quoting from a page on their website," Savannah replied.

"You don't buy it though."

"A group of law and order conservatives started the program six years ago. A few kids have complained about harsh treatment in the past. A couple even claimed racism. Nothing stuck. Like I said, their leadership has connections."

"But leads to chase down," LaShaun murmured.

"No complaints about Pattison, so it doesn't sound promising for Zulime's case."

"She was assigned to Zee and they hit it off, right?"

"The first mentors two didn't work out. Zee clammed up, wouldn't talk. Or cussed them out. Brighter Futures finally matched her with Karlene Pattison. After a rocky start, Pattison seemed to be making headway. In fact, in the month or two before the attack they seemed really close."

"Strange. Something must have happened to sour their relationship. If we can find out, it would definitely help," LaShaun said.

"We have a hearing coming up in three weeks. I'd like to get her out of detention before then." Savannah heaved a sigh. "Which is the main reason I agreed to come on this wilderness trip."

"I don't get it."

"The DA hasn't formally requested Zulime be tried as an adult yet. Mrs. Vidal won't return my calls. I need to get Zulime released on bail. Time is running out. It's a legal long shot, but damn it. She's so young." Savannah clicked her tongue.

"Hey, you're doing good for her," LaShaun said.

"My good isn't good enough. Even if I get her released on bail, the DA could have her picked up again after the adult charges. He would likely ask the judge to set bail even higher. So frustrating. All the tough-on-crime laws end up trapping the poor in a lopsided, unjust system," Savannah complained.

"Not to mention crime is still high. The 'lock 'em up!' strategy doesn't work."

"Nope, but the voters respond to scary speeches and posturing, so it's not likely to change. At least not in this state anytime soon."

LaShaun frowned as she stared out at the forest land surrounding them. "You need to build a defense that doesn't hinge on expecting mercy from the system."

"A dead woman. A teenager with a history of breaking the law. Sympathy is in seriously short supply for Zulime Glapion."

"Which means we better figure out a way to find her missing notebook," LaShaun said. "I think there are answers in it. Don't ask me why."

"Or it could be a dead end; nothing more than a relative doing Mrs. Vidal a favor by picking up Zee's stuff."

LaShaun thought it over for a few seconds before she shook her head. "I guess. But still..."

The pleasant voice from the Volvo's GPS system broke into their conversation. Their turn was one thousand feet ahead on the left. Savannah turned southwest onto a two-lane blacktop road. A worn sign said they were on Highway 339. Savannah drove on for another fifteen minutes. After a quarter of a mile, all they saw on either side were a few mailboxes on posts every so often.

"Okay, girl," Savannah said to the GPS screen set in her dashboard. "Help me out here." Silence.

"We're so far in the middle of nowhere even she's stumped," LaShaun joked.

"Why do I feel like a swamp monster is about to jump out from somewhere?" Savannah looked at LaShaun and then waved a hand at their surroundings.

Hickory, ash, and slash pine trees dotted the scenery. Between the trees, prairies of tall grass and shrubs crowded both sides of the road. Vines covered tree trunks. Huge live oaks stretched up to the sky. Shade from the still green leaves blocked out sunlight. Two houses spread far apart were set back from the road, gravel paths leading to them.

LaShaun craned her neck to get a better view of anything nearby. "Well, we're not there yet. I don't see her name on these mailboxes. Let's keep going."

"That's the last line in horror movies before the characters get snatched up. Okay, Rougarou. Your snack is on the way," Savannah muttered. She pressed the gas pedal. The SUV picked up speed but stayed at twenty miles per hour as they looked around.

"Don't be dramatic. Besides, Rougarou only creep out at night. Now the Blood River swamp monster is another matter." LaShaun let out a slow whistle imitating creepy horror movie music.

"I'm never going on another road trip with you. Definitely not into the backwoods," Savannah shot back and scowled at LaShaun.

"I'm messin' with you, girl. Ain't no monsters out here. But we should keep an eye out for jumpy country folks with shotguns. You know how we love to shoot in good ol' Murrikka."

"Thanks. I feel much better," Savannah clipped. Her fingers gripped the steering wheel tighter.

LaShaun continued to scan the countryside. "These small roads remind me of Rousselle property. Some the lanes aren't even named on maps."

"Wait, Zulime said look for twin magnolia trees. Damn it, look at all the magnolia trees. The sign with Bayou Lane on it might have fallen down. Sometimes her grandmother doesn't bother to put it back up. Says another strong wind will just knock it over again." Savannah took off her sunglasses. "This woman is serious about being left alone."

"Look, two magnolia trees on either side of a road." LaShaun pointed ahead to their left.

"A road? I don't see a thing." Savannah squinted as if doing do would enhance her vision.

"Drive another quarter mile. There's a break in the grass and shrubs where the road leads off. There's a mail box."

Savannah drove on despite a skeptical frown. "All these trees look alike to me. I feel sorry for the mail carrier with this route. You can barely see the thing with those vines covering the post."

"I can feel we're getting close," LaShaun murmured.

"Here we go with the creepy crap. Look, can we just stick to the normal everyday problem of Zee's legal trouble? I can't with the voodoo."

LaShaun rubbed hard at the tingle climbing up one arm. "You might not have a choice."

"More good news. Here." Savannah hit the brakes. She jerked a thumb a red mailbox let on a post with "Vidal" on it.

The mailbox looked surprisingly new. Beyond it, a narrow passage barely wide enough for two vehicles stretched out. Palmetto, holly, and other shrubs lined either side of it. Savannah backed the SUV up a few feet to turn since she'd almost gone past the lane. Sunlight filtered through the leaves across the Volvo as she drove. She lowered the power windows on the driver's and passenger side. Birdsong serenaded them.

"I can see why she likes it way out here. This is pretty," LaShaun said.

"Yeah. It is." Savannah's brows pulled together as she scrutinized their surroundings. "I don't get it."

"You were expecting property like the Addams family?" LaShaun poked her friend's arm and laughed.

"Exactly, only the Louisiana swamp Creole version. Hold up. We might still get there." Savannah turned the Volvo around a corner.

The lane branched off to a circle of well-maintained crushed gravel in front of a house. Honeysuckle bushes bloomed on either side of a two-story house. Wide deep green leaves on hydrangea bushes dotted the front yard along with two gardenia shrubs. The hydrangeas showed off their fall blue and pink flowers. Mrs. Vidal stood on the wide raised porch at the top of steps leading up. She leaned on a thick wooden cane.

"I made tea," she called out as a greeting. Then she turned and went into the house.

LaShaun shrugged when Savannah looked at her with wide eyes. "Well, at least she's not aiming a shotgun at us."

Savannah parked with the front of the SUV pointing away from the house. "In case we need a fast getaway."

"Looks like she's fine with us showing up. Even made us tea." LaShaun released her seat belt and opened the passenger-side door.

""Oh hell no. I'm not eating or drinking anything." Savannah hit the button to release her seat belt also. She didn't move for a few seconds but instead stared at the house.

"Fix your face. You look like the kid in a scary movie about to go in a haunted house. We need her to feel like she's part of a team." LaShaun kept her voice low. She glanced toward the house several times as she spoke. Large windows stretched on either side of the front door.

"You're right. This is ridiculous. It's the year of our Lord twenty-twenty-three. I'm letting superstition get to me." Savannah got out of the Volvo with her tote slung over one shoulder. She squared her shoulders and strode with purpose to the steps. Then she stopped and looked back at LaShaun. "Maybe you go first."

"And you were doing so well," LaShaun quipped.

With a chuckle, LaShaun mounted the sturdy wooden steps. The porch stretched on either side of them; two chairs on either side and a bench swing provided seating. Two baskets held large ferns. Savannah held open the wood-framed screen door and nodded for LaShaun to go past her. LaShaun rolled eyes and walked into the house. A hallway ran down the middle, splitting the house into two halves. A staircase faced them. Mrs. Vidal appeared in the hallway, pushing a wheeled serving cart. Her cane hung from one of the cart handles.

"Started to wonder if y'all had drove out here for nothing. Dawdling out in my yard for so long," Mrs. Vidal said. Her voice sounded strong despite the cane implying she was frail.

"Let me help. I figure we're going into the front parlor." LaShaun took the handle of the cart and guided it to their left.

Mrs. Vidal offered no protest. She picked up her cane and followed. "Thank you."

"It's the least we can do showing up unannounced," LaShaun replied with a smile.

"You was announced. That one left messages. One would have been enough." Mrs. Vidal pointed her cane at Savannah.

The long room held a sofa, a settee, three chairs and various tables. The furniture combined antiques with more contemporary vintage pieces. Mrs. Vidal nodded approval when LaShaun positioned the cart near one sturdy chair. She sat with a sigh.

"I'm not ailing, if that's what you think because of the cane. Still recovering from slipping down the back steps. Just a sprain. Thought I heard something out back the other night." Mrs. Vidal poured tea from a pot into two cups with matching rose patterns.

"Pretty tea set. Thanks," LaShaun said as she accepted a cup. She squinted a warning look at Savannah when she hesitated.

"Yes, it is quite nice. Thank you, ma'am." Savannah took the cup. She didn't drink but instead stared at the liquid in it.

"Blueberry, hibiscus, and elderberry." Mrs. Vidal smiled back at Savannah.

"Excuse me?" Savannah blinked at the older woman.

"The tea, dear. All natural from my land. Nothing sinister about it. I'm just being hospitable even though y'all came without an invite." Mrs. Vidal turned to study LaShaun.

Savannah's mouth worked for a few seconds before she could talk. "Oh, I wasn't... I mean, I didn't think—"

Mrs. Vidal waved a hand at Savannah but continued to look at LaShaun. "I know what people say about Blood Bayou. Only about a mile or so south of my property. At the end of Blood River. And what they say about me, too."

"What do they say?" LaShaun returned Mrs. Vidal's gaze with her own examination.

"That I'm mean as a cottonmouth. But they got it wrong. You see, a cottonmouth only bites when it feels threatened." Mrs. Vidal wore a placid expression. "My great-grandmother and my grandmother were both traiteurs, you know."

Savannah sent LaShaun a questioning glance. "How... interesting."

"They tried to help people. You know what it got them? Being called evil. Folks claimed they'd put spells on them. And they said worse. I like my peace out here. Life done taught me to stay away from folks." Mrs. Vidal poured tea into a cup and sipped. She nodded at the tray on the cart. "Sugar right there for you. Don't believe in that fake stuff they make. I take mine black."

"Thanks." LaShaun added two teaspoons to her tea.

Savannah shot another glance at LaShaun. She cleared her throat and put the full cup down. "I did try calling you several times."

"I got the messages," Mrs. Vidal said with a nod.

"Right. I'm afraid things have taken an even more serious turn," Savannah said. "Karlene Pattison died and the DA is going to charge Zee as an adult."

"Hmm, that is serious." Mrs. Vidal's tone or expression remained flat. She drank more tea.

"Mrs. Vidal, I don't think you understand what this means. Your sixteen-year-old granddaughter could spend decades in prison," Savannah said with force, her voice rising with each word. "You're acting like we came here for a tea party."

LaShaun leaned toward her friend. "Savannah, let's just—"

"I've been calling you for over *two weeks*, Mrs. Vidal. Two whole weeks you've ignored my messages," Savannah said with force.

"I know what's been going on." Mrs. Vidal seemed unaffected by Savannah's rebuke.

Savannah blew out a harsh sigh. "She's all alone out there in a system that eats kids like her alive. Have you even talked to Zee?"

"Yes, I have if it's any of your business. And before she got into this trouble, I talked myself blue in the face. Didn't do much good, did it?" Mrs. Vidal retorted.

"As a matter of fact, it is very much my business as her lawyer. I need to know Zulime is emotionally and mentally okay. Family support is critical at a time like this. And you need to answer when I call you on the phone. I should be in my office building a solid defense. Not wasting time driving way out here because you won't," Savannah continued with heat.

"I know why you came, young lady. What I don't know is what you expect me to do. I can't wave a magic wand and make her troubles go away." Mrs. Vidal looked from Savannah to LaShaun. Then she sipped more tea.

"I'm just…" Savannah stammered into silence; a look of stunned outrage stamped on her face. She turned to LaShaun as if seeking support.

LaShaun pushed her sixth sense hard at the elderly woman. Mrs. Vidal's impassive façade cracked a fraction. She blinked a few times and shifted in her chair. She stared at Savannah hard.

"You're a St. Julien. I don't know your people well." Mrs. Vidal placed her cup back on the serving cart with care. Then she turned to LaShaun. "What is you name again, child?"

"LaShaun Broussard." LaShaun felt a wall of resistance against her psychic energy. Mrs. Vidal had switched her full attention to her.

Mrs. Vidal's thick dark eyebrows pulled together. Even at seventy-nine years old, traces of the beautiful young Creole woman remained. "Married?"

"Yes, ma'am. My maiden name is Rousselle," LaShaun said in an even voice. She felt a jolt from Mrs. Vidal.

"You Odette LaGrange Rousselle's grandchild, the one she raised. Mama was Francine. Your mama used to run with one of my brothers. The worst one. He dead, too. No wonder, the mess they got up to." Mrs. Vidal pursed her lips.

"Mrs. Vidal, we're here to talk about your granddaughter," LaShaun clipped.

"Thought I felt something... off the minute you two crossed my property line. Odette been gone a while now. You ever hear from her? I used to get messages from my monmon when I was a girl." Mrs. Vidal's shoulders jerked and her eyes widened.

LaShaun smiled at her. The tiny finger of supernatural heat she'd sent had hit its mark. Mrs. Vidal whispered in Louisiana Creole French. Her voice was so low the words only came out as a hiss; like a snake. LaShaun closed her eyes for two seconds and tried to catch the essence of the words. The Creole Mrs. Vidal used was almost extinct. LaShaun recognized a few words from reading one hundred year and fifty-year-old family journals.

"Eunice, stop!" LaShaun said the words but not in her own voice.

"What the—" Savannah had risen from her chair and taken a step away from both women.

"Who is talking to me?" Mrs. Vidal reached for her walking cane. It fell to the floor and rolled away.

"Your stick won't help you, Eunice. Now let's stop all this playing around," LaShaun said in a voice that seemed to echoed through the house. Then she huffed out a long breath.

"LaShaun?" Savannah gawked at her but seemed afraid to get close. "You... are you okay?"

LaShaun shook her head to clear it. She gazed around the house fully for the first time. "This house holds a lot of conjure attached to it. A lot used for malicious purposes."

Mrs. Vidal drew back as if seeking to escape LaShaun's words. "No, no."

"Did you recognize the voice?" LaShaun leaned toward her.

"What do you want from me?" Mrs. Vidal rasped.

Savannah looked at the cup of tea she still held. Her hand shook as she put it on the serving cart. "I need information, about Zulime's family history or counseling she's gotten in the past. Anything that will help her defense."

"First, tell my why you got her involved," Mrs. Vidal countered and stabbed a finger at LaShaun.

"My little girl had Zee as a tutor, part of her community service. Ellie is very much on Zee's side. She even got in trouble at school trying to get a notebook for Zee," LaShaun said.

"LaShaun has experience as a private investigator of... special cases," Savannah put in.

"Zulime got no business with voodoo and spells. I kept all of it away from her," Mrs. Vidal protested.

"Really? Children are not only curious, but secrets attract them even more. You can't really think Zee didn't know what you were doing," LaShaun replied. She smiled at Mrs. Vidal and picked up her cup of tea. "This is a delicious blend. My grandmother had her own recipes as well. Did you share them?"

"I didn't fool with Odette. She stayed outta my way and I did the same with her," Mrs. Vidal snapped. "Anyway, that was all long ago between the old ones. Nothing to do with me. I never had nothing against her or the Rousselles," Mrs. Vidal said with force.

"Did you ever catch Zee reciting spells or reading your diary?" LaShaun nodded when Mrs. Vidal's eyes narrowed. "I thought so."

"None of that stuff from the ancestors got a thing to do with Zulime's troubles now," Mrs. Vidal snapped. She sat straight and lifted her chin.

LaShaun closed her eyes for a few seconds. She hummed low in her throat. "Sadness."

Mrs. Vidal breathed hard. She looked at Savannah. "Make her stop right now."

"You want to punish your granddaughter for defying you. Zulime has never had the nurturing a child should have, and for that you should be ashamed," LaShaun said. "And I didn't need anyone else to tell me. I can feel it in this house. Resentment."

"You got a nerve judging me," Mrs. Vidal shouted. She sat straight with a deep scowl at LaShaun. "My no-good second husband spent his time gambling. And getting drunk on whatever he could get his hands on. Zulime's parents were no better. In and out of jail. Like I wanted to clean up after trash in cheap motels. Driving way out to jobs that paid little or nothing. I ain't had no help. Just a bunch of layabouts always with their hands out. If you knew what I had to do to hold onto this family property..." Her voice broke and she gripped both arms of the chair.

"Mrs. Vidal, there is a lot of pain still floating around Bayou Lane. I think it's time to let it go. You need to use some of those spells to get true peace; in here." LaShaun placed a hand over her heart. "Being isolated hasn't worked."

"We can get you family counseling," Savannah put in.

"I'm not telling my business to no nosy social worker."

"Fine," LaShaun said before Savannah could reply. "Who did you send to get Zee's things from school?"

"I thought you two was bringing them with you. That uppity assistant principal left a message, but I didn't send nobody. A notebook, you say?"

LaShaun nodded. "Along with a few other items, but we think something Zee wrote in her journal might be helpful."

"The girl was always writing, but on her computer or phone. Who would want to steal her knickknacks? Zulime ain't got nothing valuable. Don't make no sense." Mrs. Vidal frown as if genuinely confused.

"And a unicorn keychain," LaShaun said.

"Don't know every thingamabob that child has collected. But none of it's worth much I don't reckon. Some teenager maybe stole her stuff. They was always pestering her at that school." Mrs. Vidal looked at LaShaun. "Your child, she got the gift?"

"She does."

Mrs. Vidal let out a long sigh. "Tell me what I need to do."

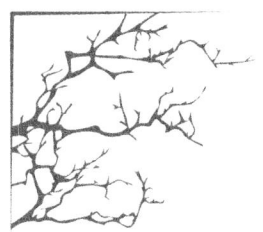

# Chapter 8

Having returned home after the visit to Blood Bayou, LaShaun put gumbo in her slow cooker to simmer. Then she chopped up seasonings for potato salad. LaShaun's mind spun in several different directions as she cooked. Beau sat watching her cook for a time. Then he strolled around the house. He sniffed the air and let out a woof; an alert that someone or something preternatural was nearby. The sound of a vehicle engine rumbled outside. LaShaun looked out to see a silver Range Rover in the driveway. She ordered the smart locks to open and went back to chopping celery. Jonah came in holding CJ by the hand.

"Hey, sweet baby." LaShaun winked at CJ.

"We went vroom-vroom down the road," CJ piped up. He raced off to follow his routine of washing up for a snack.

"Hey, buddy. Don't be a snitch," Jonah called after him. Then he turned to LaShaun. "I wasn't speeding."

"Better not. Thanks for picking him up. Saved me a trip so I could cook. And yes, I'll give you a container of gumbo as payment," LaShaun said.

Jonah waved a hand at her. "I'd do it for free. But I'm not gonna say no to Louisiana seafood gumbo. Will it come with the fixings?"

"Yes, I'll include potato salad and French bread. I might even throw in dessert." LaShaun smiled at him.

"Cool. Wait a minute." Jonah squinted at LaShaun. "I can't be bought, Mrs. Broussard."

Before LaShaun could answer, CJ bounced back into the room. He held up both tiny hands to prove they were clean. LaShaun got him settled at his own little table near the window. CJ hummed approval over his snack of peanut butter, crackers, and apple slices. Beau strolled over to sit next to him. Satisfied he was distracted, LaShaun turned to Jonah.

"What's up with my little brother?" Jonah jerked a thumb at CJ.

"Oh, he's fine."

"I mean, what's his gift? You know, the signs of what he can do. Ellie started young, which is why TEA sees her as such an asset," Jonah replied.

"No, she's a child. *My child*. Not some chess piece to move around for their agenda. CJ is going to enjoy being a kid for as long as possible. And with the infiltrations into TEA, Legion knows about Ellie, too. I don't want CJ on their radar." LaShaun brought the chef's knife down hard on the cutting board. Green onions flew across the quartz surface of the island.

"Hey, hey, relax. CeeCee and me will keep their names out of any reports we send."

Jonah glanced over his shoulder at CJ, who giggled at a cartoon on the television. He'd left his snack and turned it on using the remote. Seated on the floor, his gaze didn't waver from the antics of the colorful characters. Beau lay nearby, his head rested on his paws and eyes half-shut. Nothing about the scene suggested danger.

"Sorry." LaShaun cleaned up the mess her intense chopping had caused.

"I don't have kids, but I get it. Like I said, none of what we know points in your family's direction."

"I have more questions though." LaShaun glanced at him.

"Hmm." Jonah crossed his arms and sat back.

"I'm hurt by your suspicions, Agent Parker. An update is all I'm asking." LaShaun cut up the potatoes and put them in a large bowl. "I have a box of banana pudding from Tante Marie's just for you."

"You want to pump me for information. The kind I'm not supposed to share." Jonah shook a forefinger at her.

LaShaun went to the fridge and retrieved a container with Tante Marie's logo on it. She placed it on the kitchen island between them. Jonah eyed it for a few seconds. LaShaun pushed it closer to him. With a grin, Jonah got a spoon from a drawer nearby. He sighed with satisfaction with each taste.

"Savannah's aunt made it fresh herself today. She does her own special crust of graham crackers mixed with crushed chocolate wafers." LaShaun finished putting aside the fixings for her potato salad.

"So good. And the cookies crumpled on top. Ah, perfection." Jonah gobbled up the entire serving. "It's official. I'm bought and paid for. Ask away."

"Don't get into trouble because of me," LaShaun said.

"Trouble is the fuel that keeps me going, sis. Fire away." Jonah sat on a bar stool.

LaShaun glanced at CJ to check his attention was elsewhere. "Any connections between your case and Zulime Glapion?"

"Not a thing so far. Neesha, that was Tranicia Banks' nickname, had no notes on Zulime or any Glapion for that matter. The working TEA theory is deep cover affected her. She got hooked on drugs playing her part too well and died." Jonah shrugged.

"Seriously? Sounds iffy to me," LaShaun replied.

"Yeah, I know. The older folks in management think anybody under thirty is a drug fiend. Like our generation invented the stuff." Jonah grunted with disdain. "It doesn't help that she smoked weed and flirted with ecstasy in high school."

"And they're taking the path of least resistance. Still, you have to admit it's possible."

"CeeCee went deeper into her profile. No history of treatment for addiction. She partied like a lot of us and grew up. In fact, she didn't want anything to interfere with her clairvoyance. Drugs don't enhance gifts but impair them. After a rough childhood, she finally felt accepted in TEA." Jonah rose, filled a glass with water, and sat again.

"But you don't have any evidence that she was murdered."

"She definitely died of an overdose. But she had bruises on her body and needle marks. Neesha smoked. She never injected."

"So, she found the Legion agent or agents and they used drugs to eliminate her. Awful." LaShaun shook her head.

"They're still trying to dredge for monazite. We think there's more of it in Blood Bayou. They've been trying to buy land around there but an elderly lady told them no." Jonah raised an eyebrow when LaShaun hissed a gasp.

"The elderly lady's name is Eunice Vidal."

"Your ESP kicked in strong," Jonah said with a grin.

"She's Zulime Glapion's grandmother." LaShaun frowned as she leaned on the counter with both elbows.

"Coincidence. Hear me out," Jonah added when LaShaun gave him a skeptical gaze. "The real estate guy approached several landowners in Vermilion Parish. No indications Mrs. Vidal got special attention. Nothing about Zulime being involved. According to TEA surveyors, the possible monazite deposits cross at least three boundaries. A portion of the land is state property, protected wetlands."

"They'll have a hard time getting hold of the land then. Trying to negotiate with multiple owners, dealing with the Department of Wildlife and Fisheries, the Department of Natural Resources..." LaShaun replied.

"Not to mention having to do environmental impact studies. A slow-moving process for sure. TEA figures Neesha got bored because nothing was happening, slipped into drug use, and overdosed."

"But you and CeeCee don't buy it."

Jonah sighed. "CeeCee is keeping an open mind, but she says it happens. Being undercover is stressful. Neesha liked to party and she did use drugs in the past."

"And you?"

"I spoke to her two best friends. She only drank socially. Yes, she did like action, but they insist she was a pro at her job. They're certain she wouldn't have used. And definitely not injections. She had a phobia about needles," Jonah said.

"Or maybe she got high, her inhibitions were affected, and was persuaded by her new pals," LaShaun countered.

"Yeah, that's what senior officers say. I'm not calling you old," Jonah added quickly when LaShaun raised her eyebrows.

"Two kids, a dog, my aching back when it rains? I feel like it sometimes," LaShaun wisecracked.

"Yeah, well there are two TEA factions lining up. The old guard and the new keep facing off over everything. We try to keep our investigations out of political games, but it ain't easy."

LaShaun craned her neck to check on CJ. He had switched his attention from the television to a book. Then he put it aside to play with a toy tool box Chase had gotten him. She turned her attention back to Jonah and TEA.

"The 'old folks' have a point though. Still, those bruises." LaShaun frowned at Jonah.

He nodded. "I'll double check on the autopsy. See if the needle marks show signs of force."

"The coroner won't release info to you." LaShaun eyed his neutral expression. "TEA has someone on the inside."

"Let's just say we have ways of finding these things out. Nothing that undermines traditional authorities," Jonah added. "Try not to think about it."

"If Chase or his boss ever find out..."

"The good news is we're staying hands off of his investigation and Ellie's friend isn't hooked up with our case." Jonah glanced down when a chime sounded from his pocket. He took out his mobile phone, read the screen, and stood.

"Update?" LaShaun only got a brief glimpse of the screen. He hit the button to lock it before she could read anything.

"Thanks for the banana pudding. That should hold me for another hour or so. I'll be back for the gumbo." Jonah pecked her on the cheek. Then he strode over to CJ. "Bye, little buddy. I'll catch you on the next go-round."

"See ya later, gator," CJ chirped and waved at him.

LaShaun laughed when Jonah blinked in surprise. "His great-aunt has him talking like her and her friends. Some days he sounds like a sixty-year-old man who drives a Lincoln and is the deacon at his church."

"Gotta love this family. Talk later." Jonah headed for the door.

"If you hear anything else about Eunice Vidal, her land, or Zulime, let me know," LaShaun called after him.

"Probably won't. So, don't worry about it." Jonah winked at her and was out of the door before she could respond.

"Yeah, right. There's more to the story you're not telling me." LaShaun went to her tablet to tap into her own sources inside and outside of TEA.

THAT EVENING LASHAUN worked hard to lift the aura in her home. Ellie gave a rundown of her day in a monotone. She kept glancing at the door. For once CJ picked up on her mood. His appetite was just as robust. He especially enjoyed LaShaun's potato salad. Still, even his chatter was more subdued than usual. LaShaun patted one of Ellie's stray curls back into place. Her thick hair tumbled to her shoulders. A barrette pinned it back on both sides away from her face.

"You okay, sweet girl?"

"Braden says Zee is going to jail for a long time. He says Daddy is going to put her under the jail for killing that lady and her witch grandmother can't get her out of trouble this time.

And..." Ellie pushed around shrimp and chicken in her bowl of gumbo without eating.

"Braden doesn't know what he's talking about. And Zee's grandmother isn't a witch. She cares about Zee. In her own strange way," LaShaun murmured.

"But the teachers said—" Ellie blinked when LaShaun tilted her head as she gazed at her. "I wasn't sneaking to listen, Mama."

LaShaun really wanted to know what Ellie had overheard. She also didn't want to contradict herself about listening to gossip. The desire to get the inside scoop won. "Go on."

"Miss Dawson, she teaches fifth grade, says Miss Eunice has the devil on her tail because she's been messing with magic too many years. But Miss Allison says all the talk of voodoo is superstitious nonsense. Zee just had a bad home life and poor supervision. And maybe she'll get the help she needs. But I don't see how her going to jail is going to help her." Ellie looked at LaShaun. Her big brown eyes seemed to reflect all the questions she expected her mother to answer.

"I talked to Zee's grandmother. She just an elderly woman who likes to garden and use herbs for home remedies. It's true that Zee parents have a lot of problems. But Auntie Savannah is working very hard to make sure Zee is treated fairly." LaShaun smiled at Ellie.

Ellie didn't smile back. "You're saying Zee might still go to jail for a long time. She did hurt that lady, but she didn't kill her."

"Well, she did have injuries that resulted in—" LaShaun pressed her lips closed for a few seconds. "Listen, you shouldn't be worrying over all this stuff. Zulime is safe and we're working to get the truth of what happened."

"You and Daddy are going to help Auntie Savannah. That's good. Except..." Ellie's little eyebrows pulled together as she concentrated. Her nine-year-old store of knowledge seemed intent on solving the problem.

"Ellie, let grownups figure this out. It's going to be okay." LaShaun put as much reassurance as possible into her tone.

"Okay."

Ellie's expression didn't brighten despite her words. CJ followed Ellie around. They squabbled because of it as LaShaun cleared away their dishes. LaShaun mediated until things settled down with Ellie reading a book for school and CJ drawing pictures. It was close to their bedtime when Chase got home. He gave them all a tired smile. Ellie launched herself at him before he was halfway across the kitchen. She hugged his knees, her face pressed against his thigh.

"I'm sorry, Daddy. I'll be good and won't get in trouble in school. I won't use my superpowers so people call me a witch. You don't have to stay away from home. Sleep here in your bed." Ellie sobbed until her shoulders trembled.

CJ dropped his crayon and ran over to join them. His tiny face screwed up. "Daddy, don't go!"

"Whoa, whoa, everybody calm down." Chase alternated between rubbing Ellie's back and hugging CJ tight. He crouched down to their level as he comforted them. "Where is all this commotion coming from?"

"You stayed far away because you got mad at me because I got mad at you. And I should have..." Ellie's voice hitched as she sniffled. "My fault for being different."

LaShaun felt a stab of pain at seeing her children in such distress. She blinked back her own tears. Chase managed to picked up CJ on one hip and Ellie on the other. He balanced the weight as he walked to the family room adjacent to the kitchen. Then he sat them on the sofa.

"Daddy isn't mad at you, Ellie. I love every inch of you. We're all different in our own ways. What makes you unique is beautiful." Chase placed a lingering kiss on her forehead. When LaShaun handed him tissues, he wiped away her tears. "Anyone who says otherwise is *wrong*. Don't listen to them."

"But Grandma Elizabeth—"

"She's set in her ways and doesn't understand everything. Grown folks can make mistakes, too." Chase pulled them both into his arms. Their small heads rested against his chest. "You both are gifts."

"So, you're not going to move out and get a new family like Heather's daddy?" Ellie clutched the fabric of his shirt with one fist.

"Of course not. Never."

CJ calmed down much faster than Ellie. Chase's deep voice always had an almost magical effect on him, even as an infant. His strong presence alone convinced CJ all was right in the world. So, CJ set about trying to assure Ellie of the same. LaShaun was sure CJ didn't quite know what they were upset about anyway. Soon he was smiling again. Ellie stopped crying at least. Between the two of them, Chase and CJ managed to tease a faint smile out of her after a while. They were finally in bed when LaShaun and Chase had a chance to talk. He'd showered and changed before he sat down to eat. Dressed in tan sweatpants and a long-sleeved t-shirt, Chase looked drained. LaShaun placed a bowl of gumbo in front of him. She added a slice of French bread with garlic seasoning on a plate. He used the bread to sop up the gumbo. LaShaun ate as well. She hadn't touched dinner. She'd been too busy feeding the kids and worrying about Ellie's distress. Neither spoke for a good fifteen minutes. Chase avoided looking at LaShaun as he downed a final spoonful of gumbo.

"Don't beat yourself up. She's not damaged for life," LaShaun said softly.

"I know, it's just..." Chase sat back and crossed both arms. "I didn't stop to think how Ellie or CJ might feel. I was just pissed. I work long hours and sometimes I'm gone when they wake up."

"Chase." LaShaun placed a hand on one of his forearms.

"Listen to me making excuses." Chase rubbed his jaw hard as if the action was punishment.

"You're human. What you did was show our kids that you can screw up, admit it, and do better." LaShaun grinned when Chase's eyes narrowed.

"So, that's your way of saying I owe you an apology."

"No. Maybe." LaShaun's grin faded into a serious expression. "I owe you one, too. I should have told you CJ might be showing signs he has paranormal abilities. You were right to be mad at being the last to know."

"I shouldn't have let my parents get into my head. Mama is bad, but even my father expressed 'concerns' about what people say. He framed it as us becoming isolated as a family."

LaShaun snorted. "No way. We have friends. Aunt Shirleen, Azalei, Jonah, CeeCee, MJ, Ms. Rose, the twins—"

"Except for your aunt and MJ, I don't think my folks would be reassured. Your cousin Azalei, well she has a past," Chase joked. "And the rest are sorcerers."

"I'm going to let you slide this time because you've been under stress." LaShaun slapped one of his solid thighs. "My point is we're not cut off. We have our own community."

Chase chuckled. "True. But I have to admit it's taken me some time to get used to 'em. Still not sure about Azalei babysitting though."

"She's almost totally reformed."

"Oh, that's encouraging," Chase quipped. "We've got a few twisted branched in the on both sides of the Broussard family tree. I lost my temper and said as much to mama. Didn't go down well. She's still not speaking to me except for one-word answers."

"You're on the outs with your folks? And then you get two murders. CeeCee and Jonah show up, Ellie gets in trouble at school, and..." LaShaun got up and stood behind him. She wrapped her arms about him and kissed his neck. "You had a lot loaded on these shoulders."

"I can handle it. I'm a husband and father. It's what we do." Chase covered her hands with his.

"You're not alone though. I'll do better at keeping you in the loop on all things supernatural." LaShaun hugged him tighter.

Chase pulled her around to sit on his lap. "You feel so good. Smell even better. Like jasmine and Creole spice."

LaShaun squirmed against his pelvis until he sighed and pressed his face to her breasts. "Sweetie?"

"Um-hmmm." Chase unbuttoned her flannel shirt to kiss exposed skin.

"What's happening with the case against Zulime?" LaShaun whispered.

Chase gave her bottom a gentle squeeze with one large hand. "Shame on you, LaShaun Rousselle Broussard. Using sex to get information."

"Certainly not," LaShaun protested. "You get plenty being your usual charming self."

"I am charming, ain't I?" Chase nuzzled her cleavage. "A trade. I'll sing like a bird if you promise to wear that red satin thingy tonight."

"Deal." LaShaun stood and shook his hand. She swayed her hips as if dancing to sexy music. "Talk, mister."

He grabbed for her and laughed when LaShaun stepped out of reach. "You Rousselle women are tough."

"And don't you forget it, Deputy Chief Detective Broussard." LaShaun sat across from him.

"Pain before pleasure, eh? Fine." Chase's expression turned serious. "There might be some hope for Savannah's defense. Zulime got into a heated argument with the vic. Pattinson asked her to do something at the program. Zulime snapped back at her. They went back and forth until Pattison shoved Zulime. The girl hit her shoulder hard going down. Then she went after the vic. Pattison refused medical treatment. Just accepted first aid at the program from a nurse who also volunteers. Later she felt sick, got admitted to the ER and got worse. She had internal bleeding, but didn't show signs for almost a day."

"Self defense is plausible. Especially since she put hands on Zee first." LaShaun frowned. "The first story was Zee beat her up so bad she had to go straight to hospital."

"The program director pushed that version to avoid liability. He didn't want Zulime's family to sue. Karlene Pattison's didn't have a squeaky clean past, after all. Their background check missed two convictions for identity theft fifteen years ago."

"They were willing to sacrifice a young girl's entire life to avoid a lawsuit. I don't think much of Brighter Futures," LaShaun said with a scowl. "Makes me wonder what else is going on over there."

"MJ made a call to the state agency that licenses social service agencies. They might do an investigation. Then again, they might not. Political connections." Chase shrugged when LaShaun's let fly an expletive. "I know."

"But we still have a mystery. Why did someone steal Zee's things from school?" LaShaun tapped a forefinger on the table top.

"I don't think it matters. Admit it, babe. The notebook isn't some mysterious clue. And praise be, no magic is involved. Nothing but a troubled teen whose temper got the better of her. This time with even more serious consequences."

"Someone went to a lot of trouble for a kid's notebook. More like her personal journal," LaShaun said. She wiped the table in wide circles, her mind far from the kitchen. Chase pecked her cheek and took the cotton kitchen cloth from LaShaun.

"Hey, you've been scrubbing the same spot for five minutes."

"What?" LaShaun blinked back from her thoughts to gaze at the wood surface. "Oh, right. I'm going to ask Zee about what was in it. The journal I mean."

"And the keychain. Maybe it's worth something. You said it might have been real silver. Maybe even white gold. Mrs. Vidal might not look it, but I hear she's pretty well off in the money department." Chase loaded the dishwasher, tapped the digital settings, and it hummed to life.

"Mrs. Richardson specifically said someone came to get Zee's belongings."

"Could have been a student from her high school. An older kid who took advantage. A building full of kids and teachers, a school can be hectic. No reason she'd question it."

"Yeah, I guess. But..." LaShaun screwed up her face as if it would help her solve the puzzle. "Just doesn't feel right."

"Savannah will mount a brilliant defense. Zulime could get a smaller sentence. In fact, I'm pretty sure given Zulime's age and the circumstances the judge will take it all into consideration." Chase draped the dishcloth over a holder to dry. Then he pulled LaShaun close. "And life will get back to normal. At least what passed for normal in this house."

LaShaun looked up at him. "Jonah thinks Tranicia Banks was murdered."

Chase let out a melodramatic groan. "Now see. You had to spoil our moment."

"He doesn't think she took an overdose, not based on what he knows about her. She might have learned information someone didn't want to come out. Or her cover was blown," LaShaun replied.

"You're as bad as Schaffer. Seeing conspiracies everywhere. He's another thorn in our asses. He had the nerve to show up at the station asking about both investigations," Chase said.

"Wait, Schaffer is asking about both victims? But why?" LaShaun pushed free of Chase's embrace.

"He offered to exchange information from his 'investigation' that he thinks is related. One good thing for your wizard pals at TEA. Sounds like he still doesn't know about them or Legion.

Schaffer tried to pretend otherwise, but I could tell he was lying," Chase replied.

"He could be putting his life on the line if he starts chasing down Legion. Those ruthless demon lovers don't hesitate to use violence."

"TEA isn't much better." Chase raised both palms when LaShaun's mouth flew open. "I've seen CeeCee and Jonah in action."

"To protect people. Not unlike cops." LaShaun poked his chest with an index finger.

"Hmm, except we're official. Okay, okay." Chase pushed her hand away. "TEA isn't Legion. Sheesh, can't believe you're defending them. They get on your nerves, too."

"Yeah, well, I've got friends who work to keep them on the right path. What exactly did Schaffer ask you about?" LaShaun frowned. The obnoxious ghost chaser was a complication they didn't need.

"The woman who used to work with him is missing. Or at least according to him. He thinks she came to Louisiana and met with foul play. And a shadowy organization linked to paranormal activity, possible demon worship, is involved. His exact words." Chase yawned. "Long day made longer listening to his nonsense. Of course, the jerk wanted to yap in my ear since I'm your husband. I managed to pass him off to our information officer."

"That won't keep him away for long," LaShaun said.

"Tell me about it. He raised such a fuss demanding to be taken seriously. Dave had him in his office for almost an hour. Schaffer left sort of satisfied. Both our recent murder victims have been identified. We have no Jane Does at the morgue. At least not found in Vermilion Parish."

"Find out if Schaffer's colleague has a missing person report filed with the police where she lives." LaShaun stared off as she spoke.

Chase placed both hands on his waist. "No report. I called Philadelphia PD. Hell, for all we know the woman might be avoiding Schaffer. I know I would."

"Yeah, she's an adult. If she wants to go missing and you have no reason to suspect foul play..." LaShaun looked at Chase. "But if Schaffer stumbled on Legion she might have, too. And if Tranicia Banks didn't take an overdose we could have a connection."

"A lot of 'ifs' don't add up to me committing an officer to—" Chase heaved a deep sigh when LaShaun continue to stare at him. "I'll have one of our uniforms check to see if her description fits any unidentified bodies statewide."

"Thanks, honey. I knew you'd come through." LaShaun beamed at him.

"Okay, now," Chase said with a grin. "Where's my red satin quid pro quo?"

"Why officer, accepting gifts in lieu of services is unethical, even illegal." LaShaun affected a shocked expression. She giggled smiled when Chase headed for their bedroom.

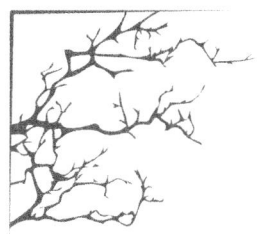

# Chapter 9

Saturday and Sunday were ordinary family weekends at the Broussard house. Chase only had to work a few hours on Saturday morning. The rest of the day he spent with the kids, which gave LaShaun time to do housework. Sunday, they attended nine o'clock morning mass at St. Mary Magdalen in Abbeville. Later they had lunch with Chase's parents. Elizabeth and Bruce Broussard hosted a large family gathering, as they had for years. Though with all their children grown, the weekly affair had become maybe once a month. Chase's three sisters, his brother, their spouses, and children usually attended. The crowd was smaller because two sisters, along with their families, had other plans. Mrs. Broussard commented on their absence, lamenting the lack of respect for tradition. LaShaun exchanged a glance with Chase. Her true complaint was not being in control. Still, they got through it with no quarreling. Ellie was on her best behavior. CJ was energized by having so many playmates. By the time they got home everyone was ready for a nap.

Except LaShaun. Chase dozed on the sofa, pretending to watch a college football game. CJ had insisted on staying with his dad. He was knocked out on one end of the long sofa, a soft throw covering him. Ellie opted for her own bed. She was fast asleep when LaShaun checked on her. Beau reclined on his doggie bed, his large head resting on both paws, eyes closed.

With the machines humming in their laundry room, LaShaun settled at the small kitchen desk with her laptop. She did a search on Schaffer's colleague. A picture of a serious-looking but pretty redhead appeared on the search. Darrah Radcliff had worked in New York and Philadelphia as a reporter for eight years before getting the gig with Schaffer. She worked as a 'correspondent' at Ghost Team USA for two and half years before striking out on her own. She and Schaffer had a beef for a time as competitors. Then it appeared they made up. Most of the search yielded dubious headlines about aliens and improbable theories about the supernatural. Nothing hinted that Radcliff had a reason to be in danger. LaShaun was about to stop when an email notification pinged. Then her cell phone vibrated. She'd put it on silent. With a peek at Chase and CJ, LaShaun answered. CeeCee's face appeared in her Whatsapp.

"Happy Sunday, CeeCee," LaShaun said quietly. She went into the laundry room.

"Hey, girl. Sorry to bother on the Lord's day of rest. Can you talk?"

"Yeah. What's up?" LaShaun sat on the bench along one wall.

"Darrah Radcliff is officially missing. At least reported as such by her parents and sister. She hasn't called them in almost a month, so they're worried. I know Schaffer went to the Vermilion Sheriff's office the other day. Seems he's finally stirred the pot enough to get the right attention." CeeCee's scowl showed she wasn't happy.

"Okay, and... you're about to drop a mini-bombshell." LaShaun's arms tingled.

"Your sixth sense is on target. Radcliff got to an unhappy TEA member. They became lovers. The woman, let's call her Gail for now, let pillow talk slip about us. They broke up but the damage was done. Radcliff, sniffing out a big story that would make her career, started following breadcrumbs."

"Which led her to New Orleans and Tranicia Banks."

"Damn, you're good," CeeCee replied.

"Don't be too impressed. I can't see anything more." LaShaun squinted hard as if it might help her second sight. Nothing.

"Tranicia wrapped up a case in New Orleans. With all of the gentrification since Hurricane Katrina, NOLA isn't the supernatural hotspot it used to be. Anyway, she got a lead to Vermilion Parish and was sent undercover."

"Chase is checking if any unidentified corpses match her description statewide," LaShaun said.

"We did already. Negative. We've got to make sure Schaffer doesn't find out about Darrah Radcliff's former girlfriend and her contact with Tranicia Banks."

"What 'we'?" LaShaun blinked at her friend.

"Sorry, girl, but we gotta coordinate with Chase on this one. We think Darrah Radcliff bumbled her way into danger. Not only do we need to keep Schaffer dumb about TEA, we might need to save his otherwise useless life," CeeCee said, her expression grave.

"Oh, he's going to blow a—" LaShaun broke off to find Chase standing in the doorway, arms crossed.

"Hi ya, CeeCee. Tell me what's going on. Then I can explain why we're not coordinating anything. No way in hell," Chase said in a firm tone.

MONDAY MORNING WAS typical. Neither kid wanted to abandon their snug beds. CJ was extra grumpy. Having Daddy home made him insist Chase take him along to work. Ellie whispered worried questions to LaShaun about Zulime. Between the two of them, Chase and LaShaun tag-team parented. They took turns laying down the law. Finish breakfast; dress in the clothes Mama laid out; on the bus for Ellie. No arguments. CJ did a miniature imitation of Chase when angry. He sat at the kiddie desk with his little chubby arms crossed, his cute face a mask of childish angst at not getting his way.

"These kids giving me more gray hairs than the job," Chase muttered. He eyed his son.

LaShaun rubbed both arms, still chilled from waiting at the bus stop with Ellie. "He'll settle down. At least you get to bounce and deal with criminals. I'll have toddler attitude on my hands until mid-morning snack time at least."

"Sorry to leave you, babe." Chase's mouth twitched as he fought not to grin.

"Yeah, I can see how guilty you feel. Go on. Lock up some bad guys." LaShaun gave his shoulder a light tap. She accepted a kiss on the cheek. "Oh, and let me know what you find out about on the Jane Doe body search."

"You're not giving me grief about refusing to cooperate with TEA. I'm suspicious."

"You have a job to do and TEA isn't an official agency. Okay, she's ticked off but CeeCee will get over it." LaShaun shrugged.

"You mean she and Jonah will find a way around me." Chase's eyes narrowed as he stared at LaShaun. Silence stretched between them for a few seconds.

"They won't break any laws," LaShaun replied with care.

"Guess that's the best I can hope for with those two," Chase retorted with a snort.

He strode over to CJ and coaxed him into relaxing his angry face. A father and son exchange went on as Chase changed from his house slippers to boots. CJ watched as Chase gathered his usual work accessories: department-issued mobile phone, Wi-Fi enabled tablet, and, last, his gun. He kept the Sig Sauer P226 secured. The case was in a locked cabinet above the washer and dryer. LaShaun smiled and left them to negotiations. She heard the rumble of Chase's deep voice answering questions from a lighter one. A truce had been declared between the Broussard men. LaShaun packed a lunch of mac and cheese, baked chicken, and green beans for Chase; leftovers from his mother's Sunday cooking. Chase strode into the kitchen again, CJ and Beau on his heels. She admired the figure he cut. He wore a navy long-sleeved button-down shirt tucked into dark tan chino slacks.

"What's on your agenda for today?" Chase put on his lined jacket, snapped it closed and look at LaShaun.

"Nothing special." LaShaun shrugged both shoulders when he gave her a look. "Aunt Shirleen invited CJ over to play with her grandkids. She's going to fix them a special lunch. Her daughter-in-law is going back to work. So, Aunt Shirleen is keeping little Ayanna and the baby. Brittany took a year off when Brandon was born."

"Thanks for the update on Rousselle family news." Chase raised both dark eyebrows in a skeptical expression. "Just a wild coincidence freeing you up to snoop."

"If you mean assist Savannah in getting justice for a frightened teenage girl, then yes. I'm going to visit Zulime and find out more about her journal." LaShaun lifted her nose in the air.

"I suppose your fixation on a kid's diary is a blessing in disguise. You won't be sticking your pretty nose in police business." Chase grinned when LaShaun hissed at him like an angry feline.

"You'll owe me an apology when I find real evidence," LaShaun shot back.

"I have a feeling the only thing you'll find in her diary are details about her latest crush, Tik-Tok dance steps, and make-up." Chase laughed when LaShaun stuck her tongue out at him.

Two hours later, LaShaun dropped CJ at her aunt's house. She texted Savannah to make sure the center knew she was on the way over. Zulime was housed in a secure residential facility. LaShaun made the drive to Lafayette in forty minutes. She parked in the lot but didn't get out immediately. Instead, she examined the two-story building. A discreet sign with the logo "H&H, Inc." gave nothing away. The official name of the for-profit that ran the program was Helping & Healing, Inc. The neighborhood surrounding it was mixed use. A few duplex homes, two sets of apartment developments, and several businesses stretched on either side. Neat shrubs lined the front of front brick walls. Windows gave a view of several offices.

"Not exactly home sweet home but better than sticking her in jail with grown women. I guess," LaShaun mumbled. She left her SUV. As she approached the entrance, a young woman opened one side of the wood double doors.

"Mrs. Broussard. I'm Shandra Sparks. Welcome."

The plump young Black woman stuck out a hand. Her smooth brown skin gave little away about her age. LaShaun guessed she was younger than her, maybe late twenties. Her natural hair was done is Bantu knots. She wore a professional smile that covered her wariness. LaShaun could sense Ms. Sparks, lead social worker, would be keeping an eagle eye on her.

"Good afternoon. Helping & Healing, Inc. runs a very efficient operation," LaShaun said and smiled.

The youth center director had required LaShaun send a copy of her photo ID. They had confirmed with Mrs. Vidal that she'd signed the consent for LaShaun to visit.

"We take our responsibility for residents seriously, ma'am. Our visitation section is down this hall." Ms. Sparks led the way. The walls of the hallway had a mural on both sides.

"This is nice." LaShaun nodded to the artwork. Female figures painted in colorful silhouettes were depicted.

"The artist is a former resident. Her way of giving back and expressing gratitude. I know it sounds cliché, but she really did turn her life around. I'm glad we played a part. Though she did the hard work." Ms. Spark opened a door and waved LaShaun in ahead of her.

"Sounds great." LaShaun looked around the room. Six tables with chairs were arranged around it. Space between them allowed for some privacy during multiple visits. More artwork was repeated on the walls of the spacious area.

"Also, we don't have pictures on the walls. Fewer missiles to be torn off and used as weapons." Ms. Sparks maintained her composed expression as she casually reminded LaShaun of potential risks. "We do house young women accused of serious offenses."

LaShaun ceased her examination of a tranquil garden scene. She faced Ms. Sparks. "And Zee's charge is about as serious as they come."

"Zulime hasn't shown any signs of aggression since admission. She's cooperative with the routine for the most part. Settled in with little difficulty."

"No sixteen-year-old girl should have to easily settle into a prison," LaShaun replied in a mild tone.

Ms. Sparks raised one eyebrow. "You do know her victim died, Mrs. Broussard. The chances of her being released were zero."

"Sorry, I wasn't condemning the work you do. I just... wish we didn't need secure juvenile homes," LaShaun said, gesturing to the room.

"Even with the pretty pictures, yes. There's no getting around it, Mrs. Broussard. We're a locked facility. Cameras, alarms on the doors, and our employees are trained corrections officers. The young women who come are either angry or depressed. Mostly angry."

"I can imagine." LaShaun nodded.

"Ms. Lockhart, one of our staff, will be close by." Ms. Sparks pointed to a framed glass window with an office beyond. Another door led to it. The tall woman looked to be a fit forty-something who could handle herself. "We also have cameras recording. In case of an incident. We don't record conversations."

LaShaun looked up. Set into the ceiling, a round glass lens was housed in a shell that matched the creamy white wall paint. "Good."

"Though you don't have attorney-client privilege."

"Right." LaShaun studied the social worker with interest. Then she glanced at Ms. Lockhart.

"Our staff have been called on to give testimony before," Ms. Sparks added.

"Understood. Thanks, Ms. Sparks."

The social worker gave a slight nod and left. Minutes later a thin woman who didn't look much older than Zulime came through the door. Zulime followed her. A third woman stood in the hallway and watched. Both wore H & H, Youth, Inc. logos on their shirts. They gave LaShaun muted greetings. LaShaun wondered at the heavy staffing. Ms. Sparks said Zulime hadn't been violent.

"You okay?" The thin young woman asked as she eyed Zulime.

"Sure." Zee nodded at her. Only then did the door close, leaving them alone. Except for Mrs. Lockhart a few yards away. Then she turned to examine LaShaun.

LaShaun saw the typical sullen expression of a distrustful teenage girl. A shock of bluish-purple locks framed her heart-shaped face. The color brought out a hint of green in her brown eyes. Her tawny skin had the youthful smoothness expected, but her hard expression made Zulime look older. She wore a plaid button-front tunic over a cream-colored t-shirt and blue jeans. Black and wide slides and white socks covered her feet.

"You're helping my lawyer." Zee's gaze swept LaShaun from head to toe one last time. Then she sat in the chair on the other side of the square table.

"I'm an—"

"Investigator. Yeah, Grandmama told me." Zulime's gaze shifted to the glass window behind LaShaun. She gave a cocky grin and a wave to Mrs. Lockhart.

LaShaun followed her gaze. The woman maintained a blank expression without responding. Instead, she went back to entering notes on a keypad. "Your grandmother called you. That's good."

"Humph." Zulime looked down. Her forefinger drew invisible circles on the plastic surface of the tabletop. "You're about to earn easy money."

"Oh?"

"Everybody knows I did it." Zee blew out a long breath. "I don't want to miss rec therapy. We're making treat baskets for old people in a nursing home."

"Rec therapy?" LaShaun resisted looking over her shoulder again at the taciturn Mrs. Lockhart. She could sense the woman monitoring them discreetly.

"Recreation therapy. To keep us calm so we won't tear up the place. Girls always beefin' over petty shit. Stuff, I meant," Zee added quickly.

"I see. I won't keep you long. Besides, I don't think Ms. Sparks will let me anyway," LaShaun added with a slight smile.

"Don't much get past her. Or any of 'em." Zee's tone implied she'd tried.

"Listen, your grandmother—"

"Let's get this over with, okay? I did it; beat Karlene's ass because she pushed me one too many times. I lost my temper. I'm a poor kid from a deprived background. Mother don't care. Daddy in prison. Bring out the sad songs. That's my defense. I get it." Zulime lost the cynical scowl that twisted her pretty face. She assumed a mask of hurt innocence. "I can say she touched my privates if that will help. Yeah, it might."

"Don't lie. Especially not about sexual abuse. Karlene Pattison might have made you angry, but she does have family. Think how such an allegation will affect them," LaShaun said.

"Like I care. Okay, you and the lawyer got a better idea? I'm a Black kid accused of killing a nice white lady. They're gonna charge me as an adult." Zulime leaned forward enough to make a point but not to seem threatening. She glanced at Mrs. Lockhart and kept her voice low. "If you think the truth is going set me free, you're living in fantasy land."

"Karlene Pattison had a criminal history. Her charges were expunged, that means—"

"I know what it means," Zee broke in. "The background check missed it. Yeah, that's promising. Oh, and she shoved me. I'll throw in she grabbed my boob to seal the deal."

"Zee, lying will—"

"Yeah, yeah, yeah. Except you get to walk out of this dump," Zee spat. She grunted and looked away. "You can afford to be all righteous."

"Look, just like we're investigating, so will the DA's office. They'll sniff out anything false and use it against you," LaShaun with force.

Zee's tough exterior wavered for a few seconds before the mask dropped in place again. "Whatever. Is that all? You drove over here to tell me stuff I already know."

"No. You didn't know about Karlene's arrest record," LaShaun shot back.

"Okay. You've delivered the good news. Collect your coins and have a great day, ma'am." Zee pushed her chair back.

"I'm Ellie's mother, Zee. She got detention for helping you." LaShaun kept her tone low.

The door leading to the observation office opened. "Okay, Zulime. Time to head on back to—"

"Ms. Sparks said I could visit for up to one hour. I have thirty minutes left," LaShaun said. She pointed to a clock high on one wall. "Check with her if you like."

Mrs. Lockhart looked at Zulime. Then she turned to LaShaun. "Ms. Glapion can leave a visit if she wants to, ma'am."

Zee looked from the sturdy staff woman to LaShaun. She pulled the chair closer to the table again. "We ain't through talking about my case."

Mrs. Lockhart went to the office gain. When the door shut behind her, the thin staff person who had accompanied Zulime entered. Their exchange was muffled as both glanced at LaShaun.

"You come to give me hell for getting her in trouble, huh? Look, I wasn't trying to... I just wanted my things. That's all." Zee switched to defensive mode as she glared at LaShaun.

"By asking her to leave the elementary school, breaking at least three rules." LaShaun squinted at Zulime.

"Wait, what? My stuff is in a locker at her school. Or it was. Mrs. Richardson probably had the janitor toss it in a dumpster." Zee frowned. Her distress seemed genuine. "Anyway, I didn't think she'd go off campus and walk all that way... Is she okay? None of those creeps at V High bothered her, did they?"

"She's fine. Don't worry. In fact, she carried out her mission almost to perfection. Besides getting caught," LaShaun said. "And going to the wrong locker apparently."

"I didn't have time to explain much to her before they snatched me up. Look, tell Ellie I'm sorry. So, she got my things. But how?"

"She figured it out."

"I'm glad she's okay." Zee's right leg bounced in a jittery movement.

"Your grandmother didn't tell you I'm Ellie's mother when she called?"

Zee snorted. "My granny is short on words. Got no time for folks, including me."

"That must be hard with your parents gone and—"

"Don't give me the poor, pitiful orphan look. I take care of me. Period."

LaShaun studied her for a few beats. "Look, if there's anything you haven't told Mrs. Honoré about what happened between you and Ms. Pattison..."

"Like you said, she wasn't who they thought she was." Zulime crossed her arms. She pushed into the chairback; arms folded.

"I understand if you're reluctant to tell me everything. But at least talk to Ms Honoré. She's in the best position to help you. Being charged with murder as an adult is serious."

"Gee, thanks for clearing that up for me. I wasn't sure if years in a prison with killers and thieves was such a big deal," Zee clipped. She rolled her eyes and stared up at the ceiling.

"Keeping information from your lawyer just ties her hands. She's trying to keep you out of prison. Reason enough to tell her everything," LaShaun insisted.

"Right. Like anyone actually listens. Some jerks made my life miserable. Nobody did anything. The teachers looked the other way. The school counselor lectured me on controlling my temper. I get a court date and community service. The other kids got to laugh at me even more. The people at Brighter Futures are phony. Yeah, Brighter Futures. What a joke." Zulime clenched both fists on the tabletop.

"If there are problems with the mentor program, your attorney can bring it out. We want to help you." LaShaun put one hand over both her fists.

"I got a body on me now. Too late." Zee's eyes went glassy with tears. "My life is over."

"Mrs. Honoré is a damn good attorney. I'm a good investigator."

"I hit Karlene and she's dead. Facts." Zee shook her head. She wiped her eyes with one sleeve.

"You're only sixteen. You were in a vulnerable position with an authority figure who had a shady background. She pushed you first. *And...*" LaShaun held up a forefinger to punctuate her point. "Karlene Pattison died hours later. Who's to say she didn't get into another fight or fall later?"

Zee's mouth dropped open as she stared at LaShaun. "Y'all been schemin'!"

"All legitimate arguments. Not schemes," LaShaun countered. She didn't mention there was no guarantee a judge would buy any of it. Still, she needed to give Zee hope.

"Worth a shot." Zee's tears dried up. Her expression turned crafty.

"One last question. What's in your journal? Someone went to the school and picked up your belongings. Your grandmother didn't send him," LaShaun said, careful to speak low but not arouse Mrs. Lockhart's suspicions.

"Him?" Zulime blinked rapidly and looked away.

"Yes. It was a man. Someone you're friend with maybe?" LaShaun's eyes narrowed as she studied Zulime.

"You know what he looks like?" Zee gazed back at LaShaun.

"I can get video from the school. Or maybe your lawyer can." LaShaun leaned forward. "Tell me the truth. Did you send—"

"Yeah, yeah. I forgot. My cousin D'Andre went to get my stuff," Zee said quickly.

"Mrs. Vidal was surprised when we told her about anybody claiming to be a relative. Zulime—"

"Look, I didn't want Mrs. Richardson snooping through my private things. Plus, some kids like to steal," Zee replied. She chewed on the nail of one thumb.

"So, your grandmother will know about D'Andre if I ask her about him." LaShaun rubbed at the tickle of electricity along one forearm.

"No, don't," Zee blurted. "Don't tell her, please. She'll get mad and quit talking to me. Maybe even won't pay for my lawyer. Gran is mean like that. You've met her."

"I won't keep secrets from your legal guardian." LaShaun tried to *see* what was going on with Zee but couldn't.

"What he's got isn't worth much to anybody but me, okay? No big deal."

"Do you know who I am?" LaShaun continue to stare at her.

"This some kind of pop quiz? You told me a few minutes ago." Zee's right leg bounced as she spoke. She chewed on an already ragged thumbnail.

"You'll get an infection or something." LaShaun reached across and tugged Zee's hand from her mouth.

Zee snatched back from LaShaun. Then she turned away to stare at a wall. "You're Ellie's mama, not *mine*. Sheesh."

LaShaun pushed against the urge to go full maternal authority figure. "You haven't read or heard about me? Gossip about me being a voodoo woman or having psychic powers?"

Zee lost the distracted frown. She faced LaShaun again with a look of astonishment. "You?"

"I've been in the news a few times," LaShaun replied in a mild tone.

"In the news for what?" Zulime's brown eyes went from surprised to teenage skeptical.

"A few investigations I've done—"

"I watched Ghost Team USA a few times. So fake, but fun. You got a reality show or something?"

"No."

"Whatever. I don't pay attention to the news. Old people doing this or that. Blah, blah, blah."

LaShaun laughed at her adolescent lack of interest in the adult world. She wasn't surprised Zee didn't know about her. LaShaun's reputation for magic spread before Zee was born. Typical of other teens, Zee was consumed with the world of her peer group. Their music, celebrity idols, fashion, and friends.

"Okay. What did D'Andre pick up for you?" LaShaun took out her phone to take notes.

"Notebooks, ink pens. Maybe my hair brush. Listen, forget that stuff. It's nothing." Zee's leg bounced again.

"A diary or journal with private thoughts? Don't lie to me, Zee," LaShaun said when she started to protest.

"Or what? You'll use your superpowers to read my mind or force the truth out of me. Yeah, right." Zee snorted. "You're as bad as my grandmama. Talkin' about a lot of spooky crap everyone knows is fake. Telling me stories to scare me into behaving."

"Like what?"

"Don't go wandering into the bayou at night. The fifolet will get you. Oh, and the legend of Blood Bayou," Zee dropped her voice low to imitate a spooky voice.

"I used to feel the same way when my grandmother told me stories. But, there's always truth behind them," LaShaun said in a quiet, somber voice.

Something in her tone brought Zee up short. Her grin vanished. She fidgeted for a few moments and cleared her throat. "I appreciate you and my lawyer trying to help. I really do. I'm gonna keep my head down, follow the rules, and not act up in court."

"Why don't you want me to know about your journal?"

"Because it's my personal business and none of yours! Now stop asking me about it," Zee snapped, her voice rising. "My grandmother probably sent you here to find out what I've been doing."

"Don't be silly, Zee. She—"

Zee slapped both palms on the table. She shoved the chair back and stood. The legs scraped loudly across the floor. "Gran doesn't care about me. Never has. She always says I got dumped on her. Well, she can go jump in the swamp and take you with her."

Mrs. Lockhart was through the door fast. She strode to stand next to Zee. "Visit over now. No more questions."

"I'm sorry if anything I said upset you, Zee. I'll let your grandmother know you're okay."

"The social worker will see you in her office before you go," Mrs. Lockhart replied evenly.

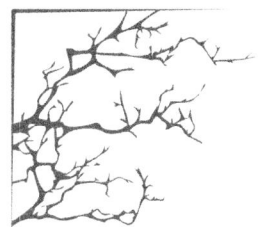

# Chapter 10

LaShaun had the feeling she was going to another principal's office to be scolded. After a few more turns in the maze-like interior of the building, they arrived at a door. A brass plate had Shandra Sparks' name on it. Mrs. Lockhart knocked once.

"Ms. Rousselle here to see you."

The door opened and Ms. Sparks gestured for LaShaun to enter. She exchanged a glance with Mrs. Lockhart but spoke to LaShaun. "How did it go?"

"Fine. Until the end," LaShaun said.

She saw Mrs. Lockhart's mouth twitch a silent message to the social worker. The older woman said nothing but closed the door; leaving LaShaun and Shandra Sparks alone in the office.

"Zulime is understandably on shaky emotional ground. I've already scheduled a therapy session with her. We also teach our girls meditation, mindfulness, and yoga. She'll be ready for any future court appearances." Ms. Sparks gestured that LaShaun could have a seat.

"I'll let Mrs. Honoré know. Thanks. Has Zee had any other visitors?"

"Only her grandmother is approved. I've encouraged her to come but so far, she hasn't shown. Only a couple of phone calls. Anything else we can do for you?"

LaShaun stood. "No, I won't take up any more of your time."

After polite small talk, the social worker led LaShaun to the lobby. She watched through the glass door as LaShaun went to her SUV. Once on the road, LaShaun called Savannah as she drove using her hands-free Bluetooth earbud. Rai answered and said Savanna would be in court all afternoon. None of Savannah's meetings or hearings were related to Zee's case. At least as far as Rai could tell from the schedule.

"Okay. Have her call me soon as she can."

LaShaun then called to check in with her Aunt Shirleen. Her aunt assured her everything was fine. The children had eaten and were taking a much-needed nap after a morning of rowdy play. LaShaun's stomach growled, a noisy signal she needed food herself. She tapped in Jonah's mobile number.

"Meet me at the Po-boy Shack on Magnolia Street. I'll text you the address. It's a new place downtown," LaShaun said in answer to his voicemail prompt. "No excuses. I'll be there in about thirty minutes."

LaShaun took a seat in a booth away from the windows. Not that it helped. James Schaffer walked in and made a beeline for her. She swore under her breath at the sight of him. A few other lunch patrons, locals, stared at him as he brushed past their tables. Their muted discussions showed they recognized him.

"Hello, Ms. Rousselle. Sorry, it's been Mrs. Broussard for several years." James Schaffer's brown hair was thinner. The fifty-something ghost chaser wore an ingratiating smile. He pointed to one of the empty seats. "You don't mind?"

"I'm expecting someone. Soon." LaShaun wrinkled her nose at him.

"This won't take long," Schaffer replied, his expression unruffled by her rebuff.

"Good, then you don't need to sit down. My answers will be 'No comment,' 'I don't know,' and 'You tell me.' I've saved you time. You're welcome." LaShaun gave a slight head shake, a signal to the approaching waitress she wasn't ready to order.

Schaffer sat across from LaShaun anyway. "Okay, so I'll do the talking. A shadowy organization is hiding behind layers of secrecy, pulling the strings. A young woman I know found out too much and now she's missing. You're either a part of said organization or you have intimate knowledge of its workings. If you're into truth and justice, then you'll help me."

"You didn't get along with Darrah Radcliff. In fact, you stabbed her in the back. She was a threat because her star was rising. You don't give a flip about where she is. Unless of course she's onto a story that will make you look small time."

LaShaun saw Jonah enter the café out the corner of one eye. Still, she kept her gaze on Schaffer's face. Jonah went to the long counter and sat on a red-covered bar stool. He picked up a paper menu. She couldn't hear his playful flirtation with the pretty waitress.

"Well, you've been doing your homework. So, they told you I'm here." Schaffer leaned forward. "I'm on the right track if they're worried."

"In your world a wild imagination comes in handy. Crazy camera angles, fog machines, and a spooky soundtrack. Presto, ghosts. Now you're building an entire *shadowy organization* to chase." LaShaun made air quotes with both hands as she chuckled. "Career not going so great, huh?"

Schaffer's smug expression slipped into a clenched jaw. "Poor little Ellie is worried about her friend. How's your investigation into the accused teenaged murderer going? I hear not so well."

"Keep my daughter's name out of your mouth," LaShaun clipped.

"Struck a nerve. Got me wondering how supernatural doings in Beau Chene are connected to my case," Schaffer replied, his smug expression back in place.

LaShaun fought against the energy pushing inside, begging to zap him. An action that would only fuel his determination to keep digging. "You're right."

"There's a connection?" Schaffer seemed ready to salivate at the prospect.

"With Zulime Glapion's family history, her lawyer has a good chance to get compassionate justice for her. But the tragedy has nothing to do with Ms. Radcliff," LaShaun said mildly.

"Right." Schaffer eyed LaShaun for a few seconds. "Darrah was following a woman but I don't know her name or have a description. Her family says she rented a car at the New Orleans airport. Then the trail ends."

"No clue. Now if you'll excuse me, I need to order lunch." LaShaun turned to the waitress when she approached. "I'll have cup of shrimp and corn soup. Can I get garlic bread on the side?"

"Of course. We baked it fresh this morning," the waitress said. She looked at Schaffer. "And you sir?"

Schaffer raised a palm when LaShaun started to answer. "I'm not staying, but thanks."

"I'll get your order on." The waitress scurried off as a bell attached to the door tinkled when another customer entered. "Anywhere is good, ma'am."

CeeCee glanced at Jonah's back, looked at LaShaun, and then waved to the waitress. She went to a table near the street-facing window. "Sure thing."

LaShaun affected her most casual expression as she looked at Schaffer when he stood. "Happy hunting."

"I know there's more going on around here. There always is in Beau Chene and Vermilion Parish."

"So true. Lots of things to do. I recommend Boudreaux's Swamp Tours. He has loads of stories to tell, too. Right up your alley."

"You know exactly what I mean—"

"Most of it is superstitious tall tales. Great for tourists, though. And reality show spirit-chasers." LaShaun sipped hibiscus tea and put the glass back down.

Schaffer's mobile phone beeped at the same time his camera guy waved at him. His jaw tightened again in an annoyed expression. "I'll be seeing you around."

"Or not." LaShaun raised both eyebrows at him. She watched him stride away while tapping the screen of his phone.

Jonah and CeeCee also watched him leave. Both rose at the same time to join LaShaun. They executed twin greetings as if they'd only just noticed she was in the café. The waitress assured them it was no problem for them to move to LaShaun's table. They exchanged friendly chatter with the young woman as they ordered food. When she left LaShaun rolled her eyes at them.

"You can stop the whole 'Fancy meeting you here!' act. Nobody cares. And Schaffer is gone."

"But we're so good at it," Jonah joked.

"Yeah, well, keep an eye out for him. He's a pain who has a unique talent for tripping over the truth. He'll take an interest in you if he sees us together." LaShaun looked out of the window, half expecting Schaffer to return.

CeeCee waved a hand, dismissing her concern. "He's not coming back. On his way following another juicy lead."

"Really?" LaShaun looked at her friend with interest.

"Yeah." CeeCee leaned back and crossed her legs.

"A trail of breadcrumbs laid down by TEA." LaShaun saw the answer in CeeCee's smug grin.

"I don't like to brag, but... all me." CeeCee winked at LaShaun.

"Bull. You love to brag," Jonah said. "But I can't lie—it was brilliant."

"Anything you can tell me?" LaShaun looked from Jonah to CeeCee.

"Not a problem. He's going after a story about a voodoo cult on Bayou Bienvenue. That will take him back to the New Orleans area. The bayou runs along the border between Orleans and St. Bernard Parishes," Jonah explained.

"He'll be following those clues for more than a minute. Damn, I'm good." CeeCee lifted her nose in the air.

They broke off the discussion when the waitress returned with a tray carrying their orders. Jonah had a footlong fried crawfish tail po-boy cut in two sections. His plate also had a mound of French fries and coleslaw. CeeCee had ordered the soup and a small side salad.

"Lord, Jonah. I'd need a three-hour nap if I ate so much food in the middle of the day," LaShaun said.

"Hey, I can't come to Cajun Country and not partake in the local delicacies." Jonah picked up one half of his sandwich. He bit into it and hummed with delight at the taste.

"He's got the metabolism of a hummingbird, as they say," CeeCee said with a sigh. "Guys have it so easy. Especially kids like him." She laughed when he scowled at her because he couldn't respond with a mouthful.

"So, you're leading Schaffer around by the nose. Sorta like you're trying to do with me," LaShaun said.

"I don't follow." CeeCee stirred her soup.

"Helping and Healing, or H&H, Inc. I know it's run by TEA," LaShaun said, careful to lower her voice.

Jonah's throat worked as he swallowed his food. He picked up his glass of cola and gulped. "Um..."

"Hold on." CeeCee sniffed the air. She jerked a nod at Jonah and he left the table.

LaShaun watched her friends sweep the area. She went on eating her lunch, maintaining her casual front. Jonah and CeeCee checked for any signs of extrasensory entities, listening devices, and discreet observers. A few other diners left. Jonah returned as if he'd been to the restroom. He gave a thumbs up. Then he winked at the waitress, which triggered a pleased blush from the young woman.

CeeCee turned to LaShaun and released a slow exhale. "Okay, we're clear to talk. Coincidence."

"Oh, hell no," LaShaun blurted out louder than she'd meant to. No one noticed since they almost had the café to themselves. The rattle and tinkle of dishes being cleared away screened their conversation.

"H&H happens to have been founded by someone with extra senses, yes. And Zulime has dormant psychic abilities. When the regional director heard about Zulime's charges, they offered their services. An alternative to the girl sitting in a jail cell," CeeCee said.

Jonah sat down. "So, partially a coincidence. You know kids who are seen as 'weird' or different get picked on. Who's weirder than a kid with extrasensory abilities?"

"Bullied kids sometimes can hurt themselves or others when pushed to the emotional brink. Having services that help all kinds of people in crisis makes sense. We're inclusive," CeeCee added.

"Yeah, the guy really is committed to helping people. Especially marginalized groups." Jonah stuffed a seasoned French fry in his mouth. He savored the taste with more humming.

CeeCee nodded in agreement with him. "So, in conclusion, Zulime is in good hands. Now, about Neesha's murder investigation. Has Chase—"

"Uh-uh, nope," LaShaun cut her off. "Back to Zulime. What psychic abilities does she have?"

"Umm, we're not sure," CeeCee said. She glanced at Jonah, but he was focused on enjoying his food again.

"Let me guess. Her grandmother, famous for being a social hermit, won't let TEA get near her so now is your chance." LaShaun studied CeeCee for a reaction.

"She's suspicious of us. A bad experience back in the sixties. Anyway, as a result she wants nothing to do with TEA. She's believes keeping Zulime in the dark about paranormal skills will be better for her."

"But you've kept Zulime under surveillance. I mean, the girl had to go to school, attend mass. All opportunities for observation," LaShaun said.

In an instant CeeCee's answer, with comments added by Jonah, faded into a faint buzz. Along with all other noise. LaShaun stared at the west wall of the café. An expansive mural had been painted to give the place atmosphere. The serene bayou scene with bald cypress trees draped in Spanish moss triggered LaShaun's third eye. The two snowy egrets depicted took flight, their white wings beating the air slowly. Figures moved on the banks of sluggish water. Blood Bayou spread out before LaShaun because now she also stood on the banks. Native peoples camped; the women skinned animals by fires. French fur trappers dressed in eighteenth-century garb tramped along through mud. LaShaun felt dizzy. She pushed away the confusing images and repeated the Glapion family name. An image of Eunice Glapion Vidal formed. Something shattered and LaShaun blinked back to the café. She picked up her glass of tea with a shaky hand.

"Sorry folks." The middle-aged man with gray hair bussing tables picked up a tray he'd dropped.

"Damn it, LaShaun." CeeCee blew out air.

"I told you she would catch the vibe. Might as well spill it." Jonah gave a blasé shrug as he dipped a fried crawfish in Creole cocktail sauce.

"The land the Glapion family owns on Blood River and Blood Bayou—is it part of the monazite deposits?" LaShaun knew the property factored in, but didn't want to let on her vision had been limited.

"Yes, but it's not the biggest one. That's Devil's Swamp. This country has a violent history. Blood River got it because Spanish explorers massacred the people in a Chitimacha settlement around 1557. It's said the water turned red and trees wept with sorrow. The Great Spirit decreed that the land should stay with The People forever. Today, the Chitimacha are the only

Louisiana tribe that still occupies a portion of their homeland," CeeCee said.

"Fascinating. Get back to Zee."

"Not Zee, her fourth-great grandmother. The Glapion ancestors got caught in the crossfire of a fight. TEA and emerging Legion founding members knew the land was important. Strong psychics were here for a reason. Both sides tried to get Esperanza Glapion to join them. She played both sides against the middle. It didn't end well for her." CeeCee hesitated before she continued. "Anyway, seems like the family went off the rails starting back then."

"Generational curse created by TEA," LaShaun muttered. "I still don't see what any of this has to do with Zee."

"Like it said, it just happens to cross into our investigation." CeeCee glanced around despite declaring their discussion safe. She dropped her voice. "You can't tell Chase what I'm about to tell *you*."

Jonah barked a laugh. He patted his mouth with a napkin. "You just guaranteed LaShaun is going to tell him."

"For sure, if what your about to say affects an active murder case. Plus, Chase and I don't keep secrets. We can't afford to, CeeCee. We're up against the world too much as it is." LaShaun thought of the Broussard family and the cool treatment of her mixed marriage. She and Chase had only just settled the latest strain on their union.

CeeCee exchanged a look with Jonah. "Humph. To hell with it. I'll ask for forgiveness from the powers that be later."

"Again," Jonah added with an amused, crooked grin.

"Easy for *you*. Dripping with privilege even within our group of outsiders. Notice most of the top positions are occupied by men. Pale men," CeeCee clipped. "My career could get sidelined fast."

"I'd make sure it didn't happen," Jonah said and placed a hand on her thigh.

CeeCee pushed his hand away. "Gee, thanks so much. Never mind I'm the more senior operative. See what I mean? Jonah isn't a regional coordinator only because he keeps turning down offers."

"CeeCee, I understand your struggles. Really, I do. But let's debate what's wrong inside TEA later," LaShaun said in a firm tone.

"You're right. I get worked up and..." CeeCee drank from her glass of cream soda. "Karlene Pattison was either in Legion or a 'normal' agent."

"Hmm, most likely normal," Jonah put in. "Nothing I've turned up says she has any paranormal talents. She was assigned to get close to Zulime, long story short. Mrs. Vidal is crafty and suspicious. Getting next to the girl seemed the next best strategy."

"A way in to figure out how to get their land." LaShaun looked at CeeCee. "But the you said the monazite deposits there are minimal."

"Yeah. There must be another reason but so far, we haven't figured it out. Manny—"

"Manny Young, recently released serial killer?" LaShaun blurted out.

"Hey, keep it down," Jonah mumbled.

He jerked a thumb at the startled waitress gawking at them. The young woman pushed a wet cloth over the surface of a nearby table. Then she looked away and scurried off.

"I think she finally recognized the famous Beau Chene psychic detective," CeeCee quipped. "Don't worry. I'm pretty sure she didn't hear anything. I'll have the owner talk to her."

"Unbelievable. Chase is going to flip when he hears. He already thinks we're part of an evil empire," LaShaun whispered.

"People with paranormal abilities have to live and work somewhere," Jonah protested. "Your buddies the Dupart sisters are part owners, so at least it's local."

"Wait a minute..." LaShaun blinked in shock. The middle-aged twins were powerful psychics. They had aided LaShaun in previous paranormal-related investigations. As did her now surrogate grandmother Rose Mouton Fontenot.

"Silent partners," CeeCee put in.

Jonah snorted. "Yeah, right. As silent as Justine and Pauline can be."

"Really, it's nothing but a café. A friendly place we can hang out. Since we always end up back in Vermilion Parish. This place is packed with supernatural trouble." CeeCee whistled a sigh. "More hotspots than anywhere in these United States. Buen Dios."

"Back to Manny being on the case," LaShaun replied, her voice lowered to avoid unwanted attention.

"I shouldn't have to remind you he was cleared. Well, mostly. There are a few loose ends about him." Jonah winced as remembering the details of their newer colleague.

"Manny has extraordinary extra-normal abilities that can't be ignored. I was a hard sell on it myself. But he's proven himself in the field twice recently. Not here," CeeCee added quickly when LaShaun started to speak.

"Yeah. MEG readings don't lie," Jonah said.

He referred to magnetoencephalography, a method TEA researches use to capture magnetic fields generated by neural activity. Manny had agreed to being studied after his release from prison on parole.

"So, what is Manny's role?" LaShaun pushed aside her now-empty, over-sized cup of soup.

"He went out to Blood Bayou. Followed Blood River to it. A family that owns land bordering Mrs. Vidal's property leased mineral rights last year. A company called Holloway Holdings LLC is digging around out there. The intelligence team is sorting through shell companies to find out who's really behind the operation," CeeCee said.

"They've been out there only in the last six weeks or so. The pandemic and supply chain issues," Jonah added. He went back to eating his food. The mound of fries had disappeared.

"Legion is determined." LaShaun frowned as if the shadowy group stood before her.

"We're not sure it's them." CeeCee shrugged at the snort from LaShaun. "Hey, we don't want to start seeing Legion around every corner. Could be nothing more than a business trying to dredge for gravel. Or look for evidence of oil."

"Yeah. With the war in Ukraine, the US is like a lot of other countries. Looking for ways not to be dependent on foreign fuel sources," Jonah agreed.

"What has any of this got to do with a sixteen-year-old charged with murder." LaShaun looked from Jonah to CeeCee.

"Activity close to Blood Bayou ramps up. I'm not paranoid about Legion, but some would argue we should throw all our resources at disrupting them," CeeCee said.

"You mean all-out war. There's a faction calling for military type operations all over the globe. The rise of dictators worldwide is one of their arguments." Jonah's smooth young face looked older as he scowled.

"TEA stays out of national and international politics. Right?" LaShaun asked.

"Hmm, yes and no. Unless there are indications extra-normal actors are involved." CeeCee sighed when LaShaun's mouth dropped open. "Nothing like encouraging coups or provoking riots. More like... steering certain events. Non-violent, of course."

"The voices calling for more active 'interventions' are getting louder. The last World Council Conference got really heated." Jonah nodded. "I thought punches were gonna be thrown at one point. But we still had fun in Amsterdam. Didn't we?"

CeeCee squinted at him. "Back to LaShaun's questions."

"We're grown-ups." Jonah gave CeeCee a wink and a grin. He crossed his arms resting on the table and leaned toward LaShaun. "CeeCee still doesn't like me bringing up our thing."

"Stop calling it our 'thing'," CeeCee snapped. She blushed when LaShaun smirked. "Karlene Pattison had secrets. She concealed her background with help."

Jonah became serious again. "Very skilled help. Unwrapping the layers isn't easy. It's not like we can run her prints like, say, a local sheriff's department."

LaShaun stared at him for a few beats. When CeeCee also looked at her with one raised eyebrow, LaShaun shook her head. "No. Nope. Not going to happen. You can forget asking me to have Chase run her fingerprints on the national database.

She's the victim. Their case isn't about chasing leads on Karlene Pattison."

"Ask Zulime's lawyer to request more background information on Pattison. She could use it to effectively represent her client," Jonah argued. He looked to CeeCee for support.

"True," CeeCee replied as if on cue and looked at LaShaun again.

"The sheriff's department has no obligation to investigate on behalf of a defendant's attorney." LaShaun drummed her fingers on the table. She repeated the verbatim quote her friend MJ Arceneaux had delivered before. "Not to mention Sheriff Godchaux would never approve the request. Same for DNA."

"Just a random thought," CeeCee said with a cheeky grin. "The shortcut would help. We have limited access to *official* resources."

"She means we don't have members planted within the FBI, DOJ, and other places," Jonah put in. "Chase can relax. We're can't be everywhere."

"Guess we'll have to keep using methods we've got. Could take longer. A lot longer." CeeCee heaved a sigh.

"I thought Pattison was upfront about her troubled past. Going back to where she's lived before is a start," LaShaun replied.

"Already working on it," Jonah said. "We'll share any intel that will help her lawyer."

"Yeah," CeeCee added. "I'm going to finish my lunch now that you're through grilling us. See what I did? We're eating and—"

"Stick to investigations, hon. Your stand-up comedy prospects are dim." LaShaun laughed when CeeCee faked an affronted scowl.

"I'm going to order their famous bread pudding." Jonah patted his flat abs. "A perfect end to a fantastic meal."

"Careful. Your six-pack might turn into eight," LaShaun teased. She pointed to CeeCee. "Hey, keep in touch you."

CeeCee, mouthful of salad, nodded assent. After more playful banter with her friends, LaShaun left to pick up CJ. He was still a bit drowsy though he'd awakened from his nap. He drifted into sleep during the drive home but perked up when Beau greeted them with barks. LaShaun started dinner from food she'd defrosted from their freezer. They would have greens, cornbread, rice, and smothered gravy steaks. The meal was one of Chase's favorites. As she cooked, LaShaun hummed a tune. Cool weather and comfort food would be perfect. The house smelled of spices by the time Ellie arrived. She seemed to have settled back into the school routine. Chase came home at almost six and they had a typical family dinner. No talk of crime allowed.

By the time the children were in bed, Chase had shed any trace of his cop persona. He padded around in thick socks, dressed in yoga pants and a t-shirt, being a dad and husband. He'd loaded the dishwasher while LaShaun got the kids bathed and into their pajamas. For once CJ's little eyes closed within minutes of being tucked in. Ellie climbed beneath her covers without protest as well.

"Well, this was a welcomed change. Both of our children went to bed without a struggle." LaShaun sank down next to Chase onto the sofa in their family room.

"Nice, peaceful end to my day." Chase stretched one arm on the back of the sofa. He continued to scroll through channels using the remote.

"Rough at the station?" LaShaun patted his muscular thigh.

"Hmm," Chase replied. "Mama isn't having the big Halloween family party this year. I think my folks are slowing down."

"Or they don't want the voodoo kids creating spooky chaos," LaShaun muttered.

"Last year Ellie used her mind thing to find all of the candy and toys in the Ghost Hunt." Chase shot a side-eye at LaShaun. "Yeah. Folks noticed. She ended up with a huge pile of loot compared to the other kids. CJ kept giggling and egging her on."

"CJ was just clapping because Ellie was good at following the clues," LaShaun said, repeating her defense of them at the time.

"Anyway, Katie is having a party. Not as big but the kids will have their Halloween bash after all. We haven't scared her away. Yet." Chase chuckled when LaShaun delivered a light swat on his leg.

"Not funny." LaShaun propped her feet on the ottoman. "Any news on the murder investigations?"

Chase hit the mute button on the remote and turned to her. "Humph. I knew my favorite dishes were a bribe to pump me for info."

"Too obvious, huh?" LaShaun grinned at him.

"And as it happens, unnecessary. We've issued a warrant for a suspect in Tranicia Banks' murder. An ex-boyfriend had been harassing her. Looks like he might have given her tainted drugs in revenge."

"Mighty convenient. I don't—"

"Human nature, LaShaun," Chase said. "Stop listening to CeeCee and Jonah. Not everything is a conspiracy from the dark side."

LaShaun started to reply but Chase continued to talk. His lecture on why most crime was ordinary faded to a muted rumble. A flash of heat shot through her chest. She saw death. No, she saw someone deliver death to another human being. A woman whose face she'd only seen in news reports.

"Chase, the complete post-mortem will show Tranicia Banks was suffocated. The drugs only made her too dizzy to fight back." LaShaun gripped his arm tighter with each word.

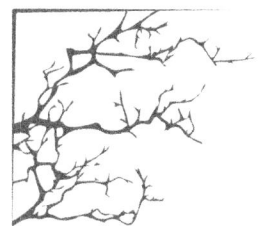

# Chapter 11

Thursday morning dawned with a layer of light gray clouds overhead. Rain was in the forecast. LaShaun gazed out at the dreary weather. A storm was coming but of a different kind. Chase had tried to reason her out of the vision she'd had. But she didn't budge. He knew better than to argue after their years together. No matter how much he wanted the world to be "normal," she'd lifted the curtain too many times. The practical lawman had to acknowledge there was more beyond his five senses. He lived with the evidence.

"Mama..." Ellie tapped LaShaun's thigh. "Mama... You're going to make me miss the bus. We're making jack o' lanterns today and learning about All Hallows Eve, All Saints Day, and Día de los Muertos. Halloween is about honoring the ancestors, really. Not ghosts and stuff."

"Huh?" LaShaun blinked out of her reverie. She looked down to find Ellie staring at her with a serious expression.

"CeeCee told me about Día de los Muertos. I tried to tell Brandon and Jamila, but I think they like being scared on Halloween." Ellie frowned disapproval of her school friends.

"Well, the holiday can mean many things to different people. Anyway, getting candy and dressing in costumes is fun. Right?" LaShaun continued packing a healthy snack for her.

"I guess. Luis says his abuela sees her mother all the time. I told him about Monmon Odette and—"

"Grandmother!" CJ chimed in from his booster chair at the table. He stuffed the last bite of scrambled egg into his mouth.

"Hush, CJ. Don't talk with a mouth full of food. Ugh." Ellie turned her disapproval onto her baby brother.

"Hmm." CJ, a bit of egg on his chin, unbothered by her reproach.

"Ellie, have you talked to..." LaShaun glanced around even though Chase had already left for work. She didn't want to hear the answer but braced for it anyway. "Does Monmon Odette visit, I mean um, talk to you?"

"You mean her ghost?" Ellie's face lit up as if the idea delighted her.

"Shh, let's not scare your brother," LaShaun said, lowering her voice to almost a whisper.

"Oh, CJ's not scared of Monmon Odette." Ellie spoke in a matter-of-fact tone as if to reassure her mother.

"She's been here?" LaShaun thought back to the many times a large white moth hovered outside Ellie's bedroom window.

"Only when I read her journals. I can almost hear her talking. Only not like the tv or music thing." Ellie's face screwed into a frown. "Is Zee going to be safe?"

LaShaun started at the abrupt change of subject. "Aunt Savannah is working very hard to make sure she is."

"I know." Ellie took out the keychain with a cute unicorn dangling from a chain. The unicorn twirled as she held it high. "CJ says she'll be okay at the place for now."

"Ellie! Mrs. Richardson took Zee's belongings from you." LaShaun stared at the pink figure. "How did you..."

"Mrs. Richardson put Zee's things in Ms. Armstead's office. I went there for one of our talks. I remembered Zee wanted me to keep her things. Zee said it was life and death important. Keeping things for a friend isn't stealing." Ellie held her chin up.

"Joëlle Renée Broussard, you're pushing my patience to the limit. You know very well—"

"The stranger didn't get it because of me. You said Zee's grandmother doesn't know who he is." Ellie raised both her dark eyebrows at her mother. In an instant she looked like her no-nonsense father.

"Hmm-umm," CJ chimed in as if saying "she's got a point."

"Finish your apple juice, young man," LaShaun clipped.

"Yes, Mama." CJ continued to look unruffled as he raised his sippy cup.

LaShaun turned back to Ellie with a stern face. "Give it to me right now."

"Well..." Ellie looked unsure. Her expression implied adults had let Zee's belongings get into the wrong hands already.

"This is not a negotiation, young lady." LaShaun held out an open palm.

"Yes, ma'am." Ellie handed it to her with a sigh.

"I'll make sure it's safe. Maybe the group home staff will let her keep it. If not, I will." LaShaun held up the keychain. She was about to drop it into the pocket of her sweatshirt when she saw it—a slot in the bottom. When pressed, a mini SD card popped out.

"Mama, you broke Zee's keychain!" Ellie crossed her arms and scowled with disappointment.

"No." LaShaun snapped the flash drive into the slot again and it disappeared.

"Oh. Good. What is it?" Ellie stepped closer to examine the unicorn.

"Something Zee wants to keep private," LaShaun murmured.

Ellie blinked at the unicorn. "Huh?"

LaShaun placed a hand on Ellie's small shoulder. "We're going to keep this between us. I'll tell Daddy, too."

Ellie gazed into LaShaun's eyes. "Because we don't keep secrets from Daddy."

"Right. I'm going to show this to Aunt Savannah and tell your father," LaShaun murmured.

"Right, tell Auntie Savannah first and then tell Daddy." Ellie's knowing expression made her look wise beyond her years.

"Um, yeah. Let's get you to school on time."

The big yellow bus pulled up less than a minute after Ellie skipped ahead of LaShaun down the driveway. CJ delighted in seeing the bright vehicle. He waved with enthusiasm and clapped his hands when the driver waved back. Then he launched into singing about the wheels going round and round. When they went back inside, LaShaun tidied up the kitchen. She started the dishwasher but ignored the laundry that seemed to beg for attention.

"Let's go into town, sport," LaShaun said and ruffled his mop of tight dark brown curls.

"Yay! We ride." CJ danced down the hallway to his bedroom.

After a brief tussle with him over which outfit he preferred, they were out the door. Then CJ whined about leaving Beau. The Great Weimar seemed to gaze at LaShaun with anticipation, his large head cocked to one side. She gave in just so she could get on the road. Savannah had said she could meet her at the office instead of heading straight to court. By the time they got there it was only eight-thirty in the morning. Savannah's legal secretary, Rai, came in at nine so the door was locked. LaShaun waited in the parking lot. She tapped her fingers on the steering wheel, checking each time she heard a vehicle engine. Savannah's Volvo arrived five minutes later. CJ had launched into the ABC song for the third time.

"Thank the Lord," LaShaun whispered. She'd been worn down trying to get CJ distracted and off the old tune.

"Hey, sweet boy!" Savannah strode up to the SUV. Her leather briefcase was in one hand, a travel cup in the other.

CJ launched into the pre-school good morning song by way of greeting. He added "Auntie Savannah" at the end. "We'll have a bright day. We'll—"

"Auntie Savannah gets the message, baby," LaShaun broke in as he launched into the second verse. She pressed the release of the booster seat strap. LaShaun lifted CJ and put him on the cement surface. Beau scrambled from the SUV right after.

"Good morning, sir. Lucky for you we're a dog friendly place of business." Savannah grinned at Beau who woofed as if he understood.

Savannah unlocked the door, turned off the alarm, and went to her office. Moments later she went around turning on more lights. Then she went to the kitchen. Savannah set up the coffeepot, then returned to the lobby.

"I see you came prepared," Savannah said, nodding at the array of toys on the floor. She leaned on Rai's desk as she sipped from the travel cup.

"It's a routine. Otherwise, he'll take an unhealthy interest in your office equipment." LaShaun looked at the dog, who sat observing the humans. "Beau, you head him off if it happens."

Beau woofed and switched his full attention to CJ. LaShaun set up CJ's tablet to access Savannah's wi-fi. A toddler video appeared. CJ, still clutching a toy dinosaur, promptly sat down to watch. Satisfied he was sufficiently entertained, LaShaun turned to Savannah. She blew out a long breath.

"Long morning already, huh? I remember those days. So glad my girls are in college. Paul had the nerve once to hint another child would be great. He narrowly escaped with his life," Savannah joked. Her twins were freshmen. One attended Spelman in Atlanta, Georgia, while the other was at Prairie View A&M near Houston, Texas.

LaShaun bypassed small talk. She raised a hand to let the unicorn dangle from its chain. "I think it's key evidence."

"I see what you did there. Cute toy, but I don't see—" Savannah chuckled. She took the keychain with two small keys attached.

LaShaun grabbed it back. The mini flash card appeared when she pressed the almost invisible slot. "Zee's too smart to do write down something anybody could find and read."

"Yeah. I did wonder…" Savannah examined the flash card when LaShaun placed it in her palm. "Okay, let's see what we've got."

Savannah sent it to Rai's desk. She turned on the sleek all-in-one computer. A wireless keyboard and mouse sat to one side. The twenty-seven-inch monitor blinked on. Then Savannah pushed the drive into a slot set in the monitor.

"Hunh. Should have guessed," Savannah said and clicked her tongue in frustration.

"What?" LaShaun went around the desk to look at the monitor.

"Password protected."

"No problem. You can go see Zee and get it," LaShaun responded.

"Not until tomorrow maybe. I've got two hearings today and a pre-trial conference. Then a status conference in the morning. I do have other clients you know," Savannah added when LaShaun huffed with frustration.

"Yes, but this could be the difference between a girl's life being ruined or exonerated," LaShaun said.

"You just took a mighty leap to a long-shot assumption. What if it has social media photos or the latest challenge she intended to upload? Or maybe her grandmother's recipes." Savannah shrugged. "Anyway, I can't not show up. Judges take a seriously dim view of lawyers who skip hearings."

"Humph, the legal system moves slower than a turtle after they've locked up somebody. But just watch how fast they move sending a Black child to prison for life." LaShaun glanced at CJ happily bobbing his head to a tune. "They deserve better."

"You're preaching to the choir and the pulpit here," Savannah said. "But look, H&H may have politically connected directors, but they provide great care. I scoured their track record. Also, if someone is threatened by what she has or knows then it's the safest place for her. They have solid security."

"Yeah, a nicely decorated kiddie jail," LaShaun retorted.

"I'm t doing everything I can." Savannah squinted at LaShaun.

"Sorry. I'm in a mood after the morning I've had. And I have to tell Chase Ellie took the keychain back. It's got to mean something." LaShaun dropped into a chair with a sigh.

"Because you don't keep secrets from the hubby. Not when it could impact his murder investigation."

"Ellie said almost the exact same thing. About secrets, I mean," LaShaun mumbled.

"Did you get a chance to eat breakfast?"

"Um, except for a sip of CJ's juice, no." LaShaun shook her head, her thoughts racing in other directions.

"I missed a lot of meals when the twins were little. I can whip you up a healthy smoothie right here. I start with one instead of coffee at first. Didn't bother with cooking since I had to meet you so early." Savannah pushed to her feet and headed to the kitchen.

"Don't go to any trouble," LaShaun called after her. She glanced at CJ, made sure the front door was locked, and followed Savannah.

Savannah took frozen bags of fruit. The compact fridge had a freezer section. "Blueberries, banana, agave nectar, almond milk, and almond butter. I can toast you up a bagel if you want some carbs."

"Hmm. Maybe I could go see Zee..." The rest of her thought was drowned out by loud buzz of the blender.

Savannah wiped her hands on a wad of paper towels. Then she used a spatula to make sure the mixture was smooth. Next, she poured the bluish thick liquid into a tall cup. She retrieved a pack of straws. LaShaun took one, stuck it into the cup, and sipped.

"Your last visit didn't end well. Yeah, I heard." Savannah nodded when LaShaun grunted in response.

"She's hiding something, Savannah. I'm worried whatever it is could put her in danger. And she could get a long prison sentence because she won't talk."

LaShaun paused at the sound of voices in the lobby. She and Savannah left the kitchen. Rai sat on the floor next to CJ. They both giggled at the antics of characters on the kids' show he watched. Rai's gray pumps lay to one side. Legs tucked under her, Rai seemed not to care that her business casual clothes, slacks and a tucked in light gray shirt, might get rumpled.

"I loved this show when I was a kid. Can't believe it's still going strong," Rai said over her shoulder to Savannah and LaShaun.

"Should I get you juice and grapes so you can really get comfy?" Savannah wisecracked.

Rai sprang to her feet. "Got lost in nostalgia for a minute. Reporting for duty."

Savannah laughed. "Just joking. Play with your little friend."

"Nah. Besides, I already had juice and grapes at the house," Rai tossed back with a sly grin. "What are you two doing up so early?"

"Trying to open files on this. We don't have the password." Savannah crossed to Rai's desk as her assistant followed. She took the flash card out of the slot of the computer and held it up.

"Hmm. Let me try." Rai inserted it again. Her slender fingers with dark gray, almost black, fingernail polish moved over the wireless keypad. She glanced at LaShaun before looking at the screen again. "Not just password protected, but encrypted. Since you're here I'm guessing this belonged to Zulime Glapion?"

"Good guess," LaShaun replied.

"The pink unicorn kind of gave it away, too," Rai said with a smile as she continued to focus on the file. "Hmm. Let me try something."

"What?" Savannah leaned over her to stare at the monitor.

"The last guy I dated wasn't a complete waste. He taught me to crack files and a few other tricks."

"Hacking?" LaShaun exchanged a glance with Savannah.

"He's a white hat. His job is to look for vulnerabilities in systems. One of his many talents. Makes a ton of money, too," Rai murmured.

Great job and taught you useful skills. Why wasn't he a keeper?" Savannah leaned forward farther to follow what Rai was doing.

"He was condescending about me studying to be a paralegal. And he had bad manners. Yelled at wait staff. After three months I'd had enough," Rai replied with a frown.

"Red flags. You were right to dump him," LaShaun said with snort.

"My mother wasn't happy. She loved Tyler. Or rather she loved his big bucks." Rai let out a huff of frustration. "This right here is beyond my skill level. Your little client has serious tech game."

"She's smart, but I don't think Zee created those files," LaShaun said with a frown. "I think she took that drive from someone and they want it back. Bad."

"Pretty advanced," Rai agreed.

"From Karlene Pattison? But she's dead, so we know it's not her. Unless..." Savannah squinted at LaShaun. "Please don't tell me her spirit has come back to take revenge."

"I'd know if she had," LaShaun replied in an offhand tone. She stared at the morning traffic outside the office's front window.

"She's kidding, right?" Rai stage-whispered aside to Savannah. Her eyes had widened.

"Nope. Mama knows things." CJ's equally matter-of-fact childish voice startled all three women. He continued to divide his attention between the tablet and a toy dinosaur.

"Oooo-kay." Rai blinked rapidly.

LaShaun turned to Rai with an apologetic smile. "Don't mind us. We—"

Rai raised a palm. "My grandmother talks about the spirit world all the time. Besides, you're the best around here at fighting demons. According to local stories, I mean."

"Superstitious gossip. Nobody mentioned demons or ghosts walking the bayou," Savannah said. She turned to LaShaun as if seeking confirmation.

"Hmm? No, no." LaShaun waved a hand as if batting away the notion as farfetched.

"I've read the news reports about your other investigations. There was the time those kids called up a—"

"Let's skip the discussion of LaShaun's colorful past." Savannah nodded toward where CJ sat. He'd turned to fully take in their discussion.

"Gotcha. So, you want me to lock this up? I could ask Tyler for a favor. We broke up as friends. Kind of," Rai added with a wry grin. "He keeps trying to cheat on his girlfriend with me."

"Maybe. He'd have to sign a non-disclosure agreement. And I'd pay him," Savannah replied.

"I should hold on to it." LaShaun crossed to the computer and accepted the drive from Rai.

"If there's evidence on the thing…" Savannah raised an eyebrow at her.

"Which we don't know yet." LaShaun slipped the drive back into its hiding place. Once again, the keychain looked like an unassuming trinket.

"Keep an eye on CJ for a minute," Savannah said to Rai. "Let's talk in my office."

"Sure. No problem." Rai winked at CJ.

Savannah led the way and closed the door after LaShaun entered. "You're going to get your secretive cult pals involved."

"They're not a cult." LaShaun laughed despite the solemn expression Savannah wore. "C'mon."

"I know there's more to CeeCee and Jonah than just old friends who come to town every now and then." Savannah pointed a finger at LaShaun.

"You always say, 'No, I don't want details.' I'm respecting your wishes. Plus, it's just as well. You're an officer of the court. You can't withhold information connected to court or police investigations. I'm not your client, so privileged communication rules don't apply."

"Right." Savannah walked in a circle as she thought. "Okay, here's what we'll do. Access whatever is on the drive if you can. Then we'll convince Zee to tell me about the information. Only if it's relevant to the murder charge. If you give the drive back to me, I'll likely have to disclose it to the DA. Even doing it this way is walking the line."

"The DA won't know where the information came from though. I mean, technically they know Zee had school belongings. Sort of," LaShaun added with a grin when Savannah gave her a look.

"Like I said, skating close to attorney misconduct." Savannah frowned and paced again.

"Good thing Rai couldn't open the files." LaShaun looked at the unicorn in the palm of her hand. "You're causing a lot of trouble for a cute doodad."

"No, stirring up chaos is your specialty," Savannah retorted as she kept pacing.

"I didn't ask for that gift. I was born to it," LaShaun shot back with a crooked grin. She studied her worried friend. "Don't wear out the carpet, girl. It's going to be okay. I'll be in touch."

LaShaun spent a few more minutes reassuring Savannah before she collected CJ and left. The rest of the day she spent between ordinary working mother duties and exchanging cryptic texts with CeeCee. The kids had finished dinner and were ready for bed by the time Chase arrived that evening. He seemed distracted and tired as he put away his duty belt. He went straight to tell Ellie and CJ good night. Their muffled voices floated back to LaShaun from the bedrooms. His laugh signaled Chase was unwinding from a trying day. When he returned to the kitchen, LaShaun debated telling him about the unicorn just yet. Chase didn't notice her sigh of relief when he declared work talk off limits.

"I just want to enjoy the peace of home."

Chase pulled LaShaun close to him with a sigh. He kissed her on the forehead and went to their main suite. She knew his routine. A warm sudsy shower, pajama bottoms, and a sports network to take his mind off crime. LaShaun decided the next morning would do; once Ellie and CJ were off to school. She checked on the children once more. Both had gone to sleep. LaShaun made certain because they'd gotten good at pretending. Only for her or Chase to catch one or both of them up. Ellie with a flashlight and a book beneath the covers. CJ would sit in his bed with a pile of toys as though it wasn't past his bedtime. Not tonight. The entire Broussard crew seemed set to chill mode. When LaShaun lay next to him, Chase's steady breathing confirmed he was asleep as well.

Her eyes popped open. Chase hadn't moved. His back was to her. LaShaun looked around. Their bedroom looked the same in the darkness. Nothing seemed out of place. And yet. Why was she up? A soft tapping drew her from the bed to investigate. She went to the window and pushed aside the drapes. The soft glow from a large lamp that topped a pole cast illumination across the backyard. Shadows from the wooded land just beyond looked peaceful enough. The tapping continued. A large white moth bumped the glass. It would have landed on LaShaun's nose if the window hadn't separated them. LaShaun drew back with a yelp. She looked over her shoulder but Chase slept on. A figure made her jump again. Beau stood in the door of their bedroom. More tapping drew her gaze back to the window. Dozens of moths beat their wings in the cool night air. They looked like tiny flashlights.

"Go."

LaShaun spun around at the word; a whisp of air more than sound near her right ear. She scanned the room. Beau had left. Or maybe she'd only woken from a very realistic dream. A familiar, insistent buzzing went off. She went to the side table where Chase's cell phone was charging but it was quiet. Her phone. LaShaun had left it somewhere. The kitchen. LaShaun stopped only long enough to slide into her slippers. She took quiet but hurried steps to follow the buzzing. Bright white light led her to the phone still on the quartz countertop. Instead of a number or *Unknown*, the word *Go* was on the display. Beau appeared at her side. She could feel warmth from his solid body. Her extra senses tingled with such force LaShaun felt as if she might combust. The phone vibrated with such intensity it moved. Fighting back the waves of dread, she tapped the screen to accept the call.

"Take care of Zulime. I should have done better," the voice rasped from the speaker.

"Who is—Mrs. Vidal, tell me what's happening." LaShaun stared at the phone as if the older woman's image had appeared.

"Something is going to get in before..." Rustling and then static came through before the call dropped.

"Mama, can I get a glass of water before you go?" Ellie stood in her pajamas and panda bear-shaped slippers. She rubbed her eyes for a few seconds. Then she looked at LaShaun.

"Go back to bed, sweetie." LaShaun held the phone tight in one hand.

"Hey, what is going on in here. Y'all ramblin' around the house like it's not—" Chase glanced at the digital clock on their smart device. "It's just after three thirty in the morning."

LaShaun followed his gaze. The clock showed 3:33 in bright green numbers. "I'll take her back to bed."

"But Mama—"

"No argument."

LaShaun took her hand and pulled Ellie along. She got the cup in Ellie's bathroom, gave her a few sips of water, and tucked in her for the second time. LaShaun rubbed her little back, willing her to drift off again. Seconds later Ellie sighed as her eyes closed. When she turned to leave again, LaShaun almost collided with Chase. He looked at Ellie and then at LaShaun.

"I have to leave," LaShaun whispered as she grabbed his arm to drag him from the room. She closed the door.

"Are you—" Chase broke off and lowered his voice. "No, you don't."

"Mrs. Vidal is in danger and the white moths appeared. Something is at her house. She called me, which means whatever it is it's bad," LaShaun blurted out the words as she whirled around and raced down the hall.

Chase followed close on her heels, his long strides allowing him to beat her to the entrance. He planted himself so that he blocked her way. "Nothing you said makes sense. Moths? What danger? You're having another of those strange dreams, visions... or whatever."

LaShaun shook her head as if to clear away mental fog. Then she pushed past him and went to the walk-in closet. "Zee's grandmother is in danger. I'll explain later. She talked like she didn't expect to survive the night. She said something is trying to get into her house."

"Dealing with intruders is my job." Chase grasped LaShaun by one arm to stop her from getting dressed.

"She said some*thing*, not someone, Chase. Dealing with dangerous supernatural threats is my job. You stay with the children. Ellie already knows I'm leaving, which means she's felt the energy, too." LaShaun brushed off his hold. She pulled a heavy sweater over her head without taking off her pajama top. The added layer would help against the chilly night.

"This is nuts. You don't know—" Chase broke off when she looked at him sharply. "Okay, okay. But you're not going alone."

"I won't be."

Chase strode out of sight. LaShaun tapped a code into a digital lock. She opened the drawer that held her antique handgun. A large silver knife in a leather sheath lay next to it. She loaded silver bullets into the derringer. When she returned, LaShaun was wearing blue jeans, her jacket, and the waterproof boots she used to go hunting. But this night she wasn't looking for the usual wild game.

"I've called night dispatch at the main station. I'm going. Not you. Stay here with the kids."

"No!" LaShaun blurted out. She grabbed his arm. "Call them back and say it was a false alarm. You've just put them in danger from something they can't handle."

"LaShaun... you don't even know what 'it' is."

"You have to trust me. Please. We don't have time for a debate. It's a long drive, so I might get there too late anyway. Trust me." LaShaun loosened her grip. "You can't come with me and leave the kids alone."

Chase rubbed a hand over his face and looked at her. "Go."

"Thanks." LaShaun hugged him tight for a second before she let go and half jogged out of their suite.

"Plug your phone in so it can charge while you drive. When you get there turn on the speaker so I can hear." Chase issued orders as he followed her through the combination laundry and mudroom. He tapped the app on his phone to turn off the alarm.

"Don't worry." LaShaun looked up at him.

"You've got to be kidding," Chase shot back.

"Yeah, that didn't make sense." LaShaun went to her SUV and opened the door. She started in surprise when Beau jumped inside ahead of her.

"None of this makes sense. I must be out of my mind to let you—" Chase continued to talk despite his words being drowned out by the racing engine.

"I'll call or text when I get there," LaShaun called before she slammed the door shut.

She hit the gas pedal. The SUV kicked up gravel as she drove off. Beau stuck his snout through the space between the driver's and passenger seats. He looked at the road ahead, his greyish-blue eyes seeming to glow with anticipation.

"Woof."

LaShaun gave him a brief side glance. His muted bark soothed her jangled nerves. Yet the tingle in her body had not subsided. "Yeah, boy. I sounded real convincing back there. Let's hope I didn't write a check my butt can't cash."

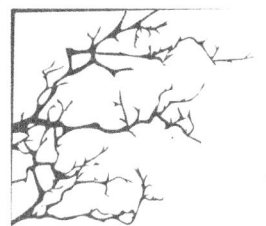

# Chapter 12

The drive to Blood Bayou took a hellishly long time. LaShaun tried calling Mrs. Vidal five times. Her mind zipped along as fast as the landscape whizzing by her window. She ignored the speed limit until she got to the turnoff onto the smaller road. Chase had called her twice along the way. The last short conversation had her anxiety soaring again.

"Look, MJ picked up on the call. And you know damn well she's not easy to fool," Chase said, his deep voice resonating through the speaker phone.

"What the hell is the head of property crimes doing up this time of night. Or morning," LaShaun complained.

"The fact is, she called me back and doesn't buy the whole 'never mind' line of bull I tried to spin. A deputy is on the way. But she's even farther than you," Chase replied.

"She?"

"Yes. Deputy Deborah Thibaut. You've met her. She insists on taking night shifts just like the guys."

"Crap!" LaShaun hit the steering wheel to let out her frustration.

"You need the backup, honey," Chase said.

"She'll get in the way or get hurt," LaShaun shot back. "But maybe... if she's on the other side of the parish I might have things under control by the time she makes it."

"Don't be surprised if MJ shows up, too," Chase drawled. Then his voice sounded distant. "Go lay down, baby girl. You got school.

"It's Saturday, Daddy. I want to know where Mama's gone." Ellie's plaintive little girl voice came through from the background. She sounded on the verge of tears.

"She'll be home before you know it," Chase replied with forced cheer.

"Can't get her settled?"

"That's the third time she's wandered in here. I should go. Be safe." Chase whispered the last words.

LaShaun worried that Ellie sensed whatever was going on. And she felt helpless to ease her distress. Instead, she needed to focus on the task at hand. What task, though? LaShaun forced her thoughts and third eye to focus on what was ahead. The weight of her weapons reassured her. Tension and excitement surged when she finally turned on the road to Mrs. Vidal's home. Pitch-black darkness made the way harder to see. A single lamp pole helped but it was so surrounded by trees, not much. The crunch of the SUV tires seemed too loud. LaShaun turned off the headlights. Beau growled low in his throat as his head swung to their left.

"What is it, boy?"

LaShaun gazed at the darkened house as she stroked his smooth dusky coat. A yellowish light from a lamp shone through one window. Remembering her visit, LaShaun knew it was the front parlor. Beau shot from the vehicle when she got out. The darkness seemed to swallow him before LaShaun could get out a sound to call him back. LaShaun eased the door shut but not all the way. In case she needed a quick entrance. A movement to her left reassured her Beau was okay. She flinched at every crackle of her boots on the stone walkway. Creaking announced her ascent up the steps to the front porch.

"Hey, sis."

The male voice whispered just over LaShaun's shoulder. She jammed an elbow back, connecting with a solid body. Then she spun with the knife in one hand, the gun in the other. When the figure approached, she slashed out. A soft grunt either meant she hit the target or pissed him off. A greenish flash lit a face. LaShaun shrieked in shock.

"Manny! What the f—" LaShaun stopped when he put a finger to his lips and shushed her.

"So much for the element of surprise."

Manny gave her a look of admonishment. He jerked his head to the west, hopped over the porch railing, and was gone. LaShaun hissed out an expletive. Still, his presence reassured her. She opened the screen door; grateful the hinges didn't squeak. Then she pushed the solid wood inner door open with care. Yellow light spilled from the parlor into the hallway. Something scuttled along the landing of the second floor. Too much to hope for only a mouse, LaShaun mused. Her extra senses sent spikes of warning along both arms.

"Mrs. Vidal?"

LaShaun glanced toward the archway that led to the parlor. In an instant she decided to go upstairs instead. A thick runner muffled her footfall as LaShaun climbed. She opted to put the silver knife back into its sheath. Someone groaned. A loud bump came from her right. An acrid burning scent tickled LaShaun's nostrils. She had smelled it before. *Focus*, a voice in her head commanded. Another sound, low growling, made her whirl around. The house was bigger than she expected. Three bedrooms. One open door. Then she heard more thumps. Before she could enter the room, a rough hand clamped LaShaun's wrist and tried to twist the gun from her hand. LaShaun pushed heat into her arm. A yelp of surprise followed by a gravelly curse word. Her attacker tried to tightened his grip but LaShaun pushed more energy into her body. Smoke came from her flesh. No, not hers.

"Shit!" The figure snatched free but raised the opposite fist to strike.

LaShaun scrambled away and raised the gun. "I don't bluff."

In the dark only the flash of white teeth, lips curled back into a feral smile, was visible. "The shot will bring my crew running. Step aside so we can get what we came for."

"Who is we?" LaShaun shivered.

"Not relevant. Now get out of—"

Shouts and a shot followed by barking brought the man up short. LaShaun pulled the trigger. A piercing scream of pain bounced off the walls, a mixture of shock and fear. Something slammed her from behind before LaShaun could turn. A second figure bent her over the thick railing. Stale breath huffed in her face as they struggled. LaShaun pushed heat again, but not as much came. She fought the weight trying to send her to the floor below. One last try. Electricity sizzled into a thin finger, a miniature lightning bolt that hit her opponent between the eyes. Not strong, but enough to stun for a few precious seconds. Gasping for air, drained, LaShaun tried to regain her balance. The wood broke and she had the weightless feel of falling. LaShaun grabbed the second attacker and yanked them along for the ride. She twisted so that her enemy landed on the hardwood.

A huge solid body cushioned LaShaun's fall. Its high-pitched scream made LaShaun's ears ache. Before she could recover from the impact, the other figured landed on all fours behind them with a snarl. A hand with claw like fingers clamped her throat before LaShaun could move.

"Grem, get up!" the creature growled, the grip tightening as it spoke.

"Help... me," came the gurgled reply.

The other creature ignored its companion's plea and continued strangling LaShaun. "Useless fool."

Unable to breathe, the dusk around her faded to black. Her arms went limp as LaShaun tumbled into a nightmare, gasping for air. She felt her children's fear so far away. Chase's face appeared like an image of hope just out of reach. Then nothing.

"I think she's coming around, chief."

MJ Arceneaux's face filled LaShaun's vision. She spoke into a cell phone. "Yes, she's okay."

"Damn!" A female voice came from the left. "What in the Halloween hell went down out here?"

"A burglary, Deputy Thibaut," MJ shot back. "Process the scene. And get more lights on in here. Like being in a dark museum."

"Sure thing. Hey, Rob, find the light switches in every room. But be careful you don't tromp your big feet on evidence," Deputy Thibaut yelled.

"Yeah, yeah. You ain't the boss of me," a good-natured male voice replied.

"Okay, so it's gonna take a while for the EMT unit to show up and give you a proper assessment. Yes, you're going to the hospital," MJ snapped before LaShaun could answer. She pushed her cellphone to LaShaun's ear. "Talk to your husband."

"Hey, babe. Ran into a bit of trouble but I'm okay," LaShaun managed to gasp. She tried to raise a hand to her neck. Her arm felt as if a fifty-pound barbell sat on it so she gave up.

"Honey, tell me the truth." Chase's voice was low on the other end.

"Deputy Thibaut trained as an EMT before she joined the department," MJ broke in when LaShaun had trouble saying more. "No broken bones or obvious head injury. Maybe she'll have a few bruised ribs."

"Eunice..." LaShaun rasped.

"What is she saying?" Chase asked.

"Mrs. Vidal is banged up. Looks like the burglars knocked her around, sleazy bastards," MJ said. "Ambulance on the way. Not sure about her condition. Gotta go. And don't stress. We got this, Chase."

MJ ended the call and strode off in the direction of a voice calling to her. LaShaun blinked away her blurry vision. A China cup full of water was pressed to her lips. The tall male deputy must have been the Rob Deputy Thibaut had teased. He wore a cap turned backwards. He nodded encouragement to LaShaun as she drank. The water revived her. When she took the cup from him, his large hands helped lift LaShaun to a seated position. She squinted against the glare of a spotlight they'd set up.

"Now that I'm sure you're not dead or dying..." MJ crouched beside LaShaun. "What the fuck?"

"Such language. Father Elliot would be shocked," LaShaun quipped. She set the cup down and tried to stand. Nausea slammed into her stomach like a punch. Her head swam.

"You're not going to move. ETA fifteen minutes, so we've got time to talk before my deputies come back," MJ replied.

"ETA?" LaShaun picked up the cup and sipped. Her thoughts scattered in all directions.

"Estimated time of arrival for the ambulance and medical techs." MJ rose and walked away. She returned after a time. "Look, I don't want crazy rumors circulating about Blood Bayou. Not with the usual Halloween nonsense we get. And James Schaffer. He chases ghost stories like a damn bloodhound."

"Manny... is he—and Beau!" LaShaun felt a rush of panic. She succeeded in getting to her feet. She gasped with relief when the Great Weimar loped into view.

Deputy Thibaut returned. She cast a nervous glance at Beau before she spoke to MJ. "Her dog, huh? Found him running around a few yards away, out toward the bayou. Is that blood on him?"

LaShaun hugged Beau and ran one hand along his taut flank. "Silly boy. Out chasing squirrels. Looks like he might have nipped one. He's not injured."

"Mighty strange you and your dog come way out here in the middle of the night." Deputy Thibaut studied LaShaun, a hand resting on er one hip.

"I'm going to get Mrs. Broussard's statement. You follow the ambulance with Mrs. Vidal; see if she comes around. If not, get a report from the doctor. Might as well be ready for the press," MJ said.

"Yeah, got ya." Deputy Thibaut lingered. "How many were there?"

"It was dark, maybe two. Mrs. Vidal called me because her granddaughter is friends with my daughter. She panicked. Plus, she's not a fan of police," LaShaun replied. She hoped her quick and smooth delivery would make a dent in the deputy's skepticism.

"Grass is disturbed. Can't see much since it's still dark out. Me and Rob will walk the scene when the sun comes up." Deputy Thibaut started to say more when a sharp blast of a siren sounded.

"That's your ride. We'll meet when you get back from the hospital. I doubt Mrs. Vidal will be in any shape for a long statement," MJ said.

"Yeah. If at all. She didn't look too good." Deputy Thibaut gave MJ a curt nod before she strode off.

MJ extended one hand to LaShaun to help her up. "They're through in the living room. We need to talk."

"I'm feeling a bit wobbly." LaShaun kept one arm around Beau and pressed the other palm to her forehead. Beau nuzzled her neck with a soft purr low in his throat.

"Don't give me the bullshit, LaShaun. You bounced back the minute you saw Beau was okay. I—" MJ broke off when a male EMT arrived.

For another fifteen minutes the medics checked LaShaun for injuries. They took her blood pressure, checked her heart rate, and examined her for obvious injuries. Beau sat to one side while his human received attention. He remained alert but calm. Which told LaShaun that whatever they'd battled a few short hours before had left. Or been neutralized.

"Okay. You should get x-rays and a CT scan just in case. I hear you took a big tumble." The EMT glanced around and then up to the broken banister. Then his gaze swept around to take in the broken furniture. "Good thing something broke the impact. What—"

"The settee over there." LaShaun pointed to the overturned bench. The cushioned seat lay askew.

"Okay." The EMT frowned but then rose to his feet. "We're ready to pull out."

"I don't need to—"

"She'll be with you in a few," MJ put in, her tone razor sharp. She scowled at LaShaun. "I have to get her first statement while it's fresh."

"No problem. I got to report in and send my assessment to the ER before we get there anyway. A good sign you can talk," he said to LaShaun. "But you could have internal injuries."

"Um, thanks. But I'm fine. I can drive..." LaShaun blinked fast as a wave of dizziness hit her again.

"Chase has already made arrangements for someone to get your CRV. No way in hell you should be behind the wheel. And yes, you're going to the hospital. After the statement. I'll sedate you myself if you don't cooperate."

LaShaun met MJ's stony glare. She had no desire to tangle with the seasoned officer. In the same circumstances, LaShaun would demand answers, too. "You're right. Of course, you're right."

"Give us a minute," MJ said to the EMT.

"Sure. I'll let Cal, the partner who's driving, know what's going on." The EMT grabbed his equipment and left.

MJ held onto LaShaun's arms as they walked to the front parlor. Her hold was firm to support LaShaun in case she became faint. Still, LaShaun also felt as if MJ wanted to make sure she didn't try to escape. She helped LaShaun ease onto the sofa. Beau remained in the hall but was visible. He sat on his haunches and watched LaShaun.

"Why didn't he follow?" MJ jerked her head in a nod toward Beau.

"He wants to make sure we're not disturbed. And your people need to finish doing a forensic sweep of the room," LaShaun said without hesitation.

"Don't say stuff like that in front of my staff. I know the dog is smart, but that's downright creepy." MJ heaved a sigh. She sat on the edge of one upholstered armchair across from the sofa. "Give me the unofficial story first."

"You mean before you take down what you'll tell Dave and the press?" LaShaun teased. Her smile vanished at the angry glare MJ wore. "Sorry."

"Where's Manny Young? I know of only one Manny you'd ask about," MJ's voice went low even though they were alone. Chatter from outside came from the EMTs and Deputy Rob.

"Alleged serial killer. He was cleared," LaShaun said, parroting Manny's own response when his past came up.

"Yeah, but only of the one murder conviction. Why was he out here? Did you call him? And—"

"Take a breath and let me answer. I know how strange this might look…" LaShaun waved a hand. The effort of lifting her arm caused a sharp pain and she winced.

"Might look strange?" MJ took in a deep breath and exhaled. "Okay, start with the beginning. Why you came out here, what happened first, etc."

"Mrs. Vidal called me. Her granddaughter is Zulime Glapion," LaShaun replied.

"I know. Why would she call you of all people?"

"Zee tutored Ellie and they got to be pals. Like a big sister." LaShaun sighed when MJ frowned at her in confusion. "And Savannah is Zee's attorney. So, I've been helping gather background information she might use in Zee's defense. Which is how I met Mrs. Vidal."

"And got to know her well enough in a short time that she called you in the middle of the night. Instead of the sheriff's office." MJ crossed her arms.

"She knows my history of... well, you know. Let's say *special* investigations." LaShaun paused when MJ still wore a dubious look. "She knew Monmon Odette."

MJ dropped her arms to rest both elbows on her knees. "So, you bonded. Go on."

"She called and... said someone was prowling around. Maybe somebody friends with the victim wanting revenge."

"Then they'd go after the granddaughter, not the old lady. Doesn't make sense." MJ cocked her head to one sided.

"Okay, the truth, whole truth, and nothing but the truth."

"I wish," MJ retorted.

"I think Zee has something related to her case. Maybe damaging information about Karlene Pattison. Her belongings were stolen from school. Some guy pretended to be a relative Mrs. Vidal sent to pick them up. Mrs. Vidal says she didn't. Looks like this room has been searched. I'll bet they went to the other parts of the house, too. Mrs. Vidal was upstairs in her bedroom."

"Or maybe it was nothing but a good old-fashioned burglary gone wrong," MJ's gaze swept the room before settling on LaShaun again. "An elderly lady living in a rural area alone.

There's antique silver, vases, too. Probably convinced she's got wads of cash stuffed under her mattress."

"And none of the antiques looked disturbed." LaShaun stood, wincing at the movement. "That vase is a Newcomb College piece. It must be worth over a thousand but it's still here."

"I doubt your common thief is an expert in antique pottery, LaShaun," MJ said with a snort.

"Even the dumbest crook would recognize silver and know it's worth something," LaShaun countered.

"I want to know why Manny Young showed up." MJ's eyes narrowed.

"I don't know. It's true, I swear!" LaShaun blurted when MJ's grunt clearly showed her disbelief. "He took off around the back of the house before I could ask. Then I got busy fighting off whatever was in the house."

"You mean whoever was in the house. Ah," MJ cut her reply. "No talk about creatures in the night."

LaShaun took a deep breath and blew it out. "I didn't get a good look. My priority was not getting pounded into a bloody spot."

"So, Mrs. Vidal heard an intruder or intruders and called you for help. You argued with Chase about zooming out here. Naturally you did the opposite of what he advised. And almost got yourself killed by a panicked burglar." MJ took out a small notepad from her uniform jacket's chest pocket. She made notes. "I'll leave out the part about Chase; and commentary on you being stubborn."

"Someone had to stay with the children." LaShaun scowled at MJ as she watched her write. "And I did suspect something more than human was involved."

"Your psychic antennae picked up signals I suppose," MJ muttered without looking up.

"Yes." LaShaun's sharp tone only brought another grunt.

MJ looked up. "You want me to include that in an official statement, with Schaffer circling? Right now, these guys think this is a simple break-in."

"Except for me being out here and this is Zulime Glapion's house," LaShaun replied.

"The legend of Blood Bayou. I'll check any deputy or medical tech who brings up that nonsense." MJ's frown seemed stamped in place.

"Folks are going to talk about it anyway. Zee's in the news. It's already been reported the DA will try her as an adult. The gossip about the Glapion family history started with her arrest."

"Can't do anything about rumors and old wives' tales. But I will rain hell down if there are any leaks from our department or emergency services," MJ said. "You mentioned the burglars might be searching for something related to our murder investigation. What would it be?"

LaShaun returned MJ's gaze and shrugged. "Hmm, I'm not sure."

MJ studied LaShaun for a few seconds. Then she went back to scribbling notes on the pad. "I'll find out eventually."

"I really don't know, MJ," LaShaun protested. "And I'm a little offended you just lowkey accused me of lying."

"Uh-huh." MJ wrote for another minute. Then she slipped the notepad and pen back in her pocket. "One thing about it, spirits don't leave fingerprints or boot prints in mud. We had a light shower out this way a day or so ago."

LaShaun fidgeted after a few seconds of MJ gazing at her in silence. "What?"

"Maybe Manny Young is the perp we're after. You knew it might be him and that's why you were so keen to get here."

"Now you're just throwing out crazy theories." LaShaun started to chuckle but MJ's relentless glare had a sobering effect. "Trust me, I wouldn't protect Manny of all people."

"Jonah Parker and Carla Cuevas are in town, too. Chase calls them your sorcery crew," MJ replied.

"What happened here has nothing to do with them."

"You gonna tell me it's a coincidence they're in Beau Chene with all that's happened." MJ crossed her arms again and studied LaShaun.

"Well, you already know they do paranormal investigations. They're always interest in local legends. All the talk about Blood Bayou..." LaShaun's voice trailed off as she shrugged.

"Uh-huh."

"They debunk a lot of stories about spirits, too. Which doesn't make Schaffer happy," LaShaun said.

"Hey, chief," the deputy named Rob walked into the living room. "I've done about as much as I can tonight. Thibaut and me will come back tomorrow. Send anything we collect to the state police."

"Okay. Search the woods down to the river in daylight." MJ nodded to him.

Rob glanced around the room. "Somebody was looking for something. A bedroom and this room have been tossed. Looks like you interrupted 'em when you showed up, Mrs. Broussard."

"Yeah." LaShaun gave MJ a pointed look. "I was just telling your boss the same thing."

MJ ignored her comment and turned to the deputy. "We'll regroup after you and Deb finish."

"Gotcha." Rob gave them a farewell wave and left.

"Time for you to get checked out. And you know it's sensible. You'd say the same if it was one of us."

"They'll just tell me to rest, which I can do in my own bed," LaShaun grumbled.

"Keep warm so shock doesn't set in," MJ said as she draped a throw over LaShaun's shoulders.

"Yeah, yeah." LaShaun tried to take a last look around for clues as MJ marched her through the house. She flinched at a sharp stab of pain in her neck. "Ow."

"Like I said." MJ guided her down the steps where the EMT waited.

He insisted on holding onto LaShaun's elbow as she descended. LaShaun felt light-headed and stumbled. MJ and the EMT steadied her. The second EMT helped her into their unit. Once they'd placed her on the gurney, LaShaun let out a long sigh. Beau hopped into the vehicle. He sniffed around, seemed satisfied with the arrangements, and sat. The EMT informed her they would go to Abbeville General Hospital. Then he gave LaShaun another once-over before he entered data into a laptop. She drifted off during the ride and woke at the sensation of movement. Over four hours LaShaun endured being poked and prodded. She winced as red and blue bruises were examined by a female doctor. The woman palpated each with gentle touches. A clear hand print appeared on LaShaun's right arm. After x-rays, a CT scan, and blood work, LaShaun was moved to the small outpatient section. Her bed was surrounded by a white curtain though the other three beds were empty. Chase showed up at eight thirty after getting the children off to school. LaShaun accepted a soft kiss from him.

"Doctor Grimes says you don't have any broken bones. No signs of internal injuries either. How's the pain, babe?" Chase's gaze swept over LaShaun.

"Not too bad. Sore, mostly. How are our kids?" LaShaun frowned with worry.

"Ellie knows you're okay. CJ is fine because Ellie's not upset. It's like she keeps him informed or something." Chase smiled. He grew serious again and lowered his voice. "Ellie announced you stopped the bad people, you'd find out who did it, and save Zee."

"I appreciate the vote of confidence. She might have doubts when she sees me limping around for the next few days," LaShaun quipped.

Chase brushed a stray lock of air from her forehead. Then he rubbed her right shoulder. "Who did you beat up?"

"Don't know. MJ is being mean and won't tell me anything."

"First tell me what the hell Manny was doing out there?"

"I'd like to know myself. We didn't have a chance to chat before hell broke loose."

"We haven't picked him up. Not a priority at this point. And your account of seeing him is 'vague.' MJ's word for it. She's not too happy with you tramping all over her crime scene." Chase grinned when LaShaun's mouth flew open.

"He's not the intruder anyway. And I went to prevent an even worse crime. I got there before the deputy, by the way. And—"

"Calm down. She's got a right. You being way out there in the middle of the night was weird. And you know MJ hates *weird*." Chase grinned harder at LaShaun's groan of frustration.

"I'm glad you find it funny."

Chase's amused expression faded. He crossed his arms over his broad chest. His wide-legged stance radiated he'd shifted to lawman mode. "So, tell me what you didn't tell MJ. And don't bother denying you withheld more than a few details."

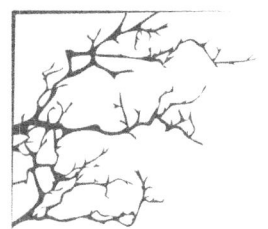

# Chapter 13

LaShaun was released from Abbeville General at almost two-thirty Friday afternoon. But not before receiving strict instructions on what she could and couldn't do for the next week. Beau had enjoyed being fussed over by two nurses. He seemed reluctant to leave his new friends. They'd taken him to visit a couple of patients. One young nurse praised how Beau's calm presence had cheered them up. Chase drove them home, joking that they should leave before the nurses dognapped him. The big Weimar sat in the back seat of Chase's Ford F10 truck. He stuck his head between them in the Chase's Ford F10 truck.

LaShaun cupped Beau's muzzle. "You big show-off. Had those folks wrapped around your paw."

"He's a charmer all right. Kind of like you and Ellie. All sugar, spice, and everything nice when you intend to get your way—or get out of trouble." Chase shot an accusatory glance at LaShaun.

"Oh, Lordy. We're going to have that kind of a talk," LaShaun said, pretending to whisper in Beau's ear. He withdrew to sit on his haunches on the rear seat. She squinted at Beau. "I'm on my own, huh, buddy?"

"I won't give you the usual 'stop risking your pretty neck' speech. Not this time anyway," Chase replied. He wheeled the truck onto Highway 14 to take them home.

"Good. Then we can skip the usual reminder that I can take care of business," LaShaun joked. Her grin faded at the stern set to his jaw. "I was armed and I had backup."

"So, you called Manny."

"MJ is such a snitch," LaShaun muttered.

"LaShaun..." Chase shot a heated glance at her before looking ahead at the highway again.

"I was going to tell you," LaShaun protested. When he grunted, she added, "I *was*! And I didn't call Manny."

"Go ahead then. I can't wait to hear this story," Chase drawled. He turned down the volume of the department-issued radio receiver. Official chatter became a soft buzz.

"I'm not sure who they were—"

"They?" Chase cut in.

"At least two of them. Beau and Manny may have chased a third into the woods. I'd ask him, but Beau ain't talkin'." LaShaun twisted around to look at Beau, who continued to stare at the passing landscape.

"Rob and Deb are both expert trackers. They'll scour the woods between Mrs. Vidal's house and the bayou."

"Okay." LaShaun looked out of the passenger-side window, her face away from Chase.

"I don't care if TEA field operatives don't like it," Chase said after a few moments of silence.

"It's just that..." LaShaun felt his rising temper beside her without having to face him. She heaved a sigh. "We would never mess around in your official investigation."

"They better not," Chase snapped. "I'd have no hesitation in hauling Jonah and CeeCee into the station. Withholding evidence, interfering with a police officer; I'll think of something to slap on 'em."

"Schaffer would be in sleazeball reporter heaven," LaShaun grumbled.

"Another reason you three better follow *my* rules. Got it?"

LaShaun clicked her tongue in irritation but said nothing. Her cell phone buzzed in her jacket pocket. She read the text, suppressed a smile, and put the phone away. "Fine."

"You've already sent them an update before talking to me. You're really pushing this trust thing we agreed on, LaShaun." Chase turned onto the smaller Highway 333 with an angry jerk.

"Hey, take it easy. I'm about to give you the full story first. Like I had time to send a report to Jonah or CeeCee. I was busy recovering from getting knocked on my ass." LaShaun rubbed her left side with a wince.

Chase's scowl eased when he looked at her. "We'll be home soon. I called Azalei to see if she could come over. Give you a chance to rest after the kids get home."

"Wow. You called Azalei," LaShaun teased and tapped his solid thigh.

"Yeah, well. She's always been a good babysitter and she genuinely loves our kids," Chase admitted.

"So, maybe you don't want to know about her selling feet pics on OnlyFans."

"Tell me you're kidding." Chase slapped the steering wheel when LaShaun shrugged a response.

"Relax, honey. We're in a whole new world where sex work is fully virtual. And what's she doing is legal." LaShaun frowned. "Although a bit questionable on the moral side."

"A bit?"

"Let's get back to what happened," LaShaun replied.

"Don't ever let Ellie know what your cousin gets up to. I sure as hell don't want to explain foot fetishes to our nine-year-old."

"Deal," LaShaun said with another giggle. She cleared her throat and assumed a serious face at the look from her husband. "I got to the house. Like out of thin air Manny showed up. On the porch. He tore off for the woods though when he heard Beau barking. I heard thumping and bumping inside, so I went in. I didn't find Mrs. Vidal, but I saw something move up the stairs. I went up and got slammed. Pretty sure I let my mark on one of them though. I got a shot off."

"I'll check to see if a local doctor reported a gunshot wound. They'd probably go to Lafayette or someplace nearby. They didn't show up at Abbeville General. I'd know already," Chase said.

"I doubt these guys would seek medical attention at a regular hospital," LaShaun replied.

"If the wound is bad, they might not have a choice."

"Don't get mad about what I'm going to say next." LaShaun shot a side-eye at him. She glanced back at Beau, who let loose a soft rumble deep in his throat. It was only then that she noticed a tuft of fur stuck to his whiskers.

"Ah, here we go. I knew something voodoo was gonna come out. Okay, let's have it then." Chase exhaled a dramatic hiss as if bracing himself.

"A little less attitude would be nice, Detective Broussard." LaShaun crossed her arms.

"Give me the rest then."

"One of the guys seemed extra... furry. And he had supernatural strength the way he hit me. I slowed him down when I threw a bolt of energy at him."

"That hot flash thing you do." Chase turned to LaShaun.

"Yeah. Anyway, I don't think those were regular crooks. I'm pretty sure my silver bullet hit the target, and judging from the scream..." LaShaun's voice trailed off when she returned his gaze.

"Damn." Chase blinked at her. A horn blast from an oncoming made them both jump. He jerked the steering wheel to take the truck away from the center white line.

"Maybe I better finish once you've parked," LaShaun said, a hand on her chest.

"Sorry, babe. We've got time before the kids get home." Chase rubbed LaShaun's arm and continued to drive.

Fifteen minutes later they pulled into their driveway. LaShaun let out a long breath at the sight of their modified Acadian-styled house. Even with the cooler weather of October, Monmon Odette's antique roses still had blooms. Two tall magnolia trees graced the front lawn. The home, though renovated with modernized features, still radiated traditional Creole charm. Beau let out what sounded to LaShaun like a satisfied short bark. He bounded from the truck the second Chase opened the back door. Then Chase went around to help LaShaun slide from her seat. She protested, but sharp pains brought her up short. She allowed Chase to fuss over her. He helped her get undressed. She eased into a cozy fleece lounge set—baggy pants with a matching t-shirt. Then they got into a skirmish. Chase insisted LaShaun should stay in bed.

"At least for the rest of today." Chase let out a frustrated huff when she shook her head no.

"Ellie and CJ will be really worried if they find me in bed this early in the day."

"They're going to notice you walking all stiff like a little old lady, LaShaun," Chase replied.

"Gee, thanks." LaShaun gave his shoulder a playful swat.

Chase pulled her into a gentle embrace. He kissed her forehead. "You know what I mean."

"I'll be careful not to do any cartwheels." The doorbell chimed and LaShaun used both palms to nudge him away. "Go, let in your favorite cousin."

"At least Azalei is on time. For once. Maybe she can get you to take it easy, Wonder Woman." Chase strode off. Two minutes later he returned wearing a deep scowl. "I started not to let them in."

"Let me guess." LaShaun brushed past him and headed down the hall. Jonah and CeeCee were already sitting on stools at the kitchen island.

"I don't think Chase is glad to see us," Jonah stage-whispered from behind one hand.

"Confirmed," Chase retorted. "For your information, my wife just got out of the hospital. The last thing she needs is—"

"Honey, dial it back. These are our friends." LaShaun put on her best sweet smile as she rubbed one of his muscular arms.

"She's not leaving this house, you two." Chase jabbed a forefinger in Jonah and CeeCee's direction. He started to go on but his cell phone rang. He walked off to take the call. He gave them a warning frown over one shoulder to emphasize his displeasure.

"Saved by the ringtone." Jonah let out a low whistle.

"We let you off the hook, girl. You called *us* to come over here," CeeCee said, keeping her voice soft.

"Yeah, we—" Jonah assumed an innocent expression. "Shush, he's coming back."

"Like I was saying, LaShaun needs bed rest. And no, I don't have to leave for work. So, don't get your hopes up. Including you, LaShaun. No running after some new madness because TEA says—"

"Sweetie, I'd already asked them to come over before the thing at Mrs. Vidal's place," LaShaun said.

"Don't 'honey' and 'sweetie' me. I'm not changing my mind because you turn on the sexy charm."

"You still think I'm sexy though," LaShaun teased. She started to hug him but stopped when Chase held up a palm.

"The doctor said rest for at least two days. Minimum. No argument."

"Agreed." LaShaun gave a good-natured salute. "Now, do you want to hear my breaking news?"

Chase cocked his head to one side as he looked back at her. He glanced at Jonah and then CeeCee. Both gave matching shrugs. "Let's go to the family room."

"I got water heating up for tea," Jonah called after them across the open floor plan. He grinned when Chase looked back at him. "Hey, I know where everything is."

"Of course you do," Chase muttered but kept going.

He insisted on getting LaShaun settled on the sofa with a throw and her feet propped on the ottoman. Then he sat next to her. CeeCee took one of the matching chairs. Moments later Jonah joined them carrying one of their trays. Four steaming cups gave off an enticing aroma. He'd also included Monmon Odette's teapot that matched the floral pattern on the cups.

"Lemon balm with a touch of Louisiana honey." Jonah sat the tray on the coffee table. Then he handed the cups around to all. He raised both eyebrows when Chase waved away his offer. "Settles the nerves."

Chase took it after a pointed look from LaShaun. "Fine."

"We're not here to whisk your wife away. Scout's honor," CeeCee said.

"You never told me you were a Girl Scout," Jonah quipped. He chuckled at the death stare CeeCee gave him.

CeeCee turned to LaShaun and Chase. "Anyway, I have an update on Neesha's murder. Information that will be useful to you, Chase."

"Really?" Chase put down the cup without tasting the contents.

"Nothing that changes any action you take. You suspect a man she was dating, right?" CeeCee studied Chase.

"Yeah. She'd broken up with him. He stalked her, more or less. She started dating a guy who was their mutual friend. Or what passes for a friend in the drug world," Chase replied with a nod.

"Correct, but he's a Legion recruit. He does sell illegal drugs, for sure. He was also part of the effort to get control of a market for monazite."

"TEA tried to keep the news quiet in the community but you know how that goes," Jonah put in.

"The community?" Chase looked at all three in turn.

"People with paranormal abilities network. The most important work is done under the radar. Including serious scientific research," CeeCee said.

"Yeah, not the reality show crap Schaffer puts out. Or the silly 'ancient alien' BS," Jonah said with a snort.

"But there are bad actors in our world, too. Legion is the largest organized group, but smaller gangs exist. And lone wolves. But back to the murder. Neesha suspected this guy had a connection to Legion. At the very least selling to them," CeeCee said.

"The psychic community's version of a drug dealer. Only in this case a substance that mostly affects people with extra senses. With some very dangerous side effects," Jonah added.

"TEA authorizes operatives using sex as leverage?" Chase raised both eyebrows.

"Kinda judgy, bro," Jonah shot back.

"It's dangerous. Intimacy means the target will be close enough to notice more about you. An already paranoid criminal will be even more watchful. He could have stumbled on who she was just because he was jealous and monitoring her." Chase looked from Jonah to CeeCee with a critical lawman expression.

"We have to rely on the operatives' decision skills. Sure, we have parameters. Neesha may have crossed a line. From our intel, we think she was trying to work her way out of the situation. Plus, she was following leads. Which is why she got closer to him." CeeCee sank against the chairback as if tired. "Doesn't matter. He killed her. Your forensics will come back with his DNA."

"His lawyer will say of course his DNA is on the vic. They were lovers. We can't prove *when* his DNA got there," Chase countered.

Jonah's affable manner vanished. He put his teacup down. "Two witnesses will report seeing him enter the place where her body was found. Also, that they heard raised voices and a muffled scream. Then the suspect left the premises."

"And did they?"

"Just to be clear, you're asking if we manufactured evidence in the form of eyewitnesses to seal a case against the man we know killed our colleague." CeeCee spoke in a level tone.

"My officers did a house-to-house sweep. All they got was 'we didn't see nothing; we don't know nothing.' We're known for southern hospitality, but that doesn't mean folks spill their guts to people they don't know. I'm just wondering how two strangers found witnesses. Assuming they're reliable." Chase returned her unyielding gaze with one of his own.

After a few seconds of charged silence, CeeCee nodded. "Video doorbell footage will back up what we're saying. We… accessed the cloud and politely asked said witnesses to revise their statements."

"Cash helped." Jonah gave a shrug when CeeCee hissed at him.

Chase pulled one hand over his face and rubbed his jaw. "That call I got earlier? Detective Anderson reported in that witnesses came forward. He picked up the suspect."

"Then he should have the footage. Your state police lab will examine the video and find that it's not doctored." CeeCee went back to sipping tea.

"No need," Chase said after a few seconds. "It corroborates facts we've already gathered."

"Dude, you did that song and dance for kicks? Calling us liars and unethical. I'm hurt." Jonah placed a hand on his chest.

"I wanted any gaps in your account," Chase said.

"And we all have a job to do. We're perfectly happy letting the criminal justice system take care of the killer," CeeCee replied.

"We have extra resources to make it happen. Find real evidence, not make up shit," Jonah added.

"Okay." Chase relaxed against the sofa again. Still, his expression remained wary.

The doorbell chimed, a break in the still-tense standoff between Chase, Jonah, and CeeCee. Jonah volunteered to get the door. Minutes later Azalei's cheery voice further broke the ice.

"Well, if it isn't the cute little snack with the mysterious job. How you doin', sugar?"

Jonah's abashed chuckle followed. "I'm fine. How are you?"

"You sure are, honey. Is your female sidekick along for this trip? I don't want to step on any toes." Azalei broke off when she saw the three of them sitting in the family room. She beamed at CeeCee. "Hey, girl. Welcome back to our lovely little town."

"Hello." CeeCee smiled at Azalei as she gave her a once-over glanced.

Azalei shrugged out of her faux fur jacket. Beneath it she wore a leopard print tunic sweater over camel leggings and matching calf-high boots. LaShaun had to admire the thick copper-colored weave that complemented her warm brown skin.

Azalei and CeeCee continued to regard each other with smiles in place.

"I didn't know we were having a party. I brought enough food, I think. I stopped by China Express. Shrimp fried rice, fried shrimp, fries, egg rolls, and wonton soup for the patient. In case her tummy can't take heavy food. I can get chicken fingers for the babies if you like. Chicken Shack is only minutes away." Azalei walked back to the bags on the island. She removed containers from bags and lined them up.

"They love eggrolls." LaShaun took her time rising from the sofa.

"Sit, honey. Four pairs of hands should be plenty to get dinner warmed up and set out." Chase pushed her down again and tucked the throw around her waist.

"I'm not helpless," LaShaun grumbled, no less annoyed that the effort of leaving the sofa had tired her.

"You'll bounce back faster if you follow medical advice." Chase brushed a hand through her hair before he joined the others in the kitchen.

"The school bus should drop off the kids any minute, right? I'll go meet them," Jonah announced. He disappeared through the kitchen door.

"Thanks, Jonah," Azalei chirped. She strolled over and sat on the opposite end of the sofa. "They're smashing hard, and CeeCee is trying not to get sprung. But I can see she's gonna lose the fight. She likes him more than she wants to admit."

"Mind your business while you're at it," LaShaun whispered.

She watched CeeCee and Chase preparing their dinner. They placed food in serving dishes that could be used to heat it up for later. Chase prepared after-school snacks for the kids. CeeCee murmured low to him, and he nodded a few times.

"Hey, I'm just stating facts. I'm a pro at spotting what people want," Azalei replied.

"Yeah, and taking advantage of it." LaShaun looked at her pretty cousin.

"I meant, I'm good at reading people. And don't give me another smartass insult," Azalei snipped at LaShaun. "Nobody is more self-righteous than a reformed con."

"Not so reformed," LaShaun muttered, thinking of the flash drive she still hadn't mentioned to Chase.

"Oh, do tell me more! And how I can get on some sneaky action. As long as it doesn't involve spooky spirits, violence, or blood." Azalei gave a dramatic shudder.

LaShaun grunted. "I thought you'd changed your wicked ways."

"Being a successful businesswoman has gotten... boring. Once you have all the money you need where's the fun?" Azalei rubbed her hands together. "So, tell me. I'll do some legwork, gather all the rumors."

"You heard about my night at Blood Bayou?" LaShaun arched her eyebrows at Azalei.

"Girl, by now everybody in Beau Chene has heard. And added to the story," Azalei replied with a laugh.

"Find out what they're saying and report back. And if there's any more gossip about Zee and her family. And about the victim, Karlene Pattison."

"Yeah, well, I already know a bit more about *her*. Seems she had a shady history. She ended up in a California prison for two years."

"Yeah. She turned her life around. Decided to mentor other young people. I found that out already," LaShaun said.

"She had two arrests for assault with a deadly weapon. Each time the victims disappeared or wouldn't testify. On the surface it looks like her rap sheet isn't so bad. But dig deeper and you get a different story." Azalei leaned toward LaShaun. "Maybe Zee was right to defend herself."

"Sounds like more information Savannah can use in her defense. Thanks. I'll see if she knows about those serious charges." LaShaun went back to watching CeeCee and Chase's muted conversation. Were they collaborating?

"Sometimes the official record is only half the story. Right?" Azalei replied.

"Yeah." LaShaun looked at Azalei again with a frown. "How did you find out?"

"A friend, Shameka Patterson, you don't know her, worked at Brighter Futures for a few months. Almost a year. She got fired. Girl can't keep a gig to save her life."

"Sounds familiar," LaShaun quipped. She gave an apologetic grin when Azalei scowled. "Sorry, keep going."

"Not everyone is cut out for nine-to-five work until you die. Or inherit riches from a grandmother who played favorites and—"

"I said sorry. Back to Shameka."

"Right. Anyway, I remembered Shameka worked there so I hit her up. She's still friends with the administrative assistant. The HR department caught hell for missing those details about Pattison's background. So did her supervisor."

"Hmm." LaShaun realized she'd never visited the program. "I should go to Brighter Futures."

"Hey, let me," Azalei piped up, her eyes bright with interest.

"More of their employees might be just as shady or worse. They won't like a stranger snooping around. I'm sure they're on edge and watchful now." LaShaun gave her cousin a pointed glance.

Azalei blinked hard at her. "You're right. I've laid the groundwork for you. Take it from here."

"Mama's home!" Ellie raced over to LaShaun with CJ trailing behind.

"Hello, my babies." LaShaun tried not to flinch in pain when Ellie gave her an enthusiastic hug. Something in her face must have shown.

"You saw a doctor." Ellie stared into LaShaun's eyes. "You got hurt fighting the bad men and—"

LaShaun pushed to erect barriers to Ellie's ability to read minds. "I'm fine. Everything is going to be taken care of by Jonah and CeeCee. Put your book bags away, wash your hands, and get snacks from Daddy."

Ellie gazed at LaShaun for a few seconds. "Okay. Come on, CJ."

"Mama, I made a picture, see?" CJ proudly showed off his abstract masterpiece."

"Wonderful, sweetie. Now go with your sister to clean your hands." LaShaun took the drawing from him.

"Snack!" CJ beamed at the prospect. He accepted a kiss from LaShaun and marched after Ellie like a dutiful baby brother.

"Does she do the baby fortune teller thing a lot?" Azalei stared at LaShaun.

"I'm usually in the kitchen. Ellie knew I left in the middle of the night because of some trouble. She saw me flinch with pain just now," LaShaun said in a matter-of-fact way.

"Humph." Azalei wore a look of suspicion.

"You have a gift for reading people. You just said so," LaShaun replied. "Runs in the family."

"True. By the way, why is James Schaffer sniffing around?" Azalei still looked skeptical enough to probe.

"I don't know. Looking for a way to save his latest show from being canceled," LaShaun replied with a shrug.

"Yeah, well he's got plenty to go after in Vermilion Parish. Blood Bayou, Devil's Swamp. *You.*" Azalei held up a palm. "Forget I asked. I want no part of the voodoo goings-on. I could use a snack myself."

"And I'm thirsty." LaShaun tossed aside the soft throw and stood.

For the next hour they talked about anything but the case. Beau trotted around the humans, happy to accept a few bites of food. LaShaun was grateful that the children were distracted from worry. Enough that they didn't think it odd so many people had greeted them after school. Though Ellie gave LaShaun a couple of thoughtful glances. Chase was aware of the unique link between mother and daughter. He stepped in to pull Ellie's attention back to mundane talk about school, Halloween costumes, and games. Things were going well. Then Chase's work cell phone shrilled the ringtone that indicated it was an urgent message or call. LaShaun moved to turn up the volume of music from their streaming device. Then she followed him down the hallway. Chase read the message, cursed, and tapped to call the number.

"Right. How the hell did they let it happen?" Chase muttered a curse word as he listened. "Okay. Let me know."

"Chase?" LaShaun glanced over her shoulder and back to him.

"Zulime Glapion is gone. She ran away from H&H."

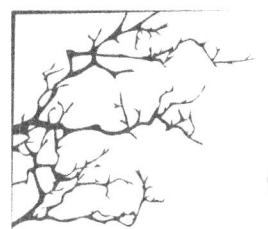

# Chapter 14

LaShaun and Chase worked hard not to disturb the fun atmosphere of dinner that night. The last thing they wanted was for Ellie to pick up on what was happening with Zee. CeeCee left early after getting a text on her cell phone, a call to report in to regional headquarters. Azalei left to get ready for a hot date. The kids settled down to watch a short movie before their nighttime routine. The adults went about clearing away dishes.

"Here's the flash drive," LaShaun whispered as she handed it to Jonah. "I don't know what's on it. And there's no reason to think it has anything to do with your investigation, Chase. So, don't give me the look."

"At least you let me in on what's going on *this* time. If you know it belonged to the victim..." Chase's dark eyebrows pulled together as he gazed at LaShaun.

"It belongs to Zee. Do you have a warrant that covers her belongings?" LaShaun closed a fist around the unicorn.

"Savannah has been coaching you, I see." Chase crossed his arms. He leaned against the kitchen counter.

"Encrypted. You need me to get in and read the contents. Got it." Jonah held out a hand. He accepted the keychain. "Smart kid. The slot at the bottom looks like a seam. Clever."

"Her scam artist daddy probably used to steal identities. Or blackmail victims if he came across secrets they'd rather not come out. He was into white collar crime for a minute," LaShaun said.

"So maybe the flash drive is his? Could be why she won't talk about it—to protect him." Jonah pressed a small tab and the drive popped out. He slipped it into a hidden zippered pocket in the sleeve of his jacket. "I don't need the whole thing."

"Okay." LaShaun took the keychain back. "You know, I hadn't thought of her father being involved. Maybe I should go talk to him."

"Let me access these files first. May not be necessary," Jonah said.

"And you're supposed to rest. We've got people out looking for Zee," Chase added when LaShaun started to speak.

LaShaun glanced over her shoulder. Ellie seemed focused on the movie. Still, she lowered her voice. "I'm worried that whoever wants the drive has her."

"There's no indication she was taken by force," Chase said. "Deputy Thibaut is back on duty. She's interviewing the staff. Zee either had help or those folks in charge are incompetent. We'll find out what happened. She's not exactly a master criminal."

"I'll talk to them, too." Jonah glanced at LaShaun when Chase frowned.

"You'll stay out of our way. What?" Chase's eyes narrowed to slits as he looked from Jonah to LaShaun.

"Young people with certain abilities tend to end up in various systems. The Third Eye Association has trained helping professionals in place to be supportive." LaShaun recited official language from TEA policy documents.

"H&H is a TEA-run group home for baby sorcerers? Unbelievable." Chase rubbed his jaw hard.

"Not 'run by,' but certain staff are part of the community. I'm not saying who," Jonah said and held up a finger when Chase turned to him. "They're qualified to help all children. They step in if a special child is identified."

Chase studied them both for a few seconds. "And you're saying Zee is one?"

"We don't know, but probably. Her grandmother had been very protective. Most think it's because Zee's parents were neglectful. Her mother took off when Zee was only a year old. Reportedly, she's been in jails across the southwest and California. You know where her father is residing," Jonah said.

"Mrs. Vidal could have let her go into foster care. She's not exactly a warm and cuddly grandma type, but..." LaShaun saw Eunice Vidal in a more charitable light. "She was in her sixties when Zee was born. It probably hasn't been easy for her."

"Sounds like you've warmed up to the old lady," Jonah quipped. He patted his sleeve with the flash drive. "I'm going to start working on this bad boy. See what's good."

"The minute you crack the thing—"

"I'll call you before anyone else," Jonah said with a grin.

"And you better tell me if there's anything related to an official investigation involving law enforcement. Either in Vermilion Parish, the state, or otherwise," Chase said firmly, his gaze on LaShaun.

"Wow, you got really specific," LaShaun grumbled.

"Yeah, I know how well you play the loophole game."

"We're on the same team. All for one and one for all." LaShaun stuck out a hand.

"In it to win it." Jonah placed his hand on top of LaShaun's.

Chase grunted when they both stared at him. "Now we're the Avengers or something?"

"We're going to share information. There's no 'I' in team," LaShaun said.

"Oh, give me a freakin' break," Chase muttered. He grunted when LaShaun glared at him. Then he tapped the top of their hands with one of his. "Fine, but if you or CeeCee withhold even a teeny bit of evidence... I'll gladly snitch to the DA's office."

"The TEA Criminal Division has never obstructed justice and we won't now," Jonah said, pitching his voice deep to sound extra official.

"Pfft, now I know you're full of it," Chase retorted.

Jonah chuckled. "Too much, eh? Anyway, I best get a move on. Things are getting hectic."

"You mean the reason CeeCee left." Chase turned to LaShaun.

LaShaun raised both palms. "Hey, I don't know any more than you do."

"Yeah. I'll catch up with her and find out. I may not be able to share anything though." Jonah walked toward the kids. "Hey, guys. I gotta go."

Chase shook his head as they both watched Jonah hug each child in turn. He even gave Beau a farewell pat on the head. "I knew you'd come with Rousselle relatives. Now I've got a whole extended family of witches and sorcerers."

"Think of them as extra hands to deal with supernatural aspects of crime in Beau Chene." LaShaun grinned when Chase let out a long groan.

"Growing up here, those were just silly old stories. I'm actually happy when a case involves everyday killers, thieves, and even drug dealers." Chase put an arm around her waist. His face turned sober. "I'm hoping Zee managed to slip off on her own. She could have found a weak spot in H&H supervision and made a run for it."

"Maybe." LaShaun waved good-bye to Jonah before he left through their back door.

"I was trying to make you feel better. Mainly so you won't ignore the doctors and take off to look for her." Chase pulled LaShaun against his body as if protecting her.

"I should at least visit her grandmother in the hospital. She should hear what's happening from me," LaShaun said.

"You make it sound like Zee being missing is your fault."

"She got upset after I met with her. Something's doesn't feel right." LaShaun walked away and checked the smart house hub. The green lights on the security system indicators reassured her.

"You think someone might find out you have the drive." Chase looked at their children.

"I don't sense anything. Beau seems relaxed, too. Let's just have a normal family time weekend. Don't go to work unless Dave orders it." LaShaun put a hand on his arm.

"The deputies can handle questioning. The usual lowlifes are taking a break for now. Nothing new on either murder that demands action. We have Tranicia's killer in custody. Movies, comfort food, and maybe Sunday mass." Chase kissed LaShaun's forehead.

"Maybe she went home. I could go—"

"Deputy Thibaut did a search of the house and property. Zee isn't there. Besides, she's smart enough to know her grandmother's house is the first place we'd look. Wait for news. Okay?"

"Right."

LaShaun looked at the kids. Beau had retreated to his snug doggie bed. She wanted the tranquil sight to reassure her. But the where, who, and why mysteries around Zee's disappearance kept her on edge. CJ put up a fuss about getting to bed. Ellie, aware she didn't have school the next day, had a new book to read.

"I can stay up and find out if the twins in the story find their way home. I don't have to get up early. Tomorrow is Saturday," Ellie pronounced.

"Me stay up, too. You can read me a story," CJ called from his room next door. His little voice carried through the open doors of their Jack and Jill bathroom.

"No, you're still too young and you need to sleep," Ellie yelled back with authority.

"Aw man," CJ replied.

"You both should go to sleep or you'll be too tired to go with Daddy. Boo at the Zoo is tomorrow." LaShaun smiled when they let out whoops of joy. The Lafayette Zoo held a Halloween event every year.

"You rest tonight, too, Mama. Zee is going to be alright." Ellie hugged LaShaun's legs before she climbed into bed.

"Have you talked to or felt Zee?" LaShaun chose her words with care. She didn't want to give too much away.

"I just know." Ellie picked up her book.

LaShaun studied Ellie for a time but saw no distress. Her mind whirling, LaShaun dimmed the lamp, leaving it bright enough for her to read. Yet the soft glow wouldn't keep Ellie from drifting off. She determined to find time the next day to visit Eunice Vidal at the hospital. Maybe Zee's grandmother would have answers.

SATURDAY LASHAUN STAYED home. Chase took the kids on outings without her all the time. He'd gotten very adept at wrangling two active children. And LaShaun did rest. At first. Then she headed to Abbeville General to visit Mrs. Vidal. The older woman had resisted efforts to transfer her to a larger hospital in Lafayette.

"Good thing I didn't listen to these fool doctors. I can't be far when my girl is missing," Mrs. Vidal said. She shot a glare at the nurse standing next to LaShaun at her bedside.

"Stubborn as the day is long. At your age ignoring medical advice is a bad idea. Your blood pressure is elevated, among other health issues. I—" The female nurse stopped when Mrs. Vidal snorted.

"Thugs broke into my house in the dead of night. Of course, my blood pressure is up." Mrs. Vidal looked at LaShaun. "You see what I been puttin' up with?"

"You should want to be fully recovered and at your best for your granddaughter," the nurse countered. She gave a satisfied smile at the effect of her words. Then she turned to LaShaun. "Maybe you can talk some sense into her."

"I got plenty of sense." Mrs. Vidal huffed as she pulled the blanket up to her chin.

"I'll get you another blanket. And a cup of tea." The nurse gave a crisp nod and left.

"Another reason my blood is up. She's always pestering me," Mrs. Vidal complained.

"Right, doing her job by taking care of you." LaShaun sat in the chair next to the hospital bed.

"I feel well enough to go home. But enough about me. Any news on my grandchild? Those fools at that group home let her get away." Mrs. Vidal found the control and raised the bed so she was sitting up.

"She managed to cover the security camera at the side exit she went through." LaShaun raised an eyebrow at Mrs. Vidal.

"Well, don't look at me. I sure didn't take her out of there," Mrs. Vidal blurted. She pressed her lips tight.

"Mrs. Vidal, does Zee have any special gifts?"

The elderly woman looked at the television. A black and white western movie played but the sound had been muted. "She's always been special to me. Maybe I didn't show it quite like I should have. Zulime is book smart, but she's got plenty common sense, too. She took to learning about herbs and such even as a little bitty thing. Why she can—"

"Let's not waste time playing word games. You know exactly what I'm talking about," LaShaun cut in. "Look, I know all about being suspicious. People with extra senses have been outcasts at best. At worst they've burned us at the stake."

Mrs. Vidal transferred her gaze to LaShaun again. She studied her for a few seconds and sighed. "Keeping secrets is a lifelong habit. I made mistakes with my children. Especially Zulime's daddy. Then he shows up with a baby one day. Says her mama took off. The girl came back for a bit. Moved in with us. I could see right off she was more than bad news. Scheming, selfish, and no interest in taking care of a child. I'm not perfect but at least I raised my own."

"Mrs. Vidal..."

"I'm getting to the point, missy. Zulime's mama noticed she was different pretty soon. Perky little thing but with an old soul." Mrs. Vidal smiled. "Had to watch her every minute with that sweet tooth. I'd put fruit out instead. Better for her."

"You aren't as bad a parent as you might think." LaShaun placed a hand on one of hers.

"Anyway, Belle, that's Zulime's mama, wanted to make money off the baby. Put her on display like some circus freak to do tricks. I overheard her telling Christopher, my son, they could train her to help them win at casinos or with lottery tickets. Christopher has his faults, but even he was shocked she wanted to use their baby. Anyway, she took off not long after that."

"She hasn't exactly earned any Mother's Day gifts. Awful." LaShaun shook her head.

"I threatened to put a curse on her. That might have helped Belle decide leaving was a good idea." Mrs. Vidal wore an impish grin.

"Poor Zee."

"She didn't even cry for her mama. Belle rarely touched the child, except to push her away. And she used to snap at her when she cried. I didn't want to raise a baby at my age, but what could I do?" Mrs. Vidal's grin melted into a frown.

"Your best, Mrs. Vidal. You did your very best," LaShaun said.

"Not good enough." Mrs. Vidal's eyes filled with tears. She blinked them away and accepted a tissue from LaShaun. "Getting weepy in my old age. My girl had a lot going against her, including me for a grandmother. But she don't deserve to have her life ruined. Find her. Please."

"I will."

"My daughter called from Houston. And my son in says he and his new wife are coming next week when they can get off work." Mrs. Vidal sniffed into the tissue.

"Good for you and Zee to have family support." LaShaun smiled at her.

"We ain't perfect, but we care for one another in our way. I didn't help Zulime run off from that place. But she's close to her two of her cousins. My sister's grandchildren Keishana and D'Andre."

LaShaun stood and took out her phone. "Do they go to her school, too?"

"Keishana graduated already. She's almost halfway through studying to be a hairdresser. D'Andre is two years older. They played together so good when they was little." Mrs. Vidal's eyelids fluttered.

The nurse returned with a wheeled cart. She parked it and took the stethoscope that hung around her neck. "You may need to rest now."

"Here she go. I could rest if you left me alone." Mrs. Vidal eyed the young woman.

Still, she didn't resist when the nurse listened to her heart and then her breathing. LaShaun sensed that Mrs. Vidal secretly enjoyed the attention. The nurse had a gentle way of chiding the irascible woman. The nurse positioned the bedside table so Mrs. Vidal could reach it. Then she placed a paper cup with hot tea on it.

"Vital signs are stable, so there's good news." The nurse took a hospital-issued blanket from the second-level basket on the cart. "Here you go. Now call when you need to potty. Don't want you trying to go without assistance just yet."

"Treating me like a three-year-old. Go potty. I'm not wearing them adult diapers yet, girl," Mrs. Vidal shot back. "Been handling my business for longer than you been on this earth."

"We all need help from time to time. Now drink your tea. And the call button is there for a reason. I'm here until six this evening." The nurse gave her should a pat before she bustled out. She pushed the cart ahead of her.

"She's sweet," LaShaun said once the door swished shut, leaving her alone with Mrs. Vidal.

"Professional busybody. But she's got her job to do, I guess." Mrs. Vidal took a cautious sip of the hot liquid. "Humph, at least she knows how I like my tea."

"How do I reach Zee's cousins?"

Mrs. Vidal patted her lips with the napkin the nurse had provided. Then she rattled off two phone numbers, their addresses, and their mother's number as well. LaShaun put the information in the notepad app on her cell phone. Mrs. Vidal chuckled when LaShaun looked at her with a surprised expression.

"I like being left alone, but I keep up with my sister at least. I knew Zulime needed to be with kids around her age. One of the few things I did right. Diane, that's my sister, and I get along all right. Better than the other two sisters. Anyway, you let me know soon as you hear something about my girl." Mrs. Vidal's worried look returned as she put the cup of tea down.

"Of course."

"Thank you. For everything you're trying to do for Zulime." Mrs. Vidal relaxed into the large pillow supporting her head. She let go of a long exhale as her eyelids fluttered again.

"You're welcome," LaShaun whispered.

She watched Mrs. Vidal drift off to sleep for about two minutes. Then she left. LaShaun felt as if a large boulder pressed down on her shoulders. She had to find out if Zee was okay. Eunice knew her shortcomings but at least she'd tried. Like Monmon Odette. LaShaun's hands gripped the steering wheel of the CRV tight as she drove and thought. Her fingers ached by the time she reached her destination. She pulled into the parking lot of Brighter Futures forty-five minutes later. She studied the entrance to the mentorship program. A wooden sign with the program's name sat on posts to one side of the front lawn. The painted double doors were a bright, inviting shade of turquoise. Her phone buzzed like an angry insect. Her arms tingled even before she touched it. Multiple notifications displayed from Savannah. She tapped one to accept the video call.

"Girl, where have you been? I hope you're going to tell me you've found Zee. The DA and judge are pissed. Mostly because of the optics. Teenaged murder suspect eludes authorities," Savannah blurted, a deep frown on her heart-shaped face.

"In other words, your weekend isn't going well either," LaShaun drawled. "I just left the hospital. Eunice is a tough lady."

Savannah sighed. "Damn, I'm sorry. How is she? Matter of fact, you should be in a bed yourself."

"Eunice is recovering. No fractures, thank the good Lord. At her age broken bones are seriously bad news. As for me, I'm sore but otherwise fine. You can't keep good women down," LaShaun quipped. "I arranged to meet two of Karlene's former co-workers at Brighter Futures."

"On a Saturday?"

"We don't have time to waste," LaShaun replied.

"Good point, but you could have delegated the search to one of your mysterious friends. Rest and spend time with the family. I imagine Chase isn't thrilled that you're—"

"Hold on a minute," LaShaun broke in.

She saw movement through the windows. A woman appeared. She stared at LaShaun's SUV and then stepped away seconds later. Then a gray Chevy Equinox pulled up in a side driveway. Four young people got out, laughing and talking to each other. A man, the driver, followed them to the entrance. They went inside without looking in LaShaun's direction.

"LaShaun, what's happening?" Savannah's apprehension radiated from the cell phone. She craned her neck as if it would help her see around LaShaun.

"Nothing. Just making observations. Look, Mrs. Vidal gave me the names of two of Zee's cousins. She's close to them."

"So, they might have helped Zee get away," Savannah said.

"Or at least given her a ride and a place to stay. I'm pretty sure Zee masterminded her own escape. I don't want them to get in trouble."

Savannah pursed her lips for a few seconds. "I know who to call. A private investigator I've used before. Text me the info. I'll get Mike on it."

"Let's quietly get Zee back to the group home. I'm sure you can deal with the DA and judge. Troubled vulnerable teen worried about her grandmother. The added stress of losing her one consistent parental figure. Something along those lines," LaShaun said.

"Oh, I've been down this road with a few other clients. Pretty much the speech I plan to use," Savannah wore a faint smile that melted into a frown of worry again. "I hope local reporters are listening to police scanners."

"Yeah, the DA doesn't like being embarrassed. I don't think the folks at H&H will be happy either." LaShaun stopped when she realized she was being watched again. The same woman stood at the window again.

"I've been on the phone with them, too. The expression 'heads will roll' comes to mind. I wasn't hard on them. The DA isn't being so generous from what I've heard. Oh good, Mike's returning my urgent text on WhatsApp," Savannah said.

LaShaun opened the driver's-side door and got out. Two more people had joined the first woman. One man vanished and moments later stood in the open door. He stared at LaShaun,

"I should go, too. Seems like my targets are getting nervous."

"Targets?" Savannah wore a puzzled expression.

LaShaun blinked when a brief vision flashed before her. "I wish psychic abilities came with a remote control. Damn it."

"Don't go in there and start more drama."

"I never look for trouble. At least not these days." LaShaun grinned at her friend.

"Channel reformed LaShaun Rousselle 2.0, please. Gotta go. And don't make things worse." Savannah's face vanished when she ended the call on her end.

"Hi, I'm here to see Aliyah Cameron and Janine—" LaShaun stopped to consult her cell phone.

"Waters, Janine Waters. You're working for Zulime Glapion's lawyer. Her assistant or something?" The man had a shock of red hair and matching eyebrows. He wore a wary expression.

"I do research for Savannah Honoré—of an investigative nature." LaShaun returned his gaze with her own impassive face.

"I see. I'm Jon Maxwell, director. We have a full slate of activities today."

"I'll try not to interrupt anything." LaShaun smiled as she walked up the paved stone path to the door. She stopped when he didn't move. "Is there a problem?"

Maxwell glanced at the cell phone in his hand. Then he looked at LaShaun. "No. Just confirmed who you are with Ms. Honoré."

"Absolutely. I was about to suggest you get in touch." LaShaun tilted her head to one side.

"Come in. You can use one of our offices." Maxwell stood to one side and pulled the door open wider.

"Thanks."

LaShaun entered the foyer. Potted plants stood in two corners. A table with brochures sat in another corner. She followed Maxwell past a large room set up with a ping-pong table, pinball machines, and chairs. A group of seven kids seemed to be having fun. Posters from comic universe movies, including the Black Panther, were in frames on the walls. A video game station was set up with two girls playing on dual monitors. Maxwell noticed LaShaun had stopped to observe so he turned to join her.

"We provide an alternative to hanging on the streets as you can see. We have two more rec rooms like that one," Maxwell explained.

LaShaun saw a van with the program's logo parked outside, visible through a side window. "Nice. You seem to be well equipped."

"Like most non-profits, fundraising is constant. A lot of what you see was donated by local retailers. We have generous supporters. You can find out more in our annual reports. All available to the public online at our website." Maxwell's ginger eyebrows twitched.

"I've read up on Brighter Futures. Very good work. Founded in 1976, your main office is in Baton Rouge. You have three contracts with the state. Construction has started on a center in Shreveport," LaShaun said.

"Yes, we're expanding. Unfortunately, business is good. A lot of young people need extra guidance." Maxwell smiled. "However, we're concentrating on prevention more and more. Offering conflict resolution training and staff in schools with high rates of suspensions and expulsions. We're funding three Dads in Schools programs."

LaShaun knew all the details already, but she was willing to let him talk. He seemed proud of the work they were doing. And he might drop his guard.

"Dads in Schools?"

"Fathers, uncles, grandfathers who go to the school and spend time with the kids. Amazing how a father figure presence does so much. More effective than a team of counselors and professional types. Just one of our initiatives." Maxwell beamed as he studied the teens engrossed in games and conversations.

LaShaun studied the tall man. Somewhere between fifty and fifty-five years old, she guessed. He had three children. All grown. One was on drugs. Information scrolled through her mind as her sixth sense kicked in. Maxwell's dedication came from the experience of trying to help his own daughter. His efforts had so far failed. She was still on the street. So, Maxwell was protective of Brighter Futures. He wasn't the one with something to hide. That left the two women LaShaun would interview.

"Sounds like a wonderful service. I—" LaShaun gawked at the scene before her.

"You have a question?" Maxwell looked at LaShaun and then followed her gaze.

"What? No. No. I'm uh, just impressed with the wide range of services. I'll talk to Ms. Cameron and Waters now." LaShaun forced herself to face him instead of staring at the familiar figure.

"This way." Maxwell wore a slight frown. The distrustful expression returned as he looked into the rec room and back at LaShaun.

"Great," LaShaun replied with forced cheer.

Manny Young gave her a carefree wave and cheeky grin. He turned around to continue his ping-pong competition against two teenaged boys. LaShaun gritted her teeth to push down the urge to collar him and demand answers. Brighter Futures must have missed "alleged serial killer" on his resume. She would find a way to corner Manny before she left. But first she had to talk to the women.

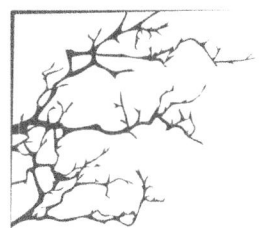

# Chapter 15

LaShaun sat across from Aliyah Cameron, trying not to think about Manny Young only a few rooms away. What the hell was he doing here? But she couldn't let him distract her. LaShaun forced her focus back to the task at hand. The office Maxwell had let them in was pleasant. A wide window let in sunshine. She watched Aliyah fidget as she chattered on. The woman was maybe twenty-two, if that. Not much older than some of the kids they mentored.

"I've been here a little over a year. Or maybe a year and half. Wow—time flies as the old folks say. I'm not saying you're old, I'm just..." Aliyah cleared her throat. "So, you're a private detective. Must be interesting. I mean, the people you meet. Do you carry a gun?"

"Sure. A knife, too. Big one."

Aliyah drew back, her eyes wide with alarm. "I was kidding, I mean..."

"So am I." LaShaun smiled at her.

"Oh, ha-ha." Aliyah shifted in the chair. She plastered on a tight smile. Her gaze shifted to other parts of the room until she looked at LaShaun again.

"Thanks for seeing me. I know this is an unpleasant conversation to have. I mean, discussing a friend after she's dead."

"Yeah. I'm not mad at Zee, you know. Not that I condone violence or anything," Aliyah added quickly. She brushed one long braid over a shoulder. "But she's just a kid. Teenagers can be impulsive, not think about long-term consequences. We've had training on child development."

"Obviously information that's helpful in your job."

"Oh, it is. Very much so. Zee wasn't especially aggressive or anything. I told the police and that guy from the DA's office the same thing when they came. I got the feeling they were trying to get us to talk bad about the girl. It's just a sad situation all the way around." Aliyah sighed.

"You were Karlene's roommate for how long?"

"The last six months until, you know... she was gone." Aliyah cleared her throat again. "I have a house my great-aunt left me. Owning is expensive. The HVAC system; the roof; plumbing. My uncle and dad are handy. But they can't do everything. So, I rented one of my extra bedrooms out. Ugh, cutting the grass in the summer is the worst!"

"So, you met Karlene at work and she moved in," LaShaun said to steer her way from homeownership complaints.

"Right. Saved her money, too. She was renting a nice new condo for over nine hundred a month. We don't get paid much here as you can imagine." Aliyah shrugged. "Not a whole lot of jobs to choose from. Plus, I like it."

Tell me about Zee and Karlene." LaShaun assumed a relaxed pose, her legs crossed.

"At first Janine was assigned to Zee. I guess that's why you want to talk to her, too." Aliyah looked at LaShaun and went on when she nodded. "Yeah, so Janine and Zee got along okay but there was no real connection. What the therapist we consult calls rapport. But Zee took to Karlene right off. After all this happened it got me to thinking..." Aliyah frowned as she gazed off through the window of the office.

"Go on," LaShaun prompted.

"Karlene made an effort to draw Zee out. Like she could tell Zee didn't really vibe with Janine. She can be a bit snippy. I mean Janine. Karlene got a feel for Zee and it just went from there. When Karlene suggested they switch, Janine was okay with it. Now though... it's like Karlene kinda low-key went on a campaign to win Zee over. Strange huh?" Aliyah looked at LaShaun.

"Maybe she was just dedicated to helping a difficult-to-reach teenager," LaShaun replied.

"Yeah. Maybe. Anyway, Karlene wasn't all sugar and spice behind that charming face. I was shocked when the cops found out she wasn't all she seemed. But then again, I wasn't. If you know what I mean."

"People can be very different behind closed doors, as they say. Really, when they're at home and comfortable."

Aliyah nodded. "Facts. Back then I just thought she was big on keeping her personal life private. Now I'd say she was a woman with secrets."

"Really? How so?"

"Once I was looking for one of my earrings. Actually, I'm always losing something around the house. Karlene had left this backpack in the living room. She came in just as I was picking it up to look under it. She snatched it out of my hand and accused me of looking through things. Then she demanded to know if I'd been searching her bedroom. I hate confrontation." Aliyah gave a dramatic shiver. "I got her to calm down finally. She acted like she believed me when I denied snooping. But I could tell she kept an eye on me after."

"Any friends you didn't know visit her?"

"Not at the house. But I got the impression she met up with someone from time to time. She'd talk on her phone in her bedroom. But I didn't eavesdrop. Looking back those conversations seemed hush-hush. Very secret agent kinda thing." Aliyah's dark eyes sparkled as if imagining some dark intrigue.

"What do you know about any conflicts she had?" LaShaun prodded.

"Karlene charmed everybody. Though Janine wasn't exactly a fan. She didn't like how Karlene low-key bragged how she'd gotten through to Zee." Aliyah leaned forward. "You're developing a list of suspects to create reasonable doubt, aren't you? I heard Karlene's injuries were more serious than her fight with Zee. She seemed fine. Someone else might have killed her."

"I can't discuss her case, but the police are still collecting facts," LaShaun replied.

"Oh. Right." Aliyah sat straight with a look of disappointment.

"What about the fight?"

Aliyah heaved a sigh. "I was off the day Karlene got into it with Zee, so I can't tell you anything about their fight. Janine was working though. She said—"

"I'll get it straight from her but thanks." LaShaun stood. "I appreciate your insights."

"Sure. Good luck helping Zee out." Aliyah stood as well after a few beats.

LaShaun had to nudge the young woman out of the office. Aliyah seemed eager to linger longer. She made a couple of clumsy attempts to get more information. When LaShaun batted away each question, Aliyah gave up and left. Janine arrived seconds later. Aliyah stood in the hallway watching as her colleague walked to the office. Janine smirked at her as she brushed past. Then shut the office door before sitting across from LaShaun. Her brunette hair was cut in a stylish modern bob. Blue eyes made for a startling contrast against her pale skin. Unlike Aliyah, Janine didn't seem nervous.

"Bet Aliyah tried to pump you for information. Girl thinks she can play detective. She's been watching too many of those old Veronica Mars episodes. She saw one movie and she's been obsessed since." Janine rolled her eyes and chuckled. Then she looked at LaShaun. "So, you want me to spread some dirt."

"I would like to ask you a few questions. I'm not here to say negative things about anyone, including Karlene Pattison," LaShaun replied with a smile.

"Humph. The best hope Zee has is to trash Karlene's name; say she got what she deserved. Self defense, in other words."

"You were assigned to Zee before Karlene took over." LaShaun kept her expression neutral.

"Took over is right. Karlene always had to be the center of attention. My grandmother used to say got to be the sun and have everybody else revolve around them. That was Karlene. But whatever. Plenty of badass kids to go around. Job security." Janine wore a crooked grin.

LaShaun was sure Jon Maxwell wouldn't be happy with this talk from a staff person. Janine's brusque manner and sardonic point of view was in contrast to his sincerity. Still, LaShaun sensed her personality would mesh well with some equally cynical adolescents. The kids they mentored had seen too much of the dark side of life. LaShaun smothered the urge to laugh. She liked Janine. LaShaun decided getting right to the point would be best.

"What do you know about Karlene's conflict with Zee?"

"For one thing Zee saw through the layer of honey Karlene spread to get close to her. Kids sniff out BS sooner rather than later. That's why I like working with 'em. Even though the money is crap," Janine said with a snort. "They got plenty money. Non-profit my big toe."

"Saw through her how?"

"Now that, I don't know. But Zee started throwing shade about Karlene. Nothing specific. Maybe she figured out her dirty past before anyone else. Kids these days can dig up stuff better than the FBI." Janine grinned.

"So, you never got close to Karlene?"

Janine shrugged. "Nah. But we didn't beef or anything, if that's what you're getting at. Look, you want to find out more press Aliyah. Karlene accused her of looking through her bedroom more than once. Knowing Aliyah, I don't doubt it. She's nosy as hell."

"She didn't find out much if she did," LaShaun replied. She'd been able to read Aliyah. The young woman had indeed looked through Karlene's belongings. Aliyah hadn't been as careful as she thought making Karlene's things look undisturbed.

"You're right. Aliyah wouldn't have been able to keep anything juicy to herself," Janine replied with a crooked grin. Then her expression turned thoughtful. "You want to find out more, ask Karlene's latest boyfriend."

"You got a name?"

"Even better. He's here right now. Court assigned community service is what I heard. Six months or something." Janine stood. "Karlene might have been secretive, but she didn't mind sharing her bed. Not that I'm judging. Anything else?"

LaShaun stood as well. She studied Janine for a few beats before replying. The woman had been attracted to the man. Janine felt a spark of satisfaction bringing him into LaShaun's probe. "Okay. Point me to this guy..."

"Emanuel Yancy. Nickname is Yance."

Janine opened the door and led the way down the hall. LaShaun's extrasensory warning system went into high gear. Her upper body tingled, not just her arms. She let out an angry hiss of air as she followed Janine. As she suspected. Janine went to the first rec room LaShaun had passed and pointed right at Manny.

SHE'D MANAGED TO CORNER him in the rec room for a whispered exchange. Only Janine seemed to notice. Janine's smirk confirmed she found a bit of revenge. LaShaun explained to Jon Maxwell that she wanted to talk to "Yance" as well. Maxwell wasn't suspicious since he knew Manny and Karlene had gone on a few dates.

Now they sat in a coffee shop in downtown New Iberia. Manny had suggested the location far away from prying eyes. His shift was almost over at the center anyway.

"Okay, before you jump all over me..." Manny held up both palms as if warding off LaShaun's wrath

"Community service. Brighter Futures does a crappy job of doing background checks," LaShaun retorted. She ignored the pumpkin spice latte Manny had insisted on buying her. LaShaun nodded toward a pretty woman behind the counter. She'd met the woman before and knew she dated Manny. "You and her broke up?"

Manny glanced at the waitress serving flavored coffee to other customers. "Nah. Look, Karlene was an assignment. Though the sex was nice lagniappe."

"Oh, that's real classy, Manny." LaShaun gave him a look of disgust.

"I had to play the part, make it real. Karlene came on strong. Refusing would have made her suspicious," Manny argued, careful to speak low.

"Uh-huh." LaShaun sipped her latte.

"I practiced safe sex and I was discreet."

"Is this the part where I give you a round of applause?" LaShaun tossed back.

"Look, it's not like me and Chrissie are married or anything. Besides, it was *work*."

LaShaun waved away his explanations. "Your business is your business. TEA told you to get close to Karlene why?"

"You know Legion has shown interest in Blood Bayou. Well, the monazite deposits," Manny whispered as he hunched forward to talk.

"Karlene had ties to Legion," LaShaun said.

Manny smiled. "I see you've been doing some homework. A low-level confederate. When she made it a point to get close to Zee—"

"TEA sent you to Bright Futures. How did you manage to get past their checks?"

"You know my parole is still in force."

"Right."

"My PO had me assigned. All legit paperwork. And I've been pretty much cleared of the murders. Bright Futures prides itself on giving people second chances. The DA confirmed strong evidence that someone else committed the crimes. All aboveboard." Manny sipped from his paper cup.

"Your TEA affiliated parole officer," LaShaun drawled. The young male social worker supervised people released from forensic prisons and treatment centers.

"A genius move. A lot of people with special abilities end up in psych wards or jails." Manny looked around the coffee shop. "I never get tired of being free. Not just from being locked up. But those hellish years with my family."

"Yeah."

LaShaun studied him for a few moments as the ordinary buzz around them continued. Just another day of people enjoying each other's company. Chatting about the upcoming Halloween parade and ghost tours around the area. Tourists mixed in with locals. None of them had a clue an "alleged" serial killer and notorious psychic sat with them.

Manny gazed back at LaShaun. "I know what you're thinking. They cleared me of those murders but..."

"Only you know the truth," LaShaun said quietly.

"I don't remember it all. I wasn't no saint by a long shot. I can't tell if things I see are memories or visions of what *he* did; or what he made me do." Manny wore a haunted look. His gaze seemed to lose focus for a few moments. He squeezed his eyes shut and then opened them. His good-humored expression returned. "Hey, the DA must grind his teeth every time he has to admit they screwed up my prosecution."

LaShaun laughed in spite of her wariness. He had a wicked sense of humor. Emphasis on wicked. "What did you find out about Karlene?"

"That she was good at not giving anything away. About her past or personal life, that is. Definitely not her—"

"Leave out the raunchy details. Please," LaShaun snipped.

Manny chuckled then grew serious. "She was trying to work her way into meeting Mrs. Vidal. Far as I can tell she never got invited to Zulime's house. But Karlene was definitely trying. She slipped up somehow. The kid got suspicious. I'm not sure what she found out. Hell, if the girl learned something before all of us TEA needs to hire her."

"Karlene may have done too good a job at getting close to Zee." LaShaun sat back in her seat, cup in hand. They shared an easy silence for a few moments.

Chrissie came to their table in the corner. "You or your sister need anything?"

"Bring me one of those king cake donuts, cher." Manny winked at her.

"I'll bring two since you're paying. It's nice y'all reconnected." Chrissie beamed at them and left.

"You told her I'm your sister?" LaShaun hissed when the woman was a few feet away.

"Half-sister. I mean, I got to explain how you're a pretty brown and I'm a white guy. Right?" Manny let out a hearty laugh at the murderous scowl LaShaun gave him. "I didn't want her to think I was a cheater. Remember we've met up here before."

"Lord, give me strength not to choke this man," LaShaun muttered. She gulped more latte to help soothe her raw nerves.

"Relax. She's from the Midwest. Came down here for Mardi Gras last year and never left. She don't really know anybody."

"In other words, it was easy to fool the poor woman." LaShaun shook her head.

"Chrissie grew up a bit sheltered but she knows my story. I'm not a complete liar. She'll be gone in a few months anyway. Moving to New Orleans to work in some film company there. Too bad. I really like her."

"New Orleans isn't that far away," LaShaun pointed out.

"Far enough. You know how it is."

"Fascinating as your personal life is, let's get back to Karlene," LaShaun quipped.

Manny glanced over at Chrissie with a wistful sigh. Then he faced LaShaun again. "I didn't get a chance to find out why Karlene was so interested in Zee. I don't think it was about monazite. I mean, Legion definitely wants to get their hands on Blood Bayou. Well, the land along it anyway. But there was something else. I came in just as the fight started and—"

"Hold up. You were there when Zee and Karlene threw hands?" LaShaun grabbed the sleeve of his jacket. "When the hell were you going to mention that small detail, Manny?"

"Hey, I'm undercover. Need to know and all that hush-hush crap. Obviously, your TEA contacts didn't think you needed to know." Manny raised an eyebrow at her and looked at her fingers clutching the fabric.

"Bull." LaShaun's temper flared at his cheeky attitude. Her fingers fired psychic heat in reaction. Manny flinched and jerked free of her grasp.

"Look, I assumed when Jonah and CeeCee showed up they'd tell you eventually." Manny rubbed his wrist where LaShaun had held onto him. He wore a pensive frown for a few seconds.

"What?" LaShaun prodded.

"I think TEA is hiding something," Manny whispered. He looked over both shoulders as if expecting to see some unwelcome observer.

"No shit," LaShaun said and grunted. "They're always hiding something."

"I mean something related to Blood Bayou or the Glapion family. But I was busy getting next to Karlene. Then this reporter disappears."

LaShaun blinked at him in confusion at the abrupt subject change. "I don't see the connection."

Manny looked around again before he leaned forward. "You know I got close to a couple of ladies at regional."

"Here we go with your love life again."

"The office gossip says some high up officers have been up to shady stuff. Certain activities that drew unwanted attention. From some ghostbuster fanatics, including digital age journalists. You know the types. They're kind of obsessed with folks like us. They've got podcasts and videos on YouTube. There's an entire Discord channel devoted to supernatural stuff, and TEA has been mentioned."

"Darrah Radcliff," LaShaun murmured.

"Who?" Manny blinked at her.

"A reporter. James Schaffer is trying to convince people she's been kidnapped. Or worse. But let's not get distracted. We need to find Zee." LaShaun took a sip from her cup and scowled at the lukewarm coffee.

"Yeah, well I've been ordered to stay put for now. Find out more about Karlene from her former roomie and other staff." Manny clicked his tongue. "Do me a favor; don't mention my little side trip to Mrs. Vidal's house the other night. I'm supposed to stay clear of the place. But I got a vision about danger that night and went anyway."

LaShaun looked at him sharply. "That's strange."

Manny shrugged. Then he signaled to Chrissie. The woman came over with hot refills and took away the old cups. They exchanged intimate flirtatious smiles before she went back to other customers. LaShaun executed a mini-eyeroll but said nothing. He waited until Chrissie left before speaking again.

"I didn't think anything about it at first. I figured they didn't want me to make Karlene suspicious of me; get her to digging into my background. Plus, turns out I'm good at this undercover stuff."

"And TEA told you they had someone else looking at the Glapion family."

"Not straight out, just that my only assignment was Karlene."

"What happened when Karlene and Zee fought?" LaShaun gazed at him. Manny still held something back. She could feel it.

"I didn't get it all because the argument started before I got there. Zee yelled something about Karlene being fake; that she'd put one over on everyone else. Karlene tried to shush her. I recognized Karlene's voice and followed the noise. I walked in just as Karlene grabbed the girl. Fists flew. Chairs got knocked over. Girls took sides. It was crazier than fights I saw in the jailhouse."

"Like I said, we better find Zee before Legion. Or TEA." LaShaun stared hard at Manny.

"We? You askin' me to ignore rules and defy authority?" Manny's eyebrows went up. Then he chuckled and rubbed his palms together. "Ah. J'ai rien a faire." (I have nothing to do)

"Since your mark is in the morgue," LaShaun replied in a dry tone.

"Hmm. I'll tell TEA there's nothing more to find out. Which isn't a lie, by the way. Technically, my assignment is pretty much done. Which means any instructions that went with it no longer apply." Manny sipped from his cup and put it down.

"So, when your boss questions you—"

"My handler, cher. I don't have a boss. Other than the Louisiana Department of Corrections." Manny winced as if feeling the weight of being on parole. "Anyway, I doubt she'll care what I get up to now."

"I'm going to find two of Zee's cousins. Her grandmother says if anyone helped her run it's them," LaShaun said.

"And me?"

"Look through Karlene's belongings. Chase says the place has been processed, so you can get in. Tell the landlord you're her ex and agreed to send her stuff to family."

Manny frowned. "Nothing of value has been found. The detectives and TEA would have it by now if so."

"I want you to use your vision. See where she's been; what she's done. I know you don't enjoy the experience," LaShaun added quickly when Manny pulled away.

"What you're asking... You know what can happen when I let that devil loose. I'm drawn to the evil. It gets to me like a worm eating its way inside out." Manny swallowed hard.

"You've had years of therapy with TEA specialists. I believe you can handle it. A girl's life is on the line," LaShaun replied.

"You said she's with family."

"I'm hope so, yes. But Legion knows she's gone. No longer under the protection of TEA-trained staff at H&H." LaShaun took out her phone and sent a text. A ping sounded seconds later in reply. "Jonah can meet you there. If you have a crisis, he'll be able to help. He's trained in first aid for people like us."

Manny drummed his fingers on the tabletop. Silence stretched between them for a few moments. "If it was anybody but you, sis... Okay, I'll do it. The manager over there has seen me visit, so he won't be suspicious."

"Good. get in touch with me if you learn anything." LaShaun stood.

"This entire case is getting too complicated." Manny shook his head. He started to reach for the frosted donut Chrissie had brought on a saucer, but LaShaun snatched it way. "Hey!"

"You don't have time for extra snacks. Move." LaShaun squinted at him.

"Main reason I don't like bosses. Always got to be telling you what to do." Manny went on to mutter low in Cajun French as he stood. He threw a defiant glance at LaShaun before he walked off. He took time to tell Chrissie good-bye and left.

LaShaun waved to the waitress and followed him out. They went their separate ways in the parking lot. Manny to his small Toyota pickup truck. LaShaun got into her CRV. She turned on the GPS system, gave voice commands to the first address. Twenty-five minutes of driving to the village of Kaplan. Keishana lived in the small house her great-aunt had left her. LaShaun knew the twenty-year-old would be home. It was her day off. But LaShaun opted not to call. No need to alert Keishana, especially if Zee was with her.

The small porch was crowded with colorful toys. LaShaun parked in the dirt-packed yard behind a 2007 Chevy Malibu. The driver's side door was a different color. One side of the back fender had been pushed in. Yet the child's car seat told LaShaun the car was in use despite its age and battered condition.

The front door swung open. The young woman, baby on one hip, stared at LaShaun. A girl who looked about four years old toddled up and wrapped an arm around Keishana's left leg. "Hey. You found Zee?"

"I'm sorry—"

"She told me about you and your little girl. Showed me your picture. I told Zee not to leave, but she got jittery. Had to go see monmon. I told her it was a bad idea." Keishana chattered on in a head-spinning flood of millennial slang.

"Stop," LaShaun said, a palm up like a traffic cop. "Slow down and translate."

Keishana swallowed hard and blew out a breath. She swept one arm out as if to explain. "She took the Subaru when I was busy cleaning up. Laundry, picking up toys. I got my hands full."

LaShaun nodded in sympathy. "You're a single parent. So, Zee left and..."

"No, I'm married. Darius drives trucks. Long hauls pay more but then he's gone for sometimes three weeks. But his company has him on the list for short hauls and—"

"Keishana, I need to know about Zee," LaShaun broke in.

"Sorry. I be ramblin' when I'm upset. Anyway, Zee took the car—" Keishana shook her head when LaShaun glanced at the Malibu. "Oh, the Malibu was my grandmama's car. She died last year. Covid. My uncle gave me the Subaru and... Okay, okay. I gotta focus."

"Juice?" The little girl tugged on her mother's pant leg. "Juice."

"Why don't I come in. Help you get the little ones settled. Then we can talk." LaShaun tamped down her own anxiety.

"Right. Right." Keishana withdrew into the house. "Okay, Shae-Shae. But this is your last cup. Then I want you to color some pictures. She had the sniffles, so I kept her home."

Ten minutes later, two sets of hands helped. Keishana put the eighteen-month-old boy down for a nap. The little girl settled at a child-sized yellow table with a coloring book and an array of stuffed animals. LaShaun got a description of the car Zee had taken and the plate number. She texted it to Chase, and over his objection, also to CeeCee. Finally, LaShaun sat across from Keishana at the table in a compact dining room. She'd made the young woman a cup of tea.

"Whew. It's been a week for sure. I thought Zee was out on a pass. Then I find out D, that's my cousin D'Andre, done helped her slip off from that home. I don't want her to be locked up, you understand? But I told 'em both runnin' made things worse." Keishana shook her head.

"Does Zee have a phone?" LaShaun took out her own and looked at the screen. No messages.

"D got her one of those cheap cell phones with some minutes loaded on it. I tried calling her. Ten times at least." Keishana's eyes went glassy with tears. One rolled down her cheek. "She ain't made to see Monmon Eunice, did she? Something bad done happened."

"I'm sure Zee is okay. I mean, look how she got away from the group home. She's probably slipped in to see her grandmother without being seen."

"Yeah, she's slick alright." Keishana sniffed and smiled.

LaShaun glanced at her phone when the text notification ringtone chimed. A deputy found the Subaru; without Zee. Her expression must have given away that the news wasn't good. Keishana gasped and covered her mouth with both hands.

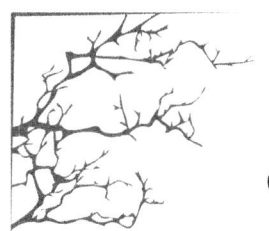

# Chapter 16

LaShaun spent twenty minutes reassuring Keishana. The young mother called D'Andre again anyway, only to learn Zee still wasn't with him. LaShaun told her they'd find Zee; that she was probably hiding out somewhere else. She put as much optimism in her voice as she could muster. D'Andre chafed at not being able to leave work. Keishana got so upset both of her kids started to whine and cry. LaShaun had to talk Keishana and D'Andre down from panic mode. She convinced both young people not to take impulsive action that wouldn't help and might well make things worse. At least she hoped they were convinced. Finally, after the cousins promised they'd call her or Savannah if Zee got in touch, LaShaun went home. She pulled up just as Chase and the kids arrived home from the zoo. After a brief exchange, Chase left to follow up with his deputies. Juggling messages, not letting her own anxiety show, and fixing snacks drained LaShaun of energy after an hour. Jonah arrived to provide a welcome distraction for the kids. Both squealed with delight when he walked into the kitchen. After the initial excitement, Ellie went to her room to play. CJ sat with his bowl of apple slices in front of the television watching an episode of Ada Twist.

"Nothing new on Zee," Jonah said, keeping his voice low. "At least not from our end. Your sheriff's department isn't sharing info with us."

"Chase sent a deputy to interview both her cousins. Zee wouldn't go to any other relatives like her grandmother said. Keishana lost her mother and grandmother to Covid within three years. D'Andre was raised by his grandparents but Zee isn't that close to them. Very strict and religious. They'd probably turn her in."

LaShaun paced the kitchen as she talked. She chopped onions, bell peppers, and celery on a wooden cutting board. Then she seasoned chicken parts and put them in Monmon Odette's deep cast iron skillet to brown. Fixing the evening meal was LaShaun's normal routine; expected by Ellie for sure. She didn't want her precocious little psychic to catch on just yet that something was wrong. Plus, the busy work helped LaShaun manage her anxiety and think.

"Manny went to her grandmother's house just in case. He'll hang out there. You never know."

"Speak of the devil, did Manny vision anything at Karlene's place?" LaShaun turned the chicken over. Then she filled the rice cooker and turned it on.

"Fond memories of hot sex in her queen-sized bed," Jonah wisecracked. He grinned at her heated look of admonishment.

"You know what I meant," LaShaun snipped.

"Nothing to give us more insight about why Pattison focused on Zee. She was good at keeping secrets." Jonah bit into an apple from the bowl of fruit on the kitchen Island.

"Well, we know she was a Legion confederate. No psychic ability. Zee would have probably sensed if she had. Pretty clever on their part."

"Yeah, and Pattison had her own 'troubled teen' history. Though she didn't mention prison time in Cali. Bright Futures is liberal about giving people opportunities, but they draw the line at major felonies."

"California. Prison." LaShaun gasped when a sharp stab of electricity raced up her arms. She almost dropped her grandmother's green ceramic bowl.

"Hey, careful. Isn't that an antique or something?" Jonah pointed to the bowl.

"Zee's mother went to California and served time there." LaShaun put the bowl down with a thump. "Get your tablet. Find out which prison Karlene was in. Zee's mother is Isabelle Glapion. She also uses two other aliases."

Jonah put down the apple. He crossed to his backpack hanging on the coat rack. "California is a big state with has thousands of women in prison. The chances of them knowing each other is a long shot."

"I'm psychic remember?" LaShaun quipped. She winked at him when he glanced up.

Jonah chuckled to himself. The screen of his smart tablet blinked on. He rubbed his chin for a few seconds. He brought out a silicon Bluetooth keypad. His fingers alternated between using the touch screen and typing. Meanwhile LaShaun put fresh green beans in a large saucepot to cook. Then she mixed up cornbread from scratch. She made gravy with pan drippings from the chicken, poured it over the meat and covered the skillet. The scent of home cooking filled the house. Shadows lengthened as the afternoon wore on. Darkness would soon follow, complicating the search for Zee. LaShaun worked to keep her mind clear of worry. She did a bit of cleaning up as she went; a practice she inherited from Monmon Odette. Then she went back to the check on the green beans. Bits of smoked ham would give them the traditional Southern soul food flavor. She stirred the pot in circles, her mind far outside the kitchen. Ellie's voice startled LaShaun out of deep thought.

"Where is Zee, Mama?"

Jonah paused in mid-swipe on the tablet screen. His gaze went from Ellie to LaShaun. Then he looked at the tablet. CJ seemed to have sensed something was brewing. He marched up to stand next to his sister.

"I'm not sure, but she's okay. A lot of people are trying to help her," LaShaun replied with care. She let go of the spoon and knelt to be eye level with Ellie. "I need you to trust me about Zee and not worry."

CJ looked from his mother to Ellie and back again. "Biscuits?"

"No, sweetie. I made cornbread." LaShaun ruffled his sandy brown tight curls.

"Okay." CJ grabbed Ellie's right hand with his left one. "Okay, Ellie."

The children looked at each other, nodded and walked away. LaShaun heaved a sigh as she watched them leave. Both now sat in front of the television. Every few moments they shared a whispered exchange.

"Well, that wasn't weird at all," Jonah murmured after a few minutes.

LaShaun scowled at him but said nothing. Instead, she went back to preparing dinner. Her sixth sense had told her she'd be feeding a larger crowd than usual. Which is why she'd cooked in the largest pots and pans she had. Her prediction came true. First, Chase arrived. Their children rushed him with whoops of celebration that Daddy was back. CeeCee arrived a few minutes later. Chase managed to extricate himself from the kids. After a curt greeting all around to the adults, he headed to their main suite. CeeCee and Jonah exchanged a glance as they watched him go.

"He's not happy about whatever he found out," Jonah mumbled to no one in particular. He went back to concentrating on his digital search for answers.

"I'm waiting for news. I won't say more until I get confirmation," CeeCee added when Jonah and LaShaun started to ask questions at the same time. She sniffed the air. "In the meantime, I'm hungry. Chicken with gravy, cornbread, and green beans."

"That supernatural nose of yours is on target again," LaShaun replied with a chuckle.

CeeCee's main gift was picking up on scents even the sensitive noses of animals missed. Especially if the supernatural was involved. LaShaun patted her shoulder and tended to their dinner.

"Yeah, well, I wish I could follow trails like a psychic bloodhound. I'd find that missing girl for you."

LaShaun's expression went somber. "How the hell did TEA staff at H&H let her get away?"

"That's exactly what I'm trying to find out," CeeCee said with a grunt. She started to say more but broke off when Chase returned.

"We're still searching for her. Hell, she might be all the way to Baton Rouge by now," Chase announced as he entered from the hallway. Dressed in old jeans and a long-sleeved t-shirt, his hair was still damp from a quick shower.

"Find any blood in the Subaru?" CeeCee asked. When LaShaun and Jonah gasped in unison, CeeCee held up both palms. "We were all thinking it."

"I was trying not to," LaShaun said quietly. She shuddered at the thought of a young life cut short. "I can't pick up any extrasensory vibration about where she is or if she's okay."

"Yeah," Jonah replied in a glum tone.

"How did you know about the vehicle?" Chase sent a scowl in LaShaun's direction.

"I haven't had time to tell them," LaShaun protested.

When Chase gave her a stony look, CeeCee shrugged. "Police scanner. I heard about the abandoned car when a deputy called it in."

"No obvious bloodstains," Chase replied. He sat down and blew out a long sigh. "We cleared the boyfriend in Tranicia Banks' murder. He has a solid alibi for the approximate time of death. He was being questioned by the Iberia Sheriff's Office in a series of burglaries. Check your messages. I sent you a photo of weird items we found in the house where she lived. Actually, squatted, since it's abandoned. The owner died four years ago with no heirs."

Jonah closed the window on his tablet screen. "Here. You can see it bigger."

He tapped the attached file in his secure message app.

A tattered carpet had been pulled back from the hardwood floor. The familiar circle with a triangle inside had been drawn in red. Symbols were carved into the wood in the spaces along the triangle. Jonah frowned at the items. LaShaun shrugged when Chase looked a question at her.

"Shit. They knew," CeeCee said. She rubbed a hand over her face.

Chase "Okay, what the—"

"I washed both my hands," CJ said as he rushed in. "Ready to eat."

"I made you do it, CJ. And his face. Boys are so dirty." Ellie, on his heels, wrinkled her nose in disgust. Then she glanced at Jonah's tablet.

"Hey, I'm starving, too, buddy. I'll follow your excellent example and clean up." Jonah stood and tucked the tablet under one arm as he spoke.

"The powder room is the door to your left, right before the laundry room," LaShaun put in.

Ellie jumped in front of Jonah to block his path. "Why are you taking the computer? It's going to get wet. I'll hold it."

"Nah, but thanks. I just..." Jonah mumbled something indistinguishable as he stepped around her.

"Ellie, help me by cutting up the cornbread," LaShaun said. She moved over to Ellie and guided her to the island again. "First, let it cool a bit more. I just took it out of the oven. But here is the butter knife you can use."

Chase stood. "Wow, I forgot about the king cake. I got one with a praline and cream cheese filling. Left it in the truck. C'mon, CJ. Let's get it."

"Yay, cake!" CJ jumped up and down a few times before he followed his father through the kitchen door.

"You know what? I've never been to Mardi Gras parades in Louisiana. But Trinidad, what a party. The costumes and music are amazing," CeeCee chattered on.

LaShaun gave her a grateful look as she talked about Trinidad and Tobago carnival traditions. Ellie nodded politely as CeeCee talked, but LaShaun knew her daughter well. They'd only succeeded in delaying her inevitable pointed questions. Thankfully, Ellie's telepathy hadn't grown past their abilities. LaShaun, CeeCee, and Jonah could put up psychic shields. Along with distractions, they could keep Ellie from "seeing" more than they wanted. For now.

For the next two hours, the adults worked hard at talking about anything other than police or TEA business. CJ seemed not to notice anything. He was thrilled to be surrounded by family. Not to mention the promise of cake if he ate enough of his dinner. He nibbled on a chicken leg and even stuffed green beans in his mouth. LaShaun cautioned him to slow down. Ellie stole glances at Jonah and CeeCee as if trying to figure out a puzzle. Beeping notifications on cell phones and Jonah's tablet only heightened her interest. They found excuses to step away and check the incoming messages. Then it was time to get the kids ready for bed, which made LaShaun let out a muted sigh of relief.

"I'll handle CJ. Ellie is all yours. I'm not psychic, so she'll crack me like a peanut," Chase whispered to LaShaun.

"You're easily wrapped around Ellie's little finger without her using telepathy." LaShaun smothered a laugh when Chase hissed in protest.

"Whatever. Anyway, I don't have anything popping off on my end. But look at the faces on those two." Chase tilted his head toward CeeCee and Jonah. Both of them wore tense expression.

LaShaun exchanged a look with him and then turned to Ellie. "Okay, then. Time to get ready for bed. I'm glad you had fun today with Daddy."

For another forty minutes or so, LaShaun kept up talk about anything but Zulime Glapion. She could feel Ellie's craving to ask questions. LaShaun managed to soothe her anxieties without giving details. Repeated assurances that Auntie Savannah was working hard to clear Zee mollified Ellie. For the moment at least. LaShaun got Ellie tucked beneath her unicorn-decorated covers and returned to the family room.

"We put up the food and loaded the dishwasher," CeeCee said as she dropped down on one of two matching recliners. "Well, I did. Jonah's been on his tablet. What exactly is he looking for?"

"To see if Karlene Pattison was in prison with Zee's mother," LaShaun replied. She sank into the soft leather of the sofa.

CeeCee glanced at Jonah, who sat at the kitchen island swiping the screen. "Damn, another plot twist."

Chase came in and sat next to LaShaun. "CJ's down for the night. He kept asking about cake, juice, or whatever excuse to get out of bed. I used drastic measures."

"Strong cough syrup," CeeCee said, her eyes on the screen of her cell phone.

"Geez, no! Never have kids, CeeCee," Chase said with a grunt.

"Not planning on it, Big Chief," CeeCee tossed back.

"I let Beau climb in his trundle bed. Being curled up next to that dog is like a sleeping pill." Chase yawned and stretched out his long legs.

"I'm going to keep an eye out to make sure Ellie doesn't tiptoe in on us to eavesdrop." LaShaun looked toward the hallway as if expecting to see their daughter.

"Relax, I checked. She's in her room. I hung her favorite stuffed bear on the door. The one with a bell around its neck. We'll know if she starts creepin'," Chase replied.

"Kind of sneaky," CeeCee said.

"Sneaky is a necessary child-rearing tool," Chase quipped. Then he crossed his arms and gazed at CeeCee steadily. "Speaking of sneaky, tell us what TEA has been up to; and don't deny it."

"Hey, bud. You're supposed to be in bed. Ok, I'll tell you one ghost fairytale; that's it," Jonah said quietly.

"What the..." LaShaun stood, hand on one hip.

"Don't worry, Mama. I'll handle it." Jonah waved her away. Then he took CJ by the hand and led him down the hall to his bedroom.

"No scary stories, Jonah. He'll be up with nightmares," LaShaun called after them.

"Actually, CJ enjoys them. Must be in his DNA," Chase put in. He patted the sofa cushion. "Sit down so CeeCee can tell us what she knows. I have a feeling this is going to be good."

LaShaun sat down as CJ's delighted giggle floated back to them. "Stop being so suspicious."

"Well..." CeeCee fidgeted with her phone for a few moments. "Okay, I wasn't told until this morning. I had no part in it."

"Spill the tea, pun intended." LaShaun raised both eyebrows at her friend.

"Let's start with the weird items found in Tranicia Banks' house. My murder case with no suspect," Chase said.

"The symbol is used to cause harm. Superstition mostly, but the items in the center draw psychic energy as a signal to identify a traitor. Basically, Legion uses it as a dog whistle to take the person out."

"Does it work? Sounds like a text would be more effective," Chase said with a snort of scorn.

"Legion is even more secretive than TEA, which is saying something," CeeCee muttered. "Anyway, not all of their agents or non-psychic confederates know each other. But they recognize the symbol. And texts, phone calls, and DMs leave a trail."

"A pig's heart with a big hatpin stuck in it," LaShaun murmured.

"Not a pin." CeeCee brought up the photo on her phone. She enlarged the image and pointed to it.

Chase sat forward to stare at the screen. "Like a small filet knife. But I've never seen one with that kind of handle."

"Looks homemade. Bone carved with images of death and Arioch, the demon of vengeance." CeeCee a grim expression as she swiped to make the image normal again. '

"Tranicia's cover was blown and a hit was put out on her. TEA found another Legion infiltrator?" LaShaun asked.

"Okay, this is where it gets complicated." CeeCee put her phone on the coffee table. She continued to gaze at it for a few moments.

"Sure it is. We're dealing with wizards and hocus-pocus," Chase muttered. He shrugged when LaShaun slapped his thigh.

"Shush and let her tell it," LaShaun said.

"A reporter started following Tranicia around. She thought Neesha was part of a cult with roots in Indiana, of all places. But they were Neesha's assignment and she confirmed they're crazy but harmless. Not part of Legion at all. But this woman saw Tranicia use a TEA device and got curious. So, she switched her focus. Followed her to New Orleans and a new case." CeeCee avoided LaShaun's gaze. She picked up her phone but didn't tap the screen to open it.

LaShaun studied her friend for a few moments. A tingle down her back and along her arms validated her psychic instinct. "TEA kidnapped Darrah Radcliff to keep her from reporting what she knew."

"Who?" Chase glanced at LaShaun with a puzzled frown.

"Not kidnapped. Exactly. She was invited to get an interview for her story," CeeCee said.

"You mean she was lured with the promise of an exclusive; something that would be a viral sensation. And then not allowed to leave," LaShaun shot back. She squinted at CeeCee in disapproval.

"Will somebody tell me what is going on?" Chase said.

Before either woman could speak, Jonah rushed in. He waved a piece of art paper with scribblings on it in colored pencil. "The key to the encrypted algorithm. CJ had it all along. The kid is a gold mine!"

"What the hell..." Chase stood and threw up both hands.

"Keep your voices down. We finally got the children to bed," LaShaun made a shushing sound at Jonah and Chase.

"Nothing but fate. When I took CJ back to his room I found the answer. He broke down the key, well the string of 'em, that unlocks the encryption." Jonah kissed the childish drawing and grinned at them all.

"I'm so confused right now." Chase rubbed his jaw hard as he stared at Jonah.

Ellie says CJ snuck into her room to play with her things. He found Zee's unicorn. Obvious he 'read' it, got signals or whatever he does. We really should let the folks in R&D chat with him. What a wonderful boy!" Jonah studied the drawing again.

"Research and Development at TEA," CeeCee explained before Chase could ask. "I'm confused, too."

"The mini-SD card with info. Encrypted. Jonah has been trying to crack it. We weren't sure it had anything to do with... anything. Your case or the murders," LaShaun said.

"CJ doesn't know what these code strings mean. He just drew a picture of what he saw when he touched the unicorn. Pretty shapes to him; answers to me. I'm going to crack that fancy encryption like an egg." Jonah strode to his tablet on the kitchen island.

"Who did you tell?" LaShaun said as she followed him.

"Huh?" Jonah was already engrossed in his task. He didn't even glance at LaShaun or the others.

"Did tell any of the tech heads at TEA about the card to help you break it? Jonah, this is important. They're holding Darrah Radcliff. Karlene might have taken it from the reporter. If she's managed to get a lot of information TEA doesn't want out..." LaShaun spun to face CeeCee.

"We're not Legion," CeeCee replied in a heated tone. "Not one official would approve such a drastic option."

"TEA has been in turmoil with radical factions fighting for power. They favor nuclear solutions to problems," LaShaun countered.

Jonah gave them his attention. He continued to hold CJ's drawing as if it was a delicate treasure. "I knew about the reporter. I'm still a counterintelligence operative inside the criminal division."

"A crime has been committed, so I'm gonna need you to give me the details." Chase swept a gaze around at the others. His casual attire contrasted with the stern cop stance he took.

"No, no. Ms. Radcliff is fine," Jonah protested.

"Being held captive is against the law. I hope you weren't on the team that snatched her," Chase barked.

Jonah blinked at him. "Whoa, everybody calm the hell down. She went to the Houston unit voluntarily. She's staying at one of the on-site cottages having a grand time. She hasn't tried to leave. So, technically she's not 'kidnapped' yet. I mean, they'll stop her if..." Jonah's voice trailed off as Chase's expression turned to stone as he talked. "It's not as bad as it sounds?"

"Mama, go get Zee. She needs you." Ellie stood barefoot in the kitchen in pink pajamas.

"Yeah, on the bayou," CJ piped up.

"You have got to be kidding me," Chase blurted out. "Both of you; to your rooms. Now!"

"But Daddy—"

"Joëlle." Chase stared down at both of his offspring. The fire in his dark Cajun eyes sent the message without another word.

"Yes, sir," Ellie said low. She grabbed her baby brother by one hand. "C'mon, CJ. They don't want to hear how Zee is near the bayou and the bad people are holding her. Not far from her great-granny's old house."

"Old house," CJ echoed and yawned.

A series of ringtones went off. LaShaun went to her cell phone on the kitchen counter. CeeCee looked at hers. Jonah checked the message app on his tablet. All three read silently for a few seconds. Jonah closed the tablet and went to his backpack. CeeCee zipped up her leather jacket to prepare against the chilly February night. LaShaun started to speak but Chase held up a palm to stop her.

"Something supernatural is going down and you three intend to jump right in." Chase spun around and marched in the same direction as the children.

"Hey, don't leave without me," LaShaun said to CeeCee and Jonah.

Then she raced after Chase to their main suite. LaShaun glanced around but didn't see him. He was already in the walk-in closet getting dressed. She entered as he was about to put on a heavy flannel jacket over the t-shirt.

"Honey, listen to me. Ten seconds." When Chase squinted at her before continuing to get dressed, she blew out a harsh breath.

"Two words. Police business." Chase pulled down the sweatpants and grabbed a pair of blue jeans. "Ten seconds up."

"Call it in. We'll give you the location. Let one of your deputies meet us out there," LaShaun replied.

"I'm not going to—"

"We can't get a babysitter at this time of night."

Chase searched for his favorite pair of warm boots. He muttered a curse word. "Can't find shit when you need it."

"Chase." LaShaun barked his name and grabbed him by one muscular arm.

"Yeah, no babysitter. I heard you. A good reason why their *mother* should be here with them. While Daddy goes out to do his job."

"Seriously; did you just spout patriarchal bullshit?" LaShaun's eyes flashed fire as she glared at him.

"Okay, that didn't come out right..." Chase huffed in exasperation. "Finding criminals and rescuing victims is my career."

Jonah appeared in the doorway. "Hey, guys. The clock is ticking. Manny says he needs backup and we got a ride ahead of us. Excuse the interruption, but we gotta move. Nice main suite, by the way. I forget how big this house is—"

"What is going on back here? Look, I'm leaving. Jonah, follow me. LaShaun can catch up later." CeeCee jerked a thumb as a signal for Jonah to comply with a command.

"Sure, everybody come right on in," Chase grumbled.

"I wasn't going to yell from the kitchen and wake the kids," CeeCee replied, already looking at her phone again. She slid it into a padded pocket of her jacket and zipped it shut. She slapped Jonah's right shoulder. "Go time."

CeeCee strode away without looking back. Jonah glanced at LaShaun and Chase, waved good-bye, and followed her. LaShaun faced her husband with a determined frown on her face. Chase's handsome face set into an equally stubborn expression.

LaShaun took a step to him until they almost touched. "What's happening out on Blood Bayou involves Legion. Those guys at Mrs. Vidal's house the other night weren't 'normals.' And they're after more than money."

"LaShaun..."

"Listen to me. Everyday crime and criminals are your territory. Paranormal crooks are *mine*. Stay here with the kids. We'll keep you in touch at every step." LaShaun placed both hands on his broad shoulders as she gazed up at him.

Chase stared at her for a few seconds before he hissed a sigh. He took off the shirt. "Frequent updates."

"Absolutely."

LaShaun kissed him on the chin before she spun around. She quickly found her waterproof boots. She grabbed her favorite jacket with all of the pockets for her weapons; an antique knife and derringer. She took both from a box on an upper shelf, ready in record time; cell phone in hand. Beau trotted in and gave a soft woof as if he knew what was happening.

"You hid my boots to slow me down, didn't you?" Chase eyed her with suspicion.

"They're in the laundry room where you always keep them," LaShaun replied as she left the closet. Beau trotted after beside her.

"You could have mentioned that while I was looking," Chase whispered as he followed her down the hall. He paused to look in each bedroom before taking long strides to catch up.

LaShaun paused at the door and rubbed Beau's back. "Okay, boy. You're coming along."

"Honey, wait."

"Yeah?" LaShaun looked into his eyes. He wore an intense expression. She felt his energy pounding, the adrenaline rush he felt when in cop mode with danger ahead. His itch for action competed with his strong paternal drive.

"Kick ass." Chase gave her a quick hug before he stood back.

"Just for you, sweet thing." LaShaun winked, blew him a kiss, and was out the door.

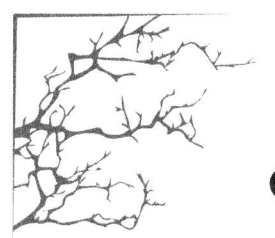

# Chapter 17

Trees and shrubs crowded the two-lane highways on either side of the SUV. They appeared as murky shadows like disinterested onlookers watching her journey. Darts of light winked in the deep darkness of night. Lightning bugs or fifolet? No way to tell. Both would cast magical glows against the almost black rural landscape. She could only pray what seemed to follow her were the little insects with built-in lamps. Fifolet could be friend or foe in a quest depending on their mercurial mood.

LaShaun kept up a running cryptic conversation via cell phone as she drove. CeeCee and Jonah had made good on their head start. They were already at the location Manny had sent them; an isolated spot not far from an old fishing and hunting shack on the bayou. The season was over, luckily, so they would not run into hunters. Manny's Cajun accent, made deeper by excitement, joined their group conversation. A secure mobile voice chat app insured their communication couldn't be monitored. So far Chase had only listened without comment. CeeCee issued instructions that no doubt matched what he would be doing. After all, CeeCee had military and police training.

"Manny, you maintain your position. I'll approach from the east; Jonah from the west. LaShaun..." CeeCee paused.

"I'll let Manny introduce me since they contacted him," LaShaun replied.

"Yeah, they found out I was her boo, so they figure I've got what they want. Saw me comin' an goin' at her place. These must be fairly new at this, or they're idiots," Manny explained again for LaShaun's benefit.

"Don't assume, Manny. They might know you're with us," CeeCee cautioned.

"Capturing a TEA agent and getting the drive would really be a win for 'em," Jonah agreed, his voice low through the speaker.

"I don't think these flunkies are that smart." Manny's words came out around labored breathing. "Okay. Waiting on you, sis."

"Almost there," LaShaun said.

Her headlights swept the surroundings as LaShaun turned the CRV. She switched them off. Then she backed up so that the front faced the way to the paved road. The dirt track leading into the woods seemed well maintained. Wide enough to accommodate two vehicles, it ran east to west and connected to Highway 35. LaShaun got out of her Honda. She pushed the driver door shut quietly after Beau jumped to the ground The big dog brushed against her thigh. To her surprise, Beau didn't race off into the woods. Instead, he trotted with her as she walked. She patted the pockets of her jacket. The solid outlines of her weapons reassured her. Beau's soft woof reminded LaShaun that he had her back as well.

"Manny and LaShaun do all the talking from here on," CeeCee said. A soft chime signaled she'd ended the call.

LaShaun turned off the speaker function on her phone. Then she inserted the Bluetooth bud into her ear. "Where are you, Manny?"

"To your right," he murmured.

She looked in that direction. A soft blue shimmer appeared. Her eyes adjusted until she saw his silhouette. LaShaun walked toward him, careful to make as little noise as possible. When she got close to Manny, she saw he had a small LED light on his jacket.

"Neat, huh? One of the buttons. You can see it, but nobody behind me can," Manny said. He touched his jacket and the light winked off. "This gal at the TEA tech unit fixed it up for me."

LaShaun grunted. "A woman. Figures. Okay, what's the plan?"

"We got us a little problem." Manny turned to gaze at the shack.

"More than one, dude," LaShaun clipped.

"Pretty sure these are the same clowns we ran into at Mama Vidal's place. Which means they'll likely recognize you," Manny replied, ignoring her sarcastic dig.

"You, too."

"Nah, I didn't get up close and personal like you. Girl, you beat their asses. So, here's what we do. I don't announce I'm here. I was too much of wimp to come but sent you alone. I told 'em you've got the goods; that Zee and her granny confided in you. Believable since your reputation precedes you in these supernatural streets." Manny jerked his head toward the house. "You're on, sis."

"Gee thanks." LaShaun took in a deep breath and let it out.

"I got your back," Manny replied, his voice no more than a whisper on the wind.

"Thanks."

LaShaun glanced at him only to find empty space. She shivered against the cold, damp country air. A sharp breeze whipped through the leaves. The thought of how terrified Zee must feel propelled her forward. Yellow light came from both windows on either side of the front door of the shack. It swung open and a figure appeared. Female. As LaShaun got closer the woman spoke.

"Stop right there. Who all you brought?"

"Yance said you'd hurt the girl if I told anybody. I'm alone," LaShaun replied. True since she realized that at some point Beau had vanished.

"He sent you way out here all by yourself. Typical lame ass dude," the woman said.

"Hey!" a male voice growled from deeper inside the dwelling.

"We'd have found it if you hadn't screwed up at the old woman's house. Let a little granny get the best of you," the woman retorted without turning around. She kept her gaze on LaShaun.

"You was in charge. Guess who they gonna blame?" came the gruff reply.

The woman grimaced as the sharp truth hit home. Legion had a reputation for being brutally unforgiving when it came to failure. LaShaun hoped the others could hear the exchange. Tension between their foes might be exploited. Eager to get inside to see if Zee was okay, LaShaun ignored the weak spot. For now. The gun in the woman's hand waved. When they were inside, a thin man with pale skin and eyes stood near table. He picked up a pistol from it.

"Move real slow. Keep your hands out from your sides. No sudden moves or tricks." The woman took backward steps as she gestured for LaShaun to approach.

LaShaun followed her instructions. "I want to see Zulime; make sure she's okay."

"And I want a beach mansion in the Bahamas and a full-time maid," the woman shot back. She grazed LaShaun from head to toe with an appraising eye.

"Point is, you ain't got no wants here, missy."

"Something don't seem right, Gina," the man muttered, his voice pitched low. His gaze darted to the door, to LaShaun, and all around the room.

"Shut up, fool. What the hell wrong with you sayin' my name in front of her," the woman barked at him.

"Where is the child?" LaShaun cut into another round of bickering between the two.

I was told—"

"Hand it over," the woman snapped. She held out the free hand, palm up.

LaShaun needed time and a distraction. Her sixth sense felt Beau's energy as he circled the house a second time. A window had been cracked open to let in air. A fire was going in the fireplace for warmth, but smoke filtered into the room. She glanced at a closed door.

"Not until you show me the girl." LaShaun shook her head slowly.

"You can either hand over the SSD, bitch, or I can do this the hard way. Drop you where you stand and take it off you. Well, hard for you anyway." The woman seemed focused on a battle of wills with LaShaun.

"I... I don't have it on me. Left it in the truck. We can get it when I walk out with the girl." LaShaun made her voice shake; her words falter to suggest fear she didn't feel.

"Look, sis, this brave act ain't healthy for you or the girl. You wasn't dumb enough to walk in here without that drive," the woman yelled. She aimed as if ready to pull the trigger.

"Okay, okay. Calm down. I'm going to reach in my jacket. Don't shoot," LaShaun said.

"Humph, I thought so." The woman glanced at her companion with a smirk.

"Just let the girl go. You can keep me while you check the drive." LaShaun unbuttoned a jacket pocket. She took out the SSD card and held it up.

"Sure thing. Maybe we'll make you a cup of tea while we're at it." The woman laughed. Then her eyes narrowed to slits. "Put it on the table. Nice and slow movements. You don't want my finger to slip."

"Like I said, Zee can leave. I'll stay until I make sure I brought the real thing. I don't know anything about what's on it and I don't want to know." LaShaun looked at the closed door. She scanned the layout of the room. A galley kitchen was to her left. The house had more square footage than she expected.

"Why you so worried about the kid? You a relative or something?" The woman looked at the drive briefly and then at LaShaun again. She appeared less on edge now that she had the prize.

"There's gotta be a reason he sent her instead of coming. Maybe she's part of a setup." The man rubbed his dry bottom lip as he squinted at LaShaun.

"Yeah; the reason is Yance is scared. Can't count on him for a damn thing. I knew he was slippin' around with another woman. Then after the heffa got herself killed, here he come shakin' like a leaf begging me to help. He ain't much use, but he's mine," LaShaun said. "The girl is trouble. I know her family. If they even think Yance had anything to do with her gettin' hurt..."

"As usual, a woman gotta deal with the mess some man done screwed up. You shoulda left his ass long ago. Now you're in it too deep." The woman looked LaShaun up and down again. Then she turned to the man. "Bring the girl out."

"Finally. I'm ready to get out of these creepy swamps. So dark way out here feels like it'll swallow you up." The man blinked at LaShaun. "Something doesn't feel right."

"Stop whining and get the girl. We got one more walk through the woods to the bayou. Them gators gone eat good for breakfast." The woman's smiled twisted her face into a cruel mask.

"Wait a minute. I won't tell anybody," LaShaun said. She rubbed her hands against her thighs as if agitated.

"Yeah, we know you won't," the man said before he pushed through the door. Moments later he appeared dragging Zulime.

Her hands were tied in front of her. A second strong rope had been wound around her arms, pinning them to her side. LaShaun's gasp was genuine alarm when he grabbed a knife from a shelf on the wall. He reached down and cut the rope that bound Zee's ankles tight. Zee seemed dazed, drugged.

"What's wrong with her?" LaShaun took a step toward Zee but stopped when the woman pointed the gun at her.

"Gave her something to shut her up. She's got a mouth on her," the man grumbled. He jerked Zee and growled the semblance of a laugh when her head bounced.

"I wanna go home. Wanna see my grandmama." Zee's eyes fluttered open as the words slurred from her lips.

"Don't worry, kid. All your troubles will be over in a minute," The woman slipped the SSD card into a pocket of the jeans she wore. She buttoned it and grinned at LaShaun.

"You sure trusting of whoever you work for," LaShaun blurted to slow down the action.

"What's she talking about, Gina?" The man, one long hand hooked under Zee's armpit, struggled to hold her upright.

"Mama..." Zee slumped more, which forced him to strain at the dead weight.

"Stop staying my damn name, asshole!" The woman screamed. Then her jaw worked as she glared at him, apparently trying to master her temper. "Look, we had a job to do. We've got the damn thing. Now let's wrap up loose ends and get the hell out of here."

"Must be a lot of valuable leverage on that thing," LaShaun said. "Somebody wants it bad. Lot of power in knowing the right info."

The man's eyes glittered with greed. He looked at his partner. "She's got a point. They ain't going nowhere. We can look."

The woman studied LaShaun. A hostile scowl twisted what might have been an otherwise attractive face. "Sit the little bitch down and keep your gun on this one. She moves shoot the girl first, then her. I'll get the tablet from the SUV."

"Shit, girl. I thought you brought in with you. And you call me a fuckup." The man grimaced at Gina briefly. He shoved Zee roughly onto a chair.

"Shut it, asshole," the woman retorted.

"You shut up," the man snapped.

"You're both assholes. I figured out Karlene was lying over a month ago. She didn't know where my mama was. She didn't care," Zee blurted out. She swiped a tear from her cheek.

"And neither does anyone else. Your mama is useless. Not even good at being a street hustler," Gina spat.

Zee sniffed a few times as her expression hardened. "Oh yeah? You lost the drive after Karlene died. Matter of fact, you didn't even know she planned to take off; use it for herself. Bet your boss is going to chew your ass big-time."

"Keep talking and I'll shoot you right here," Gina snapped.

"Kill the kid? Wait a minute. They said—"

"We can't leave witnesses, fool. We got the drive. Pattison's dead, and we can still figure out how to get the land from the old woman. Now stay here." Gina stomped to the door. "They give you a problem, shoot 'em."

"Please let the girl go. You don't need her now that you've got the card

"Yeah, right," the man said with a grunt. He aimed the gun at LaShaun, but his gaze remained fixed on the door.

"Karlene was going to steal it. How do you know Gina won't do the same?"

"She won't." The man's jaw tightened as two minutes stretched to ten.

"Going to the car couldn't be taking this long. Was that an engine I heard starting?"

"If I have to tell you to shut your mouth one more time." He darted a threatening look at LaShaun and went back to staring at the door.

LaShaun watched him swallow hard. "At least you knew enough to check the drive. No telling what your bosses would say if you got the wrong thing."

"You better have brought the real card or it won't be good for you. At all." She flinched when Zee muttered something unintelligible.

"Or what they'll do if you let her take off with it," LaShaun went on.

Zee shifted in the rickety wooden chair. She whimpered. "Hurt."

"Yance is another loose end. If me and the girl disappear, he's bound to tell somebody. He can't keep quiet when he's running scared," LaShaun said. She spoke louder to cover the sound of thumps and rustling from outside.

"Then we'll take him out, too," the man replied. His gaze shifted to the window on his right. "I heard something—"

"I know him," LaShaun broke in, bringing his focus back to her. She flinched at the cold, dead look of his eyes but pressed on. "He's probably two states away by now. No telling who all he's blabbing to along the way."

"Shut up. I can't think with you yapping at me." The man glanced at Zee. "And stop that sniveling!"

"Let me go home." Zee wiped her eyes with one hand. Her voice hitched with terror.

"I'm gonna send you off alright," the man replied as he dug his fingers into Zee's shoulder. The gun never wavered from LaShaun.

"Oh, please." Zee started to hyperventilate.

"She's just a kid, man! What kind of a monster are you!" LaShaun shouted.

She darted a glance at Zee, who stared back at LaShaun. She didn't see terror in the girl's eyes. Calculation. Zee sobbed louder, pleas to be released. The man snarled profanity-filled threats. Sweat rolled down his forehead into his eyes. An animal howl pierced through the walls from outside; then a gunshot followed by a high-pitched scream of rage. LaShaun whispered a prayer for Beau's safety.

"Wolves!" the man rasped. "They're fighting it out. You got 'em, too."

Before LaShaun could process his exclamation, Zee slammed her body sideways into his groin. Then she managed to bring a knee up with enough force to make him squeal in agony. LaShaun closed the gap between them in seconds and grabbed the wrist of his gun hand. She sent a shock of psychic fire into his flesh. The gun landed in a corner. LaShaun and Zee attacked together until he lay in a heap, moaning. LaShaun had to drag Zee away.

"He's down, Zee." LaShaun lifted the teenager, legs still flailing, away from the man as he moaned.

"He put my gran in the hospital!" Zee shouted. She followed with a string of expletives in Louisiana Creole that would have made a street thug blush.

"He's going to jail." LaShaun panted with the effort to restrain Zee.

"Not good enough."

"I need to untie you and—"

Zee shook free of LaShaun's hold on her. Then she wiggled her shoulders. The rope around Zee's torso uncurled like a snake and slid to the floor. Zee held out her wrists. The binding around them loosened as well.

LaShaun gaped at them and then at Zee. "How did you…"

"He did it. I just helped him along." Zee nodded to where Jonah stood.

"I came through a back window in the second room." Jonah panted. "Looks like y'all took care of business in here."

"Stay with her; tie him up."

Jonah turned in a circle. "Who?"

"Damn it!" LaShaun looked at the corner where the man had been. He was gone and so was the gun he'd held.

"Hands up! Police!" The shout was followed by gunfire.

More shots echoed through the woods around them. Animal snarls and barking echoed around them. Beau seemed to be battling another canine. A big one. LaShaun's heart twisted at the thought of Beau bleeding alone in the dark. She raced past Jonah.

"LaShaun, wait a—"

Jonah's protest bounced off LaShaun. She followed the battle noises, dodging tree trunks as she ran. She pulled the pistol out with one hand; her knife with the other. The words "loup garou" clanged in LaShaun's head as she ran. A scent of rank animal fur assaulted her nostrils as she passed a large swamp pine. She reached a clearing and slid in the mud to a halt. Beau snarled as he circled a large beast. LaShaun's body tingled hard as if hot needles stabbed through her. The creature's jaws dripped pink; Beau's blood mixed with its spittle.

CeeCee appeared beside her. "I got the other one. Shit. That thing is huge."

Just as CeeCee spoke, the wolf reared up on hind legs; tall as a man, its howl filled with murderous fury. LaShaun ran to draw it away from Beau; derringer ready. She ignored warning shouts from CeeCee. The mongrel bore an almost human look of glee as its snout turned to LaShaun.

"I'm right here, you mangy sack of dog shit," LaShaun screamed, her own rage fueled by Beau's pain.

The wolf dropped to all fours, crouched for a second, and then ran straight for LaShaun. A weird hush enveloped the scene as it came toward her. Muffled yells and gunshots surrounded her, yet they seemed not to matter. Her limbs suddenly felt heavy as twin intense yellow eyes bored into her. LaShaun knew she should look away, but couldn't. Mesmerized, she watched it get closer; like seeing slow motion death. Her death. Then a familiar voice sounded in her head.

"Shoot, Mama. Shoot it!"

"Va te faire foutre!" a second, deep contralto voice rang out. ("Go to hell")

LaShaun shook free of the spell the thing had cast. She fired once. It kept coming. She tried to shoot again but the huge body sliced through the distance between them faster. The wolf came on as if propelled by an invisible force. LaShaun swung her left arm in an arc. The silver blade of her knife sank into the wolf's chest. She tumbled backward, knocked hard by the force of a huge body. Beau leaped forward, slamming into the wolf, and knocking it away from LaShaun. Her butt hit the ground first, but she held onto the derringer. Dazed, LaShaun managed to sit upright. She blinked hard as CeeCee fired another shot into the buff-colored hairy carcass.

Deputy Deborah Thibaut appeared at CeeCee's side. "Mon Dieu, that's one big-assed coyote. We ain't seen them around this part of Louisiana in years!"

CeeCee spun to face her. "A suspect is at the hunting cabin. And Zulime Glapion is there."

"He's down. Wouldn't follow my command. Some crazy stuff gone down out here." Deputy Thibaut started for LaShaun.

"I'm good. No cuts, no bruises. Go," LaShaun huffed out with effort. She tried to smile but grimaced instead.

"I've got her, ma'am," CeeCee added with a nod.

The deputy blinked confusion at CeeCee. "Who are you again?"

Chase's voice boomed from the speaker of Deputy Thibaut's two-way radio. "Hey, Deb. Rob has the girl safe. He needs backup,"

"Right, boss. On my way." Deputy Thibaut backed away from LaShaun and CeeCee with a puzzled frown. Then she set off at a jog toward the hunting shack.

LaShaun gestured for Beau to come closer. He limped to her. Gashes laced his front legs and one of his shoulders. "Oh, cher. We got to get you to the vet."

"Yeah, and you to the ER. And don't argue with me. I'm not in the freakin' mood." CeeCee gingerly helped LaShaun to her feet.

Manny strolled up. He slipped a hunting knife into a leather sleeve attached to his belt. Then he handed LaShaun her own, cleaned of blood. "Big fun on da bayou tonight. Eh, mes amies?"

"Sure. A real party," LaShaun said with a grunt.

She reached out to rub Beau's head. Then she called Chase to let him know she was okay. Of course, CeeCee had beat her to it. She gave him a condensed report anyway. Chase ordered LaShaun to follow instructions and get medical care.

"I will. After I make sure Beau is okay," LaShaun said. Chase sighed deeply but didn't argue. "Is Ellie asleep?"

"Snug and hugging her favorite teddy bear. I just looked in on them both," Chase replied. "Don't you worry about them. I'm holding down the home front."

"I knew you would," LaShaun replied with a smile. His deep voice soothed LaShaun's ragged nerve endings. She let out a long, slow breath.

"Okay, time for us to get everybody that needs patching up to a doc," CeeCee ordered. "We've got the girl and the data is secure."

"What did you tell the other deputies?" LaShaun looked at Jonah as they walked toward their vehicles.

"I said Zee managed to call you before they took her cell phone. We were having dinner at your house and came along to help while Chase called it in. Just two friends who happened to be in the right place at the right time." Jonah said.

"Humph, all true. Almost," LaShaun replied with a short laugh.

"I figured leaving out the stuff about psychics and Rougarou was advisable," Jonah replied with a wide grin.

"Great idea," CeeCee wisecracked. She held onto LaShaun to support her. "Adrenaline rush wearing off. Second time you've been in a fight in the past few days. You need to crash for a good week at least. We're not as young as we used to be."

"Hey, speak for yourself," LaShaun shot back. She winced at a sharp pain in one hip. Her body seemed eager to contradict LaShaun's declaration. "Maybe taking it easy is a good idea."

"You ladies are in fine form. Nowhere near ready for a rocking chair on the front porch." Jonah winked at CeeCee, who blushed but said nothing.

As the senior officer, Deputy Thibaut took charge. She directed two other deputies to tape off the crime scene. She reported to Chase and Sheriff Godchaux via cell phone. Thirty minutes later an emergency medical unit arrived. LaShaun, though annoyed by the fuss they made, didn't argue as they checked her out. She tried to protest that she could get into the outfitted emergency medical vehicle on her own. Her knees betrayed her by buckling within seconds when she stood. Her head spun as her a queasy sensation hit her in the midsection. After a brief bout of heaving, she had no choice but submit to the indignity of being lifted onto a gurney. The medical techs left to look after the suspects again. Jonah assured them he'd keep an eye on LaShaun.

"Where is Beau?" LaShaun sat up on her elbows to look around. She shood her head to clear away a dizzy spell.

"On his way to the De Ville Animal Hospital in Abbeville. The vet assistant is meeting our operative there. CeeCee called up reinforcements. Told Deputy Deb he's a family friend." Jonah used both hands on LaShaun's shoulders to ease her down again.

Deputy Thibaut approached as if on cue. "My pal Garrett with the state police in Lafayette came through. Got a trooper who lives in New Iberia out of bed. Nice guy."

"That's great." Jonah gave her a thumbs-up sign.

"Yeah. Too bad we won't be able to get answers from the male suspect. The EMT doesn't think he's going to make it," Deputy Thibaut added.

"Did what you had to," Jonah replied with a solemn nod.

"Uh-huh." Deputy Thibaut studied him in a silence for a few beats. "The girl says there was a woman. Where is she?"

LaShaun blinked when Deputy Thibaut looked at her when Jonah didn't answer right away. "CeeCee has her and—"

"She took off into the woods," Jonah cut in sharply. "Our other friend, CeeCee, chased her but I think she got away."

"Yeah," CeeCee yelled. She seemed to appear out of nowhere a few yards away. She bent over, hands on both knees, breathing hard. "Lost her in the dark. I'm guessing you can pick up her trail when it's light."

"You went after her around Blood Bayou. In the dark?" Deputy Thibaut raised an eyebrow. "You gotta have eyes like an owl."

"I grew up out in the country. Woods at night don't bother me," CeeCee replied without missing a beat.

"Is Zee okay? She's had such a traumatic time," LaShaun said.

"She's fine. Better send out an alert. Talk to folks who live around here. The suspect is probably looking for a way to run," Deputy Thibaut said.

"Smart idea," Jonah replied with another thumbs up at her.

"I've got a pretty good description from Zulime. Anything else y'all wanna tell me?" Deputy Thibaut looked at them each in turn with an air of expectation.

"No... I think that's it for now," Jonah piped up. He glanced at CeeCee.

"Not that I think of right now. Mind kinda scrambled from running around dodging trees and bushes." CeeCee wiped sweat from her brow and gave a tired smile.

"LaShaun needs to get thoroughly checked out by a doctor. Maybe x-rays or something." Jonah turned to LaShaun and patted her on one shoulder gently. "Pretty knocked around by those crazy kidnappers."

"Yeah." Deputy Thibaut studied him and CeeCee as if working out a puzzle in her mind. Before she could say more, her two-way handset went off. She waved a hand at them as she walked away to respond.

Jonah turned to CeeCee when Deputy Thibaut was a few feet away. He spoke quietly as he glanced around. "So, did you? Lose the woman, I mean. I just took a wild guess."

"Manny is handling it. I'm going to tell them she went east. Made a track that will lead them away," CeeCee replied softly. "Our local friend will clear up the real trail south toward the bayou."

"That thing was *her*?" LaShaun bolted upright without thinking. "I've never seen a—"

"Slow down. Your husband is taking care of the kids and you dog is just fine," Jonah said loudly. He leaned over LaShaun as he spoke, pushing her flat.

"Oof, hey! Take it easy!" LaShaun started to swat him away but CeeCee stepped forward

"Deputy Thibaut is right here. She's got things under control." CeeCee jerked her head to her right.

"Everything okay with y'all?" Deputy Thibaut strode up, the handset still in one hand as a voice came over it. One of the EMTs returned before they could answer.

The man approached, rubbing his hands for warmth against the chilly morning. "Okay. Acadian Ambulance responded to one suspect to the hospital. We sedated him so we won't have much of a problem."

"Did he say anything before?" Deputy Thibaut frowned at the EMT.

"He was in pain and getting agitated. Talking crazy about spirits and whatnot. If I was superstitious, I'd believe Blood Bayou had some kind of effect on him." The EMT gave a snort as he tapped a message into his smartphone.

"Dude is out of his head," Jonah replied.

"A bullet wound will do that to ya," the EMT agreed. Then he slipped his phone into a leather holster on his belt. He walked over to the gurney and looked at LaShaun. "Tell me your full name."

"LaShaun Rousselle Broussard," she replied dutifully. She sighed and closed her eyes. "So tired."

"Okay, let's get moving. I don't intend to stay on Blood Bayou in the dark alone." Deputy Thibaut scanned the shadowy landscape with a taut expression. Blue and red flashing lights from the official vehicles gave the oak, pine, and ash trees an alien appearance.

The EMT laughed and joked with her about believing ghost stories. LaShaun saw CeeCee and Jonah exchange a look. She wanted to question them but neither chose to ride with her to Abbeville General Hospital. LaShaun let out a slow breath as the doors of the EMT van thumped shut. She'd have to get answers later.

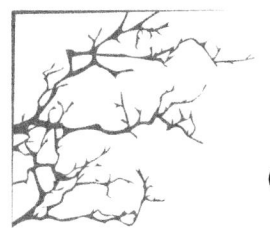

# Chapter 18

Despite feeling tired, LaShaun only dozed off once. The emergency room nurse practitioner, a woman of at least sixty, took charge. An IV had been inserted to prevent dehydration. She checked in with LaShaun frequently between trips to radiology, where x-rays and a CT scan were done. LaShaun refused pain medication when it was offered almost four hours later.

"You don't have to suffer, dear," the nurse said in a calming tone. "We didn't give you anything right off. Meds mask symptoms, and we need to know the level of pain and where you might be injured. The good news is, no broken bones. No signs of internal injuries. Of course, you're young and healthy."

As she talked, the nurse smoothed down the pillows behind LaShaun's head. Then she tucked a blanket up to LaShaun's chin as if she was a little girl. The woman, her skin a light brown, smiled down at her. Her dark hair was touched around the temples with silver. Despite being middle-aged, her plump face was smooth. She poured water into a cup and insisted LaShaun take a sip.

"Thanks so much. You've taken good care of me. I'm a little sore, but other than that I'm good." LaShaun smiled at her. Then she blinked hard into the kindly hazel eyes. "You remind me of..."

"Cher, I'm your second cousin once removed. I knew your mama, Francine. We went to high school together. She was a year ahead of me though. Oh, but that was so long ago. I can bring you my year book. Her photo is in there."

LaShaun's eyes filled with tears. She grabbed the woman's hand as she reached to take the cup away. "I would love that, and any stories you could tell me. My grandmother was the only one who talked about mama."

"Now, now. Don't you worry. I'll search this old rusty memory for you. I think a bit of something to help you sleep is in order."

The woman's soothing voice chattered on and eventually faded away. LaShaun felt a cool sensation and realized the nurse must have added a sedative to the IV. Her eyes drifted shut even though she tried to stay awake. Images of her mother and grandmother floated in her head. LaShaun tried to explain she didn't need medication, but the words seemed to drift away. Someone turned off the lights; or at least it seemed so. When she woke up, she was in a room and morning sunlight peeked around closed blinds over a window.

"Hey you." Chase rose from the chair next to the hospital bed.

"I'm ready to go home." LaShaun found the control device and lowered it.

"I'm not going to argue with you. The doctor says you're fine. Just waiting for you to wake up." Chase went to a locker-type cabinet and retrieved her clothes.

He helped her dress in the yoga pants and a top he'd brought from home. He talked to her about the kids, assuring her they'd had breakfast and gone off to her aunt's place. After a short checkout with firm instructions from the nurse, they left for home. Jonah and CeeCee were at their house when they arrived. The smell of coffee, sausages, and toast made LaShaun's stomach growl. All three fussed around, making sure LaShaun was comfortable. Beau watched the activity from his bed along one wall. He growled a complaint at LaShaun; probably about the cone around his neck.

"Settle down. It's for your own good," LaShaun said with a smile. She went to him and massaged his head. She laughed when two more woofs sounded like canine griping.

"Exactly what I was going to tell *you*," Chase put in. He walked over and led LaShaun to the dining table.

LaShaun grimaced at a twinge in her side. She eased onto one of the dining table chairs. "I'll rest once I hear the whole story. The woman's name is Gina—"

"Nelson," CeeCee put in. She set a plate of scrambled eggs in front of LaShaun. "Eat if you can. If not, I've made you a morning shake to sip. You threw up last night, so maybe solid food might be too much. Plus, you need the hydration."

"You went to medical school between TEA cases?" LaShaun quipped.

"With almond milk, banana, a bit of ginger, some vanilla, cinnamon, and turmeric. I added agave nectar, so it'll be right tasty," CeeCee continued, unbothered by her wisecrack.

Jonah chuckled when LaShaun squinted at her. "No, she's not a werewolf. Manny caught up with her. She actually had an airboat on the bayou ready for escape. Can you believe it?"

"Then what was that thing?" LaShaun pushed the eggs away and accepted a tall tumbler from CeeCee.

Jonah pulled the eggs to him and dug in. "Hmm, pretty good cook. You'll make someone a fine housewife one day."

"Bite me," CeeCee shot back. She sat across from them with a mug of coffee. "DNA will link one guy to the scene of Pattison's murder. We figure they followed her home from the hospital after treatment for the fight with Zee."

"Oh, and there's a partial print on one window in her bedroom. And at the scene where Tranicia was killed."

"Damn, they were busy. But why?" LaShaun eyed the shake with skepticism. Despite Jonah's joke, they all knew CeeCee was not the domestic type. Her stomach reminded LaShaun it was empty so she took a sip. "Umm-hum. Good."

"Don't sound so shocked," CeeCee clipped. "Anyway, we pointed Chase's department in the right direction."

"Thanks for stomping all over our jurisdiction," Chase put in. He sat next to LaShaun and put an arm around the back of her chair.

"You've wrapped up two murders. So, you're welcome," CeeCee replied with a smirk.

"To be fair, your people had the evidence. They simply needed suspects to match," Jonah said with a glance at CeeCee.

"Okay, that's true. But no way you would have found out those guys. We examined Tranicia's movements in New Orleans. Darrah Radcliff followed her there sniffing out a story. Karlene Pattison recognized Radcliff from her time on television."

"Which tipped her off that Tranicia might be TEA," LaShaun said.

"Tranicia was part of an incident that got too much media attention. Our Public Information Unit got involved, and the deaths were found to be just ordinary murders. NOPD and the Orleans Parish DA were satisfied," CeeCee said.

"You mean they scrubbed the magical stuff. Sounds more like the Public Disinformation Unit." Chase looked at LaShaun. He grunted when she shrugged.

"TEA doesn't push lies. We assure the safety of non-psychics by helping law enforcement catch human perpetrators. Like any sensitive agency, we do have levels of classified information. Also, we take into account what the public can when it comes to preternatural phenomena." CeeCee returned his steady gaze with one of her own. She was in full company woman mode.

"You rehearsed that speech for just such an occasion, didn't ya?" Chase grinned at CeeCee.

"Every word is true. Regular law enforcement withholds information from citizens every day of the week," CeeCee countered.

"Are you comparing a government body to—"

"Honey..." LaShaun squeezed his thigh and squinted a warning at him. She wanted to interrupt his potential use of a colorful description of TEA. "So, Darrah followed Tranicia to Beau Chene."

Jonah's mouth twitched as he looked at Chase and CeeCee staring each other down. "Ahem. Right, right. Darrah didn't buy statement put out by NOPD and the Orleans Parish DA."

"Karlene reported Tranicia's presence to Legion."

"And they decided to kill her," LaShaun said. "But why didn't TEA pull Tranicia out of the field?"

"By the time TEA found out it was too late. Tranicia was dead. Darrah contacted our dummy headquarters, the one which just looks like another crackpot group of pseudo-psychics. She didn't mention Tranicia at first," Jonah explained. "She's feeling a lot of guilt."

CeeCee nodded. "Legion agents were supposed to question Neesha, but the drugs didn't knock her out. She fought them but... well, she was outnumbered."

"But why kill Karlene?" Chase asked with a frown.

"Ah." Jonah rose from the table. He went to his backpack, took out the tablet, and returned to the table. "Karlene had a plan. She kept a secret file in case Legion tried anything against her."

"We think she stole it from a Legion commander. One she had an affair with a few years back," CeeCee added. "The drive had information about Legion operations in two states and Mexico."

"What does any of this have to do with Zulime Glapion?" Chase looked from CeeCee to Jonah.

"To Legion, Zee was just another assignment because her grandmother owns property on Blood Bayou," CeeCee put in before Jonah spoke. "Karlene heard stories about her and Mrs. Vidal from Isabelle Glapion. Working her way into Legion and a trip to Louisiana was a golden opportunity to use the girl."

"Right." Jonah put down the tablet. He stuffed toast with grape jam into his mouth.

"They're still stuck on the so-called magical mineral deposit?" Chase's handsome brow furrowed.

"Monazite is a potent and valuable substance. Crazy how our paths cross, but not surprising in a small town like Beau Chene. TEA and Legion are still interested in the stuff," Jonah said.

"Yeah." CeeCee raised the large mug and drank.

Chase cocked his head to one side as he examined CeeCee in silence for a few minutes. "Yeah but—"

His work cell phone went off before Chase could finish. He crossed the large kitchen to where it sat charging on the counter. The three of them watched him speak low into the phone. He stared back at them but then something said drew his attention away. Chase strode off to talk.

LaShaun turned to CeeCee "Quick, tell me the *whole* story."

"TEA classified."

CeeCee clicked her tongue when LaShaun glared at her "Fine. Zulime Glapion is a sub-power."

Her voice was so low LaShaun had to lean forward. "A what?"

"She can augment the psychic abilities of others." CeeCee glanced in the direction Chase had gone. "We think exposure to monazite over time kicked in her second ability."

"She's has more than one?" LaShaun blinked at her.

"She can see patterns ninety-nine percent of us miss. Including trained operatives. That's how the kid saw through Karlene Pattison. Who by the way planned to lure Zulime away with promises of seeing her mother," Jonah said.

"And use her abilities to her own advantage. I had a chance to talk to Zee. She's back at the H&H group home. Until her grandmother is released." CeeCee smiled. "Legion doesn't know Zulime is one in a million even among us. We're still three steps ahead of the bastards."

"Blood Bayou isn't the real prize after all," LaShaun said quietly.

"Radcliff is now an adjunct TEA member. She gets inside information. In turn, we let her release stories about supernatural incidents. Approved by the bosses, of course."

"And she's agreed to those conditions? She's got a reputation for not letting up when it comes to grabbing headlines. Ambition is her middle name," LaShaun said.

"Atonement for what happened to Neesha. She realizes lives could be in danger. Plus, loves having inside knowledge, but even she won't know everything," Jonah replied.

"But more than enough to keep her happy for years. Material for a bestselling book; or two," CeeCee added and then shrugged. "Not my choice. I would have had one of our psychic psychiatrists wipe her mind clean."

"CeeCee!" LaShaun gaped at her friend's casual statement. "That could leave her brains scrambled. Permanently."

"Yeah, well..." CeeCee sipped coffee, unperturbed by LaShaun's shocked reaction. "Not always."

"Anyway, the decision went a different way," Jonah went on. "And she gets to show up James Schaffer. Turns out he's stabbed her in the back a few times. I hear she plans to feed him leads and then debunk them. He's already left Beau Chene chasing one."

"I love it. Gonna make him look like the fool he is. So, maybe your bosses did make a better decision." LaShaun gave CeeCee a pointed look.

"Humph." CeeCee's face said she wasn't convinced. She got up and made herself a slice of toasted French bread.

"Well, at least I don't have to worry about Rougarou running around the swamps," LaShaun said with a sigh.

"Hmmm..." Jonah exchanged a look with CeeCee.

"You said the woman wasn't one." LaShaun looked from Jonah to CeeCee and back again. "Louisiana is known for coyotes with red wolf DNA. An unusually big coyote or maybe, though rare, a wolf."

"I said Gina Nelson wasn't a lycanthrope. I didn't say there wasn't one on the scene last night," Jonah said.

"Wait, so what I shot..." LaShaun's eyes went wide.

"And stabbed with a silver knife, both of which stopped it dead. Literally," Jonah said.

"And Manny stayed behind to clean up so the deputies wouldn't find the carcass. Speak of the devil," LaShaun murmured.

"Huh?" Jonah gave her a puzzled look.

"My abuela used to say it all the time. You're too young to know the old saying. Speak of the devil and up he pops. The more you talk about evil, the more it shows up basically." CeeCee returned to the table and sat. She piled fig preserves on her toast and munched.

"En parlant du diable, on voit sa queue." LaShaun remembered the sound of her grandmother's voice as she said the words.

"Yeah, well, folks around Beau Chene must be talking about him and his minions a whole lot. Supernatural shenanigans always popping off around here," Jonah wisecracked.

"Evil seeps to every part of the world, Jonah," LaShaun said.

Chase strolled back in and sat next to LaShaun again. "Zulime is going to be released. Poor Dave will have a hell of a time explaining the supernatural side of this whole mess."

"What do you mean?" Jonah put on an innocent face.

"Secret files on psychics, magical minerals, and Blood Bayou." Chase shook his head. "I can hear him yelling at me already when I dropped the bomb."

CeeCee cleared her throat loudly. "Nope. Zulime became close to Karlene and discovered her mentor hadn't given up her criminal ways."

"Identity theft using her employer's internet access to government servers. Government-funded social service do digital reporting and billing, you know. That's what's on the card we recovered," Jonah added.

"Oh, and drugs will be found at the hunting shack." CeeCee cleared her throat when Chase looked at her.

"So that's how you're going to play it?" Chase squinted at CeeCee and Jonah in turn.

"You caught the killers," CeeCee pointed out.

"And no 'wizard stuff' to explain or bring James Schaffer running back to Beau Chene." Jonah grinned back at Chase and polished off the last of his eggs.

"Two perps. One dead and one missing," Chase said.

"Umm, meant to tell you. Manny says Gina fell in the bayou. I don't think she made it out," Jonah mumbled through his mouthful. He gulped from a glass of apple juice.

"Yeah. We told Deputy Thibaut so your people will be dragging it. Time to go. Wizards or not, we still got paperwork to complete." CeeCee tapped Jonah's shoulder as she stood.

"Hey, Chase. Thanks for the hospitality, bro."

Jonah gave Chase a thumbs up as he followed CeeCee to the door. He paused to give Beau a farewell back rub. The TEA agents waved good-bye and were gone. Chase stood, hands on his narrow waist. He scowled at the door as it shut behind them.

The roar of CeeCee's Range Rover engine followed as they drove away. He stomped to the window to watch them. LaShaun finished the delicious morning shake CeeCee had made.

"All's well that ends well." LaShaun smiled when Chase turned to look at her.

CHASE, LASHAUN, AND the kids drove out to Blood Bayou the following day. Chase followed her SUV in his truck, with CJ in a booster seat. He walked the scene and spoke to deputies as they searched. A diver had been brought in from the nearby St. Mary Parish Sheriff's Department. Deputies Thibaut and Rob stood by with a small bass boat, ready to retrieve a body.

LaShaun restrained CJ, who insisted on following his dad. Instead, she took the children into the Glapion home with her. CJ pouted but brightened when Mrs. Vidal brought out a plate of freshly baked chocolate chip cookies.

"Zee, I told you Mama would know what to do!" Ellie raced over to the teen and hugged her around the knees.

"Yes, you did. I should have known you were right, little one." Zee lifted her up and planted a kiss on Ellie's cheek. "Come meet Miss Kitty and Bossy."

Zee took Ellie and CJ by the hand and led them down the center hall past the kitchen to the front of the house. CJ went willingly, a cookie in his free hand. Their merry chatter floated back as the three walked off.

"Her cats," Mrs. Vidal explained when LaShaun looked puzzled. "My child worried about them wildlings as much as she did about me. I told her, I said them cats know how to survive better than us."

She chuckled as she settled against the stuffed easy chair with a cup of tea. Zee had set the floral tray with matching teapot and cups on the cocktail table of the formal parlor. Mrs. Vidal had insisted on baking cookies for the deputies. She'd even made sandwiches for their lunch.

"You should be resting, ma'am." LaShaun raised an eyebrow at her.

Mrs. Vidal waved a hand. "Zulime did most of the fixin'. I supervised."

"And how are you feeling?" LaShaun sipped the fragrant contents of her cup. She sighed in appreciation. A hint of mint with honey and ginger tickled her tastebuds.

"Me? Pooh, I'm fine. Tough like an old hen as my grandpapa used to say. How you doin' after that scrap out in my woods?" Mrs. Vidal fixed a critical gaze on LaShaun from head to toe. "I see you walking soft so as not to worry the little ones."

"I'm a little sore, but good otherwise." LaShaun warmed under the older woman's maternal gaze.

"Do best to take it easy. No more fighting the devil for a while. Me and Zulime, we gonna be just fine. My nephew D'Andre came over. Them children been such a help, him and Keishana. You know we call 'em Zee, Dee, and Kee?"

"I'm happy your family pulled through for you," LaShaun replied.

"There's some good in the Glapion kin, thank the good Lord. At least in them children." Mrs. Vidal smiled and sipped more tea.

"Zee mentioned her mother when we were in the shack. Karlene Pattison promised she could see her." LaShaun looked in the direction Zee had gone.

Mrs. Vidal's smiled faded. She sighed and put down her empty cup. "We stayed up late talking about Belle—"

"She was released from prison in California. Then she got arrested in Las Vegas about eighteen months ago. I couldn't pick up a trail after that." LaShaun had done an online search for Isabelle Glapion. The pang in Zee's voice when she'd mentioned her the other night motivated LaShaun's effort.

"She hasn't changed. If I know Belle, she's got a new man and is up to no good. Best she stay gone." Mrs. Vidal's expression hardened at the thought of her daughter-in-law.

LaShaun thought back to the nurse whose face held traces of her own mother's features. "It's hard missing your mama at that age, even if she's trouble."

"Zulime's got me, her cousins, and her aunties." Mrs. Vidal studied LaShaun for a few seconds. "Just like you had Odette. Now your family."

"Yes, I do." LaShaun smiled when a childish whoop came from Mrs. Vidal's veranda.

"You thank that lawyer friend of yours for me again. She done her job looking out for Zulime."

"I will. Don't worry about paying her either," LaShaun said quickly when Mrs. Vidal started to speak.

Mrs. Vidal shook her head. "How she gone make a livin' not taking folks' money? I can afford it. I'm sendin' her a check."

LaShaun recognized when she'd met an unmovable force. "Yes, ma'am."

The children returned, each cradling a cat. Miss Kitty and Bossy seemed to tolerate their attention. More cookies were served, washed down with glasses of milk. Miss Kitty and Bossy strolled away as if grateful Ellie and CJ had been distracted. Mrs. Vidal and Zee entertained the children with stories. LaShaun slipped away as silently as the cats to join Chase. A ten-minute walk around palmetto shrubs and through trees brought her to the bayou. Though she tried, she couldn't see the camp. She found Chase and stood next to him watching the search.

"Nothing yet, huh?" LaShaun said after a few minutes.

"Well, she didn't get far. We found the airboat drifting on the water," Chase said, he eyes still on the bayou.

"Manny said she jumped or tripped into the water. Maybe she hit her head." LaShaun followed his gaze as the diver came up to signal he hadn't found anything.

Chase turned to face LaShaun. "Or maybe he found her."

"Manny would have said so."

"You think?" Chase raised one dark eyebrow.

"He could easily and credibly say it was self-defense. The woman was armed. Plus, Manny loves his new life. He's not going to jeopardize it for anything."

"Hmm," was Chase's noncommittal response.

Deputy Thibaut strode toward them talking into her two-way radio. "Mrs. Rousselle, good to see you up and around."

"Thank you." LaShaun nodded to her.

"Chief, I think your wife's friends are right. No sign she took off through these woods. The airboat had come untied from the ramp. Maybe she tried swimming to it to get away? Weird case all around. If a gator got her, we'll just find chunks of our suspect."

LaShaun gasped and put a hand to her throat. "Is that possible?"

"Gators are active day and night," Deputy Thibaut replied before Chase could answer. "My daddy and uncles hunt 'em in season."

Suddenly the diver popped up. He pointed to the water and gave another hand signal. Deputy Rob, seated in a bateau, waved back. The putt-putt of the small outboard motor floated back to them. Though almost a third of a mile away, they could see the action. Deputy Rob wore long rubber gloves. He accepted an object from the diver and placed it on a tarp with care. He listened to something the diver said and nodded. Then the diver went under again. Deputy Rob's voice crackled from through Deputy Thibaut's handset.

"Think it might be her, Deb."

"Roger that." Deputy Thibaut waved a hand at him in acknowledgement. "Coroner gonna have a jigsaw puzzle on his hands. Blood Bayou claims another victim."

"No Cajun legends to explain this one, deputy. Nothing but greedy crooks paying the price for crime," Chase replied in a mild tone.

Deputy Thibaut clicked her tongue as she gazed at the bayou. "If you say so."

When she walked away, LaShaun leaned closer to Chase. "I don't think she buys your plain old explanation, hon. I have a feeling a new legend is about to make the rounds of Vermilion Parish."

Chase snorted as he sent a text update to Sheriff Godchaux. "I can hear 'em now. Saying the devil stays busy."

LaShaun gave Chase an affectionate pat on one broad shoulder. She headed back to the house; and a much happier scene. "Yeah, and we'll always be locked, loaded and ready for him."

# Don't miss out!

Visit the website below and you can sign up to receive emails whenever Lynn Emery publishes a new book. There's no charge and no obligation.

https://books2read.com/r/B-A-YISG-DXCFC

Connecting independent readers to independent writers.

# About the Author

Mix knowledge of voodoo, Louisiana politics and forensic social work, and you get a snapshot of author Lynn Emery. Lynn has written over twenty novels so far, one of which inspired the BET made-for-television movie AFTER ALL based on her romantic suspense novel of the same name. Holly Robinson Peete and DB Woodside starred as the lead characters.

Her romantic suspense titles have won and been nominated for several awards, including Best Multicultural Mainstream Novel by Romantic Times Magazine.

Get exclusive offers each month in Lynn's newsletter and a free short story when you sign up! Go to:

https://www.subscribepage.com/s1y8j8

Visit www.lynnemery.com to see a full list of Lynn Emery novels.

Read more at www.lynnemery.com.

Printed in Great Britain
by Amazon